CW00381293

To Dare the Da

The Daring Daughters

By Emma V. Leech

Published by Emma V. Leech.

Copyright (c) Emma V. Leech 2022

Editing Services Magpie Literary Services

Cover Art: Victoria Cooper

ASIN No:

ISBN No: 978-2-492133-53-4

About Me!

I started this incredible journey way back in 2010 with The Key to Erebus but didn't summon the courage to hit publish until October 2012. For anyone who's done it, you'll know publishing your first title is a terribly scary thing! I still get butterflies on the morning a new title releases, but the terror has subsided at least. Now I just live in dread of the day my daughters are old enough to read them.

The horror! (On both sides, I suspect.)

2017 marked the year that I made my first foray into Historical Romance and the world of the Regency Romance, and my word what a year! I was delighted by the response to this series and can't wait to add more titles. Paranormal Romance readers need not despair, however, as there is much more to come there too. Writing has become an addiction and as soon as one book is over, I'm hugely excited to start the next so you can expect plenty more in the future.

As many of my works reflect, I am greatly influenced by the beautiful French countryside in which I live. I've been here in the Southwest since 1998, though I was born and raised in England. My three gorgeous girls are all bilingual and my husband Pat, myself, and our four cats consider ourselves very fortunate to have made such a lovely place our home.

KEEP READING TO DISCOVER MY OTHER BOOKS!

Other Works by Emma V. Leech

Daring Daughters

Daring Daughters Series

Girls Who Dare

Girls Who Dare Series

Rogues & Gentlemen

Rogues & Gentlemen Series

The Regency Romance Mysteries

The Regency Romance Mysteries Series

The French Vampire Legend

The French Vampire Legend Series

The French Fae Legend

The French Fae Legend Series

Stand Alone

The Book Lover (a paranormal novella)

The Girl is Not for Christmas (Regency Romance)

Audio Books

Don't have time to read but still need your romance fix? The wait is over…

By popular demand, get many of your favourite Emma V Leech Regency Romance books on audio as performed by the incomparable Philip Battley and Gerard Marzilli. Several titles are available and more added each month!

Find them at your favourite audiobook retailer!

Acknowledgements

Thanks, of course, to my wonderful editor Kezia Cole with Magpie Literary Services.

To Victoria Cooper for all your hard work, amazing artwork and, above all, your unending patience!!! Thank you so much. You are amazing!

To my BFF, PA, personal cheerleader and bringer of chocolate, Varsi Appel, for moral support, confidence boosting and for reading my work more times than I have. I love you loads!

A huge thank you to all of Emma's Book Club members! You guys are the best!

I'm always so happy to hear from you so do email or message me :)

emmavleech@orange.fr

To my husband Pat and my family… For always being proud of me.

Table of Contents

Family Trees

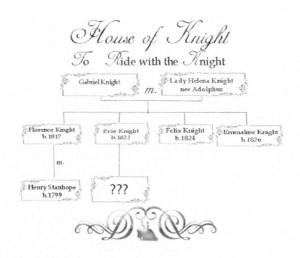

House of Knight
To Ride with the Knight

Gabriel Knight **m.** Lady Helena Knight nee Adolphus

- Florence Knight b.1817
- Evie Knight b.1822
- Felix Knight b.1824
- Emmaline Knight b.1826

Florence Knight **m.** Henry Stanhope b.1799

Evie Knight **???**

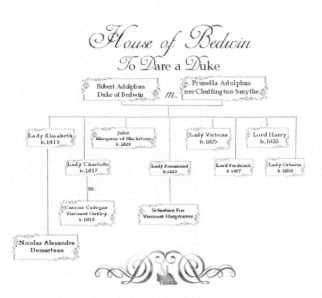

House of Bedwin
To Dare a Duke

Robert Adolphus Duke of Bedwin **m.** Prunella Adolphus nee Chuffington-Smythe

- Lady Elisabeth b.1815
- Jules Marquess of Blackstone b.1819
- Lady Victoria b.1825
- Lord Harry b.1833
- Lady Charlotte b.1817
- Lady Rosamund b.1823
- Lord Frederick b.1827
- Lady Octavia b.1838

Lady Charlotte **m.** Cassius Cadogan Viscount Oakley b.1815

Lady Rosamund — Sebastian Fox Viscount Hargreaves

Nicolas Alexandre Demarteau

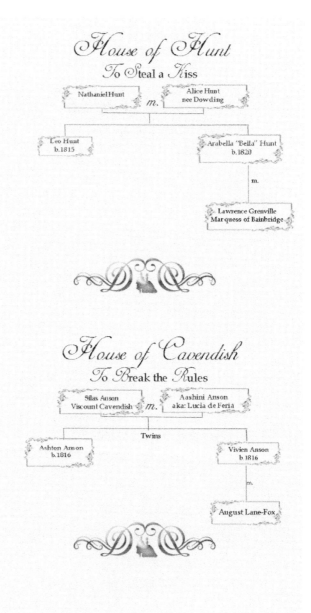

House of Hunt
To Steal a Kiss

Nathaniel Hunt _m._ Alice Hunt nee Dowding

Leo Hunt b.1815

Arabella "Bella" Hunt b.1820

_m._

Lawrence Grenville Marquess of Bainbridge

House of Cavendish
To Break the Rules

Silas Anson Viscount Cavendish _m._ Aashini Anson aka: Lucia de Feria

Twins

Ashton Anson b.1816

Vivien Anson b.1816

_m._

August Lane-Fox

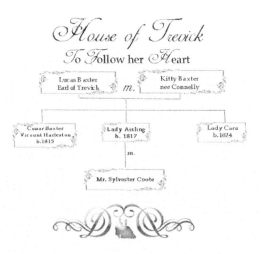

House of Trevick
To Follow her Heart

Lucas Baxter
Earl of Trevick

m.

Kitty Baxter
nee Connelly

Conor Baxter
Viscount Harleston
b.1815

Lady Aisling
b. 1817

Lady Cara
b.1824

m.

Mr. Sylvester Coote

House of St Clair
To Wager with Love

Jasper Cadogan
Earl of St Clair

m.

Harriet Cadogan
nee Stanhope

Cassius Cadogan
Viscount Oakley
b.1815

m.

Lady Charlotte Adolphus
b.1817

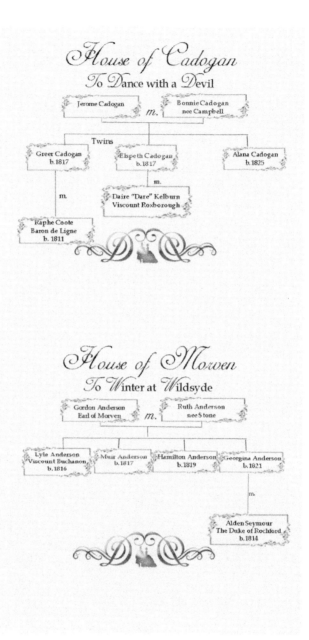

House of Cadogan
To Dance with a Devil

Jerome Cadogan — m. — Bonnie Cadogan nee Campbell

Twins

Greer Cadogan b.1817

Elspeth Cadogan b.1817 — m. — Daire "Dare" Kelburn Viscount Roxborough

Alana Cadogan b.1825

m.

Raphe Coote Baron de Ligne b.1811

House of Morven
To Winter at Wildsyde

Gordon Anderson Earl of Morven — m. — Ruth Anderson nee Stone

Lyle Anderson Viscount Buchanon, b.1816

Muir Anderson b.1817

Hamilton Anderson b.1819

Georgina Anderson b.1821

m.

Alden Seymour The Duke of Rochford b.1814

House of de Beauvoir
To Experiment with Desire

Inigo de Beauvoir *m.* Minerva de Beauvoir nee Butler

Hartley de Beauvoir (adopted at Age 6 b.1809)

Kathleen de Beauvoir (adopted at birth) b.1824

m.

Maxwell Drake The Earl of Vane

House of Rothborn
To Bed the Baron

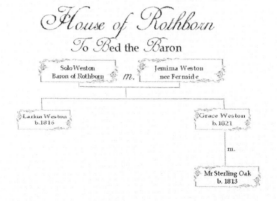

Solo Weston Baron of Rothborn *m.* Jemima Weston nee Fernside

Larkin Weston b.1816

Grace Weston b.1821

m.

Mr Sterling Oak b.1813

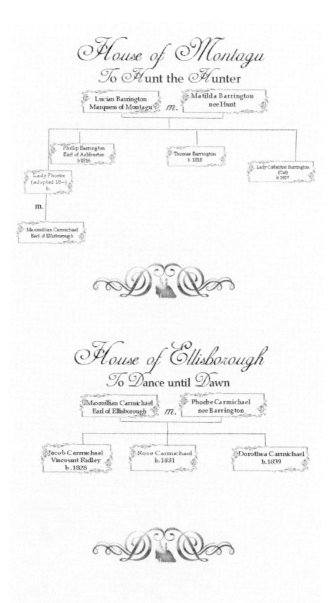

House of Montagu
To Hunt the Hunter

Lucian Barrington
Marquess of Montagu — *m.* — Matilda Barrington
nee Hunt

Phillip Barrington
Earl of Ashburton
b1816

Thomas Barrington
b 1818

Lady Catherine Barrington
(Cat)
b 1827

Lady Phoebe
(adopted 18--)
b.

m.

Maximilian Carmichael
Earl of Ellisborough

House of Ellisborough
To Dance until Dawn

Maximilian Carmichael
Earl of Ellisborough — *m.* — Phoebe Carmichael
nee Barrington

Jacob Carmichael
Viscount Ridley
b.1828

Rose Carmichael
b.1831

Dorothea Carmichael
b.1839

Content Guidance Warning

To Dare the Darkness is over 100,000 words of angst and romance, with no cliff-hangers, no cheating, and a guaranteed HEA.

Please be aware this story deals with themes of parental neglect, abandonment, physical abuse, and sexual exploitation regarding Louis César's upbringing.

If you feel these subjects are triggering to you in any way, please read with caution.

Thank you.

Prologue

Maréchal Ney is dead. I rejoice at last to see that revolutionary bastard cut down, but I will not rest until everyone who stole my life from me has paid the price for it.

Louis XVIII has not the stomach to do what must be done, but I am loyal still to France and the ancient regime. I will see them rot in hell for what they did.

—Excerpt of a letter from Armand de Montluc, Comte de Villen to an unknown correspondent, 1815.

10ᵗʰ June 1817, en route to Chateau de Naudonnet, Brantôme, Dordogne, France.

Louis César is five years old.

"Arrêtez ça! Cease your fidgeting!"

His father's sharp words made Louis stiffen in his seat, his hand falling away from his too tight cravat. It was hot and stuffy in the carriage and the journey from Paris had taken days and been long and uncomfortable. They had left last night's unpleasant lodgings at the crack of dawn and Louis suspected Père had not paid for their stay. Now his head ached and he felt sick, but he was too afraid to utter a word of complaint. In this mood, his father would strike him if he caused the least bit of irritation. Louis dared not make him cross in case his father left him again. He had left Louis' mother within days of the birth and Louis had not seen him again until two years ago. Now, apparently, Louis could be of use to him.

"Now, remember. Your job is to make Madame de Naudonnet happy. If she takes a liking to you, I am more likely to be invited to stay for a while. This is what the king has reduced me to in thanks for my service to France, begging for scraps like some mangy hound, but I will have my day. For now, you will remember your manners and tell her how pretty she is, how you wish she was your maman. You understand?"

Louis nodded, used to the routine by now, though his belly squirmed as if it was full of snakes.

Finally, the carriage rolled to a halt and his father climbed out. He did not turn back to help Louis, who jumped down from the high platform and landed awkwardly with a skitter of gravel. His father turned and scowled at him, but said nothing.

The chateau was a pretty one, with an enormous round tower all covered in green leaves. It was not nearly as grand as his father's chateau, but they had left there six months ago. Père said they could not live there any longer because the king was angry. Louis did not quite understand why the king was angry with his father for ensuring so many of the wicked men who'd wanted to hurt him died. Père said he was doing everything to make sure the king and all his kin would never be in danger of having their heads chopped off again. It was all very confusing. Père said that if he did not make sure all the revolutionaries were dead, they might come and cut Louis' head off next. That had given him nightmares for weeks.

It was cool inside the chateau and Louis hurried to keep up as a servant showed them through to a large open room, filled with elegant furniture and even more elegant people. The chatter quietened as the servant announced them. Louis hung back, hiding behind his father as the company turned their gazes upon him.

His father was all smiles now, his voice softer and more melodious, his manner charming. Père said charm was like magic. If you used the right words and spoke to them just so, you could get anything you wanted. Louis had discovered he was right, up to a point. He could get ladies to fuss over him and feed him sweetmeats easily... but that did not work on his father.

Louis stood quietly, the image of an obedient child, although he was dreadfully thirsty, and hungry too. He'd not eaten a bite since breakfast and then only a stale croissant. His father spoke to everyone, ignoring Louis and making the assembled company laugh. Père could make anyone like him—until they didn't. Then they were frightened of him. Louis was frightened of him, too.

At last, the woman Père wanted Louis to charm for him appeared, smiling and laughing quietly at the soft words Père spoke, though Louis could not hear what he said.

"May I present my son, Madame? Louis César de Montluc. Vicomte Sainte-Apre."

Madame's face lit up as Louis stepped forward and gave a smart bow. "Oh, what an enchanting child. Why, Monsieur, he has the face of an angel, and he is your son?" she asked with a coquettish laugh. "It hardly seems possible."

Louis' father laughed too. He seemed to enjoy his satanic reputation, which Louis did not really understand, though ladies flocked about him like so many pretty butterflies.

"Come and sit beside me," Madame said, settling herself on a lovely silk-covered settee of the same shade of pink as her gown. She beckoned for Louis to come to her.

He hurried over, aware of his father's gaze on him, though he was happy to sit beside Madame. She was pretty, dressed beautifully in silk and lace. The heady scent of flowers clung to her. Louis suppressed the urge to sneeze and gazed up at her from under his lashes with the besotted expression his father had taught him.

"Vous êtes la plus jolie femme que j'aie jamais vue."

Madame went off into peals of delighted laughter, as ladies always did when Louis told them they were the prettiest he had ever seen. Sometimes it was even true, like today. Madame really was lovely.

"Why the divine creature has inherited your charm, Armand! That, and his mother's looks. Dear me, but he will be a devastating creature when he is grown."

Madame stroked Louis' cheek, and he wriggled closer on the settee, staring at her with genuine interest now.

"J'aimerais que vous soyez ma mère," Louis said, unsurprised when the woman's lovely eyes filled with tears.

"Oh, child. Oh, you poor, sweet boy."

Louis knew if he looked around, he would see her reaction had pleased his father. Père believed Louis was obeying his orders and doing just as he ought by telling the woman he wished she was his mother. Père did not understand, though, that Louis was not trying to charm her now, only telling the truth. Each time he said the well-rehearsed words, he clung to the frail hope that one of these pretty, sweet-scented ladies would want to be his maman too. Sometimes they only laughed, but often they cosseted and made a fuss of him, perhaps for an afternoon, sometimes for a few weeks, but never any longer than that. They never wanted him to stay for always. Louis knew that there was something wrong with him. There must be, for Maman had died and Père had left him and threatened to do so again if he didn't behave. Père was always angry with him too, and no matter how sweet and nice he was—and he tried very hard to please them—the ladies always sent him away eventually.

Madame gathered him upon her lap, and Louis snuggled up, resting his head on her soft bosom. He sighed and closed his eyes, enjoying the sensation of comfort and security as a bejewelled hand stroked his hair. It was an illusion. He might only be five, but he knew that much. He knew too those illusions were so much kinder than reality, and so he clung to them, determined to hold on for as long as he could.

24th June 1818, Chateau de Naudonnet, Brantôme, Dordogne, France.

"Alors, what am I supposed to do with the child?" Madame asked her friend who had come for tea. The two women fanned themselves, shaking their coiffured heads and sighing.

"It was terrible of Armand to just abandon the child here. I admit, he's an angelic creature, but he is hardly your responsibility."

Louis shifted uncomfortably, his ears burning. His father had left him here two weeks ago and he knew Madame was becoming bored with playing the part of Maman. She had no children of her own and her interest in him was waning with each passing hour. Louis had done everything as Père had taught him—reciting poetry from memory, making her drawings, picking flowers for her—but nothing seemed to impress her now and he did not know what to try next. If he had any money, he could buy her something pretty, but he didn't. He didn't think Père had any, either. Louis shrank back against the overstuffed armchair, hoping if he kept silent and caused no trouble, she might not send him away. He didn't even ask for one of the sweet pastries that the ladies were eating, afraid to draw attention to himself. If only Père would come back for him. At least he knew where he stood with his father.

More visitors came later in the afternoon and, once again, Louis found himself the subject of discussion. One man stood out in the throng, seemingly out of place among the beautiful, laughing aristocrats. Monsieur Boucher was a large, aggressive-looking man dressed all in black, his features strong and uncompromising. He seethed with restless energy, making him different from those around him, whose expressions of studied ennui rarely altered. A cigar hung loosely from the man's thick fingers, and he flicked it carelessly, sending ash tumbling to the marble floor. The smoke tickled Louis' throat and made him want to cough. Every time Monsieur Boucher's gaze settled on him, Louis shrank back behind Madame's skirts as a hot and cold feeling swept over him. They were discussing his father now, their voices low.

"Really, Joseph, you were foolish to come here when you know the comte might return at any time. Do you want him to kill you? He's tried hard enough these past months."

Joseph laughed, an unpleasant sound that made Louis' stomach tighten with worry.

"I'm afraid I have bad news for you then, ma chère, for your darling Armand is the foolish one. The king has banished him."

Madame gasped, pressing a hand to her heart. "Mais pourquoi?"

"Because the king knows France has not yet lost her taste for revolution so he is trying to walk the middle ground and can no longer tolerate ultraroyalists like the comte for fear of another uprising. In short, Armand killed the wrong man this time and caused too much of a fuss. He's fled to Belgium and there he shall stay."

Louis was breathing very hard. His fingers curled in Madame's copious silk skirts, despite knowing she would be cross with him for creasing the fine fabric. Yet he could not seem to let go. Père had gone. Père had gone away and left him behind and Madame didn't want him. Louis looked up, a terrible feeling pressing down on him as he met Monsieur Boucher's eyes.

"I'll take the child off your hands, if you like. He's a little younger than my son, but it will be good for Etienne to have a playmate."

Madame looked from Louis to Monsieur Boucher with a frown. "But you despise Armand. Why would you do such a thing?

I won't have you be cruel to the child, Joseph, for he is a dear creature and I'm quite fond of him."

"Really, Madame, you think so little of me you believe I would take my revenge on a mere child? Come, now," he chided.

"Oh, no," Madame said with a regretful sigh. "Of course not, Joseph. Forgive me, and in all honesty, I should be grateful, for he is not mine to raise, and it was too bad of Armand to just abandon him."

"Indeed, it was. How foolish of the comte to leave his son and heir to fend for himself, but it seems I have more Christian charity than a man who would have seen me dead in a gutter. So, little vicomte, you will come along with me," Monsieur Boucher said, smiling at Louis.

Louis stared at him in horror. Finally, he pried his fingers loose from Madame's skirts and backed up.

"Non," he said, shaking his head. Père had taught Louis how to lie, and how to recognise one too. Louis had inherited his father's instincts and he knew this man hated him, that he did not mean to take care of Louis for the sake of Christian charity. "Non," he said again, tears pricking at his eyes.

"Don't be foolish, boy," the man said impatiently. "Madame has been more than kind, but she can't keep you. You cannot possibly be so very spoiled and selfish to expect more of her. You're not her problem and your worthless father has gone without you. You'll come with me and be grateful for the roof over your head."

Louis turned to Madame, who avoided his gaze.

"See to it, will you, Joseph? You know I cannot abide a scene," she said.

With this, Madame hurried away, her silken skirts rustling as she left the room.

Monsieur Boucher smiled at Louis. The sight made his heart skip in terror.

"All good things come to him who waits," the man murmured, and then laughed softly.

Louis ran.

24th July 1819, Place de Coderc, Périgueux, France.

Louis is seven years old.

"Come along, Louis," Etienne said, impatient now. "That's good enough. I'm bored with waiting for you."

Louis bit back the observation that Etienne would not have waited so long if he had helped Louis finish his work. There was no point. Etienne was the son of this household, whereas Louis…

He shut his mind against descriptions of what he was, reminding himself fiercely that he was the Vicomte Sainte-Apre, a nobleman's son, descended from the old kings of France. Except that his father had abandoned him, and he was on his knees, blacking a fireplace grate, and hunger was gnawing at his belly. Louis ignored Etienne, which was a dangerous game. The boy was around three years Louis' senior, though he often found that hard to believe. Etienne was not a clever boy, though he was cunning when he wanted something. Occasionally, they played together, going down to the river to fish or catch frogs. When he was in a good mood, Etienne was fun to be with. He could be kind too, sometimes, and if he was feeling generous, he would steal food for Louis. But those acts of kindness usually came at a price, and Louis knew better than to trust him.

"I must finish my chores, and then I must collect the bread for supper," Louis replied, though Etienne knew it well enough.

His days had an endless, mind-numbing quality that sometimes felt like being dragged into thick grey mud. But he must not think like that. His father had once told him only fools despaired. Clever men made plans and waited for their moment to act. Louis had realised that he was clever, compared to Etienne at least, who plodded over his lessons and despised books. At night, Louis would creep into the schoolroom and devour everything that Etienne had been studying, absorbing the information as greedily as he might a fresh baguette. Of course, Monsieur Boucher only hated Louis even more for that, knowing he could do complex calculations in his head while Etienne could barely manage basic sums with a pencil and paper.

Patience was the key. Louis had forgotten that in the first years he'd been here, trying repeatedly to escape and finding himself black and blue for his trouble. He had discovered Monsieur Boucher was an important man here, feared and respected, and he had spies everywhere. Louis could barely set foot outside the house without a dozen people knowing it. So, he allowed them to believe they had broken his spirit, that he was without hope, without pride, whilst a fire burned in his heart. One day. One day, he would be free.

One day, he would have his revenge.

"I want to go fishing, and I want to go now," Etienne said, his tone belligerent.

"Vas-y alors. Then go," Louis said, struggling to keep his tone even. Did the thick-headed idiot think he preferred to stay here and work? Did he think it was a choice? "You know I am not allowed to go, Etienne."

Etienne folded his arms, his lip jutting out in a pout. Really, he was too old for such behaviour. "I want you to come."

"Non."

With a furious snarl, Etienne kicked the pot of thick black iron paste. It hit the white wall, leaving a dirty black mark and a large dent in the plaster. Both boys froze as heavy footsteps paused outside the door before it swung open.

Louis' heart sped as he felt Monsieur Boucher's gaze settle on him. He kept his eyes down, kneeling before the hearth unmoving, knowing better than to look up.

"Who did that?" monsieur demanded, his voice cold and furious.

Louis said nothing, trembling with fear and hating himself for it. There was no point in saying it hadn't been him. If monsieur believed him, he'd be beaten for tattling on Etienne, and Etienne would take his revenge on him too. There was no way to win. So he held his tongue, waiting for it to be over. It would be over, he promised himself. Nothing lasted forever. Patience. He must endure, that was all. Except it was so very hard to do.

"Well? Answer me. Etienne, what happened?"

Etienne sighed. "I did not like to say, Papa, but I was going fishing and Louis wanted to come too. I said I was sorry, but that he must finish his chores first. He got angry. I'm afraid he kicked the blacking pot. But it is a very fine day for fishing, so I don't blame him for being a bit upset," Etienne added, sounding so very understanding.

Louis gritted his teeth so hard his jaw hurt, tears pricking at his eyes at the unfairness of it.

"Is this true?"

Louis concentrated on breathing, deep breath in, deep breath out.

"Is this true, chien?" Abruptly Louis was hauled to his feet by one arm, monsieur's powerful hand gripping his upper arm in a punishing hold. "Well?"

Louis closed his eyes against the burn of tears, knowing the man would only humiliate him further if he caught him crying. He nodded, a taut bob of his head. The slap made his ears ring, but he barely had time to register it before he was being dragged through the house, down the stairs to the cellars.

Non, non, non, he cried silently, but did not speak the words aloud. It would not help. Indeed, he felt monsieur enjoyed it when he begged. He would not give him the satisfaction. Louis flinched as he heard the squeak of iron hinges.

"Get in, dog."

Obediently—for what other choice was there? —Louis got on his hands and knees on the dirt floor and crawled into the cage, curling up with his back to the man who stood over him, the only defiance he could offer. He heard the door close, the lock slide into place, and closed his eyes. With a sigh, he reminded himself he did not have to finish blacking the grate now and allowed his mind to take him away. He remembered things that had made him happy, such as the first time he had seen his home, his actual home, when his father had come for him. It was a splendid chateau with a view over a river and the countryside spread out for miles and miles before him. It was all theirs, his father had said, and if Louis was as clever as his Père and did what he was told, one day there might even be more than this… carriages and horses, and money for whatever he wanted.

Louis was as clever as his father, he promised himself, squeezing his eyes shut. He would have fine clothes again, and a beautiful house and he would never be hungry—and he would make Monsieur Boucher pay for everything he had done.

Chapter 1

Her words and those becoming tears mastered e'en that rude heart as Pluto first learned to feel love's longings. The tears he wiped away with his murky cloak, quieting her sad grief with these soothing words:

"Cease, Proserpine, to vex thy heart with gloomy cares and causeless fear. A prouder sceptre shall be thine, nor shalt thou face marriage with a husband unworthy of thee. I am that scion of Saturn whose will the framework of the world obeys, whose power stretches through the limitless void. Think not thou hast lost the light of day; other stars are mine and other courses; a purer light shalt thou face marriage with a husband unworthy of thee.

— "The Rape of Persephone" by Claudian, circa 395 A.D.

7th July 1842, Peregrine House, Grosvenor Square, London.

Ten days prior to Mrs Belvedere's Ball...

Evie jumped as her maid, Rachel, dropped her hairbrush on the floor with a clatter.

"Sorry, miss," she said, wincing.

"That's quite all right." Evie smiled, wishing she could get her nerves under control. It was taking everything she had to sit quietly. She set aside the poem she'd been reading, or trying to read.

"Not ideal if you've a headache, though, me throwing hairbrushes about," Rachel said with concern. "Are you certain I can't get you some willow bark tea?"

"No, thank you. I'm just tired, that's all. An early night will put me to rights, I'm sure."

"Very well then, Miss Evie. Good night."

Evie replied in kind and sat staring at the candle that burned on her dressing table. Her heart was beating too fast. No. She ought not. She knew she ought not. Deliberately, she ignored the candle and picked the book up again, rereading the same words. She could not shake the story of Persephone and Hades, or Pluto, as Claudian called him. Ever since her father had spoken to her, Louis' image had taken shape in her mind as the beautiful dark god, come to steal her away into the darkness.

She smoothed her hands over the page and sighed, knowing she had long since decided and was only pretending otherwise. Louis might as well have fed her a magical pomegranate seed when he had first kissed her, and then touched her so wickedly, for she was bound to him now, no matter how much it scared her. Evie did not consider herself ignorant. Indeed, compared to most young ladies, her education was scandalously broad, for her mama had no interest in her girls being compromised because they were too uninformed to make good choices. Yet Louis had awakened something in her she had not known even existed. Desire burned in her blood, consuming her, making her restless for him, making her want him above all else.

It was dangerous and wicked, and she ought not to do it, but… she would summon him to her, like conjuring a demon, and he would come.

Moving slowly, as though in some hazy dream, she set the book aside once more and got to her feet, untying her wrap and setting it aside. She undid the neat plait that restrained her hair and ran her fingers through it until it cascaded down her back, to her waist. Then she walked to the dressing table and picked up the candle, tugged open the curtains at her bedroom window, and set the candle down on the sill.

It was almost an hour before she heard the door handle turn, and only then because her nerves were strung so tightly that she was listening intently to every sound that disturbed the quiet. Her breath caught as the dark shape entered her bedroom, moving silently. Candlelight caught the glitter in his eyes, vibrant blue like the dazzling glint of a kingfisher darting across still water. He had covered his face with a black silk scarf and now tugged it down. He smiled at her. Evie's heart skipped helplessly.

"Louis," she said, and ran from the bed into his arms.

He caught her up and kissed her as if he needed her to breathe, as if he had been waiting for this moment his whole life. It was intoxicating to be wanted like this, and by this man of all men. Louis released her and drew back to study her face. She studied him in turn. The most beautiful man in Europe, they called him. Thick dark hair, golden skin, and a face so exquisite artists clamoured to paint him. Louis always refused them, which only made his mysterious aura increasingly tantalising. Beneath the thin black fabric of the clothes he wore, she felt the flex of powerful muscles, and shivered. She wanted to see him without these clothes on, to learn what lay beneath and discover everything she could only guess at. And yet he was so much more than this. She adored him. He was her friend, her confidant, and had been for years, and the simple pleasure of his company was a joy. He was the man to whom she had entrusted her secrets and shared her private hopes, never once considering that he might not think of her as just a friend, but something more too. It had taken her a long time to find the courage to listen to him, to hear what he'd been trying to tell her for so long. Evie did not like change, she did not long for excitement as some girls did, and yet somehow everything had changed, nonetheless.

"Are you well, *mon amour*?" he asked her, tracing her cheek with the backs of his fingers.

Evie nodded. "Only terrified we will be discovered. I have been fretting myself to death, afraid to put the candle in the window and yet wanting to see you so much."

"I am here now."

She nodded and pulled away from him, suddenly overwhelmed. Evie took the candle from the sill and replaced it on the dressing table before closing the curtains again. She could feel Louis' gaze upon her like the heat of a fire burning her back. Her instincts prickled with fear and anticipation.

"You promised me we would talk," she said, striving for a normal tone of voice and dismayed to hear herself sound so breathless.

"I did. It was not all I promised, if I remember correctly," he said, his dark voice caressing her, making her intimate muscles contract with longing, highlighting the hollow ache deep inside her that clamoured for him.

She heard the smile in his words, but could not look at him. If she lost control of this conversation, he would divert her with kisses and, before she knew where she was, she would be lost in him, in her desire for him which had become an unwieldy thing that stole her sense and made her forget about everything else she wanted. When he kissed her, his touch was all she could think of, and her longing for more and more, no matter the danger.

"You promised me we would talk," she said again, firmer now.

Louis lowered his lashes, frowning at the carpet beneath his feet. "I did," he admitted. "If you are sure you wish to hear it, *mon amour*. It is not a pretty bedtime story."

"You lived it, Louis," she said, putting her chin up. "And if I am to understand the man you are, the things you have done, then I can hear it. I have no need for you to protect me from real life."

"Real life is crueller than you can imagine," he said softly.

"That only means we must be kind to each other, not that we ought to live with lies. You promised me the truth a long time ago. Don't let me down now."

His expression darkened for a moment, but he nodded. "As you wish."

She watched as he sat down in the chair she had vacated earlier, and picked up the book she'd been reading. "*The Rape of Persephone*? Well, you do have a taste for dark stories before bed."

Evie ignored the comment, not wanting him to pursue her interest in the poem. Instead, she moved to sit on the bed opposite him.

Louis tsked. "*Mais non,* you are too far away. I cannot talk to you if you are all the way over there."

Evie rolled her eyes and got up, moving to sit on the footstool instead, but Louis grabbed her wrist, pulling her closer.

"I'm too heavy," she said uncomfortably, realising he wanted her to sit on his lap.

Louis snorted with amusement. "You say the most ridiculous things." With a sharp tug, he pulled her down, and she fell with a little squeak of indignation. Louis settled her against him, pressing a kiss to her forehead. "There. Now we are both comfortable, *oui?*"

"Yes, Louis," she said with a sigh, resting her head on his shoulder.

He made a contented sound, his arms closing around her, and they sat like that for a moment, neither of them speaking.

"Louis," she prompted.

He sighed. With heartbreaking simplicity, he outlined the early years of his life with little embellishment and less emotion. His mother had died when he was a baby. His father had left him with distant relatives who had not much wanted him and gone about his life. When Louis was three, his father had returned, and he had travelled through France with him, visiting people he needed favours from, and tracking down opponents of the king and destroying them, whether financially, socially, or however he could. Often, they paid with their lives. Then, when he was five years old, his father's most despised enemy and a man the comte had tried to kill on several occasions had found Louis and taken him away.

Evie's throat was tight as she stared at him. He had stopped speaking, but she felt the tension in him, sensed his reluctance to continue.

"Louis," she said gently, reaching up to turn his face towards her.

"I don't want to talk anymore," he said, an edge to his voice.

His sensual mouth set into a hard line, and she had no time to protest before he kissed her. Something like panic stole over Evie as she realised how easily he could do this to her, steal her wits and summon her desire for him as if he held her spellbound. She was helpless to deny him anything he wanted, for she wanted it too. He tugged at the ribbon that secured the gathered neckline of her nightgown and loosened it, pulling it down over one shoulder to expose her breast. He broke the kiss, gazing at her. His breath hitched, his eyes dark with want, and Evie stared at him, not understanding why this stunning man was so in love with her, so entranced by a body that many people dismissed as too plump to be beautiful. She gasped as he touched her, stroking the generous curve of her breast.

"Si belle," he murmured reverently, caressing her and toying with the pink tip until it was hard and aching, sending jolts of pleasure directly between her thighs.

Everything feminine in her contracted, aching with need, quivering with anticipation. It was on the tip of her tongue to beg him to touch her, more and more and… and if she gave in, she would never hear any more of his history. Drawing on reserves she had not known she possessed, she caught his wrist and stilled his clever fingers, though her body screamed at her to let him continue.

"Louis," she said again, reproving this time. "You promised."

His expression darkened. *"Non,* I do not want to…." She stared at him, and he muttered a curse. "You don't want me to stop," he countered.

"No. But I shan't let you use my desire for you to get your own way. That is a dangerous road."

"A pleasurable one," he teased, his eyes glinting wickedly. "I want to put my mouth on you, Evie, like I promised."

The breath snagged in her throat as she remembered his promise, and he chuckled.

"Stop it," she said, her voice hard now, her resolve fraying.

He fell silent, looking away from her. "I am sorry, *mon amour.* Forgive me. I…. It is difficult to speak of and I do not wish to tell you. I don't want you to know my past, everything that happened. It will change the way you look at me, and…."

"And you're afraid," she finished for him. "I know that. I understand. But I love you, all of you. That won't change. You ask me constantly to trust you. Well, now I am asking the same of you. Trust me, Louis. Tell me. *Please.*"

She slipped her hand into his and squeezed his fingers, silently encouraging him.

"Very well," he said, and she heard the resignation behind the words. "If you must hear it, so be it. Monsieur Boucher took me to his home. He stripped me of my fine clothes and gave me others that were little more than dirty rags. It was explained to me that my kind—the aristocracy—were parasites, leeching off the common man. So now we were to be treated in kind. I was graciously allowed to live by the Christian generosity of this family, which meant I was allowed to work for them, to fetch and carry. I was to empty their bedpans, clean the grates and light the fires, and to do any menial task they saw fit. In exchange for this, I had the privilege of sleeping on the stone floor of the kitchen before the fire, without so much as a blanket. My meals were the scraps they left, tossed to the floor. To begin with, I refused to eat, but eventually hunger drove me to accept even this indignity. They laughed and mocked me, and I could only endure it. I was too small, too weak to fight back. I learned to fear Monsieur Boucher's fists, and I discovered there were worse things than being beaten."

For a moment, she just stared at him, shocked into silence. Tears rolled down her cheeks as his words sank in, disbelieving he had survived such treatment, unable to comprehend the horror he had endured. She was not so naïve that she believed this was the worst of it. This was an expurgated, clinical retelling of facts, nothing more. He did not look at her, his face set into hard lines.

"How long?" Evie managed, her voice thick with emotion. "How long did you live like this?"

He did not bat an eyelid, utterly impassive, his reply cool. "Almost five years. Until Nic found me."

His breathing was even, controlled, but she sensed he was waiting. For what, she was uncertain. Perhaps for her to draw back, to consider him diminished for the way he had been treated. Her heart contracted.

"Louis," she whispered. "Look at me."

Reluctantly, he turned his head, and she saw only the beautiful face of the Comte de Villen, the mask he wore so well.

It was hard to speak when she wanted to weep for him, to hold him and kiss him and make up for all he had endured, but she suspected he was too raw for such a show of emotion from her and would not welcome it. He would likely view such a reaction as nothing more than pity. So, she steeled herself and attempted to talk to him without sobbing her heart out.

"I am so proud of you. Such cruel treatment, such a terrible way of life would have broken most people, but you survived. You made a success of yourself, and you did not let it damage your beautiful heart. I do not understand how you did that, my love, but I am so, so proud that you did."

His expression flickered, something like bewilderment in his eyes that she should say such a thing. He shook his head.

"Don't pity me," he said, sounding annoyed. "I may have been a victim in the past, but I have not been helpless for a long time. I took my revenge on those who hurt me, I learned to take from those who would take from me. Do not look at me and see an abandoned little boy, for he is dead and gone. I survived, and survival means doing whatever you must to stay alive. I stole, I cheated, and I lied and, when I had to, I killed. There, now. Have you heard enough?"

Evie watched him, sensing the turmoil inside him no matter how well he hid it, and knew she could not ask him for more now. She reached out and stroked his face, wanting to calm the storm within him. She held his gaze, and he shifted, uncomfortable with her scrutiny.

"I am proud of you," she said, her voice firm.

He made a dismissive sound but leaned his head closer to hers. "Evie," he whispered.

She kissed him then, hard and needy, understanding that he could give her no more tonight. He needed to feel in control again and this was his way. They had time, and with time she could make him understand that she would accept him if only he would trust her with the truth. All of it. Besides, she wanted him too badly to deny him, or herself. The passion she had fought so hard to restrain broke free and she laughed with delight as he lowered his head to her breast, his hot mouth closing over her nipple. He suckled and she had to smother her cry, burying her face in his hair, holding him to her. Liquid heat flooded her, and she tugged at his shirt, wanting to feel his skin.

"Take it off," she demanded, surprised when he refused. Instead, he lifted her, startling her with the ease with which he did so. Such a powerful body lurked beneath that elegant exterior and she wanted to see it. "Louis, take it off," she said again, but he settled her on the chair, spreading her thighs.

"Hush," he commanded, sliding his hands up her legs. "Did you do what I asked of you?"

Evie blushed, remembering very well he had asked her to think about him pleasuring her with his mouth, touching herself until she came. She nodded, and he smiled.

"Good girl. More than once, I hope?"

Evie made a sound of protest but nodded and he pressed a kiss to her inner thigh, pushing her nightgown higher. "Such a good girl," he crooned against her skin, his warm breath fluttering over her. "Let us see if I can live up to your fantasies."

Louis sank to his knees before her and Evie held back a smile, for he was her fantasy, her friend and her lover, a man she wanted to trust with her whole heart, with her future, though she did not know if she dared do such a thing.

Her breath hitched as he pushed up her nightgown and pressed a kiss to the dark triangle of curls.

"I'll stop if you tell me to," he murmured, and kissed her again, using his tongue to tease through the curls, seeking her most sensitive flesh.

Evie gasped and shook her head, but it felt so decadently good, too good to stop. She moaned, her hands clutching at the arms of the chair. He laughed softly, grasping her bottom and pulling her to the edge of the chair, opening her to him. He glanced up at her, his beautiful blue eyes dancing with mischief.

"Shhh," he whispered, pressing a finger to his lips.

Evie swallowed and closed her eyes. Oh, lord. This was wicked. This was so very bad of her and yet she could not deny the excitement thrumming beneath her skin. There was nothing that could have made her tell him to stop. The pleasure of it was just too delicious. His sinful tongue licked and teased, toying with the sensitive bud of her sex until she wanted to scream, the sensations he brought bursting to life were so overwhelming. Evie clutched at his hair, holding him in place, demanding more of him. She trembled, struggling to keep quiet, and then his fingers slid inside her, caressing deeper until the world whited out. Evie gasped, whimpering with pleasure, fighting not to cry out as waves of joy made her giddy and disorientated.

Just as she thought she would slide off the chair and onto the floor, Louis stood, lifting her into his arms and carrying her to the bed. Her head lolled against his shoulder, her body utterly drained, limp as a rag doll and tingling pleasantly. He laid her down and settled behind her, pulling her close, wrapping his body around hers.

"Sleep, *mon amour*. I shall watch over you."

Evie sighed, closing her eyes, trusting him to do just that.

Chapter 2

Louis,

Where were you tonight? No, don't answer that.

This will not end well, my friend. Please take care.

—Excerpt of a letter from Mr Barnaby Godwin to Louis César de Montluc, Comte de Villen.

15th July 1842, Peregrine House, Grosvenor Square, London.

Louis waited in the darkness, staring up at the imposing façade of Peregrine House, waiting for Evie to put the candle in place. He suspected she would be nervous about doing so tonight. The death of Lady Hargreaves four days earlier had caused quite a stir, with rumours of murder circling the *ton*. Everyone had instinctively tightened their security, watching the shadows for a killer lying in wait.

Her husband was the prime suspect, of course, though Louis doubted Gabriel Knight believed that any more than he did. Hargreaves wasn't the kind to take a life, especially not a woman's. Even a woman who had destroyed his world with such obvious glee. He was too thoroughly decent to do such a thing. Hargreaves was not a killer… unlike Louis. Though it appeared he had not killed one man as efficiently as he'd hoped, for the bastard had risen from the dead. Etienne was here in London, he knew it, and the only reason he was here was to finish what he had failed to accomplish last time. The neat scar on Louis' side twinged. He rubbed at it irritably.

He pushed thoughts of Etienne away, considering instead the last time he had seen Evie. He smiled, remembering how she had struggled to keep quiet as she came for him. *Merde,* but they needed to marry and soon. He did not want to keep sneaking about behind her parents' backs, stealing moments with her like the thief he was. It was not supposed to be like this. Louis dreamed of a life where he could be a good man in reality, instead of just playing a part. Though he had tried to be as honest with Evie as he dared, his life had been too full of lies and deceit, of getting what he wanted through his looks and charm, and he was sick of it. He needed to escape, to have something real and whole like his brother had found. Nic had turned his back on his past and created a happy future. Surely, he could do the same. He had wanted to court her, to do everything properly in full view of the world, but his life had never allowed him to take the straight path, even when his intentions were honourable. It hurt, though, to be cast in the role of villain, when he did not want to take from her, but to give her everything. If only she would let him.

Closing his eyes, he remembered holding her as she slept in his arms, and just how that had felt. The feeling had engulfed him, overwhelming him as he recognised what he had been searching for his whole life. Somewhere to belong. Someone who was so generous, so kind and giving that they would love him, even though he was bad and broken and wrong in so many ways. Someone who would not send him away when they grew bored… though he'd let no one have the chance to grow bored with him since he was a child. He had never stayed for long enough for them to realise they could.

Louis opened his eyes, blinking in the dark, and saw the flicker of a candle flame.

2ⁿᵈAugust1821, Place de Coderc, Périgueux, France.

Louis is nine years old.

Louis took the baguette in its neat little twist of paper from the boulangère and handed over the coin he'd been given. The bread was still warm, the delicious scent making his stomach clench with hunger. The temptation to break just a tiny piece off was palpable, but he knew better. Stealing from Madame Boucher was a terrible idea. Her husband might be a brute, but she had her own brand of spite that was almost as bad.

He made his way back to the house, keeping to the back streets, his head down. There had been too many fights with the local boys of late and he was tired of their taunting. It had been his own fault, of course. He should know better than to stand up to them, but Etienne had told them his name was 'chien' and that had been too much. He had reacted with fury as they had barked and treated him like a dog, shouting at them he was the Vicomte Sainte-Apre, which had naturally been greeted with howls of laughter. Now they addressed him as 'monsieur le roi' or 'le roi de la merde'—the king of shit.

His temper, which he had grown used to keeping tamped down, had unravelled. He had felled two boys twice his size before they'd had a chance to react and had been pummelling a third before it had dawned on any of them he was outnumbered. They'd beaten him until he threw up, and left him curled in the dirt. Somehow, he'd got back to the Boucher household only to get slung in the cage for his behaviour. He'd been relieved. At least he didn't have to move.

The bruises had almost faded now, but the memory hadn't, and he did not want to see any of those boys again.

"Psst!"

Louis stiffened, but did not look around.

"Psst!"

The insistent sound came again, and Louis glanced around to see a boy lingering in the shadows. He was around the same age as Louis, with grey eyes and dark blond hair, a scattering of freckles over his nose, and he was smiling, gesturing for Louis to come.

Instantly suspicious, Louis scowled at him. The boy was clean and better dressed than him and Louis bristled with indignation. "What do you want?"

"Venez ici," he insisted, gesturing to the alley where he lingered.

Louis snorted. "What, so you and your friends can kick my head in? Non, merci."

The boy paled, shaking his head frantically. "They're not my friends," he said in disgust. "They beat me up too, you know. Look, I only came to give you this." He unfolded a piece of clean linen to show the three neatly cut slices of baguette within.

Louis stared at the bread, his stomach clamouring, before his gaze returned to the boy. Hunger warred with pride. "I don't need your charity," he said coldly, though the words nearly choked him.

"It's not charity," the boy said at once, looking alarmed. "It's a... a gift, from a friend. We had some left over and I thought you might like it."

"I don't have any friends," Louis snarled at him, angry now that the boy would force him to make the point.

"Neither do I, but... but I could be your friend. If you want," he said, giving a crooked smile. It was a nice smile, genuine, and it crinkled his nose. The boy held out his free hand—the one not holding the bread. "I'm André."

Louis hesitated. "Why?" he asked, perplexed.

"I don't know, my mother liked the name, I suppose," André said, frowning.

Louis tsked. "Non, why do you want to be my friend?"

André shrugged. "Because I never saw anyone who looked like they need one more. Well, except for me, I suppose," he added sheepishly.

Louis felt the corners of his mouth quirk upwards, a strange sensation, unfamiliar but... nice. Cautiously, he shook André's hand, amused when the boy beamed at him.

"Tiens," he said, thrusting the bread at Louis. "I'd better not stay, I have jobs to do, and I'll catch it if I'm away too long, but I'll see you in the morning if you like? When you get the bread, first thing?"

Louis stared at the three slices of fresh bread, taking them with a sense of unreality. "Demain," he agreed, nodding, but by the time he looked up, the boy was gone.

Rather to Louis' surprise, André was waiting for him early the next morning, this time with a croissant. The boy talked nineteen to the dozen, trying to fit an hour's worth of conversation into the scant ten minutes it took Louis to walk to the boulangerie and back. He told Louis about his father who had been a baker and had taught him to cook, but who had died, leaving his mother to do the best she could. The day after that he was there again with three slices of bread, and the next a brioche bun his mother had baked, so tender and sweet Louis had almost cried. He had blinked hard, furious with himself, not wanting this strange boy to think him foolish, but André had studiously looked away, chattering like he always did, though Louis knew he'd seen.

One morning, after they had been meeting in secret for some weeks, André handed Louis a small golden biscuit sprinkled with sugar. He was trying very hard to look nonchalant, Louis realised. Louis, however, primed to respond to the tiniest shift in atmosphere or mood that might leave him with bruises or locked in a cage, knew this was no ordinary biscuit. He studied it carefully, lifting it to his nose to smell it. Butter and sweetness, the delicate unfurling of vanilla filled his senses. André was watching him avidly, practically jittering with impatience. Finally, Louis bit into it and did not need to feign his pleasure as the warm, buttery, crumbly flavour exploded over his tongue. Memories flooded back of fine china tea sets and plates of sweetmeats and pretty little cakes; of sitting on silk-covered settees and reciting poetry to ladies in fine gowns who smiled at him and played with his dark, curling hair. For a moment, the biscuit almost choked him. Then he remembered André had made it for him—his friend—and suddenly he could taste it again, taste the butter and the sugar, and the kindness with which it had been given.

"That," Louis said gravely, once he was steady enough to speak again. "Is the best thing I ever ate in my life."

André gave a little yip and ran around Louis in circles. The boy never seemed able to keep still, full of energy and exuberance and happiness. "Can I tell you a secret?"

"Bien sûr, if you want to," Louis said easily, filled with sudden pride that André trusted him.

André blushed, looking awkward. "You won't laugh?"

"Of course not," Louis replied, indignant.

"Non, of course not," André repeated, grinning. "Sorry. You're not like anyone else, are you? I keep forgetting."

Louis frowned at that. André had clearly meant it as a compliment, but he did not like that André could see he was not like everyone else. Père had taught him he was better than someone like André, though Louis did not understand how that could be true, when André was so gentle and good and kind. His Père had also taught him to lie and to cheat, how to manipulate and charm people, but then the king had banished him. Then Louis had been banished too, punished in the same way. So, he must be as wicked as his father. Why else had this happened to him? It was disconcerting, though, to discover even André, who was his friend and seemed to genuinely like him, could see that he was all wrong, different somehow, perhaps even wicked for the things he'd done, the lies he'd told. Père had been wicked too, lying and cheating and killing. What if the men his father had killed had not been bad men like his Père had told him. It was an illuminating thought. It had been wrong of Louis to tell the ladies lies, to use their kindness to get things from them. Lying was wrong, he'd known that even then. Manipulating people to get what you wanted was wrong too. Surely good people would never do that, only liars, and liars were weak and worthless, and people didn't want them around. Little wonder that the ladies had not wanted him to stay.

"You see that old shop?"

Louis forced his attention back to the conversation to look at a small, rather dilapidated building, the name above just visible in peeling paint. Thick cobwebs draped the glass front like tatty grey lace and children had scrawled rude words in the dirt. He nodded, though, curious why it interested André.

"I want to buy that shop. I made that biscuit, Louis, and I'm good at it, like my father was. I want to make pastries and cakes and biscuits, all kinds, the fanciest you ever saw. I will be the finest pâtissier in Périgueux, perhaps in the Dordogne." André grinned and then blushed furiously.

Louis studied him, his expression serious, realising that— despite the grin—this was André's dream. It was like Louis' dream of showing the world that he was worthy, even if it wasn't true. The dream was necessary, as necessary as air and water.

"That sounds like a good idea," Louis said carefully. "This part of town only has the boulangerie, you must go right down to the other side of the river for pastries."

"Oui!" André exclaimed, jumping up and down on the spot. "See! That's what I said." He gave a triumphant laugh. His

laughter died abruptly, though, and he sent a wistful glance at the shop and shrugged.

"What?" Louis demanded.

"It's only a dream," André said, his shoulders slumping. "Papa died last year and we're doing well enough, we have enough to get by with, but I shall never have enough to buy a shop. If I'm lucky, someone might take me on as an apprentice, but..."

Louis frowned, wishing he could help, which was a joke, as he could not even help himself. "If I had the money, I would have bought that biscuit. I'd buy all the biscuits you could make," he offered.

André smiled, a wistful smile this time. "Merci."

"Non, I mean it. Why not sell them? You don't need a shop. Just take a trayful out at lunchtime. There's the market on Wednesday morning and the stallholders can't leave their stalls to buy things, you could sell to them as well as the customers. Then use the money to buy more ingredients. Perhaps in time you'll get enough to have a stall yourself."

André looked at him as if he'd run mad. Louis made an impatient sound and grasped the boy's thin shoulders. He was scrawnier than Louis, and that was saying something. "Only fools despair, André. Clever men make plans."

André stared at him, eyes shining with admiration. "You're clever, aren't you, Louis?"

Louis snorted. "And a fat lot of good it does me. But it is a good idea, André. Promise me you'll try it. It might take time, but it's worth a try at least."

André nodded. "I promise," he whispered.

15th July 1842, Peregrine House, Grosvenor Square, London.

"We can't keep doing this."

Evie pulled out of his embrace and walked to the window. She removed the candle and then set it on her dressing table. She was anxious tonight, no doubt after being the object of her family's love and attention all day.

"It's your birthday," Louis said, unnerved by her jittery mood. "I had to see you on your birthday."

She turned and smiled at him, but it was a wistful smile, as if they were living in a fantasy and she, at least, was prepared to admit it. "So it is, but what about next week, Louis? What will be the excuse then? And the week after, and the week after that? We are going to get caught eventually."

"Then marry me," he said, frustration making the words sharper than he'd intended. "Stop all this dancing about and come away with me. We can go now, this minute. I'll take you to France. We could go to Provence and swim in the sea. It is so blue and clear, Evie. You would love it, I know. We could walk through the lavender fields and drink wine as pink as your blushes. We would be together, you and I. Always. I will buy us a house overlooking the sea and we will make love with the windows open, and the sound of the waves can lull us to sleep in each other's arms."

"Oh, Louis," she sighed with frustration. She moved to him, cupping his face with her hands. "That sounds like a beautiful dream. But what of my family? I cannot just go against their wishes. They love and care for me too and I won't hurt them that way. What of the secrets you are keeping? What of the men you have killed? Are there more men like this? Will there be more killing? Have you got enemies? For I have the strongest sensation you are preparing to run away, and you want to take me with you."

"And will you come?" he demanded, angry and hurt, even though she was absolutely right.

He had enemies. He had one man determined to see him dead and if that man discovered his love for Evie, she too would be in danger. He ought to tell her, he ought to tell her everything, but he feared if she knew it all she would be afraid of him and turn away. The idea that his past would be the reason for ruining his future made him feel sick, panic filling his chest until it became hard to breathe. Yet he knew it was likely the way this would play out. He was too difficult, too tainted, too immersed in the kind of dark world in which she wanted no part... but not telling her would be betraying her trust in the worst way. She might never forgive him for that. If only she would choose him marry him, and not care about the rest. Then he could keep her close, keep her safe, but what had he expected? She was far too intelligent to do something so risky, so very foolish. Why would she choose a man like him over her family? He wasn't enough. He was never enough. Hadn't he been told over and again that he was the devil's instrument, leading the innocent into darkness? He had so wanted that not to be true, but here he was, doing his best to tempt Evie to leave her family and everything good in her life for him, a man who had spent his life lying and thieving and cheating to survive. Just because he'd had no choice did not make it right. Perhaps he really was the serpent in the garden of Eden after all. A sudden chill washed over him at the thought. No. Not that. That could not be true. He had been bad, wicked even, but he *wanted* to be better. Evie would help him to be better. Unless she saw what he was and ran away, leaving him alone in the dark again.

Louis swallowed down a surge of panic.

"Will you come with me, Evie?" he asked again, the question tinged with desperation now no matter how hard he tried to hide it.

She stared at him in exasperation. *"Tonight?* No. I will not come tonight. A spiteful woman who has since been murdered has ruined one of my dearest friends, you might care to remember. Poor Rosamund is in trouble. The scandal is out of control, and she needs her friends to help her, Louis. All of us."

The reproach stung. "Fine. And when the scandal has faded, will you come then?"

"Will you answer my questions?" she countered.

"Haven't you heard enough?" he replied, trying to tamp down his growing panic, wondering if he was pushing too hard. She would get tired of his evasion soon, she would see through the façade to what lay beneath. Would she tell him it was over?

Instead of withdrawing her touch, she reached up on tiptoes and pressed her mouth to his cheek. "No, Louis. I want to hear it all. I will not marry you until I have heard everything, all of it. *If* we marry, then it will be with the truth spread out between us, or not all."

Louis made a sound of frustration and caught her in his arms, pulling her close and kissing her because he could not think of what else to do, and because he needed her too badly not to be selfish. The kiss was hard and deep and more than a little frantic. She melted against him, responding instantly as he'd known she would. Thank heavens. He still had this, at least. She still desired him. Evie slid her hands into his hair, tangling her fingers into it. She liked his hair, liked pulling it tight when she was in the grip of a climax. He liked that too. But now she pushed him away, dragging her mouth from his with a groan.

"No. No! Stop. You're doing it again. I won't let you divert me. We must talk."

"I do not want to talk tonight," he bit out, stubborn now as anxiety reasserted itself. Every time he revealed more of his past, it was like stripping away another layer of paint on the mask he wore, and he feared what—if anything—would remain when it was all gone.

"Then you had better go," she said, not unkindly, but with a steely note he did not underestimate.

He had never underestimated Evie. That was the rest of the bloody world, not him. There was one thing left to do though, one last chance tonight to tempt her to choose him.

"I have not given you your present yet," he said, holding out a small, square box.

Evie stared at the velvet box sitting in the palm of his hand.

"Oh, Louis," she said with a helpless sigh.

She took the box and opened it, her breath catching as she saw the ring on the bed of white satin, the huge, flawless emerald glittering in the candlelight.

"It's beautiful," she whispered, a catch in her throat, and then snapped the box shut again. "But I can't take it. I've had to hide the other gifts. I can't even look at them, Louis. It's all hidden. All of us is hidden. I don't want to hide anymore. I don't want to run away like we've done something shameful. I don't want people to discuss our elopement over their coffee and wonder why on earth you chose me."

She held the box out to him, but he refused to take it.

"Why do you care what those people think? You know what I think. I love you!" he said fiercely. "I would do anything for you, you know that. Why isn't that enough?"

"Because you're hiding from me, Louis! I won't run away, abandon my family, my life, everything I know, for a man who does not trust me enough to give himself to me entirely. You want my entirety. You have it, Louis. You know all my secrets, all my dreams. You have my heart, but you will not have my life until you learn to trust me as much as I trust you."

"But you *don't* trust me!" he raged, immediately mortified that he had said such a thing.

What had he done to earn her trust of late? Since her father's revelations, he had gone out of his way to persuade her to love him, to run away with him without ever giving her the only thing she consistently asked for. The truth. But he dared not give her the truth, for surely she would turn her back on him once the entire sordid story was laid before her. The tightness in his chest increased, the desire to give her everything, anything she wanted, warring with his certainty that she could not love him if she knew it all. She was too good, too kind, to ever wish to hurt him, but he knew she was strong enough to walk away too, and there would not be a damned thing he could do about it.

"Perhaps," she admitted slowly, staring at him as though she could see into his soul, making him want to turn away and hide his face in shame. "Perhaps I don't trust you enough. Perhaps I do not trust in your love enough to believe it will not fade, that you will not tire of me and grow bored when I no longer amuse you, or when I am bad-tempered, or difficult, or unreasonable. For I can be all those things, Louis, as you are discovering."

Louis jolted with shock, astonished that she of all people could think that? How could she believe that he would be the one to grow tired of her when the truth was so obvious to him. Keeping her, proving to her that he could deserve her love would be his life's work. No one else had ever wanted him to stay. No one else had ever known him like Evie had without bedding him and still sought him out. No one ever came back, but she did. She always had, and she thought *he* would be the one to run away from that?

"You think I would grow tired of *you*?" he said, struggling to hide how badly that accusation hurt. "You think I'm playing at this?"

"I never said that!" she exclaimed, annoyed now.

"You're right, I should go," he said, aware that she was becoming impatient with him.

He did not know how to make it better, to make it right. She wanted from him the one thing he was afraid to give her, because if he gave it she would decide it was too much, that *he* was too much. She did not want to live in the darkness with him, and no matter how hard he tried, it always came for him in the end. Perhaps he ought to leave her, ought to do the honourable thing and let her marry someone more deserving of her. But he had tried to stay away, tried to give her the chance to find another man, a better one, and it had been impossible. He was not strong enough to let her go.

No woman had ever loved him like she did and that was so impossibly precious he did not know how to let it go.

What was wrong with him? He was too on edge, reacting badly. Rationally, he knew she was not being unreasonable in what she was asking of him, but she did not understand what he was holding back. She had been raised in a loving home, with a sense of security, of her place in the world. How could she possibly look at the vileness of what his life had been and not see at once how tainted he was by it? Evil was drawn to him, just as Etienne had become obsessed with him. His belief that Evie was his guiding light, a talisman so powerful it would keep the darkness at bay, was not something he could explain in words without sounding like a lunatic. But time was running out, he was too aware of the clock ticking, of things moving beyond his control. A cold, panicky sensation kept sliding down his back, foreboding pressing down on him, smothering all his hopes.

"Louis!"

She caught his hand as he reached for the door, and he hesitated. He frowned as she pressed the ring box against his palm, giving him no choice but to take it. "Keep it for me," she whispered. "I want to wear it. I swear I do, but with my eyes wide open."

Louis nodded though he wanted to beg her to change her mind, but he knew too well she had a will of iron. If he wanted her, he must tell her everything. All of it. And no doubt he'd watch her walk away from him the moment he was done. He nodded reluctantly.

"Come to me again after Mrs Belvedere's ball, the day after tomorrow. Perhaps we will both be in a better frame of mind. We'll talk, and you'll tell me the rest of it. All of it?"

He made himself say it, though it felt like agreeing to cut out his heart. *"Oui."*

Evie must have heard his reluctance for she pressed the point. "Promise me, Louis. No trying to distract me with kisses." She stared at him, serious, though there was a smile on her lips.

What choice did he have? *"Je promets."*

She leaned in and kissed him softly. Louis closed his eyes, sighing.

"Be careful, Louis. I love you."

He nodded and stole another kiss before slipping out into the dark hallway.

Barnaby was outside his front door when Louis returned to his apartment. He started as Louis slipped in through the window onto the landing. Louis could hardly be seen walking through the front door of the building dressed as he was and looking like a thief, though.

"Oh, thank goodness," his friend said, his relief palpable. "I was certain you'd get caught. I came by earlier and left a note. Knew where you'd gone, of course. It's her birthday."

Louis nodded and headed to the door.

"Did she like her present?" Barnaby asked.

"Not enough to accept it," he said darkly, and then shook his head, annoyed with himself. "Yes, she liked it, but I am still winning her over. It seems trusting me means knowing every dreadful thing I've ever done. It's not a comfortable experience, baring your soul."

Barnaby made a sympathetic sound as the door swung open. "Don't suppose it is at first, but think how it would feel to have someone who knows every terrible thing about you, and know they still love you. It's worth the pain of ripping off a plaster, isn't it? Just get it over with. I should."

Louis huffed out a laugh and smiled. "As ever, you give the best advice, *mon ami.*"

He stepped inside the apartment and went to the lamp Elton had left for him, turning it up. As he lifted it, he froze, his instincts prickling. There was a used glass beside the decanter of Cognac. Elton had cleared everything away earlier. Louis had watched him do it, and he knew Elton well enough to know he would never sneak his employer's liquor. Even if he would do such a thing, he was far too intelligent to leave the evidence on view. Louis' stomach plunged, his breathing becoming fast and harsh as he realised Etienne had been here again. He shuddered at the idea of the man poking around among his personal belongings, touching his things.

"Louis?" Barnaby asked, staring at him cautiously.

No doubt he thought Louis was losing his mind. The man sniffed the air, evidently remembering what had happened last time, and how Louis had gone mad because of the stench of Etienne's foul cigars.

"No cigar smoke. Not a trace," Barnaby said, his voice soothing, as if he was placating a fretful toddler.

Louis ignored him, staring about as if expecting an attack from any side. Barnaby watched him with concern, but Louis didn't care how it looked; he knew the bastard had been here. He went to his study, his stomach twisting as he opened the door. Here, the telltale scent of a French cigar reached his nostrils, making him want to retch. The window was open, had been since the last time on Louis' instructions, for even days later he could not shake the scent of the damn cigar. The warm night air ruffled the curtains, dispersing the smell, but it was there again.

"You smell it now?" Louis demanded.

Barnaby pulled a face. "Faintly, I suppose," he allowed, moving to the window. "But it probably just drifted up from the street. Loads of fellows out strolling. Look, see for yourself."

45

Louis moved to the window to see Barnaby was right, but he didn't care. Etienne had been here. Etienne was not dead. His heart picked up speed. If Etienne had been here, he'd want Louis to know it. But he'd tease him first, like the lingering scent of a French cigar, the same brand his father had smoked. Etienne had never been an original thinker, but he liked to believe he was clever. He'd left something. There was something else, Louis knew it.

He moved to the shelves and began pulling out books, shaking them out and tossing them onto the desk.

"Louis? What the devil are you about now?" Barnaby demanded.

Louis didn't answer, well aware he must look like a madman but not prepared to stop. He pulled the cushions off the sofa, thrusting his hands down the sides and sliding along to search all the hidden corners. He looked under chairs, under rugs, behind pictures, even shook out the curtains.

"Louis, there's nothing here," Barnaby protested in alarm as Elton came to see what the fuss was about.

"There's been no one here, monsieur, I swear it," Elton said, wringing his hands together. "I locked the door after you, just like you said, and no one could climb up to the study window, we're on the fourth floor."

"I could," Louis muttered grimly, and though Etienne had never had his skills or anything like, he was obsessed and bloody mad, and that counted for a great deal when impossible things needed to happen.

Louis moved to his bedroom next, ripping the covers off his bed, flinging the mattress aside, pulling out drawers while Elton watched in mute dismay. He did not know what time it was when he heard voices and the sound of the front door opening and closing but the apartment was in disarray, and he was moving to Nic's old room.

"Qu'est-ce que vous foutez? Have you run mad?" Nic demanded, catching him by the arm.

Louis started in surprise at the sight of his brother, realising that Barnaby must have sent for him. He glared at his friend, who blushed and threw up his hands. "I didn't know what else to do, Louis! You're overwrought."

"Etienne," Louis said urgently. "He's been here."

Nic sent him a worried, slightly pitying look. "Louis, Etienne is dead. He's been dead a long time now. You know that. He was badly wounded, unconscious. Wolf only just got you out of that building alive and Etienne was still in there. I saw what remained after the fire. No one could have survived it."

"He did!" Louis shouted furiously. "I know he did. He's been here, and more than once now. He's toying with me. The bastard is coming for me, Nic. He's left something here, I know he has. You know how he loves his games and letters, his vile little parcels."

Louis tugged his arm free and carried on his search of Nic's room, very aware of the three men standing together, talking in low voices. They thought he was losing his damned mind. Perhaps he was. He felt sick, a thrill of panic rolling down his back. He knew what he was saying, knew Nic was right. When Wolf had hauled him out after the fight, he'd been half dead and had taken months to recover, but Etienne had been unconscious too, bleeding from a gunshot wound, the fire raging around him. Wolf had barely carried Louis three steps into the street before the building had collapsed, sending fire billowing for miles up into the darkness. Etienne could not have survived that.

Yet Louis would stake his sanity, his life, on the fact that he had.

Chapter 3

Dearest Aisling,

I am writing on behalf of Sultan. He is most terribly sorry for eating your gloves and hopes that you might forgive him for his unacceptable behaviour, and he begs you to remember that even though he is very large — as Great Danes are — he is still only a pup. He begs me to send you a replacement pair of gloves which he hopes might allow you to think kindly of him.

The poor darling is giving me the most mournful look as I write this, so you simply must forgive him. Please do.

—Excerpt of a letter from Lady Cara Baxter (daughter of Luke and Kitty Baxter, Earl and Countess of Trevick) to her sister Mrs Aisling Cootes—on behalf of her dog, Sultan.

11th November 1823, Place de Coderc, Périgueux, France.

Louis is eleven years old.

November was a cruel month, icy cold with a bitter wind that howled through the narrow streets of Périgueux, cutting through

Louis' threadbare clothes. Shivering, he dusted icing sugar from his frozen fingers and grinned at André.

"C'était délicieux. The best thing I ever ate," he said with approval, licking his lips and laughing as André turned scarlet with pleasure.

Not that it took much these days to make André blush. Louis had noticed the change in the way André looked at him, the way most people looked at him, spoke to him. Despite the Bouchers' meagre rations he was growing up fast, catching Etienne who was three years older. Louis was getting taller, broader, and judging by the way the girls looked at him, they approved of the changes. They giggled and whispered and followed him about on his daily trip to and from the boulangerie, much to André's annoyance.

Louis knew André was jealous, but did not know what to do about it. Louis tried to shoo them off, growling at them to keep away from him, but his bad-tempered displays only seemed to make them more insistent. Not that he wouldn't have liked to have spoken to them, but he knew the way the girls stopped and stared at him disgusted Monsieur Boucher. He said Louis was made in the devil's image, that he was Satan's spawn, come to tempt the righteous down into darkness. He was the serpent in the garden of Eden. Louis did not know what that meant, but he knew if the man saw the way those girls followed him about, it would be he who would suffer for it. If Monsieur Boucher saw the way André looked at him, it would be far, far worse.

André had begun a stall in the marketplace earlier in the year and it was doing well. Not anywhere near enough to buy or even rent the shop he dreamed of, but it was a start. He was growing in confidence too, and that was wonderful to see. Louis wanted his friend to be happy, though he feared for him. André was slight and delicate and easily bullied. The local boys had stopped picking on Louis, knowing to fight him was to get their noses broken, but they had also figured out the best way to hurt him was to hurt André and then tell stories about him to Monsieur Boucher, which usually got him locked in the cage or lashed with monsieur's belt.

Louis dreamed about running away, but during the day there were too many eyes upon him and his chances of getting far were poor. At night, the house was locked up tight, but Louis lived hoping a chance would present itself.

Though it was incredibly risky, he had stolen items he'd need to survive on his own and buried them down by the river, wrapped in a piece of rag. He had a knife, stolen from the butcher's shop, small but wickedly sharp; a tinderbox swiped from inside an open window when the opportunity had presented itself; and a fob watch. The watch was old and rather beaten up, but Louis thought it might be silver. Silver he could pawn.

He had literally bumped into a man strolling through the town some months back. Not a local, or at least not one who still lived here. Louis had been running to avoid a gang of boys in case they meant to cause him trouble and had ploughed into him. He'd put his hands out to steady the fellow, and the watch had been right there, and... it had been the work of a moment. The man hadn't even known it had happened. Louis had apologised and run away as fast as he could, the watch clutched in his hand. He'd been terrified and elated all at once and had not slept a wink that night, certain that someone would wake the household by hammering on the door and calling him out as a thief, but no one did. He'd stolen other things since then and now had a few coins set aside. Only from people who looked like they could afford it, and never from the locals. André didn't know. Nor did he know Louis was planning on running away. Louis didn't know how to tell him.

Louis said goodbye to André and hurried back to the house, irritated to discover Etienne waiting for him.

"Shouldn't you be in lessons?" Louis said, trying to keep his tone even. Etienne always needed careful handling. Louis was usually clever enough to manage him, to divert his attention, but sometimes Etienne was just belligerent and pig-headed and there

was nothing to be done with him. There were other times too, like when Etienne had caught a rat and found it endlessly amusing to prick the creature with a pin tied to a stick to hear it squeal. Such casual cruelty, even to a rat, made Louis look upon the boy with revulsion, but he kept such emotions hidden, as he hid everything.

"The teacher is sick, so I have the whole day to myself," Etienne *crowed, grinning at him. "Come down to the river with me. I want to see if the ice is thick enough to skate on."*

"I can't. I have to work in the kitchen. Thérèse is sick and there's only Jeanne to prepare lunch."

"Women's work," Etienne said in disgust.

Louis shrugged. "You want to eat, don't you?"

He had always preferred working in the kitchens, especially in the winter. Thérèse knew better than to be kind to him and incur her employer's wrath, but she was not unkind, which was boon enough to be pleasant.

"But I want you to come with me. You never spend time with me anymore. You're supposed to be my friend."

Louis wondered in what world Etienne could ever see them as friends, but held his tongue. Etienne seemed oblivious to the life Louis led, believing the things his father told him. Etienne believed they were helping Louis be a better person by teaching him how real people lived, by saving him from becoming corrupt like his Père.

He had been careful to keep his friendship with André secret from Etienne. The few times Etienne had seen Louis talking to his friend, Etienne had been suspicious and jealous, not liking the fact Louis spoke to anyone but him. Louis had lied, saying the boy had been trying to sell the household biscuits and wanted him to ask Madame Boucher if she would like some. Etienne had appeared to believe this, but had watched Louis like a hawk for days afterwards, following him about like his shadow. Thankfully, Louis had warned André that Etienne was not to be trusted and his friend had wisely kept clear.

"I can't come. Your mother expects me to work."

Etienne grumbled, folding his arms. "Well, then later. At bedtime. Come to my room and play cards with me."

"If you want," Louis said with a reluctant shrug, and left Etienne, hurrying down the stairs with the baguette.

"Alors, at last," Jeanne said, wiping dirty blonde hair from her eyes with a floury hand. "Thought you'd got lost. Get peeling those potatoes, will you? If we don't get them on soon, lunch will be late and then we'll be up to our necks in shit."

No change there, Louis thought darkly, but picked up the knife and began peeling the potatoes. He'd done perhaps three when he felt Jeanne's eyes on him. Louis looked up, but she was rolling out pastry dough and he dismissed it. The next time he caught her looking and she blushed, turning away from him. Louis frowned. Jeanne was two or three years older than him and skinny as a pole, though that hadn't stopped Etienne from trying to kiss Jeanne and get his hands under her skirts. Louis had heard the commotion when Madame Boucher had walked in on Etienne. Of course, Jeanne had got the blame for leading Etienne on. Not that Jeanne had said otherwise, what was the point? Louis had looked out for her since then, trying to ensure she was never left alone with Etienne.

"You got a girl then, Louis?" Jeanne asked.

Louis stared at her in disbelief. Did no one see what went on in this house? Did they not realise he was a bloody prisoner here? Monsieur Boucher always told people how Louis was a charitable case, a bad lad with a propensity for lying and stealing, and he was doing his best to put the boy back on a righteous path. Lying bastard.

"When and where would I get one of those?" he demanded. "If I'm not back from the boulangerie inside of fifteen minutes, all hell breaks loose."

"You ever had a girl?" Jeanne asked a moment later, looking at Louis oddly from under her lashes.

Louis felt colour creep up the back of his neck and did not deign to answer.

Jeanne wiped her floury hands on her apron. "I'd let you… you know… If you want to."

Louis shook his head, unnerved. "Non."

"You shy?" Jeanne wheedled, sidling around the table towards him. Louis jumped as she squeezed his backside and stared at her in shock.

"Jeanne! Take your hands off that boy."

Louis could not remember ever being relieved to see Madame Boucher in his life before, but in that moment he was. Except then he saw the way she was looking at him, not at Jeanne. There was disgust in her eyes, her thin lip curling.

"Ca suffit," she said, shaking her head, her dark eyes glittering malevolently. "I suppose it was inevitable, but I thought we'd a year or two yet before you caused that sort of trouble. I should have known better. It's in your blood. Tainted and debauched, it is. It's time we got rid of you before you infect the entire damn town. I've seen the way you bat your lashes at everyone. Don't you think I haven't seen," she sneered at him.

Louis went hot and cold, wondering what that meant. Did he do that? He supposed Père had taught him something of the sort. Guilt squirmed in his belly. She swept out of the kitchen and Jeanne returned to her work, acting as if Louis didn't exist, which suited him fine.

A week came and went and nothing more was said, so Louis hoped whatever Madame had been threatening to do with him had been forgotten.

As with so many things Louis hoped, he was proven wrong.

In the early hours of the morning, Louis was rudely awoken by Monsieur Boucher. Louis was curled in a tight ball on the stone floor before the dying embers of the kitchen fire. Monsieur's boot came down on his side and gave a hard push, sending Louis sprawling. He woke instantly, gasping.

"Levez-vous," the man said, his voice cold, flicking the ash from his cigar at Louis with an expression of contempt.

Louis got up as instructed, knowing better than to hesitate. Monsieur Boucher was looking older, Louis noted in the flickering light of the candle the man carried. His thick dark hair was greying now, and harsh lines scored his face, highlighting the bitter expression that he habitually wore. The eyes were the same, though: hard and merciless. His once fine clothes were shabbier now, too, and the meals the family ate were not as lavish as they'd once been. Louis wondered what that meant.

Monsieur gestured for Louis to move, guiding him up the stairs to the front parlour. Outside of the door, he grabbed Louis' hair, yanking his head back.

"You will be nice to my guests and do exactly what they tell you to do? Do you understand?"

Louis wanted to say no, he didn't understand, but that would gain him a slap, so he said nothing.

Monsieur's grip tightened on his hair. "Do you understand, you little shit?"

Louis nodded, seeing no other option.

Monsieur nodded, opened the door and pushed Louis inside. Louis staggered, blinking in the bright candlelight of the room, to discover a man and a woman staring at him.

"Well, well," the man said, with a cultured English voice. "I admit I am surprised, but you are every bit as pretty as he said."

Louis' father had taught him some English. A prerequisite for any nobleman, his Père had said. Louis remembered very little of it, but 'pretty' he understood. The man switched to French, addressing the gaudily dressed woman who sat watching Louis with unnerving intensity.

"He'll do nicely, eh, Liane?"

"Oui," the woman purred, getting to her feet. "He'll grow up big and strong, I reckon."

Louis stepped away up, finding the door at his back.

"Oh, but he is shy, monsieur," the woman chuckled, moving closer. "Don't be shy, little man. We won't hurt you."

Louis' gaze darted from one to the other, not knowing what to think. The man was big, far bigger than Monsieur Boucher, and an Englishman. A nobleman, if Louis had to guess. Did he know who Louis really was? The woman was harder to judge. French, certainly, but not from around here; her accent was harder. She might have been attractive, but her eyes were like chips of pale blue glass, utterly cold, making her look older than perhaps she was, though she was younger than the man, maybe in her thirties.

"How would you like to come and live with Liane in a lovely big house? You'll have a nice room and no hard work to do, regular meals." She touched a finger to the ragged shirt he wore and grimaced. "Smart clothes too. Wouldn't you like that?"

Instinctively, Louis shook his head.

Liane made a moue of displeasure. "Well, that's not very nice. I think you were told to be nice to us, weren't you?"

Louis flushed, now having a vague idea of what that was supposed to mean. Knowing he would be beaten for it and not caring, Louis turned, snatching at the door handle, only to find it locked.

There was a soft chuckle from behind him and the man caught his arm, gently but firmly forcing him to turn around again.

"Don't tell me you want to stay in this hellhole? You're a clever boy, I'm sure. Can't you see how much easier your life will be with us?" he said, his voice kind enough but a look in his eyes that made Louis' chest tight.

This man was not going to make his life easier. Not at all. Though he could not have put into words why, Louis knew this man was worse than Monsieur Boucher, that his life would never be his own again if he went with them.

"He's not very friendly," Liane said with a sigh. "Come on, lovely, don't be a silly boy. Come and talk to me."

She went and sat down on the settee and patted the seat next to her. Though Louis would rather have tried to climb out the window, the man guided him to the settee and so he sat.

Liane smiled at him. "There. I don't bite. Now, tell me your name."

Louis tried to answer, but the words wouldn't come. He glanced up at the man's face, wondering if he would hit him for it. Monsieur Boucher would have hit him, but the man only smiled pleasantly. Louis' skin crawled.

"Louis César," he choked out.

"A pretty name for a pretty boy," the man said, exchanging a glance with Liane.

Louis jolted as Liane took his hand. "Good grief, dearie, I'm not going to eat you!" she exclaimed with a laugh.

Louis wanted to pull his hand free but that would have been rude, and he did not want them telling Monsieur Boucher that he had been rude.

"Now, then," Liane said. "When we come back to get you, we will take you to Paris. We have a big house there, with lots of boys

and girls, so you'll have so many friends. You'll have your own room too, all to yourself, with a proper bed, and a fire in the winter. Won't that be lovely?"

Too lovely, he thought, looking from Liane and her blue glass eyes to the man whose gaze upon him made Louis feel sick and anxious. He wanted to get away from them both. He wanted to pull his hand free and wash it and wash it and go somewhere they could never find him. Louis did not say that though. Instead he steeled his nerve and lied through his teeth.

"It does sound lovely," he said, hoping they would think the way his voice trembled was simply from nerves and not revulsion. "W-When will we go?"

"Oh, he's eager now!" Liane said, beaming at the man, whose gaze had never strayed from Louis' face. "What a good boy."

"Are you eager, Louis? Do you want to come with us?" the man asked, and Louis knew this was someone who understood human nature, who could read a lie as easily his father could have done.

But Louis had been taught to lie too, to charm and deceive. So he looked at his feet, hoping he looked shy and naïve.

"Monsieur Boucher b-beats me," he said in a halting voice. "And I have to sleep on the kitchen floor. I'm always hungry," he added for good measure.

"Oh, poor lamb," Liane said, and he glanced at her, wondering if that was truly compassion in her eyes or if she was as good at dissembling as he was.

He dared to look up at the man, a shy glance from under his lashes, one his father had taught him all those years ago. The fellow smiled and ruffled his hair.

"Well, that's all over now. You'll be far more comfortable with us. We'll have a grand time together."

Louis forced himself to nod but could not make his mouth return the smile, no matter how he tried.

Liane got to her feet and held her hands out to Louis, pulling him up too. "Well, we'll be off now, but you'd best pack your things, for we'll be back in two days, and then you can begin your new life."

"I don't have any things," Louis replied, not having to try too hard to sound pitiful.

Liane tsked and stroked his face before grasping his chin and pressing her red painted mouth to his. She made a kissing sound and then pulled him into a hug, his face pressed against her bosom.

"Such a lamb!" she said with a sigh, before turning to the man again.

She let him go and Louis had to fight the overwhelming need to scrub at his mouth, to remove the taste of her from his lips. The door opened and Louis thought he had never been so relieved to see Madame Boucher in all his life.

She looked at the couple with obvious distaste. "Alors?"

"Oui, Madame," the man said. "We'll come back this way on our return to Paris in two days. Make certain he is bathed and made presentable. I'll send some decent clothes for him, not those disgusting rags. We can't have our beautiful young man dressed like a pauper, can we, Liane?"

"Non, indeed, monsieur, we cannot."

"But don't cut his hair," the man instructed, reaching past Madame Boucher to tug at Louis' dark curls. "It's so pretty as it is. It's hard to tell if he's a boy or a girl."

With that, he laughed, and the two went out. Once the door closed behind them, Louis turned to Madame Boucher, his heart thudding behind his ribs.

"Madame," he said, the words almost choking him as he'd sworn he'd never beg this woman for anything. "Please. Please, don't... don't let them take me. I'll work harder. I'll be good, I swear."

"Good?" she said in disgust. "You can't be good. You're the serpent in the garden of Eden is what you are, tempting decent folk to act licentiously, and it's only just begun. It will get worse as you get older. See what you did to Jeanne, making her act like a bitch in heat."

"I'm not!" Louis cried, shaking his head, trembling so hard he had to lean against the wall. "I didn't!"

Madame snorted. "You don't even know you're doing it. Away with you now. I don't want to look at you."

Somehow, Louis made his way back to the kitchen to the last embers of the dying fire. He did not sleep, silent tears slipping down his cheeks. He could not stop shaking as he conjured images of what his future would hold.

He was not innocent; he did not think he ever had been. Louis knew what a whore was, how they earned their keep, and that beautiful women earned more than ugly ones. Monsieur said he looked as pretty as a girl and Louis had a horrible feeling he knew what that meant for him. There was no other choice now, he had to get away. He had to leave, because he knew he would not survive that life. If either of those vile people touched him, Louis would kill them, or he would die.

15th July 1842, Peregrine House, Grosvenor Square, London.

Louis sealed the note to Wolf, knowing he was likely the only person in the entire world who did not think Louis had lost his mind. Wryly, Louis conceded that he himself was uncertain he had not, but he would rather act like a madman than risk being caught unaware. Elton had put his office back to rights and Louis could still hear him moving about the bedroom, tidying up the havoc. Louis felt bad about that. Elton got a generous wage and Louis was not an exacting employer, but tonight's behaviour had caused the fellow a deal of distress and a lot of work. He would have to make it up to him.

Louis sat back in his chair with a groan, massaging his temples. His head ached, and he had not had a decent night's rest since the first time he'd smelled that disgusting cigar smoke. Nightmares plagued him, disturbing his sleep to the point he was reluctant to try for fear of what hellish scene his mind would make him relive. He wanted to sleep with Evie in his arms, wanted to wrap himself in her goodness, in her love, as if she were a living amulet, protecting him from evil. A foolish idea, but one he could not seem to shake off. He missed her fiercely and castigated himself for spoiling his time with her. He'd known he would have to confess the truth of his life eventually, but he did not want to think about a time when he'd either been at the mercy of others, or using people in turn for his own ends, let alone share it with the woman he loved. She ought to be protected from such a world, from knowing he had lived such a life, but she demanded his honesty. She did not understand what she asked of him. Louis would have given her the world if he could, and happily, but to tell the truth? To tell the truth was to expose everything he hid from the world. How could she not be sickened by it when it sickened him? How could he share the things that gave him nightmares and woke him sweating with terror in the middle of the night and imagine she would still choose him?

She deserved his honesty. He had always known that, and had always tried to give it to her, but it was becoming harder to do. Every time he thought about his life, about the things he'd done, he became more ashamed, more aware of how little he deserved her. What if she realised that too? What if she looked at him and realised there was nothing behind the pretty façade except a rotten interior? He had tried so many times to change his life, but it always ended the same way, repeating the same cycle. Would it be that way with her too? If he let her see everything, know all of him, would that be the spark that illuminated her view of him, let her see him with too much clarity and ended everything?

He sighed and opened his eyes, and his gaze snagged on a tiny triangle against the blue-painted wall, the corner of a piece of paper perhaps, slipped behind a crack in the ornate white plaster moulding. With a sick feeling swirling in his guts, Louis got up and pulled the chair from behind his desk. He stood on it and reached up to where a leak in the roof had slightly damaged the plasterwork, making it pull away from the wall in places. An artisan was due next week to make repairs, but *that* had not been there before. Carefully, Louis tugged and withdrew a small square of paper. It was old, yellow with age. Louis unfolded it. Inside was a curl of dark hair.

"Putain!" Louis exclaimed in shock, dropping it as if he'd been burned.

Chapter 4

Duval,

Take as many men as you need and watch the English ports the comte is most likely to use. If he needs to leave fast, he'll need help. Make certain he has it.

—Excerpt of a letter from Wulfric 'Wolf' De Vere to Gaston Duval.

17th July 1842, Mrs Belvedere's Ball, Bloomsbury Square, Holborn, London.

Louis rubbed the back of his neck as he scanned the ballroom. No matter how many times he assured himself he was merely being paranoid, he could not shake off the sense of foreboding. Yet he had not lived this long by ignoring his instincts and, although he knew Evie's parents were here watching over her, he could not bear to allow her out of his sight. He did not approach her directly, not wanting to cause her trouble.

The entire *ton* was twittering like so many birds this evening, thoroughly over-excited by the appearance of the new Lord and Lady Hargreaves. Louis had to admire the man's nerve, marrying Lady Rosamund when his last wife was barely cold. Louis watched as Evie crossed the ballroom to intercept Lady Rosamund. The two women spoke, heads together for a moment, before turning and hurrying off, side by side. Evie looked up as she went, perhaps sensing his gaze upon her, and their eyes met. She stared at him for a long moment, before turning away, and carrying on with Lady Rosamund. Louis went to follow them, only to be halted by a hand on his arm.

"Monsieur le Comte?"

Louis turned to see one of Lady Belvedere's servants. "Yes? What is it?"

"I was asked to give you this, sir." The servant held out a sealed note.

Frowning, Louis took it. There was no crest on the seal, no writing on the outside, nothing to mark its sender. "Who gave you this?"

"It wasn't given to me directly, but to another servant. He said a gentleman left it at the door with instructions that you got it at once. Said it was important."

"A young man? An old one?" Louis demanded.

"I'm sorry, I can't say. Will that be all?"

Louis nodded, frustrated, and the man hurried away.

"What was that about?" Barnaby demanded, having seen the exchange. "Letters at a ball? Bit odd."

"Indeed," Louis replied, breaking the seal. He stared at the page.

The writing was an untidy scrawl, but legible enough. One word written in large letters: *Chien.*

Louis' stomach plunged as he stared at the word, his heart beating too fast, though somehow he had expected it. At this point, it was almost a relief.

"Louis? What is it? What does it say? You've gone white as a sheet."

Louis folded the paper again and handed it to Barnaby. "Give that to my brother," he told him. "Ask him if he believes me now. I must find Evie."

Louis pushed through the crowd, not caring who he elbowed in his need to get to Evie, but he found no sign of her. He searched the refreshments room and lingered impatiently in sight of the ladies' retiring room until he was certain she could not be in there, either. He searched the gardens, all the public rooms and some of the private ones, interrupting a tryst in one before he hurried away again. Back in the ballroom, he fought to keep his panic under control, only dimly aware that something was happening amongst the crowd of people. Raised voices reached him and then a scream.

A fight, Louis realised. He forced his way through to discover a scene with Lord Hargreaves and that vile little shit, Mr Price. Louis had never liked the insinuating bastard and hoped Hargreaves broke his nose for his part in ruining Lady Rosamund. Ignoring the scandalous scene unfolding, he looked around for Evie, for if she knew her friend was in trouble, she'd be here, beside her. She wasn't.

Non, non, non, he repeated silently. *Please God. Non.*

The crowd shifted, more screams and people pushing and shoving as further fights broke out. *Damnation.* This was just what he needed now. Louis pushed through the crowd again, seeing Barnaby.

"Have you seen her?" he shouted over the increasingly frantic gathering.

Barnaby shook his head.

"Find her!" Louis told him, relieved to see Barnaby give a sharp nod and hurry into the fray. He turned to see Lord Hargreaves carrying his new wife to safety.

"Lady Rosamund! Have you seen Miss Knight?" he called, shouting to make himself heard over the noise.

"Evie?" Rosamund said, shaking her head. "No, not for a while."

"When?" he demanded, seeing the young woman's face crease with concern at his sharp tone. "When did you see her last?"

"Not since you sent her that glass of champagne," Lady Rosamund said.

"Champagne?" he repeated in confusion, then felt a shaft of ice skewer his heart. "Excuse me," he muttered.

With sheer force of will, Louis held back the burgeoning panic that was threatening to overwhelm him, to cloud his mind. He needed to think. It seemed likely Etienne had drugged Evie. If so, she would have felt unwell. Dizzy, perhaps. She must have sought somewhere quiet. Etienne would be waiting to grab her, but at least this chaos might make that difficult, for Etienne must have assumed most everyone would be in the ballroom. Hard to escape unseen now, especially carrying an unconscious woman. Where might she have gone?

Louis plunged back into the crowd, shoving people out of his way as he fought to get through. Thankfully, the retiring rooms were empty now as everyone had hurried to leave before they got caught up in a minor riot. Louis searched to no avail and ran down the corridor, fighting against the crowd surging in the opposite direction. He flung open doors, searching rooms until he came to a large, ornate parlour. His heart skipped as he saw a swathe of cream silk spilled out over the floor.

"Evie," he cried, running to her. He knelt beside her, sick with terror, petrified by her stillness. An empty glass lay on the rug beside her. Pulling her into his arms, he patted her cheek, trying to rouse her. "Evie, *mon amour?*"

To his eternal relief, he discovered her breathing was deep and even, and he swallowed down a burst of emotion that threatened to sweep over him. Not now. No time for that now. She was sleeping only, drugged but unharmed. But if Etienne had drugged her, who knew what else he'd planned? The hysteria among the guests must have spoiled whatever he had intended, thank God, and Louis would not give him a chance to regroup. For all he knew Etienne was armed or had employed more men to help him commit whatever vile crime his twisted mind had envisaged. He could not simply wait here with Evie in this state when that madman might find them at any moment. There was only one door in or out of the room, and so Louis lifted Evie into his arms and carried her out into the crowd. There were gasps as people saw him emerging from a closed room with her in his arms, whispers and exclamations, but he could not help that. He'd just ruined her, and he didn't give a damn. She'd have to marry him now.

He hurried out of the house, searching for his carriage, ignoring the people staring as he carried her away.

"Rémi!" Louis shouted, seeing his coachman. The man's eyes widened as he saw Louis and the young woman in his arms.

"Monsieur! Que s'est-il passé? Is the young lady well?"

"Non, she's been drugged. We must get her out of here."

The coachman nodded, his expression filled with concern. "It's Mademoiselle Knight? Shall we take her to her father's house?"

Louis climbed into his carriage, laying Evie carefully against the velvet cushions. He hesitated, staring at her beautiful face, a shaft of pain lancing through his heart. It was the right thing to do. It was what Evie would *want* him to do, and yet… and yet if he did, Gabriel Knight would know this had happened because of Louis. Knowing what he did, Knight would refuse to let them marry even now Evie was ruined. He would not let his precious daughter end up with a man like Louis, no matter how damaged her reputation. He would take her away, give her a fresh start somewhere new, somewhere far away. Knight would hide Evie away, Louis would stake his life upon it. Panic slithered down his spine. What if he couldn't find her next time? What if Etienne found her? His breathing quickened as fear sped his heart, clouded his mind with the terror of losing her. Her father did not know what Etienne was like, did not understand his obsession with hurting Louis. No, he must keep her near him. It was the only way to keep her safe, to *know* that she was safe. In France, with all the resources at his disposal, he would be able to ensure her safety until he had dealt with Etienne once and for all.

"Non," he said, his mind made up. Evie would hate him for this, but he would have the rest of his life to beg her forgiveness. "I need to get to France. We must get the train to Folkestone. We must make haste, for Knight will hear I've got his daughter shortly. What time is it now?"

Rémi fished out his watch, showing it was almost ten o'clock. Ridiculously early for a party like this to have broken up. Once again, Louis thanked his lucky stars for the confusion and the fight, and for all the chaos that must have interfered with Etienne's plans. If he'd not found Evie first... his blood turned to ice in his veins.

"Hurry," Louis instructed the driver as he closed the door.

Cocooned in the darkness, Louis gathered Evie into his arms, stroking a lock of dark hair from her cheek as he bent to kiss her forehead.

"Forgive me, *mon amour,"* he whispered, though she could not hear him. "I cannot lose you. Not now. Not ever."

12th November 1823, Place de Coderc, Périgueux, France.

Louis is eleven years old.

Louis went about his morning chores in a ferment of terror. He was certain Madame Boucher would stop him from going to fetch the bread now in case he ran away. They must have felt secure in the knowledge than too many people watched him and feared Monsieur Boucher's anger to help him leave, though, even by just turning a blind eye. So, he was sent to the boulangerie as usual. He had until tomorrow night to leave, but his chances of success would be greater if he had the items he'd stolen, and he had the maximum time to get as far away as possible.

So, this morning he would collect his things and smuggle them into the house, and say goodbye to André. That last bit he was uncertain how to do, for he knew the boy would be distraught. Louis only hoped André would not do anything to give him away. Instead of walking to the boulangerie, Louis ran, skidding in the snow and arriving just as the man turned the sign on the shop door. He snatched the baguette, setting the coin down on the counter and running out again.

André's eyes widened as Louis caught up with him near to his home. He was still tying a scarf about his neck, having only just set foot outside.

"Come with me," Louis said breathlessly, tugging at André's hand.

"Where are we going?" André demanded, but when Louis didn't answer he ran after him all the same.

Louis picked his way across the icy banks of the river to where he'd stashed his belongings, turning over the large stone and feeling a surge of relief as he saw the dirty piece of linen. He unwrapped the knife, already having decided he'd not go anywhere without it now. Louis stuffed the dented silver pocket watch, a few coins, and the tinderbox into his pockets, all the while feeling André's eyes upon him.

"Louis?" he said, his voice quavering. "You're leaving?"

Louis looked up, seeing misery in André's eyes, and resignation. He'd known. All this time, he'd known Louis would leave.

"I'm sorry," Louis said, wretched at having to leave the boy. "I don't have a choice."

André nodded. "You need to find your father. You're a vicomte, and you don't belong here. I always knew it."

Louis felt a swell of gratitude towards the boy, who had never doubted his story, never teased him for insisting he was of the nobility. Not that he had any intention of finding his father, even if he knew where to begin. Père had abandoned him without a second thought, and Louis was damned if he would go begging to him now. He would make his own way. Somehow.

"I'll miss you," he offered, knowing he could not give André anything more than that.

The boy's eyes swam with tears. "You too."

Impulsively, Louis took the knife and cut off a thick curl. "Here," he said, feeling a little ridiculous but needing to give something of himself to this boy who had been brave enough to be his friend.

André took the lock of hair, staring at it in wonder. "Merci," he said, tucking it carefully into a pocket. "I'll keep it always. I'll never forget you."

Louis nodded, uncomfortable now, not knowing what to say.

André's voice quavered, and he wiped his eyes as tears rolled down his cheeks. "Will I ever see you again? Will you return here when you're back where you belong? Do, Louis. Come back and spit in their eyes. Turn up with your fine clothes and a fancy carriage and show them they were wrong. Please. Promise you will."

Louis hesitated, unable to consider such a scenario, or a world where he would ever willingly return here.

"All right, I promise," he said reluctantly, though he thought it wrong of him to do so, but he could do nothing more for André. There seemed no harm in giving him the promise that he would do as he asked if he could. It was a small thing if it made André happy.

André flung himself at Louis, wrapping his arms about him and holding on tight. Awkwardly, Louis patted his shoulder before giving in and hugging him back. He was a fair bit taller than André, who looked up at him, a shy but determined glint in his eyes before he took Louis quite by surprise and kissed him.

After last night's revulsion, the taste of which still lingered on his mouth, this was quite different, sweet and innocent, taking nothing but giving Louis a glimpse of the depth of feeling André held for him. So he did not protest, and held still until André pulled back, blushing scarlet and looking at him fearfully.

Louis smiled and ruffled André's hair, and would have said something to diffuse the rather odd atmosphere if a roar of fury hadn't filled their ears. Louis turned to see Etienne running full tilt at André. Etienne tackled the boy, sending him sprawling in the frozen mud before pummelling him with his fists. Louis fell upon Etienne, pulling him away by his shirt as Etienne flailed and lashed out.

"Run!" Louis shouted as André scrambled to his feet. "Go. Now!" he cried, struggling to keep hold of Etienne.

André took one last tearful look at Louis, and ran.

Louis held Etienne until the boy ran out of steam, panting with effort and fury.

"Papa was right!" he screamed. "It's you! You corrupt everything, everyone. It's your fault. Your fault! You shouldn't do it. Shouldn't make me feel like this! It's wrong. You're wrong!"

Louis stared at him in shock, not understanding.

"You look like a stupid girl. You're prettier than Jeanne, than any of them here. It's your fault. I shouldn't... shouldn't...."

Etienne gave a yell of frustration before tackling Louis to the floor, fists flying. Louis held him off, pushing Etienne away, and scrambled to his feet, snatching up the baguette. He stumbled away, staring at Etienne in shock as he realised what he was saying. Too startled by what that meant, he ran, knowing he had already been away too long. He dared not waste another moment.

With hindsight, he should have expected Etienne to tattle on him, to tell his father that Louis was a deviant, worse than they had ever guessed, for he had kissed a boy. Yet, to his eternal relief, Etienne never mentioned the boy by name, so Louis too held his tongue and did not deny it had been his fault, his doing, did not explain that monsieur's son was only angry because it hadn't been him Louis had kissed. Somehow, he did not think that would help.

Monsieur used his belt, and when Louis lay down to sleep, he whimpered with pain as the bruises pressed into the cold stone of the kitchen floor.

"Tomorrow," he promised himself, as he closed his eyes, ignoring the tears that slid down his face. "Tomorrow I'll be free."

He did not hear the kitchen door open and close, the stealthy feet padding over the flagstones. He was aware of nothing but his own pain and misery until an icy hand pressed down over his mouth, silencing him. Louis smothered a gasp, his eyes flying open, his hands grasping the thick wrist, but the man leaning over him was powerfully built and, as ever, there was no point in fighting. Staring in disbelief, Louis looked into the face of his father.

No.

No, that was impossible. This man was far younger than his Père, handsomer, and his eyes were kinder, full of sympathy. Louis stared and stared, certain he must be dreaming.

"Quiet," the man who was not his father said, his voice stern. "I've come to help you. Do you want to get out of here?"

Louis froze, and the man moved around to face him, his expression one of shock as he looked into Louis' eyes.

"I'm not going to hurt you. If you come with me, I'll make sure no one ever hurts you again. D'accord?"

Louis almost wept then, hearing the words and believing them, knowing instinctively this man meant what he said. He gave a sharp nod.

The man softened his voice, encouraging. "I'm going to take my hand away now. If you shout for help, this will be your life, sleeping on a kitchen floor, working for that miserable bastard who treats you worse than a dog. Understand?"

Louis stared at him, unblinking, and nodded again. The man took his hand away.

"Will you come with me?" he asked.

"Yes," Louis said at once, without a moment's hesitation.

The man smiled, amusement in his eyes. "Don't you care where we're going?"

"No."

"You trust me?" the stranger said, looking vaguely appalled by that.

"Yes." Louis' answer was fervent, determined.

The man frowned, and despite their need to escape at once, it seemed as if he could not help but ask, "Why?"

"Because you're my brother."

Chapter 5

Mr Knight,

By the time this reaches you, Evie will be my wife. I am sorry. Sorry for any hurt or anxiety you have suffered since the moment she disappeared. I could not let you take her from me. I swear to you I would move heaven and earth to make her happy, to keep her safe, but I cannot leave her. Perhaps a better man would have, perhaps a better man would have walked away and allowed her to find someone worthy of her. We both know I am not that man. I am not better and never will be, but I shall try to be the best I can – for her.

Do not try to find her. You will not succeed. There are certain matters I need to settle. As soon as this is done, we will return to visit you. I have no desire to keep her apart from her family, for that would make her unhappy, and her happiness is all I wish for. I do not blame you for trying to keep her from me. Had I a daughter, I would do just as you have done. But though you do not wish to see it, and though I do not understand why fate has been so very kind this once, Evie loves me. She would not give me up, even though you demanded it of her. Do not make her choose between us.

—Excerpt of a letter from Louis César de Montluc, Comte de Villen to Mr Gabriel Knight.

18th July 1842, The Port of Folkestone, Kent.

Wealth and influence counted for a great deal, Louis reflected, as he carried Evie from the train to the waiting carriage. If he had been an ordinary man with no title, carrying an unconscious female away in the dead of night might have been difficult. For a man who could throw gold sovereigns about like confetti and claim the title of Comte de Villen, there was no one around—certainly at this hour of the night—to gainsay him. His wife was unwell, he said, and he needed to get her home to their family doctor in France. Who could contradict him? Who dared when he met their eyes with his arctic expression, promising they would not like his reaction if they did not leap to do his bidding? Louis was uncertain what they saw in his eyes. Likely he did not wish to know, for they could not hold his gaze. They only nodded and did as he asked, which was fine by him.

He had sent a note to Elton, telling him to leave everything and get out. Elton would understand. He would know where to go to find him. He had also written a note to Gabriel Knight. It was not fair to the man to leave him with no clue if his daughter was safe or not. Of course, Knight would not consider Louis' company safe either. Louis could not blame him for that. Of all the things he had done in his life, this was the most reprehensible. He had taken Evie's choices away from her. The thing he had sworn never to do, he had done without so much as blinking. She would wake to discover there was no option but to marry him. By morning the story would be on everyone's lips, how the Comte de Villen had carried her away from the ball and taken her in his carriage, alone, that he had carried her off to France with him. Everyone would be gossiping about them as they broke their fast.

Louis tamped down a flicker of panic as he considered Evie's reaction. Surely, she could not stay angry forever? Could she? There was enough doubt in his mind to make his stomach roil and his heart beat too fast. If she were like any other woman he had ever wanted, he could manage her, soothe her temper, he could make love to her until she could not remember her own name, never mind why she was angry with him. But she wasn't any other woman, and Evie wouldn't stand for that. He did not truly want her to either, not at heart. It was why he loved her when no one else had ever touched his soul as she did, but he had never loved anyone before and did not know how to manage the unwieldy emotion that made him act like a damned lunatic.

Not only that, but Louis believed he had never had anyone love *him* before, either. Not real love, despite their impassioned words. Infatuation, yes, certainly, but not the look he saw in Evie's eyes, the affection and love she had for him. His breath caught as he wondered if he'd ever see that again, or if he'd killed it for good. *No.* No, he would not believe that. Evie was too good, too kind. He might need to spend the rest of his days making up for this, but she would forgive him. She would.

The unprepossessingly named Widgeon was a wooden paddle steamer, due to leave port at first light. The early start was not for the convenience of passengers, but to get the day's post to the French capital as quickly as possible. It suited Louis, however; Gabriel Knight would pick up his trail soon. Once they were on French soil, they'd be safe. Until then, he could not rest easy. A chill breeze whipped across the harbour and Louis held Evie tighter, aware of her bare arms. He needed to get her on board, and quickly.

"Monsieur!" Louis started as a familiar French voice hailed him.

"Duval?" he said, recognising one of Wolf's most trusted men. He was six feet tall, almost as wide at the shoulder, and completely bald save for a luxurious moustache, which was his pride and joy. "What the devil are you doing here?"

"Looking for you, monsieur," the fellow said, grinning as he raised an eyebrow at the lush armful of femininity Louis was holding to his chest. "And it seems with good reason."

"Wolf knew I'd be coming?" Louis said, shaking his head. Damned man was part witch, he'd swear, or he knew Louis far better than was comfortable. Either way, he could not deny relief at seeing Duval. Now everything would go smoothly.

"She's got no passport, Duval," Louis said in an undertone. "But she's the Comtesse de Villen, do you understand? I need her added to my papers. and to leave with the minimum of fuss and gossip."

Duval returned a crooked smile. *"Oui, monsieur.* I understand perfectly. Leave it with me."

Louis nodded, relieved, and turned his attention to call out to a harried looking porter who dropped whatever he was attending to at a word from Louis and showed them to their private cabin.

He gave the man a generous tip, which smoothed the fellow's brow considerably, and warned him he wanted no one to know who was in this cabin, and that any gossip about the Frenchman and his lady was to be stamped on at once. The fellow nodded his understanding and left.

Louis lay Evie carefully on the bed, where she stirred uneasily.

"It's all right, *mon amour.* Everything will be all right," he told her, stroking her hair, and wondering if that were the truth.

He hoped to God it was.

14th November 1823, Limoges, France.

Louis is eleven years old.

Nic stared at the boy standing beside him, anxious in case he was expecting too much.

"You're certain you can do it?" he asked again. They were both exhausted and frozen to the marrow after walking all day and much of the night for two days now.

His little brother stiffened, obviously offended.

"Oui," he said, blue eyes blazing.

Nic stared. He'd never seen eyes that colour before. Hell, he'd seen no one like Louis César before. He was going to cause one hell of a stir among the circus folk, that was for damned sure. Still anxious, he nodded, for there was no other choice. The boy might look slender, far too thin in all honesty, but there was a steely note in his voice, a hardness to those blue eyes that told Nic he had endured too much in his brief life. Too much to fail now.

"Right," Nic said. "We're going to wait, out of sight of the inn, under that bridge. When the carriage passes under the bridge, in the shadows, then we're going to climb up on top of it and hold on for dear life. You got it?"

Louis nodded. His face was set, pale with apprehension, but determined. The shrill blast of a whistle pierced the frozen air and the seven horses that pulled the lumbering diligence coach stepped out as the carriage swayed and creaked. Usually, the upper deck of the carriage would also be packed with both passengers and luggage piled to the heavens. This late in the day and with snow falling in fat white tufts, anyone with the least bit of sense was inside the carriage or leaving the journey until tomorrow with the hope of a better day. It was the first bit of luck they'd had and Nic wasn't about to waste it. They'd walked miles already and Louis was exhausted. Not that he'd complained. Not so much as a word of protest. The boy had hardly said a word at all, just cast curious glances at Nic when he thought he might not notice. His silence, the way he had put his entire trust in Nic, was daunting and *troubling, but Nic had not dared to ask questions, too afraid of what the answers might be. He'd glimpsed the livid bruises beneath Louis' threadbare shirt and had been sorely tempted to go back and beat the bastard responsible to within an inch of his life. But their father had not asked for that. He wanted Louis back, that was all. So that's what Nic would do: bring his brother home.*

The diligence lurched forward and Nic hugged the shadows under the bridge, aware of Louis beside him. As soon as the carriage came through, Nic grabbed Louis by the arm, making him wait until the last moment, and then yanking him forward. For Nic, who was used to hard physical activity and adept at climbing and acrobatics, it posed no problem. He scaled the carriage using the ropes lashing the luggage on top down with little effort, turning at once to give Louis a hand and somewhat startled to discover he didn't need it. The boy collapsed down beside him, grabbing hold of a thick rope that secured several enormous trunks as the carriage lurched sideways.

"Well done!" Nic said, grinning at Louis.

Louis beamed at him, so obviously pleased and surprised by the praise that Nic's heart hurt. They hunkered down, side by side, huddling together for warmth as the carriage swayed.

"We've got a long way to go like this, I'm afraid," Nic said apologetically. "I have little money for travelling."

"Our father doesn't have any money?" Louis asked, his piercing gaze studying Nic.

"Not that I've seen," Nic replied with a shrug.

Louis nodded, apparently unsurprised by the information.

"But he sent you to get me?"

Nic nodded. "He found me especially because he wants you back. Father's been anxious about you," he added, though he wasn't certain that was true. He suspected their father worried about no one but himself. Nic wanted to believe everything the comte had told him, wanted to believe he mattered to his father too, not just this boy who was his legitimate heir, but his mother told him he'd be a fool to listen to a word the man said.

Louis said nothing, and his lack of response unsettled Nic. His gaze was placid, accepting of the fact that he would go with Nic, back to his father, but Nic sensed the comte would not easily manage him. Underneath that calm surface was something entirely different, something that was waiting for an outlet.

"Has he always known who I was with?" Louis asked casually, though Nic knew better than to think it was idle curiosity. He had lingered in the town for a few days, observing Louis, listening to gossip about Monsieur Boucher. It had not taken long to form a picture of Louis' life, a boy treated like a slave, beaten and mistreated, isolated from everyone because they feared his master.

"I don't know," Nic said, which was the truth, thank God. "He came to me about three months ago. I had never seen him before that. He was never interested in me before; I am his natural child, not legitimate like you. It was a shock to see him, to hear I had a brother. He said he had people looking for you. We waited until one of them came back with a report that they'd found you, and then he sent me to get you."

"Pourquoi? Why did you come? Why did you do anything for him if you'd never met him before then? You don't owe him anything."

Nic shrugged, wondering about that himself. The Comte de Villen was a force of nature, charming and beguiling. It had been fascinating to Nic to see the man who'd sired him, this elegant nobleman, a creature from another world who looked so much like him. Even though he'd abandoned Nic and his mother, Nic could not hold on to his resentment. He'd wanted to please the man, to make him proud, and he'd very much wanted to meet his little half-brother.

"You're my brother. I've never had one of those before," he said, smiling.

"Me either," Louis replied, staring at Nic in wonder. "You're very strong."

"Working in a circus will do that for you," Nic said, grinning at the admiration in his brother's expression. It was rather nice to be looked up to like that.

At the mention of the circus, however, Louis' eyes widened with astonishment.

"The circus? You work in the circus? Ce n'est pas vrai !" Louis exclaimed, his excitement palpable.

Nic laughed. "I do. I'm a rope dancer."

"What's that?"

All at once, the boy's calm demeanour had fallen away, and he was alight with interest.

"I walk the highwire, but also tumbling tricks. You'll see when we get to Paris. I'll show you."

"Will you teach me?" he demanded, clutching at Nic's arm.

Nic gave a nervous laugh. He did not think the comte would wish for his son and heir to learn such tricks. It was fine for an illegitimate son whose mother was a circus performer too, but for the Vicomte Sainte-Apre? And yet it was the first time Nic had seen anything like animation in the boy's too placid eyes in the two days since they'd left the place of his incarceration.

"Alors, if you like. Sure. I'll teach you."

Louis beamed at him.

18th July 1842, The English Channel.

Louis muttered a curse as the paddle steamer lurched and Evie groaned. She was sweating and wretched. Whether she'd had an adverse reaction to whatever Etienne had given her, or was merely seasick, or a combination of the two, he did not know. He only knew she was miserable, and it was all his fault. Her eyes flickered open, hazy and unfocused.

"Louis? W-What—?"

"Don't try to talk, *mon amour*. It will be all right."

She moaned, fidgeting on the narrow bed before making a panicked sound. Louis snatched up the bowl he'd sent for and shoved it in front of her just as her stomach rebelled for the second time that night. The poor girl vomited, coughing and choking before subsiding again, utterly spent.

"What's happening?" she sobbed, clutching at the bed as the boat lurched again.

"Just rest, Evie," Louis said, wondering if she would ever forgive him for this night's work. He covered the foul basin with a cloth and opened the cabin door. Duval was there in an instant and a second later a servant appeared, spiriting the disgusting bowl away and bringing a clean one with a fresh towel and a pitcher of water.

Louis soaked the cloth in the water and wiped it over Evie's face. She whimpered, turning towards the cool cloth. Once she was calm again, Louis reached for the fastenings on her gown and loosened the ties of her corset, which could not be helping her poor stomach. Patiently, he took the pins from her hair until it was loose, cascading down her back. Louis combed his fingers through it with care, stroking the nape of her neck and gently massaging her scalp. She sighed, relaxing by degrees and slipping back into an uneasy sleep.

They'd soon be in France, he told himself. Then Gabriel Knight would be hindered by the French authorities, authorities which would fall over themselves to do Louis' bidding. This was only partly because of his title. He and Wolf had created a network of paid retainers throughout the country, people who could be bribed to look the other way, to create paperwork where it was required or to lose it when it wasn't. Louis and Evie would simply disappear, and no one would remember seeing them or have any information to give. Mr Knight might also discover his paperwork was in some way lacking, which would no doubt cause him some irritating delays.

Relieved that Evie was calmer now, Louis lay down beside her, bracing her body from the ship's motion by holding her carefully against him. Closing his eyes, he wondered just how furious and unhappy she was going to be when she came to. He suspected he had a fine idea, and it wouldn't be pretty.

18th July 1842, Calais, Pas-de-Calais, France.

Evie had never felt so ill or wretched in her entire life. Her head was splitting in two, her stomach was sore, and she felt sick and exhausted. Worse than all of this was the strange sense of unreality. She tried to open her eyes, which felt heavy and swollen, but the bright sunlight seared her brain, and she closed them again with a sharp exclamation.

"Evie? You're awake?"

"Louis?" she murmured, clutching at her head. What on earth was Louis doing here? Except… where was *here*? Her heart gave a panicked thud, and she struggled to open her eyes again, squinting at her surroundings. They were in a carriage, an expensive one judging by the thick green velvet seats and the fine finishings. Evie blinked against the glare and Louis shifted, tugging a thick curtain across the window to shield her eyes. The movement made her realise she was laying across the seat and had been sleeping with her head in his lap. Startled, she pushed upright and then gasped as her stomach roiled, threatening to misbehave.

"Easy, *mon amour*. You've been very unwell," Louis said, his voice gentle.

Unwell? Evie was never unwell. And if she was unwell, why was she alone with Louis? Why was it daylight? Where were they going? Fighting through a jumble of distorted memories, she looked down at herself to see she was wearing a cream ballgown. The gown she had worn to Mrs Belvedere's ball. But it was daylight. And she was in a carriage alone. With Louis.

She gasped, turning to stare at Louis, who gazed back at her, his expression wary. He looked a little rumpled himself, not nearly as immaculate as usual. His usually smoothly shaved jaw was dark with stubble, giving his angelic face a wicked, disreputable edge that did nothing to diminish his beauty. Annoyingly, he looked more handsome than ever. Evie stared at her crumpled gown, the beautiful cream silk grubby now. Her hair was loose, tumbling about her shoulders, and she had the unwelcome thought that there was an unpleasant smell in the carriage, and it was coming from her.

"What did you do?" she demanded, her voice raspy.

Louis held out his arms to her. "Come here, *mon amour,* I shall explain, but—"

"No," she said, shaking her head, and then wishing she had not as pain exploded behind her eyes. She sucked in a breath, holding up a hand that warned Louis not to touch her. She felt disgusting, grubby and smelly, and utterly awful. She needed a bath and a bed, and a very long sleep, but first she would have an explanation about what the *hell* was going on!

"Explain. Now," she said curtly, breathing carefully as her stomach still felt most peculiar.

Louis nodded, his expression remote now. "Someone tried to take you away. They drugged you. I believe they intended to kidnap you. There was a disturbance at the ball. A fight started. Happily, this interfered with the kidnapper's plans. I was able to find you before they could figure a way to get you out. But people saw us, Evie. They saw me carry you out of a room where you had been alone with me. You were ruined, *mon amour*. There was nothing I could do. I needed to keep you safe, so I decided we would be best off in France. We'll be married as soon as I can arrange the paperwork, don't worry. All will be well."

Evie stared at him in disbelief and then tugged at the curtain he'd pulled across, staring out.

"W-We're in France?" she stammered, too shocked to take it in.

"Oui."

"But my parents, what did they say? H-How…?" She stared at him in horror as the pieces fell into place. "Why would anyone want to kidnap me?"

Louis' complexion, usually such a golden tone, was stark white, making his eyes an unearthly blue against his thick, dark lashes. "To hurt me."

Evie gasped, a thrill of fear rolling down her back. "The man who gave me the champagne. He was badly scarred. Burns I think."

Louis muttered a furious curse that did nothing to ease her anxiety. *"Oui,* I know this man, but I would let nothing happen to you, Evie," he said urgently, shifting closer to her, taking her hands in his. *"Mon amour,* I would die before I let anyone hurt you."

Evie snatched her hands free of his grasp, staring at him. "And where is this person now? This person who wants to hurt you by hurting me?"

His expression grew taut. "You need not worry about him. He will be dealt with."

"Dealt with?" she repeated in horror. "You mean to kill him, then? More blood on your hands."

Louis shook his head, a flash of anger in his expression. *"Non!* Not more, for I thought I *had* killed him. I had believed him dead this many years. I shall just make certain he stays dead this time."

Evie gasped, horrified by his casual words. Who was this man who spoke of killing so easily? Was this really *her* Louis? "Where is my father? You can't mean to say he knew about all this and did nothing?"

"Of course not," Louis replied, and she heard the weariness in his voice. "I took you before he knew what had happened. I am sorry, Evie. I had to keep you safe."

"And so you brought me with you to France, where I suppose this madman will follow? You didn't think to return me to my home, to my parents? You didn't think that might be safer?"

"Non! I did not believe that. They do not understand this man, what he is like, besides which, you were *ruined!"* he shot back. "You must marry me, Evie. There is no choice now."

Evie stared at him in disbelief. "Oh, but you thought there was. You thought there might be another choice, or you would not have taken me away. Oh, Louis! How could you?" she demanded. "You did this. You did this on *purpose!"*

His face shuttered up, wiped clean of expression and he turned to stare out of the window, avoiding her gaze as he spoke. *"Alors,* you have had a dreadful experience and I've no doubt you are still feeling very unwell. Once we reach Lille, we will stay in the best hotel, you will have a bath and rest for a while. Then we shall talk again, when you are calmer."

"I do not think I am going to be calm for a while yet," Evie said, trying not to give in to the hysteria that was threatening. Oh, her poor family. Mama and Papa would be frantic by now. Oh, how could Louis have done this to her? "I trusted you," she said, her voice quavering.

He turned then, eyes blazing. *"Non!* You did not, and I suppose you were right not to. I warned you from the start I was no angel. If you think I was going to let your father keep us apart, you are out of your mind! He would have taken you away from me. You know this. Is that what you wanted, Evie, in your heart? Did you want never to see me again?"

"N-No!" she exclaimed, stung by the unfairness of the question. "But—"

"But you wanted not to hurt your family, or me, I know this. I understood that you did not want to decide until you had heard all my sordid tales of woe. Well, there was no time left for that, and now I have decided for you. I have done this terrible thing and inflicted the hurt, so you do not have too. You are not to blame. It is entirely my fault. Your parents can hate me all they want. Fine. Be angry with me. Fine. But do not ask me to regret it, for I shall not."

She was not certain she believed that, watching as he folded his arms, rigid with tension, and staring out of the window.

"I wouldn't bet on that," she said darkly, huddling on her side of the carriage.

But he was right about one thing. She could not think straight in this state. Her head throbbed and everything ached, she felt sick and wretched and frightened and very unhappy. She needed a bath and some sleep and then... and then... Evie bit her lip and tried very hard not to cry.

Chapter 6

Lucian,

It appears the rumours are correct. Villen has Evie. He took a train to Folkestone, then a paddle steamer to Calais. I am booked on the next boat. Tell me you have contacts in France? I suspect the bastard will keep away from the railways such as they are, for there I have influence at least, but I am stepping into his world now. I am at my wits' end. Was Evie a part of this? Did she agree to it? I can only think not, for she would not have us worry so. Which means he did this against her will, and if that is the case, I'm going to make him wish he'd never been born.

—Excerpt of a letter from Mr Gabriel Knight to The Most Hon'ble Lucian Barrington, The Marquess of Montagu.

18th July 1842, The Black Bull, The Port of Folkestone, Kent.

"You're blaming me for this?" Gabriel stared at his wife, hurt and incensed.

Helena's face softened at his reaction, but she still threw up her hands in exasperation. "You ought never to have forbidden her from seeing him. Have you not noticed how out of sorts she's been? You put her in an impossible situation, torn between her family and the man she loves."

"Loves!" Gabriel said, shaking his head vehemently. "She doesn't love him. She's just… just—"

"Just what, Gabe? Bedazzled by a pretty face? Charmed? Had her head turned by flattery? Does any of that sound like Evie?" Helena demanded.

Gabriel clenched his fists, wishing he could control the damned tides. They were sitting in the private parlour of the Black Bull, and doing nothing was driving him insane. He turned as his wife slipped her hand into his, prying open his stiff fingers. "I tried to warn you, my love. Surely, you know by now that the women of this family will go to any lengths to be with the men they choose."

"Evie did not choose this!" he insisted. "If I had a letter in her hand telling me she had run away with him, it might be different. He did this. He took her. You know Evie doesn't like excitement or adventure or being away from home. She likes things to stay the same, familiar things, people she cares about."

Helena gave a soft laugh. "Oh, my love. That is just what Evie tells herself, because she is afraid of the truth."

"What the devil does that mean?"

"It means she has always been the daring one, the one who would befriend a man whom no one else would speak to because he was too beautiful and remote. She is the one who will end up doing something wild and reckless because she has a passionate nature and eventually she is going to stop trying to smother it and embrace it. She is my daughter, Gabe. I know her. Perhaps she did not choose this, but she chose Louis César a long time ago whether she knew it or not. She just didn't want to hurt you when she knew you disapproved."

"She is too innocent for him, Helena. He's got blood on his hands, his life is tainted by violence and crime, and this is the man you want for *Evie?"*

Helena sighed and squeezed his hand. "It has little to do with what I want, but, darling, I wish you would see. Evie is far stronger than you realise, than even she realises. Yes, perhaps she is innocent, she has been sheltered by us, but that does not mean she cannot handle what life throws at her. If we wrapped her up in cotton wool, she would be miserable. There is a spark in her I recognise, for I had it too. It was what made me goad you into racing me from London to Brighton. It was what made me elope with you against my brother's wishes, because I knew you were the one I wanted. You do them both a disservice by believing her to be a swooning victim and him a wicked villain. It's not so black and white as that."

"So what? I shouldn't go after them, is that what you're saying?" Gabriel asked in frustration, though Helena's words were a comfort to him.

Evie had a backbone, there was no denying that. With a bit of luck, she was giving Louis César hell right now.

"Of course not. We both need to know she is safe and happy. You must find them, but don't go at it like a bull in a china shop, Gabe. I believe they love each other. Louis César has acted rashly and selfishly, but we do not know the full story yet. Remember that and try not to lose your temper."

Gabriel huffed with irritation but pulled his wife into his arms. "You're too romantic, too tender-hearted, that's the trouble."

"Perhaps," she allowed, resting her head on his chest. "And you guard your heart and those who dwell in it with a little too much zeal, but we are none of us perfect."

20th November 1823, rue du Faubourg du Temple, Paris, France.

Louis is eleven years old.

Nic could not help but grin at Louis' expression as he took in the enormous circus tent. His mouth seemed shaped in a permanent 'o' of wonder as he saw the brightly coloured costumes of the performers, the exotic animals, and all the painted accoutrements of the surroundings. It was late in the evening and the performance had ended some time ago, for which Nic was relieved. He was too worn out to perform, but he knew his presence would have been sorely missed. If they'd arrived earlier, they would have persuaded him to go on. He rather wanted to perform in front of his little brother, for he had quickly become accustomed to the admiration in Louis' eyes. That the boy looked at him as his saviour was obvious, and rather gratifying. It was also very clear to Nic that Louis was terrified he would be abandoned again. They'd taken shelter one night in an empty barn and when Nic had woken in the early hours and got up to relieve himself, Louis had snapped awake, demanding to know where he was going. There had been sheer terror in his face, and it had taken Nic sometime to reassure him he had not been about to abandon him in the middle of nowhere.

What were the comte's plans for Louis, though? Nic suspected he would not be a part of them. What would happen when Louis discovered his father meant to take him away from Nic? Perhaps Louis would not care once he had his father back in his life. Nic did not like to believe that to be true. On the long, arduous journey back to Paris, they had come to know each other, a little at least. Louis had confided something of what his life had been since the king had banished their father. Nic had endured the story with as stoic an expression as he could, aware that Louis was very much on his dignity and that any show of pity would alienate him. Last night's revelation had been the worst, though.

"You nearly missed me," Louis had explained, over a frugal supper of bread and cheese, bought with the last of Nic's carefully eked out coin.

"What do you mean?"

Louis frowned, chewing the bite of cheese he had taken and avoiding Nic's eye. "I knew I had to leave. No matter what. I would not go with that man and that... that awful woman. Not for anything. I'd rather have died."

"What man? What happened?" Nic demanded, unsettled by the sincerity he heard behind the boy's words.

Haltingly at first, Louis described the Englishman and the over-painted woman, a whore by the sound of his description. His breathing quickened, and he blushed scarlet with shame as he told Nic what had happened. He kept glancing at Nic, as if he thought Nic might not believe they'd had vile intentions for him, that he had made it up, but Nic knew enough of the world to trust Louis' instincts and to believe he had been entirely correct. The thought of how close he'd come to being too late, to his little brother ending up in a situation Nic did not wish to contemplate made his skin crawl.

Nic shifted closer and slung his arm about Louis' shoulders, pulling him into a rough hug. "Alors, you're safe now. I won't let anyone hurt you."

Louis rubbed at his eyes, swiping away tears before they could fall and embarrass him. "But those people, they came from Paris."

Nic shrugged. "Paris is a big place. An easy place to disappear into. Besides, I just told you, I won't let anyone hurt you. That's a promise, Louis. I don't break my promises, and you said how strong I was, didn't you?" Nic added, making a show of flexing his muscles to amuse his brother. "Think anyone can make me do anything I don't want to?"

Louis gave an uncertain smile and then shook his head.

"Voila, of course not," Nic said, ruffling the boy's hair.

"Now finish that bread and cheese, for we'll get no more till we get to Franconi's and there's still a long walk ahead of us tomorrow."

Louis did as he was told, taking another bite of cheese. He regarded Nic solemnly, and Nic wondered if anyone could stand the scrutiny of those extraordinary blue eyes.

"What?" Nic asked, shifting uncomfortably.

"Do you think I will be as strong as you one day?" Louis asked.

Nic considered this. The child was far too skinny, but his shoulders were broad, and he was already tall for his years. "Oui. With good food and plenty of exercise, I reckon so."

Louis grinned, delighted with this information, and devoured the rest of his bread and cheese.

18th July 1842, Hôtel Clément, Lille, France.

The elegant Hôtel Clément had nothing that Evie could complain about. They did not bat an eyelid at the state of her when she arrived, but leapt to do Louis' bidding. It was clear he was known to the hotel staff from the way they practically fell over themselves in their eagerness to please him and his new comtesse. The state in which circumstances forced her to present herself mortified Evie, and though she heard and understood Louis' explanation to the concierge about a rough sea crossing and his wife's indisposition, it did nothing to soothe her mood.

The suite of rooms to which the manager himself showed them were simply stunning. Done throughout in shades of pale blue and white, it was bright, opulent, and comfortable. Louis nodded his approval, ordered a bath and a light meal suitable for madame's delicate constitution, and made a dozen more demands that Evie did not bother attempting to decipher. His rapid French was beyond her skills, and she felt too tired and wretched to bother with understanding.

Once the manager had shown himself out, they were alone again.

Evie looked longingly at the bed, torn between collapsing on it and awaiting her bath. If she laid down, she doubted very much that she could force herself up again, and the thought of waking up in this same state made her feel worse than ever.

"Let me help you out of that gown, *mon amour,*" Louis said, his voice gentle.

Evie stiffened, shaking her head. "You may have a maid attend me."

"Evie," he protested. "I am not about to molest you. The hotel staff believe we are married, which will be true enough when we get to Paris. I have sent word ahead so that everything will be ready for us. I only want to help you feel more comfortable."

"You've done quite enough, I thank you," she replied, too wretched to modify her tone. And why should she? He'd behaved abominably and if he got away with it now, heaven knew what kind of life she would be in for.

"Won't you let me make it up to you?" he said, moving closer to her. Despite having endured the same crossing and wretched journey she had, he still looked beautiful. She wished it was as easy as he said, to let him make amends, but he had betrayed her. Her friend, the man she had trusted, had made decisions for her, against her will, and she did not know if she could ever forgive him for that, or ever trust him again. She had always seen beyond the beautiful façade, had seen a troubled, lonely man who did not know how to find his place in the world and her heart had gone out to him. Now, though, she did not know what to think, what to feel, and his perfection, even with his rumpled clothes and unshaven chin, only made her feel worse, made her wonder if she had been a fool all these years. The idea of him coming near her, let alone touching her in this state, only made her want to weep for what she had lost.

"No," she said, folding her arms and turning her back on him. She stalked to the window and looked out over an elegant formal garden. "I am furious with you, Louis. You have broken my heart if you hadn't understood that much. So, no, I don't want to speak to you right now. I am tired and my head aches and, if you persist, we are going to have a dreadful row. I suggest you find yourself another room and leave me be."

There was a taut silence.

"Very well. If you need anything, you need only ask for it. Send for me if you change your mind."

"I won't," she muttered.

A moment later, she heard the door close quietly and, when she turned around, he was gone.

19th July 1842, Hôtel Clément, Lille, France.

Louis approached Evie's room the next morning with trepidation. He was tired and anxious after a sleepless night and the fool the hotel had sent to valet him had not helped matters. The man had clearly been nervous, which had set Louis on edge, considering the fellow was close to his throat with a deadly razor and hands that trembled. The entire experience had not got his day off to a good start. Then he discovered his *wife* had already breakfasted in her room, alone, and was awaiting him downstairs in the salon.

Retracing his steps, Louis entered the salon to find Evie at the open door, looking out into the gardens. The gown she wore had cost a small fortune from the best modiste in the city. He'd had people tearing the city apart trying to find something suitable, hoping to please her. It had been made for another wealthy client, who would no doubt kick up hell to discover someone else had taken it. Not that he cared about anyone else, or the cost, he had only wanted her to feel happier and more herself after the trauma of the past hours. The modiste had come this morning to fit it to Evie's splendid curves, and Louis' critical eye had to admit she had done an excellent job. It was a blue-grey shot silk, the colour shifting in the light as she moved.

She turned as she heard him approach but did not smile and Louis' heart sank. Not that he had expected anything else, but he had hoped all the same. He had known he was taking a terrible risk in the decision he'd made, but he had panicked, had feared he would never see her again, that Etienne might find her, and he would be powerless to stop him. Now, though, in the cold light of day, he saw how badly he had betrayed her, how deeply he had hurt her. A thrill of fear ran through him as he began to doubt if she would ever forgive him for what he'd done. He had known she would be angry with him—furious, and rightly so—but in the moment he'd made the decision he had thought her anger would be short-lived. He had believed he could charm her into forgiving him. What an unutterable fool he had been to think that, even for a moment. His charm, his looks, had never worked on Evie. He knew himself well enough to know that was why he'd fallen so hard. She thought nothing of his looks, and she liked him anyway. Or at least, she had.

"Did you sleep well, *mon amour?*" he asked, striving to sound relaxed and wondering why it was so damned hard to hide his feelings around her when he was so practised at keeping his thoughts to himself.

"I did, thank you," she replied, her gaze lingering on his face. "You did not, I think," she added, a slight frown furrowing her brow.

Louis shrugged, unwilling for her to know he had spent the night fretting himself to death over her. His pride could not stand that. "If you are ready, we should be on our way."

"Why are we going to Paris?" she asked him, her green eyes cool, utterly composed.

"Because that is where I live, where I can make the arrangements for our marriage."

"That is where you can create false documents, you mean," she corrected. "Where you can use your influence to make everything happen the way you want it to."

"*Oui,* if you like to put it in such terms. I can circumnavigate the need for permissions and delays and proof of identity. We may be married at once."

"How efficient."

Louis stiffened at her tone and its implied criticism. "The marriage will be legal, Evie, and it will still mean everything to me, I will make my vows with sincerity and never break them. No matter the nature of the paperwork the ceremony will be performed properly as it ought to be."

"Oh, just as it ought to be," she said lightly. "With forged documents, a kidnapped bride, and my family worried out of their minds. Just what any girl would want."

She swept past him, regal as a queen, heading out to the carriage without him.

Louis fought the desperate urge to run after her, to pull her into his arms and beg her forgiveness. Instinctively, he knew that kind of behaviour would not work on Evie. Not in her present mood, anyway. He needed to make amends, to show her he could be trusted, that she could rely on him. There was a cold, panicky sensation in his gut though, and a hateful voice that whispered to him, telling him she would never forgive him. A chill sensation prickled down his spine, warning him she would leave him. He could promise her the world, he could give her expensive presents and pretty words, his heart on a platter and she would still leave because it wasn't enough. He'd always known it, but he had wanted to hold onto the illusion so badly this time, perhaps forever, because Evie was everything that was good and kind, and he... he was....

His breath hitched and though he tried to calm himself his mind could not help but consider the words that had been thrown at him so many times in a new light. He paced the room, but the vile accusations repeated in his head, over and over until he couldn't breathe, could think of nothing except how much he feared they were true. Were they true?

You're the serpent in the garden of Eden, that's what you are.

He shook his head, as if he could shake the words out of his mind, but they carried on, repeating themselves over and over, echoing in his brain until he felt sick and hot and like he was going to go bloody mad.

You use your looks to get what you want. The devil made you look like that, to tempt the innocent into sin.

He sank his hands into his hair, pulling hard, trying to calm himself. He was being ridiculous, but the more he considered what he'd done the more credence he had to give the accusations. His chest felt painfully tight. He'd stolen Evie away, hadn't he? He'd taken her from a family that had loved her because he wanted her for himself, because he couldn't persuade her any other way, could not charm or seduce her. She saw past his looks, she knew that was just a façade, and perhaps now she would see she was mistaken, that there was nothing on the other side of any value. Not to her, not to anyone.

You're Satan's spawn, Louis, come to tempt the righteous down into darkness.

He caught sight of himself then, in the gilded mirror over the fireplace, saw the elegant reflection of the Comte de Villen and did not know whether to cry or scream. Nothing but a pretty face, after all, not worth staying for. He'd had the lesson drummed into him for long enough. Women never stayed. Not for long. He ought to know that by now.

7th December 1823, Rue du Faubourg du Temple, Paris, France.

Louis is eleven years old.

Nic had been shocked and disappointed to discover their father was not awaiting them with open arms, joyous to discover both of his sons returned to him. Louis had pitied him for that, saddened that his brother must learn the lesson he had learned so long ago. In some ways, Louis was relieved. Thoughts of Père were complicated, stirring too many emotions for him to contain easily. Instead, he pushed them down, ignoring them, and concentrated on the facts of his new life. His brother was a good man, strong and honourable, someone he could admire. Louis wanted to be just like him.

He was less certain of Nic's mother, who was a hard woman, though not unkind. Compared to Madame Boucher, she was angelic. She clearly had their father's measure, though, and had no faith in the possibility he would return.

"If the boy stays, he works," she said implacably to Nic before turning to Louis. "I don't care if you're the King of England. If you want to eat, you earn your keep, you work."

"Oui, madame," he said at once, terrified lest she find a reason to make him leave. "I can do whatever you want. I'm a quick learner."

He had set out to prove this, doing whatever task he could find without complaint. So he helped to clean out and feed the animals—those it was safe for him to go near, at least. He did not like the monkeys that bared their teeth and made angry chattering noises, but he loved the horses. Louis extracted a promise from Nic's maman to teach him to ride, for in her youth she had danced upon the horses' backs like a ballerina and could still ride better than anyone he'd ever seen. He learned to sell snacks and souvenirs to the audience and impressed everyone with his ability to charm people and add up in his head with astonishing speed. Louis even learned how to sew so he could help repair the costumes, which needed constant upkeep. To his surprise, he had quickly become a favourite among the other performers, who always welcomed him with a smile and a kind word, happy to teach him some new trick to help him fit in.

Nic's admiration and approval was what he longed for though, and it was that which made him push himself, demanding of anyone who could be persuaded to teach him something new, and practising balancing on the low wire for hours on end so he could emulate his big brother.

"He's a natural."

Louis grinned, surprised to have gained such praise from Nic's mother. She stood with her arms folded and Louis realised she had been watching him for some time. Madame Demarteau was too old to perform now, having suffered an injury that had hurt her back.

Nic frowned, shaking his head. Though he had been generous with his time, he was still adamant that Louis would never perform and had refused to teach him in earnest.

"This isn't the life for Louis, Ma. The comte will come back for him to teach him how to be a gentleman, to take his place in society. This life isn't what he's made for."

Nic's mother gave her son a pitying look and shook her head. "Teach him the wire, how to perform. If Armand comes back, all well and good, and if he doesn't, the boy has a skill and a place to work. Don't take the opportunity from him when he clearly has the ability."

"S'il te plaît, Nic," Louis begged, certain he'd not see his father again and not much caring.

Nic's expression grew troubled, but he could not withstand the pleading in Louis' eyes, so he sighed and nodded. "D'accord, I'll teach you."

Chapter 7

Dearest Cara,

I wish there was something we could do to halt this dreadful gossip. Everyone is talking about the comte and Evie. They dominate every scandalous headline and print shop cartoon. What makes me the most furious is those who speculate why on earth he would have abducted her when there were so many more beautiful women ready to throw themselves at his feet. Honestly, people are idiots.

I don't know what happened, but the comte was clearly afraid for her, he was searching for her. I saw the terror in the man's eyes when I told him I hadn't seen her. Sebastian agrees with me that the comte truly loves Evie, and I know she is in love with him. Whatever happens, they belong together. I am certain they will work things out. Love will find a way, for I believe neither of them will accept anything less.

—Excerpt of a letter from Lady Rosamund Hargreaves (daughter of Their Graces, Robert and Prunella Adolphus, Duke and Duchess of Bedwin) to Lady Cara Baxter

*(daughter of Kitty and Luke Baxter,
Countess and Earl of Trevick).*

19th July 1842, Compiègne, France.

By the time they reached their destination, Evie was
exhausted. The after-effects of whatever had been used to drug her
still lingered, making her head ache. Her stomach was still sore
and unsettled and she dared not eat much. In consequence she was
hungry and fractious, worried about what her parents must be
enduring, and wondering what on earth she was to do about Louis
and their impending marriage.

Louis had been unfailingly solicitous and patient with her,
enduring her silence with nothing resembling reproach. During one
of the many stops they made to change horses, he had come back
to the carriage carrying a single white rose, offering it to her with a
smile. She had taken it too, not so churlish as to reject his offering,
though she still refused to speak to him beyond any necessary
conversation. Though she knew they needed to talk, she was still
too angry to speak to him, afraid of what she might say, perhaps
afraid of what he might say too. Why had he so stubbornly refused
to talk to her before now? Was what he was hiding so much worse
than what she already knew that she would not be able to forgive
him for it? Had she misjudged him so badly?

Evie did not want to believe that, did not want to consider the
idea she could have been wrong about him. She wanted her friend
back, but she feared she had lost him, was very afraid he had not
existed at all. If she was wrong about him, how long before he too
realised he had made a mistake? It seemed increasingly clear he
had not thought this through.

He had told her he loved her, and she had believed that, but
was his love the kind that would endure? Louis had loved no one,
had never stayed with anyone long enough to try. Could he really
love her enough to put up with her when she was cross and

unreasonable, or would he go running into the arms of a more agreeable companion? What about when she had children and got tired and fat? He professed to love her curves but… was that really true? There were many other far more beautiful women who would welcome him to their beds. It was a fact she had always been aware of, but one that had struck her forcibly as they travelled. Whenever they stopped, Louis caused a stir. Women fell over themselves for him, infatuated on sight, eager to do his bidding, everyone from serving girls to married women sending him come hither looks bold enough to make Evie blush for them.

Evie forced herself to calm down, to take a breath and consider things more rationally before she became a hysterical mess. Because she knew Louis never returned those looks, indeed, half the time he seemed oblivious, and the rest…. She thought back to times in the past, before this awful journey, when she had been present and women made great idiots of themselves to get his attention. He had always seemed uncomfortable with such adulation, embarrassed even, as though Evie would judge him for their behaviour… which, now she thought about it, was rather strange. It was hardly his fault they acted so, or did he believe otherwise?

She frowned, wondering how that could be possible.

To Louis' consternation, there was a grand fete in progress as they arrived—the marriage of some local nobleman—and the hotel was full to bursting. Evie waited whilst Louis negotiated with the manager. After an interminable wait, they were shown up to an impressive bedroom and promised that a bath would be prepared at once.

"I am sorry, there are no other bedrooms. The manager has already caused a ruckus by giving this one to us. You must endure my company, but do not be uneasy, I shall sleep in the chair."

"Where did you sleep last night?" Evie asked him, torn between guilt and curiosity, and a tiny, anxious seed of doubt that rcminded her he could have easily found another welcoming bed if he chose.

"Not with you," he said, his tone brisk as he tugged at his cravat. His hand stilled, and he took a breath. "Forgive me. I am not thinking clearly. I am tired and hungry, *mon amour*, and I have no doubt you are too. I slept in the carriage."

She turned to frown at him. "Why did you not take another room?"

He shrugged. "I played cards until the early hours. There seemed little point."

Evie nodded, wishing she could simply forgive him for what he'd done and run into his arms. She missed her friend, and having him so close to her all day without speaking to him was wearing on her nerves.

Wearily, Evie went to the window and opened it to let in some fresh air. The weather had become close and oppressive, and she could smell thunder in the air. There would be a storm at some point.

"You... You wish to talk?" he asked hesitantly.

Evie snorted, not turning to look at him. "No. Not at the moment. As you said, I am tired, and unhappy too. I've asked and asked you to talk, and you've refused me at every turn. You prefer to take my decisions out of my hands rather than discuss things with me. Well, I cannot change that, but do not expect me to forgive you for it."

There was a long silence.

"I am sorry, Evie."

Her heart ached at the regret in his voice, and she blinked hard as her eyes grew blurry.

"Are you?"

"Oui, mon amour. I am very afraid I have lost you."

Evie fought not to cry, not to just turn around and run into his arms for that would resolve nothing, would do neither of them the least bit of good.

"Evie?" he said, such uncertainty in his voice she could not speak her answer but only shook her head. Pain lanced down her neck at the movement and she gasped, raising her hand to squeeze the taut muscles.

"Let me," he said at once, and she stiffened as she felt Louis' hands settle on her shoulders.

"Relax," he murmured, his strong fingers working the tight muscles at the base of her neck. "I know you want to murder me, and with good reason, but you'll have a megrim if you don't let go of some of this tension."

Evie bit back a sigh, wanting to tell him to stop but too relieved by the touch of his clever hands, easing the pain that made her head ache and her shoulders sore. She closed her eyes, her body relaxing beneath his skilful touch. His hands sought the tight muscles in her neck and shoulders, calming her fraught mind, beguiling her.

"I know how badly I have hurt you," he said, his voice low. "But I swear to you, I'll never again make a decision that affects you without discussing it with you first. Please, Evie, you must believe that."

"Why? Because you say so?" she whispered, too weary for this discussion now.

"Because it is true, because I love you and regret the damage I have done."

She swayed, tiredness catching up with her, the temptation to lean back against his hard body tantalising. She was considering the foolishness of the idea when she felt his lips against the curve of her shoulder, his mouth warm upon her skin. Desire lanced through her, undermining her resistance, making her breath hitch, reminding her of just how out of control this man made her feel.

Fear fluttered in her belly like the unfurling of butterfly wings. Evie twisted away from him, putting distance between them.

"No."

Louis said nothing, but the hurt in his eyes was hard to miss. He nodded and stepped away from her, but his expression shuttered, closing off his feelings, and Evie was torn between regret and relief. A knock at the door broke the frigid silence and Louis called for whoever it was to come in.

Servants carried in a large copper tub and more followed, hurrying through with buckets of hot water. They set a small table beside the tub with a selection of perfumed oils and soap.

"Alors, I shall leave you to your bath," he said once the servants had finished and gone. "I am sorry that the hotel cannot accommodate you with a maid this evening, for they are overrun. If you will allow me to, I will undo your ties. I won't touch you; I give you my word."

His voice was perfectly relaxed, but Evie knew she had upset him. She realised in that moment that the calmer and more composed he became the harder he was hiding behind the mask he wore so well.

"Thank you," she said.

Louis approached her and deftly undid the ties of her dress before making quick work of her corset. "I'll be back in an hour. Is that long enough?"

Evie nodded, not moving until she heard the bedroom door close. She let out a shaky breath and stepped out of her gown and the heavy layers of petticoats, wriggling the corset off with relief. Laying the gown out carefully so it did not crease, she undid her garters and finished undressing. The bath water was blissfully warm, and she soaked for as long as she dared, allowing herself the indulgence of a good cry before telling herself not to behave like such a ninny.

She knew her father would be in France by now. He would track them down and would let nothing get in his way. The question was, did Evie want him to find them before or after they were married? Did she *want* to marry Louis? The idea of her life without him in it filled her with dread and sorrow, but she could not pretend the idea of being his wife was a comfortable one, either. He had already proven himself to be ruthless in getting what he wanted, just as her father had warned her. Papa had told her he was dangerous, and that was clearly true as well. She had seen the way some people treated him, and not just women. Powerful men and officials reacted to his name, and she was not so naïve as to believe it was only because of his title. Yet he was her Louis, her friend, the man she had put her trust in a very long time ago, and she wanted to believe he was still that man.

Evie stepped out of the bath and dried herself, slipping into the nightgown and wrap that the modiste had supplied her with in Lille. It was a delicate cream silk, edged with lace, and the cool fabric clung to her curves, making her feel self-conscious. It was the kind of thing a bride might wear for her new husband, and the knowledge made her edgy, knowing Louis would be back soon.

As if she had summoned him, there was a sharp knock on the door and, a second later, Louis entered the room. He stopped in his tracks as he saw her, his expression such that nerves exploded in her stomach. His hungry gaze roved over her, making heat prickle over her skin, a molten, liquid sensation pool low in her belly. Suddenly, Evie remembered how it had felt to be in his arms, the pleasure he had given her, the wicked sensation of his tongue between her thighs. Her breath hitched, and she turned resolutely away from him.

"It's been a long day," she said, aware her voice was trembling. "I'm tired and I wish to sleep. The bath water is still warm if you wish to use it, though."

He must also be tired and hot; it seemed childish to refuse him the opportunity to bathe.

"Thank you. I won't take long," he assured her.

Evie went to the dressing table, where she could keep her back to him and give him some privacy and sat down to brush her hair. She concentrated on taking all the pins out, ignoring the telltale sound of water sloshing that told her Louis was getting in the bath. Raising her head, Evie placed all the hairpins in a neat pile and then stilled as she realised she could see Louis in the reflection of the looking glass.

He was working soap over his chest and shoulders, and her heart gave a panicked little kick behind her ribs. Good God, but he was magnificent. Evie's mouth went dry, and she told herself not to look, told herself to turn her gaze away, but she could not.

Efficiently, Louis finished washing himself and stood, water sluicing down his body. Evie's breath caught as her gaze travelled over him, drinking in the sight of him. Her chest ached as much as her body as she acknowledged her desire for him, how thoroughly her heart was in his hands, and just how vulnerable that made her. Unable to stop herself, her gaze fell to that most masculine part of him, and her pulse sped up as she saw he was aroused, his cock standing proudly to attention. A slow, insistent throb began between her thighs, demanding she go to him and take what she wanted. With difficulty, she tore her gaze from his arousal and glanced back at his face, jolting as she discovered his piercing blue eyes watching her watch him.

"I never pretended I didn't want you," he said softly. "And I am yours, Evie, entirely, if… if you want me too. Do you? Do you still want me?"

"You're beautiful, as you well know," she replied, knowing that was not what he'd asked, wishing she had not heard the doubt behind the question. She turned her attention back to brushing her hair, looking anywhere but at him.

"So are you."

Evie made a dismissive sound. Not that she was fishing for compliments. She knew her strengths. She knew she was a good friend, intelligent and fun, and that people sought out her company. Yes, she was attractive, in a pretty, abundant sort of fashion that appealed to some, she supposed, but *beautiful*? No.

"You think my body lies?" he asked impatiently, and she could not help but turn to look at him then. He finished drying himself and cast the towel aside, gesturing to his erection. "You've not touched me, not given me the slightest encouragement. Every inch of you is covered up, and yet here I am, desperate for you. I love you, Evie, and I need you so badly I do not know how to manage these feelings. Does this not please you, to know how much I want you when you clearly don't want me?"

There was an edge to his voice, something between anger and frustration.

She forced herself to turn away again, trembling with a dangerous combination of lust and fear. "You just want what you can't have, that's all. How many times have you been told no, Louis?"

He made a harsh sound that might have been a laugh if it had not sounded so bitter. "That depends on what you mean, *mon amour*. If I merely want to fuck someone, never. For anything else I've ever wanted, it's the only word I ever hear."

Evie glanced back at him, startled by the misery in his voice. He snatched up his shirt and pulled it over his head before reaching for his trousers. There were twin crests of colour high on his cheeks and something told her he had not meant to speak so candidly. She hesitated, aware of his unhappiness but too uncertain of what to do about it. She wondered what he meant by those angry words. Was that really true? If so.... Her heart ached.

"Louis?" she tried, not knowing what it was she wanted to say, but needing to try.

He ignored her and dressed haphazardly, tugging on his boots before stalking to the door.

"Louis, wait. Where are you going?" she asked, not liking the idea of him leaving her in such a temper.

"What do you care?" he demanded. He paused as he got to the door and took a deep breath. When he spoke again, his voice was a calmer, something like hope audible in the words. "Do you want me to stay, Evie? You need only say so."

Evie hesitated, uncertain of what it was she did want.

Louis closed his eyes for a moment before he spoke again. *"Non,* of course not. Why on earth would you."

He went out and closed the door behind him.

10th March 1824, rue du Faubourg du Temple, Paris, France.

Louis is twelve years old.

Their father returned the night of Louis' first public performance. Nic had been anxious about allowing Louis to perform, but everyone else had badgered him so much he'd had no choice but to allow it. Louis was popular among the circus folk, and it was easy to see why. He was beautiful, kind-hearted and quick to smile, eager to please. Louis wanted to perform, and everyone wanted Louis to be happy. What choice had Nic but to allow it?

It had only been a short act but, unsurprisingly, the audience had loved him on sight. The appearance of the stunning young man running across the highwire, surefooted as a cat, had the audience beguiled, and Louis was a born showman. He grinned at them and winked, playing to the crowd, blowing kisses at the ladies. He pushed himself to perform with such utter fearlessness that even Nic could only stare with admiration, for he knew Louis' teeth had been chattering with terror before he'd gone on. At the end of the highwire act, when Nic went to find him, Louis had been glowing with pride and happiness.

"Did you see?" he demanded.

"I saw," Nic replied, pulling his brother into a rough hug. "Well done."

"How dare you!" thundered another voice, making them jolt as the refined accent cut through the noise of the audience cheering the next act. "How dare you have my son, my heir, behave in such a fashion, no better than a performing monkey! He is the Vicomte Sainte-Apre, not some gutter-born lowlife."

Nic stiffened, the heat of humiliation suffusing his body.

For a heartbeat, no one said a word, and then Louis pushed past Nic.

"Now you care what I do, Père?" he demanded with quiet fury, regarding the father he had not seen in years with such rage that Nic's breath caught.

He had never seen Louis lose his temper with anyone, never seen a show of frustration or irritation despite the punishing schedule and hard work required to attain the skills he needed. Truthfully, it had bothered Nic, for it did not seem normal for a boy of his years to be so utterly contained, but whatever force of will kept his emotions in check was gone now. Louis was chalk-white with anger, his eyes blazing an uncanny blue. Louis might not have raised his voice, but his tone made the hairs on the back of Nic's neck stand on end.

"Did you not care when you abandoned me to the mercy of a vile man that despised me and everything I stood for? A man you'd tried to have killed. Did you care when he stripped me of my clothes and dressed me in filthy rags, when I was reduced to eating scraps from the floor for his amusement, and emptying his bedpan? I have lived these past years being called 'chien', Père. Where was my title then? Where were you?"

Finally, Louis' voice broke, and he shouted the last words, tears glittering in his eyes.

The Comte de Villen stared at his son, his shock clear, and for a moment Nic hoped he would fall to his knees and beg his son's forgiveness. He hoped that their father would have something kind to say, some words that would make Louis understand he had not been forgotten, that only circumstances had kept them apart. But Nic saw the flash of anger that followed and knew it was not guilt on the man's face; he just did not like being spoken to so by a boy.

The comte raised his hand and Louis stiffened but did not cower away, merely waited for the blow to land. Nic's hand shot out, and he grabbed their father's wrist, stilling the motion with ease. The comte glared at him, outraged.

"Non. Louis has been beaten enough for one lifetime. When I found him, he was black and blue. No one will touch him again. No one." Nic tightened his grip on his father's wrist, illustrating the ease with which he could turn the situation if he chose to. The Comte de Villen was getting old. He was no match for Nic, and they both knew it.

"He will not perform again," the comte said coldly as Nic released his grip.

There was a snort of mirthless laughter from behind them. "Are you going to feed the boy, then? I've raised one of your sons without so much as a sou from you. I'll not raise another. If he stays, he earns his keep, or are you going to take him with you?"

They all turned as Nic's mother appeared, regarding her onetime lover with contempt.

The comte flushed, and now Nic looked at him critically, as he had not done before. Previously, he had been too dazzled by his father's lofty title, his entitled manner, and that effortless charm to see that his fine clothes might be clean and well kept, but they were old and worn. The seams were wearing thin, the colour fading in places. Moreover, he looked ill, his skin grey and drawn, and his coat seemed rather too big for his frame, suggesting he had lost weight.

"If people see him performing, he will never take his rightful place in society," the comte said icily.

"So, keep it a secret, which will be easier if you don't come here again. You think anyone can recognise him under that greasepaint up on a highwire? Don't be daft, Armand. And unlike your kind, we are loyal to one another here. We will keep the boy safe, keep his secrets for him, which is more than you ever did."

The comte gritted his teeth, but it seemed like the fight had gone out of him, and like he had little choice in the matter.

"Very well. Do as you please, but if anyone finds out who he really is—"

"They won't," Nic said at once. He knew what it meant for Louis to have a future, even if the boy himself seemed less than thrilled at the idea.

"Louis has much to learn, as it seems he has forgotten all his manners. He barely sounds like my son anymore, that accent…" the comte said, shuddering, regarding Louis with such disdain that Nic wanted to shake the old man until his teeth rattled. Instead, Nic laid a reassuring hand on Louis' shoulder, instantly aware of the fine tremor running through his body. "If he is to have a chance of taking his place in society, he must learn how to speak properly again, how to behave like a gentleman. That is going to take time."

"I'm not learning anything from you," Louis said at once, but Nic tightened his grip on his shoulder.

"Louis, you need this. If you can take your place in that world, it could change everything," he said, willing the boy to understand what he would throw away by refusing to do as their father wanted.

"I have a home here with you," Louis said, staring at Nic, such panic in his eyes that Nic's heart clenched as he understood

why he was so afraid. Louis rarely let Nic out of his sight for long, certain that his brother would simply leave and disappear one day, despite Nic promising he would never do that.

"And you always will have, Louis," Nic said gently. "You'll stay here, with me, for as long as you want to, but this will give you power in the world, power that none of us here have."

Louis snorted, shaking his head. "It never helped me before now, it only ever made things ten times worse."

"It will be different with your father's backing," Nic insisted. He hesitated, not wanting to use guilt as a reason for making Louis do what he wanted, but he knew this was an opportunity Louis would be mad to ignore. The Comte de Villen might be penniless, without a friend in the world, but Louis would grow to be a handsome, charismatic man, the sort of man who could get what he wanted. Add to that a legitimate title, and he could hold the world in his hands. Nic would not allow him to walk away from that. "Think of what it could mean for us both," he said under his breath.

Louis frowned, his dark brows drawing together. He regarded Nic, confusion and anxiety in his eyes. "You... You want me to do this?"

Nic nodded. "I do."

Nic hated himself for the misery he could see on his brother's face, but it was for the best. It was Louis' best chance for a future. "Then I'll do it for you, Nic," Louis said tonelessly, glaring at his sire. "Not for him."

"You think I care?" their father said with a snort. "Hate me all you like, boy. I hated my father, and he hated his in turn. The title is all that matters now. You're the next Comte de Villen. It is your duty to help me regain all that we lost. It is your duty to see our properties returned to us, to sire the next generation so your son may carry on the line. You want your revenge on that bastard that treated you so badly, then prosper. Knowing you've taken

your rightful place in the world will fill him with rage the likes of which you cannot possibly understand. Kings come and go, but our family has endured for too many generations to fade away. Have a little pride in your blood. Our name was one of the oldest and most revered in the land before the revolution, and I'm damned if I'll let it die out with my son performing in a circus, of all things. God help us!"

Louis said nothing, but Nic could tell he was holding onto his composure by a thread. He needed to get him away from their father, and quickly.

"What do you need us to do?" He asked, aware now that his mother had been correct. Their father thought nothing of either of them. Louis was only a means to an end, and Nic... Nic was merely incidental.

The comte handed them his card. "You had best come to me in the mornings. At first light, so no one sees you. We'll begin tomorrow. Do not be late."

With that, the Comte de Villen turned and strode away.

Chapter 8

Wolf,

I pray this letter reaches you before I do.

I suspect you know more than I, but it seems Etienne Boucher is not dead. I will never forgive myself for not having believed Louis at once. I should have known better than to dismiss his concerns. He is in a deal of trouble.

I have been trying to track Etienne down and found the rooms where he has been living, but too late. He has crossed to France. I am doing my best to pick up the trail, but the man is a damned magician. From what I have learned, his face is badly scarred, burns I assume, though how he got out of the fire you described is beyond me. Despite that, no one ever seems to see the bastard. He's like a ghost, disappearing into the background. For heaven's sake, get your men on alert looking out for him.

To make matters far worse, Louis has a young woman with him. Miss Evie Knight. This is the woman he wishes to marry, but I am uncertain if she has agreed to do so or not. I

*believe Etienne drugged her and Louis took
her with him to keep her safe. Her father is the
English industrialist, Gabriel Knight. He's a
powerful man with influential friends,
including the Marquess of Montagu and my
father-in-law. Needless to say, I am in a
difficult position now, but my brother needs
help. You know what Etienne will do if he
catches up to Louis. For the love of God, keep
him safe. I will send news when I have it and
be with you as soon as I can.*

**—Excerpt of a letter from Monsieur
Nicholas Alexander Demarteau to Wulfric
'Wolf' De Vere.**

20th July 1842, Compiègne, France.

Evie did not see Louis again until the next morning, when she joined him in the carriage. He was clean shaven and neatly turned out, but there were shadows beneath his eyes, and he looked exhausted.

"Where were you?" she asked, aware that he had not returned to the room at all last night, for she had not slept well herself and had woken each time to find herself alone.

"Playing cards," he replied, not looking at her.

Evie studied his face, wondering if he would lie to her. No. She did not believe that of him, but he must have felt her scrutiny and turned towards her.

"My, I have fallen from favour," he said, regret and hurt flashing in his eyes for a moment before he returned his gaze to stare out of the window.

"No," Evie said at once, shaking her head as she realised, he thought she believed him to have been up to no good. "I am only worried about you. Where were you, Louis? You look worn to a thread."

"I told you, playing cards," he said again, his voice weary. "This journey has been expensive and, as I left unexpectedly, I had little in the way of funds on me. I needed money, which I now have. I'm sorry if I worried you, there was no need."

"You won?" she said, offering him an uncertain smile.

"Oui," he replied, not seeing her smile for he stared out of the window still, not looking at her.

He looked tense and unhappy, and she remembered his parting words last night that suggested he believed she did not want him. He had said he'd been denied everything he had ever wanted, unless he wanted to take someone to bed. She considered this, wondering what that would do to him over time.

"Louis," she said, keeping her voice soft. She was tired of being angry with him, it was exhausting, and she could see no good resolution to this situation unless they worked it out between them. They loved each other. Surely, they could find a way forward. He had promised to tell her everything he had been hiding from her, and she needed to know his secrets if she was to decide what came next. "I'm sorry, I know you are tired, but I think…we need to talk."

He stiffened, the little colour in his cheeks blanching. "As you said, I'm tired. Perhaps later."

Louis closed his eyes, forestalling any possibility of a conversation. Evie sighed and resigned herself to a long journey.

Louis tried to force his body to approximate the relaxed posture of a man trying to sleep, but his limbs would not obey him. Tension rang through his muscles, his heart beating too fast. She was going to tell him she would not marry him. Evie was going to tell him it was over, that there was no place in her life for him any longer. There had been too much gentleness in the way she had spoken when she had been so cool with him until now. She was trying to soften the blow, for Evie was always kind. Even when she broke his heart into a million pieces, she would try to be kind.

Something like panic seethed in his blood. He told himself to stop. He was being ridiculous. Evie loved him. Yet that cruel voice kept murmuring in the back of his mind, reminding him he was worthless, that no one could love him because he was corrupt and wicked and brought out the worst in everyone. Though he was horribly afraid there was more truth in the accusation that he wanted to believe, he shut it out. Not Evie, he insisted. She was different and, when they were done with this interminable journey, they could spend time together, he could show her Paris. He was certain that she would love it.

It was a beautiful and seductive city, so much more uninhibited than London, with all its rules and snobbery, just as Evie was so much braver and bolder than even she realised. Like when they had been trapped in that hot-air balloon, miles above the ground. She would have been well within her rights to have been terrified and hysterical, but instead she had adored every moment. Yet if anyone had asked her to do such a thing, she would have run a mile, insistent that she was too afraid. She simply did not have enough confidence in herself yet, that was all, but if she did—if she realised everything she could have, that *they* could have—she would be magnificent. He wanted to see her become the woman he knew she was, bold and full of life and laughter. Louis wanted that so badly it was an ache beneath his skin.

They could have the best of both worlds if they wished to. They could enjoy all the decadent delights of Paris, and then to return to the home he had bought them in England. A safe, beautiful place where they could be at peace together, raise a family together. That dream had lingered in the back of his mind for so long now. For years he did not have a specific place in mind, or a woman, just the longing for a home, for a place to belong, a place where someone wanted him to stay. He had never really believed it was possible, had allowed no one close enough to make it a possibility, and then Evie had slipped beneath his defences before he had seen the danger. She had worked her way into his heart and suddenly the image had taken shape, had taken root in his mind and refused to shake free. He had pinned everything on the vision of that future, and if that was taken from him....

He drew in an uneven breath, willing his pulse to slow. *No.* He would not give up on that future. Not yet. Not for anything. Evie loved him, and even if she did not love him enough to forgive him, to marry him, she desired him. He had seen the look in her eyes last night when she had looked upon his naked body. She wanted him, and perhaps he had damaged her love for him, but it was not entirely gone. Not yet. Other women had professed to love him madly when he'd done nothing to deserve it. With bitter amusement, he realised he finally understood the long, pleading letters, begging him to change his mind. Now the hysteria, the scandalous behaviour, the tantrums and the threats all made sense. He knew just how those poor unhappy women had felt when he had ended things, for he was perilously close to acting like a madman himself. But surely, if he had roused such feelings in those women, he could make Evie love him again if he tried hard enough? Couldn't he?

The endless rocking of the carriage finally lulled his troubled mind as exhaustion swept over him. He had barely slept for two nights now, and he did not have the will to fight it as sleep tugged him under and back into the past.

14th May 1824, rue François Miron, Paris, France.

Louis is twelve years old.

Their father's rooms in Le Marais had once been grand. Before the revolution, this area had been full of the best of French high society, from le Duc de Richelieu and his ilk to the intellectuals and philosophers, musicians and artists of the age. Now, it was rather down at heel, and though the buildings still impressed Nic, to Louis' eye they looked shabby and showed signs of neglect. He tugged his coat a little tighter about himself, wondering if he was out of his mind.

He was late for his father's lesson this morning, and he knew Nic would be worried about him, for he had not come home last night. Louis had rowed with the comte yesterday morning. Hardly a rare occurrence, but Nic had been quiet on their walk home and Louis had felt bad, knowing it was his fault. Nic was disappointed in him and his reluctance to do as their father wanted.

That they needed money lay at the heart of the problem. His father had discovered Louis' ability with numbers and had taught him to play cards. Having discovered his son was nigh on unbeatable, he wanted to take him out with him, playing for money. But he could not do that if Louis was not properly dressed. But they could not dress him as befitted the son of the Comte de Villen without money. Frustrated by this circular problem, the comte had lost his temper as he was wont to do and taken it out on Nic. Furious to see his brother treated so badly, Louis had told his father to go to hell because he'd not do a damned thing he wanted ever again and stormed out.

Nic had followed him, but Louis had seen the disappointment in his eyes and known he would have to eat his words. But to have a chance of acting the part of Vicomte Sainte-Apre, Louis needed to look the part as well. It was simply that to him now, too. A part to play. In his mind, the Vicomte Sainte-Apre had died years ago, destroyed by Monsieur and Madame Boucher and Etienne, and all the relentless bullying from the other children who lived around that awful house. The creature who had survived was not that boy, he was different, harder, more resilient, and he did not give a damn what his father wanted. Nic, however, was a different matter. Nic wanted Louis to succeed, wanted him to become this fine, well-mannered creature who seemed a million miles away from who

Louis was now. His brother dreamed of a time when Louis would return to the home that he had known all those years ago and make it his own. Why Nic wanted that so much for him, Louis could not fathom, he only knew it to be true.

Well, if that was what Nic wanted, then Louis would do it, because he owed his brother everything, and he would not let him down. Not for the world. Gritting his teeth, he knocked on the door that led to his father's rooms and was drawn into a fierce hug the moment the door opened.

"Dieu merci," Nic said, before thrusting Louis away from him again, his expression fierce as he gave him a hard shake. "You rotten little sod! You've had me worried sick. You missed last night's performance too, which means you're in trouble there as well. I looked everywhere for you. Where the hell were you?"

Louis muttered an apology, startled and overwhelmed by his brother's anger. No one had ever worried about him before, and he was rather taken aback.

"You're late," his father said coldly, eyeing him with disfavour.

Louis glowered back at him and reached into his pocket, throwing something at his father's feet. Nic gasped as he bent and picked up the bracelet Louis had thrown down, the diamonds glittering in the light.

"Where did you get this?" Nic demanded.

Louis shrugged. "What does it matter? It's valuable, isn't it?"

This time, his brother was too stunned by the jewels in his hand to halt the blow his father aimed at Louis. The slap resounded through the sparsely furnished apartment, and Louis sucked in a breath at the sting as his cheek burned and he staggered backwards.

"Thieving now?" his father said in disgust.

"Oui, Père, for you've not a pot to piss in," Louis replied calmly, knowing how badly it would rile the man. It delighted him to make his father angry, to know that his sire could not claim the same power over him that Monsieur Boucher once had. He would let no one make him afraid like that man had, would not allow them that power over him. And so he taunted his father and deliberately angered him, because his Père could knock him down, perhaps, but he could not terrify Louis as that man had, he did not haunt him in the same way that Monsieur Boucher slid into his dreams and made him wake in a cold sweat.

The comte's eyes flashed with anger at his words but he snatched the bracelet from Nic. He held the bracelet to the light, turning it this way and that. Finally, the comte laughed, shaking his head. "Well, I'll be damned if this thing isn't real. You've an eye for quality, son, I'll give you that. Can you get more?"

"Louis, non," Nic said urgently, shaking his head.

"Oui, Père," Louis said, seeing the spark of satisfaction in his father's eyes as he returned a curt nod.

"Très bien, mon fils. So be it," he said, and went to walk away before thinking better of it and turning back, slapping Louis again, so hard this time Louis fell back against the door and smacked his head. He gasped as stars exploded before his eyes. "And if you ever speak to me like that again, I'll make you sorry, you little shit."

"Louis! Louis, wake up!"

Louis sat up with a start, blinking in the daylight, utterly disorientated. The dream still clung to him, and he put a hand to his cheek, expecting to find it sore. How strange to have dreamt of that day, one he had not thought of for a long time. It was almost a pleasant memory compared to the ones that had plagued him of late, for despite getting the back of his father's hand twice in one day, he had won. He had solved the dilemma, providing the finances his father could not. The old comte had hated him for that and Louis had been glad.

Waking fully, he looked down, suddenly aware of a small hand clutching his arm. He turned his head to find Evie watching him with concern.

"A bad dream?" she asked, and Louis fought a blush, realising he must have said or done something to worry her.

"Where are we?" he asked, ignoring the question.

"In Paris, close to our destination from what I gather," she replied carefully, removing her hand.

"You should have woken me earlier," he said, realising he had slept through several changes of horses.

"You were worn out and needed your rest. I'm afraid I stole some money from you to pay for things as we went along, though," she said with a slight smile.

Louis sat back, regarding her cautiously, encouraged by her lighter mood. "What's mine is yours, *mon amour*. You may have whatever you want from me whenever you want it."

She blushed, hearing the suggestive tone in his voice. "Louis," she protested, the warning note quite audible.

Louis ignored it and took her hand, raising it to his mouth. "What? I love you and I want you, and I think you want me too. Don't you? Why must you keep denying us? You did not before. When I came to your room—"

She silenced him, pressing a finger against his lips. "That was before you broke my trust, Louis."

He nipped at her finger, and she blushed but withdrew her hand, shifting away from him. Louis studied her, noticing the rapid rise and fall of her chest. "Do you remember how it felt when I touched you, how hard you came for me?"

She let out a harsh breath, shocked and visibly flustered now.

Thunder rumbled ominously outside the carriage and the light dimmed as dark clouds rolled in. The storm that had threatened in Compiègne had followed them to Paris and seemed set to break at any moment.

Longing for her rose inside him, an ache in his heart that echoed throughout his body, to his very bones. "I remember the taste of you on my tongue, sweet and tart. *Délicieuse*. I am hungry for you, Evie."

She shook her head, refusing to look at him, but he saw the way her eyes had grown dark, the flush that stained her cheeks, her throat. Oh, she wanted him.

"I could do that now, if you'd like me to. I could push up your skirts and put my mouth on you, with the driver sitting up front and the footmen behind, people walking past us in the streets outside. I think you would like that, my wicked Evie."

"No, that's… that's not…" she protested.

"Not true? I don't believe you. I think you like the idea, the scandalous thrill of it."

He glanced outside, dismayed to realise he recognised the streets they passed though, and they were closer to their destination than he had guessed. If he was going to do this, he needed to work fast.

Louis shifted closer to her, not touching her, but aware of the way her body stiffened, like some wild creature ready to bolt. "Open your legs for me and pull up your skirts," he begged, discovering he was breathless, too.

She shook her head, her mouth clamped shut, as if she did not trust herself to speak.

"We both know you're aching for me, *mon amour,*" he whispered, leaning in close so his breath fluttered over her skin. She shivered and closed her eyes. "You're wet, aren't you? You can feel your pulse throbbing between your thighs. It's saying *yes, yes, put your mouth on me, Louis.* Isn't it? *Isn't it?"* he demanded.

She made a small, desperate sound.

"Ask me to do it," he said, feeling as though he'd lose his damned mind if she didn't. For as much as he was tormenting her, he was doing worse to his own sanity. "Spread your legs and tell me to get on my knees. Demand that I pleasure you," he ground out.

He jolted as she surged out of her seat and rapped hard on the door of the carriage. The driver pulled them to a halt so suddenly that Evie almost fell on her arse, but she exploded out of the door the moment they stopped, not waiting for anyone to let the steps down.

"Merde!" Louis cursed, leaping down after her.

Thunder cracked overhead, illuminating the narrow street briefly before the heavens opened. Rain fell in a torrent, soaking Louis to the bone in a matter of seconds as he hurried after Evie. He caught up with her, taking hold of her arm and pulling her to a halt. People stared at them as they ran for shelter.

"Evie, get back in the carriage," he said urgently, furious with himself for taking the wrong tack with her yet again. What was it about this woman that made him do everything wrong? Now she would get drenched in the downpour and catch her death of cold.

She shook her head, staring at him, her green eyes wide and wild with panic.

"I won't touch you, I swear it. I won't say another word," he promised her, needing to get her out of the rain.

She had refused him again. Louis knew she had been desperate for his touch, so aroused she would have shattered the moment he put his mouth on her, and she had still run away from him. Cold dread seeped into his bones, chilling him to the marrow as he knew he must face the truth. He was losing her. He had broken her trust in him and proven himself to be everything she had feared he was. All he had left was the fact that she desired him, but it wasn't enough for her. It was never enough for anyone. She would leave him. Her father would come for her, and he could not hide her away, could not compound his villainy by keeping her a hostage. Gabriel Knight would come and take her away and that would be an end to it.

"I'm sorry," he said helplessly, wishing he was different, wishing he was a different kind of man, one who knew how to love her as she deserved.

She deserved so much better than he could give her when he was so twisted up and ugly inside, but he had only seen salvation, a light in the darkness, and he had wanted it so badly he had snuffed it out with his own selfish desires.

She stared at him as the rain pelted down over them both. Impossibly, it was coming down even harder now. People ran past, heads down as they ran for cover and in moments the slick streets were all but deserted, except for the two of them. They stood toe to toe, both breathing hard, water trickling down their faces as rivulets sluiced from the rooftops.

With a cry of frustration, Evie grabbed hold of his lapels and dragged him closer. She caught hold of his neck and tugged, pulling his mouth to hers. Louis snatched her up, crushing her against his body so tight she could not hope to get free, but instead of struggling she pressed closer, as if she could not get near enough to him. Her kiss was frantic, demanding, as though she would die if he did not kiss her hard enough, deep enough, and still she demanded more.

She dragged her mouth from his to kiss his jaw, his throat, and Louis groaned, uncaring that they were in full view of anyone mad enough to still be on the streets.

"Evie, Evie, *mon amour*, my God, I am going to lose my mind."

Suddenly, as if his words had broken a spell, she gave a startled little yelp and pushed away from him. Louis held on, reluctant to let her go but she struggled and cursed so he released his hold on her.

"Oh!" she cried, glaring at him. "Oh…. *You!*"

He stared at her uncertainly. "You kissed me, I didn't—"

"You… You started it," she said, stamping her foot so that water splashed them both. "Oh, and now I sound like a five-year-old. It's all your fault. You are turning me into a lunatic!"

"I know it's my fault," he said, utterly wretched, staring at her and wondering how much longer he had. Days? Hours? He was cold and soaked to the bone, vibrating with sexual frustration, and perilously close to losing what little remained of his sanity. He did not know which way to jump. She had only just begun to see the worst of him, if she saw everything he was, everything he had been, he would lose her, but if he did not let her see, he would lose her anyway. It was like balancing on the highwire with his hands tied behind his back, knowing it was only a matter of time before he fell.

A dark shadow fell over them both and Evie gave a little scream, scurrying closer to Louis as an enormous man appeared from the mouth of the narrow alley beside them.

The fellow grinned as he looked Louis up and down, then shook his head. *"Bienvenue à Paris, mon ami.* And by the looks of you, not a moment too soon. Is this what life in England has reduced you to? What the hell is the elegant Comte de Villen doing in the middle of the street, looking like a drowned rat?"

Louis glowered at his old friend, frustrated to meet him again under such circumstances.

"Mind your own damned business, Wolf."

Louis held out his hand to Evie, who took one look at Wolf and did not protest, hurrying to stand beside him.

Wolf stared at Evie, whose bonnet was a sodden mess, her dark hair plastered to her face and her gown mud-splattered, the fine material losing its shape under the weight of water.

He raised an eyebrow, turning back to Louis with a look of mild surprise. "That's surely not…?"

"Pas un mot," Louis said, enough warning in his voice to make Wolf snap his mouth shut.

"Not a word," Wolf repeated, holding his hands up in surrender. "Well, let's get you both indoors and out of the rain, and then perhaps you can explain to me what the hell you've been up to."

Chapter 9

Dearest Eliza,

Do you mean to say Nic has gone after them, too? Good heavens, I thought the scandal I had caused with Hargreaves would have the ton gossiping for years to come but they barely mentioned our names. I am glad of it, but wish it were anyone else they were talking about instead. All anyone can speak of is how the Comte de Villen carried an unconscious Evie away in the dead of night. He seems to have become a villain overnight, though that does not stop most of the women wishing it were them he'd carried off.

What did Nic have to say? Did he have any idea why his brother did it?

—Excerpt of a letter from Lady Rosamund Hargreaves (daughter of Their Graces Robert and Prunella Adolphus, The Duke and Duchess of Bedwin) to her sister, Lady Eliza Demarteau.

20th July 1842, Amiens, France

Barnaby stepped out of the diligence coach with a groan, cursing the French for not having made as much progress with their railways as in Britain. He was tired and aching and in a very bad skin. His lamentable French was causing him no end of trouble and getting away from the *douaniers* at the custom house had taken him hours. Privately, he was certain they had understood a good deal more of his broken French than they let on but were entertained by his incompetence and had a bit of fun at his expense.

He was not entirely certain what he hoped to achieve by undertaking this mad journey, except that he knew damn well that Louis was in trouble, and… well, when a friend was in trouble, one did whatever one could to get them out of it. What exactly Barnaby thought he could achieve was another matter, however. He felt certain Louis was mixed up in things Barnaby himself would do well to stay far away from, and Louis was far better equipped to deal with such matters, but Barnaby hoped he'd figure that out when he found him. Assuming he *could* find Louis. He knew his friend was tied up with the notorious nightclub Rouge et Noir in Paris, though, and so that seemed as good a place to begin as any.

Thunder gave an ominous rumble and the early evening light faded as dark clouds boiled overhead. Well, he had better get a room booked, and quickly. There was still a good deal of ground to cover before he reached Paris, and he was dog tired. He turned and looked up at the coaching inn before which the carriage had deposited him. It looked like a decent place, with sparkling clean windows and jaunty boxes of colourful geraniums outside. His Aunt Hester always said clean windows were a good estimation of what you'd find inside, so that boded well.

Out of the corner of his eye, Barnaby caught sight of something scurrying by. He turned, frowning as he saw a boy duck out of sight, hurrying into the stable yard. Well, that was odd, because it looked very much like the lad he'd seen at Calais, skulking about in the shadows. Barnaby had particularly noticed him because he looked shifty, and he'd suspected the boy of being a pickpocket. Ah, well. He was gone now. Steeling himself to face

the proprietor of the inn and murder the French language a bit
more, Barnaby strode up the steps to the inn and went inside.

20th July 1842, Rue de la Bièvre, 13th Arrondissement, Paris, France.

If Evie had ever doubted Louis was a dangerous man involved
in questionable activities with the criminal underworld or all the
other troubling things her father had said of him, the next ten
minutes swept those doubts away. The man Louis had called Wolf
took them to a place he unnervingly referred to as The Fortress. It
was a large, unwelcoming building, a chateau of considerable age
and with walls so thick it was clear why it had gained the name.
Wolf took them in past an entrance bristling with men Evie would
not want to meet in a dark alley, or any other circumstance going
by the knives and pistols they were equipped with.

Everyone stopped and stared as Louis passed, the men tugging
caps from their heads with haste and nodding respectfully. That
they all knew and even feared him was written all over their faces.
Evie swallowed her misgivings for now, keeping her head down,
utterly mortified at having to arrive with Louis in such a wretched
state, sodden and mud-spattered and hardly looking her best. Louis
gripped her hand, but she could not help but wonder if he was
reconsidering. He could hardly be proud of her in this state when
the men here must be used to seeing him with the most glamorous
women Paris had to offer. Certainly, Wolf had made no secret of
the fact she was not at all what he had expected. The shock in his
eyes when he had looked at her might have been comical if she
hadn't felt so much like sobbing. She rather hated him for that, not
that she'd say so. He was the most terrifying looking man she'd
ever encountered.

Miserable and anxious, Evie shivered, though she suspected
that was as much nerves as the fact she was cold. Her damp clothes
were clammy against her skin. They entered through a narrow
corridor which led to an inner courtyard. Here, a large cart was

131

being piled with crates, the occasional chink of glass suggesting the crates were full of bottles.

Once inside the fortress, a thick oak door closed with an unnerving finality that echoed through the vast entrance hall.

"My wife needs a hot bath and a meal," Louis said to Wolf. "I take it my rooms have been made ready, as you were prescient enough to have Duval waiting at Folkestone for me?"

"They are," Wolf replied, studying them both with unapologetic interest. "But I thought you weren't married yet?"

"Not yet," Louis replied, sounding a little terse. "But no one else is to know that."

Wolf's eyes flickered to Evie with curiosity, and she blushed, having a good idea of what he was thinking.

"It's good to see you," Wolf said, speaking in English this time, and Evie was surprised by the upper-class English accent.

Louis sighed and nodded. *"Oui,* it is good to see you too."

Wolf gave a bark of laughter and hugged Louis with enthusiasm, slapping his back so hard Evie winced. "Ah! I've missed you!" the man exclaimed, grinning broadly now.

"Wolf! *Arrêtez ça! Mon Dieu,* you are like an overgrown puppy. Pack it in, you great oaf," Louis protested, though there was no heat in his words.

"It's been four years!" Wolf said, reproach in his eyes.

Louis laughed, nodding, and hugged him again. "So it has, *petit loup."*

"Little wolf?" Evie repeated dubiously, eyeing the big man.

Wolf glowered at her, but Louis grinned. "It was not ironic when I named him that, *mon amour,* but how was I to know he was half mountain when he was a such a scrawny boy?"

"I was a late bloomer," Wolf replied, addressing his comment to Louis, his lip twitching with amusement.

Louis snorted. "Enough of this. My lady will catch cold if you keep on. We will speak later, *mon ami.* For now, we are tired and chilled to the bone. It has been a long journey. I trust you to keep anyone from finding us here."

"Like her father?" Wolf suggested, the innocent expression sitting ill on his harsh features and leaving Evie in no doubt he found this exceedingly amusing.

"Oui," Louis replied, curt now. "Exactly like her father."

Evie frowned, and Louis avoided her gaze as he guided her up a winding staircase and along a gloomy corridor. Evie hardly knew what to expect when he opened the door to what he'd referred to as his rooms, but she gasped in surprise. Though it was July, fires blazed in both the large, high-ceilinged rooms. The dark stone walls that gave the entire building such an oppressive feeling had been painted off-white here, and thick blue damask curtains framed the one narrow window. The thickly planked oak wood floor shone in the firelight, and lamps cast a warm glow on everything. There were elegant pieces of furniture, including a writing desk and chair, and a comfortable-looking sofa upholstered in soft, luxurious fabric stood by the fire. Bookcases lined two entire walls, their glass fronts reflecting the flickering light back into the room. Evie moved across to a door that led to a cosy bedchamber, dominated by a large, ornate bed. The same dark blue was on the bedcovers with crisp, white linen sheets. Evie's heart picked up, and she turned away, inspecting the comfortable sitting room instead.

Evie looked around to see Louis watching her.

"It's lovely," she said truthfully. "This is your place?"

Louis shrugged, peeling off his sodden coat with a grimace. "It used to be. I haven't stayed here in years, but Wolf keeps it as I left it, just in case."

"In case you need to escape from people who want to kill you?" she asked pointedly.

He stilled for a moment before giving a taut nod. *"Oui.* Exactly so."

"That's why it's called the fortress."

"It is. There is only one real entrance in and out, though there are many secret tunnels. It is nigh on impenetrable. It was the first property I ever bought for myself."

"Somewhere you felt safe," Evie guessed, her heart aching as she remembered the little he had told her about his childhood. That much had made her want to protect him too, and explained a good deal about the man he was now, but how much else was he hiding? Nothing good, judging by his reluctance to tell her.

He hesitated for a moment before he replied, as if the thought had not occurred to him before now. "I suppose so."

There was a knock at the door and Louis opened it to allow a stream of servants to enter, carrying buckets of hot water. Two men hefted in the biggest bath Evie had ever seen in her life, big enough for a man like Wolf, she guessed. Once the huge bath was filled, a maid entered, carrying a basket of toiletries. She was a lovely woman, slender as a reed and in her mid-twenties, with dark eyes and glossy black hair. The woman bobbed a curtsey to Evie, but her attention was all for Louis.

"C'est très bon de vous revoir à Paris, monsieur," she said, blushing prettily as she stared at him with undisguised admiration.

Evie's jaw tightened as she mentally translated the girl's welcome back to Paris... along with the flirtatious manner in which she had spoken it.

"Merci, Irène. That will be all," Louis replied politely, barely giving the girl a second glance.

Irène cast an appraising glance at Evie, barely concealing a smirk as she took in her bedraggled appearance. She set down the basket on a table beside the bath and returned her attention to Louis.

"S'il y a quoi que ce soit dont vous avez besoin... rien du tout."

Evie stiffened, understanding the girl's offer to supply anything Louis needed. The brazen invitation in her tone was implicit.

"That will be all, thank you," Louis repeated, with an edge to his voice this time as he opened the door for her. Chastened, the girl hurried out. Louis' gaze flicked to Evie's as he closed the door.

"I make a point of never bedding the staff," he said tightly.

Evie nodded her understanding, grateful to know that, even if he appeared cross with her for having wondered. Well, and why shouldn't she wonder? Irène had certainly made her availability obvious. Evie had always known he was a libertine, long before she had cared who he took to his bed. From the start she had guessed that he was lonely, that he was searching for something more, but now he had decided she was the more that he needed. To have a man like Louis pin all his hopes upon her was... daunting, and this glimpse into the reality of his life had not helped one bit.

"Why not?" she asked, suddenly curious.

Louis frowned. "Why don't I bed the help? Because their situations are tenuous enough without getting involved with the person who pays their wages. How do you refuse a man who holds your ability to buy bread in his hands?"

Evie nodded, pleased and reassured to learn that this side of Louis was exactly as she had expected, but something restless was simmering inside her and she could not help but pry deeper, despite knowing he was every bit as out of sorts as she was.

"She did not look as though she cared about that."

Louis threw his waistcoat aside with obvious irritation. "Am I to be held accountable for what other people want of me? I assure you, *mon amour,* unlike you there are many who would willingly take me to their beds. But you know that, don't you? And you *do* hold it against me."

Evie flushed at the accusation, but could not deny it. "Yes. I suppose I do. I know it's not your fault, but it is hard, Louis, knowing that people will always try to tempt you away from me."

"And when will you believe me when I tell you I will not go?" he demanded.

She could hear anger vibrating behind his words, though he did not raise his voice.

"I don't know," she said, her voice trembling with regret. "Perhaps when I trust your feelings run as deeply as you say they do, when I trust you to always be true to me and to my wishes. I might have found it easier if you had not abducted me, not taken my choices away when you knew very well it was not what I wanted."

She saw the anger leach away as the rigid set of his shoulders lessened. Suddenly, he looked weary and sad, and she was consumed with guilt… but then a wave of frustration hit her that, of the two of them, *she* should feel guilty.

"You should take your bath before it gets cold," he said, his voice devoid of emotion. "Shall I help you undo your clothing, or do you prefer I send Irène back to you?"

"You do it, please," Evie replied in a small voice.

The idea of having Irène attend to her was more than she could bear. She turned her back to him, nerves leaping as she heard him move closer. His touch was impersonal as he undid the fastenings of her dress, without the slightest hint of seduction, and yet her skin burned with his nearness, her heart crashing about behind her ribs.

"So, this place is… what? The centre of *Le Loup Noir's* criminal world?" she asked, struggling to keep a grip on her emotions, which seemed to career from anger to sorrow to unbridled lust and back again with dizzying speed.

"*Oui.* Everything your father told you was true. I never denied it." The dress sagged as he reached the last button and Evie clasped her arms about the bodice, holding it in place. Louis turned his attention to her corset strings.

"And how much do you have to do with it now?"

"Nothing. But I was a part of it for a long time, and all in Paris know it. Besides which, Wolf is loyal to me. That means something here."

"People fear you," she said, and he must have heard something in her voice, something that reminded him that this was not what she had looked for in a husband.

"They do."

His hands settled on her shoulders, and he turned her to face him. "I never hurt an innocent, Evie. I only did the things I did to stop people from getting hurt, to protect those who had no one else. I never meant to become this… *this* man. I don't even know who this man is, if you want the truth. I am not sure I ever did. I was just so very tired of being powerless, and the only way I could see for that to happen was to be the person who held the power."

Evie nodded, her heart aching for him. She reached up to stroke his face, wishing she could just forget everything and remember this feeling, the love she held for the man before her, but she was in a building that Louis himself admitted was at the centre of Paris' criminal underworld, and he had brought her here against her will.

Louis closed his eyes, turning into her caress, pressing his mouth to her palm. He covered her hand with his own, holding it there.

"Marry me," he whispered, such desperation behind the demand Evie felt tears prick at her eyes.

But any decision she made in this state, with her nerves so raw and her heart so exposed, would not be one she could rely upon. It was the rest of her life that hung in the balance, and for a decision of such magnitude, she needed a clear head. Despite her turmoil, she almost smiled as she realised—she was her father's daughter, after all. How many times had he counselled her never to make any important decision when in the grip of powerful emotions? *A fool decides on the turn of a coin, Evie, on the second hand of a clock. Always, always step back, and take the time you need to consider.*

"Don't demand an answer now, Louis," she said softly. "Not after such a day."

His blue eyes fixed upon hers, dark with desire, and her breath hitched as he nipped at the fleshy pad of her thumb before kissing the place where his teeth had been. His mouth moved to the underside of her wrist, and he pressed his lips there.

"Your pulse is racing, *mon amour,*" he observed, his voice dark with the promise of making it run far faster than it already was.

Louis reached out, pressing his hand over her heart before sliding down to her breast. Her dress and bodice had sagged, only her thin chemise keeping his touch from her skin. Evie's nerves skittered with anticipation as the heat from his palm burned her, sending desire thrumming beneath her skin. Her body came alive under his hand, every part of her alight with the anticipation of his touch. The longing to give in, to give in to this mindless passion for him was like being caught in a riptide. Fighting it was such hard work, straining her nerves and her will, when it would be so easy to let go, to drown in her desire for him.

"Go on," he dared her. "Tell me to stop."

"I-I will," she promised, putting up her chin, seeing frustration flare in his eyes.

"Because you are afraid, because you know how good we are together, because you know if I get you into bed, you'll deny me nothing," he accused.

Evie couldn't help it, she laughed. "Yes, Louis. That is exactly why, and that is why I cannot have a conversation with you without you trying to seduce me."

He dropped her hand at once, liked she'd burned him, and stepped away from her. "And what choice do I have?" he shouted, and hearing him raise his voice to her, the sudden fury seething in his entire frame was a shock.

Evie jolted at the rage in his voice, having never heard him lose his temper so before, but it was the look in his eyes that troubled her the most, the stark resignation she saw there.

"Louis," she said, taking a step closer, but he held up his hands and shook his head, his expression taut.

Before she could say another word, he backed away and left the room, slamming the door on his way out.

Evie stared at the space where he had stood with dawning comprehension. There had been a part of her that believed Louis used his beauty as a weapon, as a tool to undermine her resolve and get his own way. Now she saw with sudden clarity that it was no such thing. It was a shield, a protective layer that guarded his heart, because he did not believe anyone could want him for any other reason. Even she, whom he knew to be his friend, who had loved him as her dearest friend and confidante for years before she ever thought of him as anything more... he did not trust her to love who he really was underneath the beautiful façade. That made her want to weep for him.

Suddenly her father's warnings, her need to make a clearheaded decision about her future, all of it went out of the window, her resolve dissipating like so much smoke. She loved Louis—all of him, including the faults and flaws—the entire man who had done things she did not want to face, but she would face them, because he needed her to. He was a tangled mess of imperfections, and her life would never be the safe, comfortable existence she had once thought she wanted, but she loved him, and that single fact trumped every other consideration. She let out a sigh, all the anxiety she had held inside for the past days disappearing as her decision gave her a sense of peace. Though she still did not have the slightest idea what their lives would look like, she trusted her own judgement, and Louis needed her. He had tried to tell her as much. She realised that now. Louis had begun to explain what it was he wanted, but she had been so wrapped up in all the reasons he ought not want her she had not stopped to consider all the reasons he should. Even her father had told her the truth.

Believe me, I understand all too well why he is drawn to you, too. Your sweetness and innocence fascinates him. When one has led a life in the darkness, one does long for the light, and that is you, love.

Tears pricked at her eyes, and she swallowed hard, wishing he had not run out on her, but that was Louis all over. He did not know how to ask for what it was he wanted and, if he could not beguile her into a good mood, could not use his charm and his obvious attractions to make her want him to stay, he would leave before she had the chance to tell him to go.

"Oh, Louis," she said, wiping her eyes as tears rolled down her face.

Well, no more. She would make him understand the truth, now that she finally understood it herself. As soon as he returned, she would tell him yes. Yes, she would marry him. Then she would make him tell her everything: all of it, every sordid detail. Perhaps, when he knew she would not leave him, when there were no more secrets to hide—when she knew the very worst there was to know and still wanted him with all her heart—perhaps then, he would learn to trust her as she was learning to trust him.

Finally at peace with her decision, Evie cast her damp clothes aside and stepped into the warm bath with a sigh of relief.

Chapter 10

Gabriel,

Why the hell did you not mention the fact Le Loup Noir was Wulfric De Vere? If you had mentioned his surname, I would have placed him at once. No wonder the association with Villen is such a concern. I'm certain we are of a like mind but, if he takes after his father, he is not to be trusted. Though, with a father like his, it is little wonder the man decided a life of crime was his best option.

—Excerpt of a letter from The Most Hon'ble Lucian Barrington, Marquess of Montagu, to Mr Gabriel Knight.

27th July 1824, rue François Miron, Paris, France.

Louis is twelve years old.

Louis stared out of the window of their father's empty rooms. The lack of furnishings revealed the true state of the building, from the damp patches to the peeling paint. Père had a new home now, opulent and beautifully furnished. He still grumbled that it was a modest sized property for the Comte de Villen, but Père had plans to transform the adjoining houses to make something the whole of Paris would speak of with awe. He had bought the entire row of houses and begun making his plans. Louis had plans too, though *he had learned to keep them close to his chest. Still, the knowledge that he played a deeper game than his father realised was comforting, a defence against the comte's constant machinations.*

Louis stifled a yawn. Fatigue clung to him, as thick and unpleasant as the scent of stale cigars and brandy that perfumed everything he wore, making him want to tear the fine clothes from his body and fling them away. Instead, he stood still, the picture of calm. Paris shimmered in the sun, the heat already climbing though it was barely past ten in the morning. He had a sudden longing to be somewhere green and peaceful, with someone who wanted nothing from him but his company. He wondered how André fared and if he was still selling his cakes and pastries. Would he have made enough to buy his shop yet? Louis doubted it and resolved to do something to help his old friend as soon as he was able to.

"That's the last of it," Nic said, handing a heavy crate into the arms of the removal men he'd hired.

He was unreasonably cheerful, given he'd been reduced to lugging their father's boxes of belongings about all morning alongside the labourers. Irritation seethed beneath Louis' skin at the way their father treated Nic. Of the two of them, Nic was the only one who held any regard for the comte, somehow still a little awed by the man's charm and power, despite the truth of what they knew. Louis knew Nic longed for their father's approval, though his brother would have fiercely denied it if he'd suggested as much.

Seeing the contempt with which the comte treated his illegitimate son made Louis want to murder him with his bare hands. To return after a night of gambling with their father to discover the man was using Nic as unpaid labour had made him wild with fury. Well, not for long. The comte might have plans for their future, but Louis had his own. Already, he had gained quite the reputation, with people flocking to the clubs and private parties he attended to try their hand against the comte's long-lost son.

His father had told some ridiculous story of their becoming separated when the king had banished him, speaking with a quavering voice about his years of searching for his beloved son, and his joy at finding Louis again. Society devoured the story. They saw no trace of the abandoned child, the boy who'd scrabbled in the dirt for survival. Louis had studied until he remembered how to speak with the accents of his class, had adopted his father's mannerisms and learned how to address a duke or a chevalier, and which cutlery to use at the endless lavish meals they attended. At his father's behest, he studied the subjects boys of his class would have learned over years at school, including how to speak English, though only on the condition that Nic learned too. Louis did everything that was asked of him but, though his father had demanded it, Louis did not do it for him. He did it for Nic, and because he knew this way lay a chance at power, at a life where no one could ever push him around and make him helpless again.

So, he swallowed his ire as his Père played the part of doting parent, charming everyone as usual, taking pride in Louis and giving him lavish compliments that turned his stomach. It was all Louis could do to keep his countenance, to hide the loathing in his eyes and not to give himself away by word or deed, but he had become adept at hiding himself beneath a façade. Why change now? Instead, he went along with the lies, fabricating many of his own, darkly amused when society ate them up with a spoon. But whenever he could he concentrated on the cards he'd become so skilled with. There was peace in following the numbers, calculating the odds, judging the skill of his opponent. These little outings into his father's world offered other opportunities, too, such as the knowledge that a certain man's wife had a king's ransom's worth of diamonds.

Louis' pickpocketing had not yielded quick enough results. For them to be free of the comte's influence, they needed their own money, and fast. The comte might think Louis had forgotten the lessons he'd taught him long ago, but that was not so. Louis remembered how to charm, how to beguile, and he had been careful to make friends who could be of use to him. Once Louis was established in society and had made friends with the right people, even his father could not shift him, and his power over them would wane. A shaft of longing struck him for the life he had begun at the circus. For the first time, he had felt a sense of belonging, of being home. Not that Nic's mother had been particularly warm towards him, but she had accepted him without complaint, at least.

Nic still performed most nights while Louis was out gambling but, at least once or twice a week, Louis dug his heels in and performed too. His father had raged and thundered with fury, but Louis refused to stop. The thrill of performing, the adulation of the crowd, was the greatest high. For those few moments, Louis felt loved and approved of in a way he had never known in his life before. He would not give that up. Not yet. So he painted his face and put on his costume so no one would recognise him as he performed for them, just like stepping into the clothes of the Vicomte Sainte-Apre, or a thief dressed all in black, keeping to the shadows. Now he lived a strange half-life, playing different parts until he was no longer certain which was real, or if there was anything of himself left at all.

If he must leave his life at the circus behind, then it would be on his own terms.

At a function his father had taken him to, Louis had been struck by a magnificent sapphire necklace around the elegant neck of some man's paramour. The men often brought courtesans or their mistresses to such games, parading them about dripping jewels like any other acquisition, as if they were racehorses or a new carriage.

The whores looked at him with curiosity, sometimes teasing him and enjoying his discomfort when they flirted with him, laughingly offering to make him a man. Their presence made him anxious, reminding him of the woman called Liane and the man *that had come for him. He had not forgotten the kiss forced upon him and had no wish to repeat it. The lady with the sapphires had watched him all night, and it had made him uncomfortable. Sometimes he feared Liane would be at one of these events, that she would call him out as an imposter. Because even though he was the comte's legitimate heir, he felt like a fraud.*

It had not been difficult to locate the address of the lady with the sapphires and break in one night after she had gone out, when he knew she would not return for hours. In fact, it had been child's play. It had been sheer chance she had not worn the sapphires that night, but for once his luck had held. He had given the necklace to his father, who had received it with his usual mix of avaricious delight and disgust that his son was a common thief. What he did not know was that Louis had kept the bracelet and earrings for himself. There had been other jewels that night too, but Louis had felt bad stealing from a woman forced to work for her place in the world. The man she was bedding was fat and old, and Louis thought she must earn every gewgaw he had given her ten times over. He had decided then that he would only steal from those who could well afford to lose it, and there were plenty of those among the company his father had thrust him into.

After that he had noted conversations, introductions to ladies who wore lavish diamonds and precious stones, and he and Nic had cut a swath through the jewellery collections of society who were beside themselves as news of the daring robberies circulated. Many people could not fathom how the thieves had got into their homes unseen and got away again, never realising that skills such as Nic and Louis possessed were ideal for the dangerous work.

Nic was uncomfortable with their crimes, but went along to keep Louis safe. He had restricted their list of victims further, insisting they only steal from people who were known to be corrupt, or were cruel to those beneath them. Louis had laughed and agreed at once, for it had made little difference to the list he had already compiled.

"We have a job tonight," he said as Nic came to stand beside him, his voice echoing in the now empty rooms. Louis could feel Nic frown, even though he did not turn and look at him.

"Is that necessary? The comte is rich again. He's got his fine home and is living in the style he's used to. You still win plenty at cards. Your progress has pleased him, and he told us to stop thieving now. Everyone is talking about the rash of jewellery thefts. It's going to get harder, Louis. We'll get caught. Perhaps you should stick to gambling and—"

"Non," Louis said, shaking his head. Their father knew how much he made at cards and could control what happened to his winnings. He turned to his brother, excited by the idea that had been forming over the past days. "It's not enough. Tonight, we work for ourselves. Père is to know nothing about it. As far as he's concerned, someone else is copying our crimes and we are innocent. We need our own funds, Nic. We're going to open our own gambling establishment. It will be yours and mine. You will run it and I will make all the fashionable people come to us. They will come to play me, and we will make it the most exclusive place in all of Paris."

Nic's eyes grew wide. "But… But that's impossible. I work in the circus, Louis, I can't—"

"You can! You can do anything you like. Look, if you want to keep on at the circus, that's fine by me. We'll tell the comte to go to hell and go back to how things were."

"Non!" Nic objected at once. "Not after how far you've come. You need to get out of that life before someone recognises you. Besides, it's dangerous. You take far too many chances, and you were born for better things."

Louis snorted. "Then the same applies to you. We're brothers. Whatever we do, we do together. You want me to return to society, to live up to my title? Well, so be it, but I do it on my terms, and I'll only do it if you come too. If you don't want to, I'm happy to give this up. Just say the word and I'll take off these fine clothes and concentrate on performing. I'd be delighted to tell the old bastard to go to the devil."

"I don't belong in that world," Nic objected at once, shaking his head.

"Non, you don't," Louis agreed, his voice hard and cold. There was a flash of hurt in Nic's eyes, he hid it quickly though and nodded his agreement, but Louis carried on. "You're good and honourable and kind, Nic, that's why you don't belong with those people, but you want me to live in that world alongside them. Very well. I'll do it, but not without you. We go together, we succeed together, or not at all."

Nic stared at him but knew by now he would not move Louis once he'd made up his mind. He sighed. "Fine. What's the job?"

Louis grinned. "Diamonds."

20th July 1842, Rue de la Bièvre, 13th Arrondissement, Paris, France.

Evie took her bath and ate the supper that was sent up for her but still there was no sign of Louis. He had been gone for hours and it was getting late. She badly wanted to speak to him, to reassure him and tell him she would marry him, and sitting here twiddling her thumbs was making her increasingly anxious. Yet, the idea of setting foot outside of these rooms and trying to find him—especially if it meant facing Wolf—was an uncomfortable thought.

Another hour passed with no sign of him, and she could stand it no longer. If he meant to stay out all night gambling again, she was going to have something to say about it. Determined, she found the clothes a narrow-eyed Irène had brought her earlier. That Irène begrudged Evie's presence was obvious; Louis might have no intention of ever touching the girl, but it was clear *she* did not believe that. It was with some frustration that Evie was forced to ring for her to help her dress. She must engage her own lady's maid as quickly as possible, for she did not put it past Irène to singe her hair with the tongs or send her out looking a fright. For now, Evie was too anxious about Louis to give a damn about the girl's resentful gaze or pouting and, as soon as she was dressed, she asked her where she might find the man they called Wolf.

"Dans son bureau," she said sullenly, before stalking off.

Evie ignored her rudeness, deciding she could locate Wolf's office herself if she put her mind to it, and left the safety of Louis' rooms.

It was easier to find Wolf than she had expected, for the first servant who saw her was an older lady, perhaps a housekeeper, who gasped and curtsied with great formality. She greeted Evie with deference, addressing her as Madame la Comtesse, a title which startled her rather as she realised it would belong to her once they were married. The lady introduced herself as Madame Moulin and seemed eager to please her.

"Où est mon mari?" Evie queried nervously, deciding to ask where Louis was first, as the lady seemed far friendlier than Irène. She was anxious about speaking French, having only done so with Louis, but Madame Moulin beamed at her and seemed happy at the effort. Sadly, she did not know where Monsieur le Comte was. She readily agreed to take Evie to Wolf, however, addressing him as Monsieur De Vere.

Madame Moulin led her to a thick oak door, flanked on each side by a guard. Evie thanked her, nodded, and steeled her nerves before giving a sharp rap on the wood. An impatient reply from inside bade her come in, and so she did, her heart beating too hard as she came face to face with the man named Wolf.

She had not really looked at him before, too overwhelmed by her row with Louis, by the storm, and by finding herself in this strange and rather terrifying place. She had only gained an impression of a large and frightening man and nothing in his expression now changed that opinion. That he did not like her was obvious, though she could not fathom why. Evie regarded him as he studied her. His features were uncompromising, though not coarse: thick dark brows, a forceful nose that had been broken more than once were she to guess, and a firm, stubborn jaw. His eyes were dark and watchful, mistrustful, and gleaming with intelligence.

"What can I do for you, *comtesse?*" he asked, not bothering to hide his mocking tone at the title, which was not yet hers to command.

Evie ignored him, reminding herself severely she was granddaughter to a duke and her mother would be furious with her if she let a man like this know he'd rattled her. "Where is Monsieur le Comte?" she asked, her tone cool. "I wish to speak with him."

He snorted and set down the pen he'd been holding, sitting back in his chair. "Oh, you do, do you? Well, why don't you snap your fingers, perhaps he'll come running? That's what you have him doing, isn't it, running after you? Though God knows, I can't figure out why you've got the poor bastard tied up in such knots. You must be a wildcat in bed, is all I can think." He gave her a scrolling look which was at once dismissive and lewd, and Evie fought not to blush.

She put her chin up, refusing to let him see her embarrassment, but his eyes grew wide and somehow she must have given herself away.

"*Putain,*" he said on a breath of shock. "It's not possible he hasn't…? What the bloody hell have you done to him? Are you a witch?" he demanded, so obviously outraged by the idea she was still a virgin, she almost laughed.

"Oh, don't be tedious," she snapped. "You don't like me, I know. I'm not nearly beautiful enough and besotted enough to be Louis' wife. Yes, yes, I quite understand that I do not live up to your high expectations. Believe me, I am quite aware of my shortcomings, but I am Louis' choice, not yours. If it helps, I will tell you now that I dislike you too, but I really don't care about your feelings one way or another. I must speak to Louis at once. It's… It's very important to both of us."

Wolf stared at her, and she had the satisfaction of knowing she had surprised him. He studied her for a long moment before he spoke again.

"He didn't say where he was going, but I can take a guess."

Evie smothered her impatience, trying her hardest to modify her tone. "Then would you mind doing so, please?"

"I'll do one better," he said, getting to his feet.

Evie took an instinctive step back, although the desk was between them. "Oh?"

His eyes flashed with amusement as he walked towards her. "I'll take you to him."

"Thank you," she replied, before asking with some trepidation. "And where is it you think he might have gone?"

Wolf grinned, which was the most unnerving thing he had done since she'd entered the room. He opened the door for her, gesturing for her to precede him, and somehow managed to make the gentlemanly gesture mocking.

"Home," he said, chuckling darkly and following her out.

Chapter 11

Well, Fred, I don't care what you think! The Comte de Villen is very dashing, and I think it's romantic. So there.

—Excerpt of a letter from Lady Catherine 'Cat' Barrington (daughter of the Most Hon'ble Lucian and Matilda Barrington, Marquess and Marchioness of Montagu) to Lord Frederick Adolphus (son of Their Graces, Robert and Prudence Adolphus, Duke and Duchess of Bedwin)

20ᵗʰ July 1842, Avenue des Champs-Élysées, 8ᵗʰ Arrondissement, Paris, France.

Evie endured the stony silence in the carriage for as long as she could before demanding. "Where does Louis consider home?"

Wolf's sloe-dark eyes slid to hers. "I'm not sure there is anywhere he really considers home, but this place is the closest thing he had to it when he was a boy."

"Was this before or after he was left in the hands of Monsieur Boucher?" she asked, remembering the story Louis had told her with a stab of pain for all he'd suffered.

Wolf's eyes widened, and he sat up in the carriage, staring at her. "He told you about that?"

Evie nodded. "Yes, some of it. Not everything by any means, but—"

"You're lying. He never speaks about that time to anyone but me and his brother," Wolf said furiously. "What exactly did he tell you?"

Stiffening with annoyance at the way he spoke to her, Evie's reply was cool. "They dressed him in rags and forced him to eat leftovers tossed to the floor. He slept on the floor of the kitchen and was abused horribly. Is that what you want to hear? For I tell you now, if I ever set eyes on the man who did that to him, I'll kill him myself!"

Wolf looked at her with blank astonishment. That her words had shocked him was undeniable, and Evie realised how much trust Louis had put in her to share that much of his past. Gradually, he relaxed back into his seat, his gaze less hostile but more curious than ever. When he spoke again, there was challenge in his expression. "There's no need to do murder, comtesse. Louis did that some years ago."

He meant to shock her, she knew, but she had known Louis had killed and was unsurprised to hear he had taken his revenge.

"Good," she said, folding her arms and turning to look out of the window.

Wolf laughed and it was a dark sound but strangely put her more at ease.

When the carriage halted, the first thing that struck Evie was the noise.

"What is this place?" she asked, stepping out and regarding the huge circular building. It was rather grand, with great marble pillars flanking the entrance.

"*Le cirque d'été*," Wolf replied, gesturing for her to proceed to the building.

"Louis is here?" she asked in confusion. "Why should he consider this place home?"

"He never told you about the circus, then?" Wolf asked with obvious satisfaction.

Too curious to pretend an understanding she lacked, Evie shook her head.

"Of course, this wasn't where they began. This building is recent and far grander than the tent that housed the circus before, but Louis knows a lot of the people here. I expect he came back to catch up with old friends."

"Where who began?" Evie demanded, hurrying to keep up with Wolf, who was striding inside.

Even if Wolf had deigned to answer, Evie doubted she would have heard him as the crowd were chanting, such a din she could barely hear herself think. They passed the ticket desk, the fellow taking one look at Wolf and waving him through without a word of protest.

"What are they shouting?" Evie said, raising her voice to make herself heard.

Before her eyes, she saw all the colour leave Wolf's face as he stilled, listening.

"Putain," he murmured. "Oh, no."

Before Evie could say another word, he grabbed hold of her arm, almost yanking it from its socket as he towed her behind him and into a vast arena.

Evie blinked as her eyes became accustomed to the light from the dozens of enormous chandeliers hanging from the impossibly high roof. Gradually the sound of the crowd's chanting permeated her brain until she understood they were saying the same word, over and over: *l'aigle, l'aigle!*

"What's the eagle?" she demanded, grasping Wolf's arm to get his attention, but he was staring up at the ceiling and ignoring her. "What does it mean?" she asked again, frustrated as a strange, anxious sensation uncoiled in her belly.

Though she did not know why, all the fine hairs on the back of her neck stood on end and her heart thudded. Slowly, as if in a dream, she followed Wolf's gaze to where a thin, taut wire spanned the width of the tent. Impossibly, there was a man balanced on the wire, and the sight of him so far above the crowd, with only the unforgiving ground beneath him, made her stomach pitch. Resolutely, she turned her attention back to Wolf.

"Where is Louis?" she demanded, cross now that the circus performance should distract the man so thoroughly, no matter how daring it was.

Slowly, Wolf raised his hand and pointed to the man on the wire, and she was so frustrated she was tempted to hit him, but then she saw the terror in his eyes. No. Oh, no… It couldn't possibly….

But she remembered how easily Louis had scaled the walls to her bedroom, remembered the sight of him climbing and jumping to catch the monkey at the fancy fair. Her stomach plummeted, and she spun around. A terrified sound escaped her, and she clapped a hand to her mouth.

The man on the wire was wearing tightly fitted black trousers, the waistband glittering with brilliants that caught the light as he moved. His chest was bare, but his skin gleamed gold, as though it had been painted. A black mask hid his eyes, but his hair was dark, his shoulders broad and powerful, the muscles in his arms and across his abdomen flexing as he moved. It was Louis. Even from this distance, even painted and masked, there was no doubt in her mind.

"Stop him!" she cried, taking Wolf's arm and tugging at him for all the good it did her.

155

Wolf shook his head, though he looked as stricken as Evie felt.

"I can't," he said, his voice hoarse. "Not now."

Evie had seen a highwire act only once and had been overwhelmed by the skill and fearlessness of the artist, but that man had walked slowly, holding a long pole to help keep him stable. Louis was at least forty feet up in the air and used only his arms to stabilize. He moved with reckless speed, almost running along the rope. As she turned back to watch, though she could hardly bear to look, Louis dropped. Evie screamed, but Louis only sat on the wire, using the spring to bounce up again and balance once more. Too terrified to turn her gaze away, she watched as Louis danced on the wire, at one point running backwards before returning to the centre of the wire and growing still. He stood, finding his equilibrium. The audience held their collective breath, Evie's heart pounded in her ears as Louis flipped backwards. He landed on his feet, but swayed violently, taking a moment to regain his steadiness as the crowd screamed and cheered.

"Sainte Mère de Dieu!"

The familiar voice, laced with shock, was the only thing that could have torn Evie's gaze from Louis as she turned to see his brother, Nic.

"Nic!" she shrieked, running to him. "Oh, please, please, stop him!"

"Wolf, if you've played a hand in this…" Nic raged, apparently too overcome to pay Evie much mind.

Wolf held up his hands. "I swear to God I had no part in this. You think I would have let him had I known? I had no idea he was contemplating this madness."

Nic's hands sank into his hair as though he would tear it out as he watched his brother perform.

"Tell me he's been practising in England," Wolf said, his voice laced with anxiety.

Nic shot him a look that might have shrivelled a lesser man.

Wolf groaned. "I'm going to kill him."

"I pray you get the chance," Nic replied darkly, "but I'm first."

Evie turned back to where Louis was performing, to the delight of the crowd. He ran across the wire, pretended to fall, and caught the wire in both hands on his way down. Evie screamed as he fell, relief coursing through her as he held the wire tight. She felt dizzy with terror, her heart beating out of control as every muscle in her body turned to stone. Sweat trickled down her back, but she barely noticed, entirely focused on the man she loved and the death-defying performance he was giving. Still hanging from the wire, Louis swung back and forth, levering his feet back to the wire and standing once more. He paused, steadying himself, his concentration absolute as the crowd grew quiet, and Evie knew this would be another trick.

Please don't let him fall. Please don't let him fall. Please don't let him fall.

She repeated the words in her head over and over, too frantic not to watch. Louis threw himself forward into a somersault, spinning in mid-air and landing back on the wire as it swayed back and forth. The crowd cheered as he righted himself, finding his balance again as Evie swallowed down the urge to be sick.

"And now," the voice of the ring master echoed out over the crowd as everyone grew silent once more, "for one night only...."

"Non!" Wolf said, shaking his head. *"Merde, non!* Louis!" He shouted this last, moving as though he would run into the ring and bring Louis down himself, but Nic grabbed hold of him.

"Tenez votre langue!" he exclaimed, though he was chalk white, his eyes fixed on his brother. "He won't stop now, but you distract him and he's a dead man."

As one, the crowd surged to their feet and Evie moved until she could see Louis again. He was standing on the highwire but looking off to one side. Now she saw the trapeze swing back and forth on his left side, what seemed to be miles below the highwire.

"What…?" she began, hardly able to force the words out. "What is he going to do?"

"This is why they call him the eagle," Nic said, no inflection in his voice as he stared at his brother, as if he could keep him safe by sheer force of will.

"No," Evie said, shaking her head. *"No!"*

But Louis turned to face the trapeze, staring at it as it swung back and forth below him.

He leapt.

All Evie saw was Louis falling through the air, and then everything went black.

Nic was only vaguely aware of Evie crumpling to the floor between him and Wolf, unable to take his eyes from Louis as everything stopped and the world hung, suspended. His brother dropped, and his usual impeccable timing was a fraction of a second out. Not for nothing had they practised and practised until their muscles burned, but Louis hadn't performed in years. Nic's heart dropped to his guts as he saw the error. For the briefest moment, Louis' grip faltered on the bar of the trapeze, one hand fumbling until he grasped it, both hands tightening as he swung up to stand on the bar and made a theatrical bow.

The crowd went wild.

Nic exhaled.

"Fuck," Wolf said, rubbing a hand over his face. "I think I just lost ten years of my life."

"I am going to murder him with my bare hands," Nic replied savagely.

Wolf nodded, apparently in complete accord with this plan, but he shifted Nic's attention to the crumpled figure at their feet. "I'm in," he agreed cheerfully. "But what are we going to do about that?"

"Merde!" Nic exclaimed, immediately contrite that he'd left the poor young woman out cold. Stooping, he lifted her into his arms and carried her out. He was unsurprised to see several other females exiting the circus in a similar manner. Louis' performances had always been too much for some. For once, he completely sympathised. He felt giddy with relief and in need of a strong drink to settle his nerves.

Wolf followed behind as Nic made his way backstage to where the performers congregated. He could already hear the whoops and cheers of congratulation as Louis returned to them, through the crowd made up of the other entertainers. Nic studied his brother, wondering why he did not look elated, as he usually did when he'd delivered such a successful show. Instead, Louis only looked weary and rather lost, his smiles as much a part of his performance as everything else he'd done this night.

Wolf forced his way past Nic and on through the crowd to Louis and shoved him hard.

"You son of a bitch!" he roared as Louis staggered backwards. "What the bloody hell were you thinking? Were you hoping to kill yourself?"

Louis righted himself before he hit the floor and glared at the furious man standing over him. "Wolf, I assure you, I am not in the mood for your histrionics."

"Oh, is that right? Well, I wasn't in the mood for watching my best friend plummet to his death, but it seems like we're none of us happy tonight."

"Well, unless it disappointed you because I did not plummet, I do not see what your problem is," Louis snapped.

"You don't see…?" Wolf began in disbelief before throwing his arms up in the air. He turned back to Nic with an expression of outrage. "He doesn't see what the problem is!"

Louis' attention shot to Nic, his eyes widening, and then to the woman he held in his arms. Before Nic could speak, Louis was moving, shoving people out of the way.

"Evie!" he exclaimed, his blue eyes settling on his brother with fury. "What did you do to her?"

"What did *I* do?" Nic said, every bit as outraged as Wolf. "Well, seeing the man she loves performing forty feet up in the air seems to have come as a bit of a shock to her. I can't think why, because it's not like you to keep secrets, now, is it?"

Louis blanched, his jaw tightening but he knew damn well he had nothing to say in his defence.

"Give her to me," he demanded instead.

"Why should I? You left her to come here and perform like a lunatic. Whatever possessed you? Did you even get any practice before you did such a thing?"

"Of course," Louis retorted.

Nic snorted, furious with his brother for his recklessness. "For how long?"

"A few hours," Louis admitted gruffly.

Nic uttered a curse.

"Nic, please… let me take her," Louis begged.

Nic relented, seeing the anguish in his brother's eyes and not wanting to make matters worse. Louis only acted rashly when he felt backed into a corner. Whatever had driven his brother to act as he had tonight, it was nothing good, and he wasn't about to make matters worse for him, although he so richly deserved to be raked over the coals. Nic only hoped Evie would do that well enough for them both once she came around.

Louis took Evie into his arms and carried her through to his dressing room. Nic followed, darkly amused to discover they had given his brother top billing for the night and there was a star on the door. Unsurprising. *The Eagle* had filled the circus every night he had ever performed from the time he'd taken the name as his own. Because he had to hide his identity and did not perform regularly like most others in the circus, his mystique had grown to epic proportions, until the adulation had become intrusive and Nic had finally persuaded Louis to stop before he was discovered and ruined everything. He had not wanted to, though.

Nic lingered in the doorway as Louis lay Evie down on a chaise. She came to with a soft moan, obviously disorientated. Louis rubbed her hands, his gaze on her full of anxiety.

"Evie, *mon amour,* are you well?" Louis said, the concern in his voice quite audible. "Is there anything I can get you?"

Nic turned to see Wolf watching with bemusement, startled to see how obviously besotted Louis really was.

Evie stiffened in shock as she came properly awake and focused on Louis.

She stared at him for a long moment and then threw herself forward, wrapping her arms about his neck and holding on tight. "Louis!"

Deciding this was their cue to leave, Nic guided Wolf out of the dressing room and closed the door.

Louis let out a breath of relief as Evie's arms went around him. She held on so tight she was in danger of choking him, not that he cared. He was sweaty, the gold paint on his body smearing over a gown which had cost him a small fortune, but if she did not care about that, neither did he.

Evie burst into tears, clinging to him and sobbing incoherently.

"Non, non, don't cry, Evie," he pleaded, feeling wretched for having frightened her so badly.

She sat back, running her hands down his arms, up his neck, her touch frantic as she searched him for injuries. "You're not hurt? You didn't fall?"

"Non, not in the least. I'm sorry. I'm sorry I scared you."

She grew still, her tears stopping abruptly. "Scared me," she repeated slowly. *"Scared* me?"

Louis tensed as he recognised the glint in her eyes as something dangerous.

"You bastard!" she shouted, shoving him so hard he fell back in surprise, sprawled on the floor. Evie followed him down, pounding at his chest with her fists until he caught hold of them, keeping her still as she struggled with fury. "You selfish, pigheaded, stubborn, inconsiderate *bastard!* How dare you! How dare you run out on me and... and do *that!"*

"I'm sorry...." he tried again, startled by the force of her anger. Though he had seen Evie angry before, this was a new and rather impressive experience. She did not let him speak.

"You're sorry? Oh, well, that's all right, then. Never mind that you left me alone in the middle of an argument. I wanted to talk to you, Louis. I wanted to tell you something important and you ran out on me. Is this the way it's going to be when we're married? Whenever I'm the least bit cross with you, are you going to go out and do something ridiculous instead of discussing it with me like a rational person? Because I tell you now, I shan't stand for it!"

Though she was clearly irate, and with good reason, Louis picked out a few words from her furious tirade that made his heart skip.

"When we're married?" he repeated, unable to keep the hope from his voice.

"Of course, when we're married," she snapped. "That's what I wanted to tell you, and if you'd have come back, you would have heard me say so. Instead, we have theatrics and drama and—"

He kissed her, too relieved to do anything else. For a moment, she remained rigid in his embrace, but then the anger left her as quickly as it had arrived and she kissed him back, hard and with all the passion he knew she possessed. Euphoria flooded his system, a buoyant sensation he had only ever found after performing for a crowd, until now. Suddenly, she broke the kiss and sat up, regarding him with an expression he did not know how to read. Exasperation was there, certainly, and a lingering sense of anger, but also such warmth and affection that an odd sensation filled his chest, almost like pain.

"You never told me about this, Louis. How could you keep something that was so important to you from me?"

Louis drew in a breath, but she knew now anyway, so.... "I thought you might look at me differently. You fell in love with the Comte de Villen, not... not whoever this person is."

He made a sweeping gesture to encompass the paint and the mask and the circus they were in, wracked with uncertainty even though her expression had softened.

"Oh, Louis," she said, her voice aching with sadness. "That's simply not true. I fell in love with the man who kept me company at balls and shared my dinner with me without ever making me feel bad for liking cakes and sweet things, the man who made me laugh and made me feel good about myself, the man who designed a dress for me so I would not feel anything less than beautiful."

"Because you *are* beautiful," he said, his voice unsteady.

Evie gave a choked laugh and nodded. "I believe you. I do."

"But... do you forgive me?" he asked cautiously.

She let out a breath of frustration, and he waited.

163

"Of course I forgive you, though I don't know what on earth I am supposed to do with you," she said, shaking her head.

"Love me?" he suggested.

She laughed again, an incredulous sound this time. "As if I could stop now, you impossible creature!"

Louis tugged her down, so she sprawled over his chest. She sighed and brushed her mouth against his. A desperate sound escaped him, and he tried to deepen the kiss, needing more, but she pulled back, her expression fierce.

"If you think I'm going to let you make love to me on the dressing room floor of a circus, you've another think coming, I assure you."

Louis felt his lips quirk into a smile. "I would not dream of doing such an appalling thing, though I admit it's tempting."

He rolled his hips, and she gasped as his arousal became obvious to her. He saw her eyes darken, and his breath caught as she trailed her hand over his bare chest, her fingers coming away sparkling with gold paint.

"Take off the mask, Louis," she breathed.

Louis hesitated, wondering what she saw. She did not seem horrified that this had been a part of his life, but then she was clearly still in shock. He reached up and tugged at the ribbon that held the narrow mask in place, putting it aside. She stared at him, and Louis stared back, knowing she was seeing his eyes lined in black kohl, knowing she was seeing him. He felt raw, stripped bare, and vulnerable.

Evie traced a finger around the curve of his lower lip, never taking her eyes from his. "And what about the other masks, Louis? Are you going to take them all off for me?"

He let out an uneven breath, shocked that she had seen that much of him, that she had understood. But then, Evie had always seen past the façade. He should have remembered that. Even so, the idea of giving himself up entirely was still daunting, and yet she was smiling at him now, her expression encouraging.

He nodded, determined to be whatever she needed, even if he must remake himself all over again. *"Oui, mon amour,* or at least, I will try my best. The truth is, I don't know any longer what is a mask, and what is really me."

"But I do," she replied, leaning down and kissing him again. "I know you, Louis, and I love you, all of you, the good and the bad, the kind and the wicked. You belong to me now, and I will not let you go."

"Swear it," he demanded, hardly able to believe her words.

She laughed then, stroking his cheek. "I will, before God, when I make my vows. As soon as you can arrange it. For now, I shall only tell you, *yes*, Louis. Yes, I will marry you."

Louis pulled her down into his arms and kissed her again, his hands skimming down her sides to her hips. He wanted to lift her skirts and find his place inside her, to lose himself in her lush heat. He wanted so many things his skin felt too tight, unable to contain everything he needed from her. Want and desire burned beneath his skin, a delicious torment, but she was right, she deserved so much more than a quick tumble on the dressing room floor. Especially after everything he'd put her through tonight.

"Promise me something, Louis."

"Anything," he said, too unguarded and happy to not to agree to anything she wanted.

"Never walk out on me and disappear like that again."

He stared up at her and nodded. *"Je promets."*

"You were magnificent," she said quietly, tracing a finger around his nipple, teasing him, the look in her eyes making it clear she knew damn well what she was doing to him. He shivered, delighted by her boldness. "I was quite terrified, but… my word,

Louis, however did you learn do such a thing? I died a hundred times watching you."

"Nic taught me."

She shook her head, staring at him in wonder. "What an extraordinary man you are."

Louis frowned, not wanting her to believe such nonsense, to make him out to be anything more than a performer, for that was at the heart of everything he did. *"Non.* Do not go believing that, *mon Evie.* I shall disappoint you."

"You never could. When the gold paint washes off, when you get old and grey, even if something spoiled your beautiful face and you were no longer handsome, I will love you, Louis. Always."

Louis' breath caught, and he stared at her, for the first time in his life believing what he heard when a woman professed to love him. His Evie loved him, and she always would.

"I cannot promise I shall never make you angry again, *mon amour,* but I swear upon my life I will always be true to you. I shall never betray you, not by word or deed. I will do my best to be a good husband, to make you happy. I swear I shall," he said, needing her to believe this much of him.

Evie nodded, reaching down to caress his cheek, and smiled. "I know."

Chapter 12

Dear Aunt Hester,

Thought I had best drop you a note to stop you fretting unduly. Sorry I left without a word. I've gone after Louis. You probably guessed that. Never slow on the uptake, are you?

Please don't believe all the dreadful things they're saying about him. I don't know exactly what happened, but I know Louis loves Miss Knight and wishes to marry her. He would never do her any harm, and if he took her away, I feel certain it was with the best of intentions. He's a jolly decent fellow. A good friend.

In all honesty, I don't know what the devil I'm doing (no surprise there, I hear you say) and I doubt Louis needs any help from me, but, well, I'm here. Oh, here is in France. Forgot to mention. Anyway, doing my best to track him down. Not sure what I'll do when I find him. Thought you ought to know.

Yr obt svt,

B Godwin.

—Excerpt of a letter from Mr Barnaby Godwin to his Aunt Hester Henley, Lady Balderston.

20ᵗʰ August 1825, Rue de la Bièvre, 13ᵗʰ Arrondissement, Paris, France.

Louis is thirteen years old.

"Don't you dare walk away from me! You owe me everything, you conniving little shit!"

Louis did not bother to respond to his father as he prepared to leave for the evening. He did not know how his father had discovered he – or rather Nic, on his behalf - had bought the decrepit old chateau that had once been a fortress, but the comte had appeared on the doorstep half an hour earlier, ranting and bellowing about deceit and treachery. The idea had entertained Louis deeply, and he was too inured to his father's insults and vile temper to pay it much mind. This place was his, a place no one could touch him, a place that belonged to him, and he'd let no one take it from him. The walls were thick, strong enough to keep out an army, or anyone else Louis did not wish to see.

He had been tempted to leave his father ranting on the doorstep and leave by one of the many hidden exits, but he was not afraid of the comte and cared little enough what he thought about anything. The man held no power over Louis any longer. He had his own friends, had made his place in society, had stolen enough to make him richer than he could have believed possible a few short years ago.

"If you perform in that crass circus tonight, I'll disown you. I'll let everyone know who you really are. You'll be ruined, a laughingstock!" his father bellowed.

Louis glanced at him with undisguised amusement before turning back to the mirror and adjusting the scarf he'd tied about his neck. He scowled as he regarded the shabby clothes he wore to go to and from the circus unnoticed. It was ridiculous, but he had become used to the finery his father insisted he wore and, though he would have died before admitting it, he rather enjoyed dressing well.

"Really, Père, you ought not to get so irate. Look at you, all purple in the face. Your poor heart won't stand it. You know what the doctor told you, and I shall be displeased if I am late for my performance because I must dispose of your wretched carcass when you expire at my feet."

"Did you hear what I said?" the comte raged, his eyes flashing with rage, his fists clenched.

Louis paused, looking down his nose at his father with a supercilious expression he had copied directly from his sire. It was nicely calculated to make the man wilder than ever. "Oui, monsieur, my hearing is excellent, I assure you. The trouble is, I know you're lying. You will never betray my identity, for I am your last hope for the survival of our noble bloodline. The next Comte de Villen. How the knowledge must vex you. A pity Nic wasn't the legitimate heir. He's so much easier to deal with, whereas I...."

He shrugged as his father glowered at him with loathing in his eyes, before swinging a fist at Louis' head.

Louis stepped back, avoiding the blow with ease. He smirked with defiance. It had been some months since the man had succeeded in hitting him. His heart troubles were making him old and slow, and he was no longer a match for Louis' youth and vigour.

"You'll fall and break your neck!" the comte spat after him.

Louis only laughed as he headed for the door. "Oh, mais, non," he said, shaking his head. "You know as well as I, the devil looks after his own."

169

"You're a madman!" Nic exclaimed, eyeing Louis with a mixture of awe and frustration as he returned backstage. The crowd were still screaming for him, and the sound of their approval fizzed in his blood, ringing in his ears. "I swear you get more reckless with every performance."

For the first time, Louis had performed the trick he had been practising for months, and the crowd had gone wild. Several people had fainted, believing he would plummet to the floor, but the eagle had been a terrific success and Louis was elated.

He grinned at his brother and embraced him, kissing his cheek. "I am marvellous!" he retorted, flinging his arms wide, still buzzing with the adulation of the crowd. "Everybody says so, therefore it must be true." He winked at Nic and laughed, about to hurry back to change out of his costume, when a soft hand caught his wrist.

"Bonsoir."

Louis turned, frowning at the girl who had waylaid him. She was pretty, with a sweet smile and a knowing look in her eyes. Perhaps a year older than Louis, her parents owned one of the food stalls that lined the street leading to the circus. She came to every performance and, as she was friends with many of the staff, she often came backstage to follow him about, batting her eyelashes at him. Much to Louis' consternation, she was not the only one. Nic had insisted they pay for guards to stop people slipping backstage to bother him, aware Louis needed to keep his identity secret, but Delphine knew the performers and must have bribed someone to let her in.

Louis nodded to the girl. "Bonsoir, Delphine. Excuse me, but I need to change." He tugged his hand free and carried on his way. "What?" he demanded, aware Nic was watching him with amusement.

"Rien!" Nic said, holding up his hands, though he was smirking.

"Oh, spit it out," Louis retorted as Nic followed him into the curtained off area that served as his dressing room. His brother plonked himself down, straddling the single chair, leaning his arms on the back. Louis tried not to fidget under his gaze, aware Nic was studying him.

"I just don't understand why you run away from the girls that chase you?"

Louis blushed, and then scowled, furious that his brother had gained such a reaction. "I do not run away!"

"You do, though, and Delphine likes you. She likes you a lot," Nic said with emphasis, failing to hide his smile. "Rumour is she's, er... free with her favours, too."

"Good for her." Louis set his mask aside and began wiping the paint from his face.

Nic was quiet until Louis had cleaned his face and began peeling off his costume. He was working on something else for his next performance, something far more dramatic, and was careful to stand facing his brother so he could not see the half-finished tattoo on his back. Nic was going to kill him when he saw it. For now, he wore a loose-fitting black shirt and pair of black trousers with soft leather shoes, the only colour a red silk sash tied about his waist.

Nic cleared his throat, looking strangely awkward. "Louis, do you...er... do you like girls?"

Louis paused with his shirt half on, half off. "What do you mean?"

A look of mortified impatience chased across his brother's face. "I think you know very well know what I mean, and to be clear, it wouldn't matter to me either way, but... I was just wondering."

"Wondering what?"

"About whether you liked girls or... er... boys."

Louis frowned, staring at his brother with dawning understanding. He bit back his amusement, deciding the sight of Nic in a sweat of embarrassment was too entertaining to miss. "I don't understand what you mean," he said, feigning innocence.

Nic shifted uncomfortably and cleared his throat again, speaking in a rush. "Well, only that if you don't want to spend time with Delphine because you'd rather be with... say, David, I, I just wanted you to know that's all right with me."

Louis flung his shirt down and stared at his brother, who was now the only one of them blushing. Taking pity on the poor devil, Louis' lips quirked in a smile.

"Non," he said, remembering the kiss André had given him. It had been vastly preferable to the one that had preceded it, but it had not made him feel anything. At least nothing but affection for his friend and regret that André was doomed to disappointment. "Non, I do not prefer David over Delphine."

Nic nodded, letting out a breath. "Fair enough. Why don't you follow up on those dazzling smiles Delphine gives you, then? Are you shy? You know, if you want any advice, or... have any questions. I'm happy to help."

Louis hesitated, uncertain of what to say, uncertain himself of what held him back. He did like girls, could not help but notice the female circus performers in their outrageous sparkling costumes, noticed too the way some of them looked at him in return. He could not pretend he wasn't tempted, wasn't curious.

"Ah," Nic said, getting to his feet and walking over to lay a hand on Louis' shoulder, his expression sympathetic and so full of understanding Louis felt like a prize twit. "It wouldn't be like that. It wouldn't be anything like that, Louis. Not with someone you liked."

Louis scowled and shrugged Nic's hand away. "I know that," he said irritably. "I'm not an idiot."

"Why, then?" Nic persisted.

Louis ignored him, dressing quickly.

"Louis?"

"I don't know!" he yelled in frustration before snatching up his things and stalking out.

Chapter 13

Dearest Mama,

I don't expect Papa is with you, so I address this to you alone. There is little doubt he is tearing France apart with his bare hands, looking for me. I am sorry for it, for making you both worry for me, though I think perhaps you are not so worried as he has been.

Tomorrow morning I will marry Louis César. I love him, Mama, with all my heart. Papa was right. Louis is everything he warned me about, but he is so much more than that, too. If you knew what he has endured, what he lived through to become the man he is, you would understand better. I have only learned a fraction of his past, and I am in awe of all he has survived, all he has achieved. I hope when we return you will give him the chance to show you just how extraordinary he truly is.

You must have realised I did not go with him willingly, for I would never cause you such anguish on purpose. I do not wish to explain everything in a letter, but Louis had his reasons for what he did. He acted rashly, and you must believe me when I tell you I have not let him off easily for that.

Since we left, I have learned far more about him, and about myself. <u>I am your daughter, Mama</u>, far more than I ever realised. I am braver and more capable than I ever expected, and Louis knew that better than I did. He saw something in me I never knew was there, though you did.

Thank you, Mama, for always believing I was more than I realised myself, for pushing me to learn things I never thought I needed to know. You have always been bold and brave and everything I admire, but until now, I never thought I could be those things too, but I can – I am – with Louis.

—Excerpt of a letter from Miss Evie Knight to her mother, Lady Helena Knight.

20th July 1842, Rue de la Bièvre, 13th Arrondissement, Paris, France.

Evie was relieved when Madame Moulin came to help her get ready for bed. She was weary to her bones and in no humour to deal with Irène. Louis had obviously had someone rouse the poor woman from her own bed as her hair was plaited and she wore a thick robe over her night things. She was kind, though, and seemed pleased to help Evie, making no remarks about the streaks of gold paint on her new gown.

Once she was ready, Evie sat and wrote a letter to her mother, hoping it conveyed everything she needed to say. The rest would need to wait until they returned to England, but Evie was surprised to discover she was in no hurry to go back. Perhaps she would invite her family here instead, it might be easier for Louis to face them all here too. Evie wanted to experience Paris for herself, to see the place through Louis' eyes, to visit the decadent night club he had created with his brother. She wanted to learn everything there was to learn about the man to whom she was about to commit her life, and she felt instinctively the secrets would be easier to reveal here, where it had all happened. Besides, there was still the matter of the man who had threatened Evie, and what Louis meant to do about him. Evie did not like the idea of more blood on his hands, though she had to admit it was less from a moral perspective and more because she knew it would damage Louis further to take such action.

Evie sealed the letter and set it aside at a soft knock at the door, which opened as she turned towards it.

"I've just come to say good night," Louis said, smiling at her from the doorway. "Everything is ready for tomorrow. We'll be married before midday."

Evie smiled at him. "Good."

His brow furrowed, his expression one of regret. "I'm sorry, Evie, sorry that your family won't be there, that it won't be the kind of wedding you dreamed of."

Evie got to her feet and moved towards him. "I never actually dreamed of what my wedding would look like. I know girls are supposed to, the happiest day of your life and all that, but… I never did. I dreamed of you, though," she added.

It was the right thing to say and the smile he returned was a dangerous thing, making her remember this man could turn her heart inside out and upside down with very little effort, but now she trusted him not to abuse that fact.

"I'll make it up to you," he promised, and she heard the sincerity in his voice. "I don't know whether your family—your father—will ever forgive me, but I'll do everything I can. We'll hold a ball to celebrate when we return, and we'll invite everyone we like and no one we don't. It will be the most fabulous celebration London has ever seen; I promise you. Should you like that?" he asked her, his eyebrows tugging together as he judged her response.

Evie considered it. She must be infamous now, the scandal sheets full of how Louis had carried her off. Though the truth startled her, she discovered she didn't much care. In fact, if she were completely honest, she might rather like the idea of being the scandalous Comtesse de Villen, wife to the most beautiful man on three continents. She grinned.

"Yes," she said, giving him a decisive nod. "I should like that very much, but not yet. I don't want to go home yet."

"You don't?" he replied, obviously surprised.

"Before I've seen Rouge et Noir, and Paris, and all the places you've lived and performed, the things you've done? Certainly not! I want a tour of your life, Louis. I want to hear all of it, see it if I can, and I think perhaps you need to see it too, so you can appreciate how far you've come."

His expression darkened, and she thought perhaps he would refuse her, but he only let out a breath, eyeing her uncertainly. "This is what you want?"

Evie nodded.

His jaw tightened, and she knew he was deeply unhappy about the idea, but he nodded. *"D'accord."*

"Merci, mon beau."

Louis' lips quirked at hearing her address him with an endearment in French. "I like that. I like your accent."

"It's terrible," she laughed, shaking her head.

"Non, not terrible. It's charming," he corrected, taking her hand and lifting it to his lips.

He held her gaze as he brushed his mouth over her fingers, and Evie shivered with pleasure from even that brief contact. She was exhausted after the days of travel, the stress of all that had happened, the terror she had experienced this evening, but it all fell away under the weight of his gaze. His eyes were such an impossible shade of blue. Nothing in her life had ever matched that startling azure and she doubted it ever would.

"I hope our babies have eyes that colour," she said in a rush and then wished she'd not said anything. They'd never discussed babies, she had just assumed, but Louis had gone still.

"The thought of my child growing inside you," he said, his voice wistful as he placed a hand on her stomach, the heat of his touch and the reverence of his words creating an ache in her heart, the desire to give him what he wanted startling her with its force. Evie's breath caught. "But their eyes should be green like yours, like spring and new beginnings, though perhaps one or two could take after me," he added, watching her intently.

"One or two?" she queried. "How many do you hope for?"

"As many as you'll give me," he answered at once, and she realised in that moment that this was something he had thought about a great deal. "I'd have a dozen. More, if you like, but only… only if you are well, Evie, and only if it is what you want. If we have none but I have you, then that is enough, more than I dared hope for, but I have always wanted… hoped…."

He broke off, looking uncertain.

"You want a family, you want somewhere to belong."

"I belong to you, whatever that means," he said roughly, pulling her into his arms, and she knew she had struck too precisely for him to say more than that.

Evie sighed and rested her head on his shoulder. "I'm yours too, Louis. No matter what."

She felt the tension leave him, felt him bend to kiss the top of her head. "I should say goodnight. You need your rest."

Evie looked up, recognising the wicked glint in his eyes as something hot and anticipatory unfurled deep in her core. Tomorrow, she would be his wife.

"I'd better go to bed, then," she agreed, and could not help the ridiculous smile that curved her lips as he chuckled and pressed a lingering kiss to her mouth before leaving her alone.

They were married the next morning by the mayor's assistant, who looked to Evie to be in the grip of nervous hysteria at the presence in his office of not only Le Loup Noir, but the Comte de Villen and his half-brother. The man sweated profusely as Wolf handed over a thick sheaf of papers, all of which were required to allow the marriage to proceed. Evie had tried to hide her shock when she had stolen a peek at the papers and realised that they had provided her with a false birth certificate and passport. There was a forged document purporting to be written by her father, too, giving permission for their nuptials, and a marriage contract. Anxiety niggled at her as she wondered if they would truly be married. Obviously, her father would never contest the documents, but still.

"Louis?"

He turned to look at her, and Evie hesitated. "Could we marry again, in England, in the church on my uncle's estate? I know you're Catholic, so perhaps you might not want...."

She relaxed as he smiled at her and nodded.

"Of course," he said, squeezing her hand. "There is nothing I would not do for you, have you not realised that yet? Though in truth I have no faith, not anymore. God and I have not been on speaking terms for a very long time. Perhaps, though... after today, I may have to rethink that."

He smiled, his expression one of such sincere happiness that Evie's lip trembled, and she had to blink hard to hold back tears.

She jumped as a clean, neatly folded handkerchief was thrust into her face and turned to see Wolf. He stood, glowering straight ahead, the handkerchief in the palm of his large hand as he watched the mayor's assistant slide a heavy bag of coins into his desk drawer and rifle through their forged documents.

"Thank you," she said.

Wolf grunted and folded his arms.

Evie wiped her eyes and glanced at Louis, who was watching Wolf with amusement. He leaned in, whispering in her ear. "I hope he brought another, or he'll need that back."

Evie frowned at him.

"What for?"

"Because he'll cry," Louis said with a sigh. "The most feared man in Paris, and I swear he's got the heart of a marshmallow."

Evie shot a sceptical glance at Wolf, who was going to give the poor mayor's assistant a conniption if he didn't stop glaring at him. Evie huffed out a laugh, shaking her head. "I don't believe you," she whispered back.

Louis shrugged. "See for yourself, but either way, I'm going to weep so you'd best prepare for the worst."

Evie smothered a giggle, and Louis winked at her. Happiness filled her, as though her heart would sail away like a hot-air balloon if it were not securely contained within her chest. She wished her family and friends were here; she wished she could share this with them, but she did not regret this moment, not even a little, and she knew she never would.

Though Louis had been teasing Evie about crying during the ceremony, he discovered his voice shook as he said his vows, even though there was little of a romantic nature to be found in the civil service. The enormity of the chance she was taking on him, the belief and trust she was putting in him was humbling, though, and he knew he would never forget how he felt in this moment, the hope and joy and sheer relief of knowing she was his at last.

When they had signed a ridiculous amount of papers, which had taken an interminable time, Louis glanced up to see Wolf rubbing irritably at his eyes. He hid a smile and pretended not to notice, turning to his brother instead, who was grinning broadly.

"Félicitations, petit frère," Nic said, hugging him and slapping his back with enthusiasm. "I'm so happy for you."

Louis thanked him before turning to Wolf, who had got himself back under control.

"Congratulations," the man said gruffly, his dark brows drawing together. "I suppose you'll be going back to England now?"

"No, actually," Evie replied before Louis could speak. "We're staying, for a while at least. I want Louis to show me Paris, and… and I would like to get to know his friends, for they are my friends now too. Or, at least, they are if they want to be."

She held out her hand to him and Louis felt a burst of pride in her, for her courage, her generosity, and simply because she tried so very hard to be kind.

Wolf regarded her small hand for a moment before sighing and taking it, bowing low.

"If you are to be friends, I think a formal introduction is in order," Louis said as Wolf rolled his eyes and Evie sent him a quizzical glance.

"Madame la Comtesse," he said, revelling in the ability to call her by her title. "May I introduce to you Wulfric De Vere, Viscount Latimer."

Evie's eyebrows shot up. *"Viscount Latimer?"* she repeated, eyes widening.

"Oh, now you've done it," Wolf said, shaking his head. "It's shock enough I've a title but *that* title. Yes, madame, *that* Viscount Latimer. My father was an unremitting bastard, a traitor, and a vile excuse for a human being."

His expression was stony, his stance defiant, waiting for her to despise him, but Louis knew what Evie's reaction would be, far better than his friend did.

Louis watched her, unsurprised when her face fell, her eyes sparkling.

"Oh," she said softly. "Oh, you poor man. To be forced to live with the weight of his crimes upon your shoulders, to be exiled through no fault of your own. I'm so very sorry."

She reached out to touch his arm and Wolf jolted, taking a step back and staring at her with such shock Louis had to hide a smile.

Louis stepped forward and embraced his friend, patting his back. "And now you understand," he murmured in Wolf's ear, and guided his wife out to the waiting carriage.

The moment the carriage door closed, Evie snuggled against him, raising her face to his for a kiss. Louis brushed his mouth over hers but sat back, staring at her, hardly able to believe she was really his.

"That's it?" she replied, looking a little exasperated.

"For now," Louis agreed, hiding a smile.

"You've been pursuing me for how long, and all I get is a measly peck on the lips?" she retorted, and though he heard the teasing note to her voice she was obviously more than a bit put out.

"Unless you want to lose your maidenhead on the seat of this carriage, that is all you get," Louis replied firmly. "I have waited for you a very long time, *mon amour,* and I have been living in a ferment of sexual frustration for longer than I care to consider. Do not test me on this," he warned her.

"Oh," she replied, her eyes growing wide and looking inordinately pleased by his reply.

Louis snorted. "Ah, yes, you like this, my wicked Evie. You like to think of me aching and in pain, all by myself in my lonely bed, wanting you until I thought I might run mad."

"Yes," she admitted readily. "I do. I like that very much."

"Cruel," he said with a sigh. "I always knew you had a cruel streak beneath that sweet exterior."

"How long?" she asked, narrowing her eyes at him.

Louis shifted uncomfortably, partly because he really was in a ferment of sexual frustration and was counting the seventeen minutes it would take them to return to his rooms at the fortress—including the time it took to walk up the stairs—and partly because he was uncertain he wanted her to know exactly how long he had waited.

"Long enough," he said gruffly.

Her mouth fell open as she stared at him. "Louis… when you say you've been waiting, what exactly…?"

Louis let out a harsh sound and leaned in, taking her mouth in a short, fierce kiss. He pulled back, regarding her flushed cheeks and breathless state with satisfaction. *"Oui, mon amour,* I have been faithful to you alone for a very long time. Even though you did not see me, did not want me, I have wanted none but you. I will want only you for the rest of my days. So your fears about my fidelity are groundless. I have proven to myself that I can be loyal to you, and now I shall prove it to you, too."

Evie touched her mouth with a trembling hand, the sight sending a jolt of lust directly to his cock. Louis smothered a groan and looked resolutely away.

"Louis," she whispered, sounding shaken by his words. "I had no idea."

He laughed a little at that. *"Non, amour de ma vie,* I know you did not."

She fell silent for a while and Louis tried hard to concentrate on the streets he knew so well as they passed outside the carriage window.

"Louis?" she said, her voice low and intimate, holding a note of something that sounded terribly dangerous. "All those lonely nights, did you think of me, when you were in your bed, all by yourself?"

Louis' breath caught, and he turned to glare at her. "Truly? You wish to torment me *now?"*

She bit her lip and nodded. "I'm afraid I do," she said apologetically, not looking the least bit sorry.

"Of course I thought of you!" he growled, outraged. He turned on her, crowding her with his body until he'd backed her into the corner of the carriage, his arms bracketing her head. "Oh, *mon amour,* all the things I have thought of, the things I dreamed of doing with you, how you would blush to know."

She did blush, her cheeks turning that delicious rosy tint that he wanted to chase over her body, to see how far it bloomed, to see if her nipples were a darker shade still. But she did not look the least bit coy, instead curiosity blazed in her eyes and Louis' heart skipped, his arousal so fierce it hurt. He was going to have to take the edge off before he made love to her or risk disgracing himself and disappointing his new bride.

"Tell me," she demanded, her lush mouth curving into a smile.

"Why? So you can provoke me into spending in my breeches like a green boy, hmmm?" he said, narrowing his eyes at her.

"Could I?" she asked, all innocence.

"Petite diablesse," he murmured, catching his breath.

"Did you touch yourself, Louis?" she asked in a breathy whisper, leaning in to press a kiss to the corner of his mouth. "When you thought such wicked things about me, did you make yourself come?"

Louis closed his eyes and groaned, concentrating fiercely on not doing as she was so clearly set on making him do. Muttering a curse, he retreated to the opposite corner of the carriage and sent her a dark look.

"Wicked, wicked girl," he said approvingly, and counted the minutes until the carriage rolled to a stop.

Chapter 14

Dearest Aggie,

I beg you will forgive me for the way I left. There was no time to do otherwise but I deeply regret not being able to take my leave of you or warn you about what happened.

You must have heard by now what I have done. Your Miss Knight was very cross with me, and I have a good deal to make up for. I promise you, I shall do it. She has had the goodness and kindness to forgive me, though, and we will be married this morning. I believe you understand how happy this makes me.

I have not yet had the chance to speak to her about where we shall live and how that might work — her forgiveness is quite recent — but do not think for a moment that I have forgotten you. I never shall.

I am coming back, Aggie, and you will be the very first person to wish us happy. My word upon it. In the meantime, I send you much love from us both. Try to behave yourself, mon enfant.

—*Excerpt of a letter from Louis César de Montluc, Comte de Villen, to Miss Agatha Smith.*

21ˢᵗ July 1842, Rue de la Bièvre, 13ᵗʰ Arrondissement, Paris, France.

When they arrived back at the fortress, Louis led her back to his rooms, where a delicious lunch was ready for them, including a bottle of chilled champagne in an ice bucket.

Evie fell upon a plate of delicate little pastries with a sigh of delight, chewing contentedly on a tiny mushroom tartlet as Louis smiled at her and reached for the champagne. He opened it and filled their glasses, handing one to her.

"To us," he said, his voice soft. "To a future I never dared dream of until you."

"To us," Evie repeated, her voice quavering as she saw the happiness shining in his eyes. She took a sip of her champagne, sighing with pleasure. "Oh, that's good."

"Let us see what else is good," Louis said, drawing his chair around to sit beside her and selecting another pastry. He lifted it, holding it to her mouth. Evie leaned in, holding his gaze, taking it from him and making certain to brush his fingers with her lips.

Louis' eyes darkened and Evie felt a surge of satisfaction. It had taken her a long time to accept that this beautiful man desired her so very much, but there was no doubting his reaction to her now. She shifted closer, placing her hand on his thigh, aware of how the muscles tightened under her touch.

"More," she demanded, licking her lips.

Louis' gaze went to her mouth and lingered there for a moment before he turned to choose another pastry, a tiny little choux bun with an herby cream filling.

"Mmm," Evie said, closing her eyes to better appreciate the fresh, green flavour. "Delicious."

She opened her eyes again to find her husband's gaze riveted upon her. Her husband. Evie felt her mouth curve into a slow smile as she considered that.

"You look like the cat that got the cream," Louis observed.

"That's because I did. You're the cream in that analogy, in case you were wondering."

Louis laughed. "I beg to differ, but we can haggle about that as much as you like. We had better do justice to this wonderful lunch, for I promise you it will be sometime before we leave this room again."

"Promises, promises," Evie said wistfully. "From a man who delivered a stingy peck on the lips."

"I'm still not forgiven for that, I see," Louis replied, taking an oyster from a dish arranged over a bed of ice. Evie watched as he tipped it into his mouth and swallowed.

"Indeed not. Aren't those supposed to be an aphrodisiac?"

"Apparently. In which case I ought not eat any more or one of us is going to be in a lot of trouble." His lips twitched, and he drank his champagne, watching her with amusement.

"Louis."

"Oui, mon amour."

"I'm not hungry," Evie admitted. She was alight with anticipation, her stomach a fluttering swirl of butterflies. Not because she was the least bit nervous, because Louis was and always had been her friend, and she trusted him. It was nothing less than excitement. "Take me to bed, please."

Louis watched her, his blue eyes bright and intent as he drained his champagne glass and got to his feet. He held out his hand to her and Evie took it, standing to face him.

"Take this dress off me," she said, unable to keep the impatience from her voice.

Louis chuckled and turned her around, his hands undoing one button at a time, his movements leisurely.

Evie shot him an exasperated look over her shoulder. "Faster," she said, jittering with impatience.

Her only reply was the touch of his lips to the nape of her neck. The warmth of his mouth sent shivers running over her skin and Evie closed her eyes.

"I like this dress on you," Louis observed. "It's lovely."

"Not as lovely as the ones you designed for me. Where did you learn to do such things?"

"At the circus. Before I was good enough to perform, I had to learn many jobs, including repairing the costumes. I designed some too. I always preferred it to dealing with the monkeys," he added darkly.

Evie let out a breath of laughter. "Ah, that's why you don't like them."

"They have very sharp teeth," he protested, and leaned in to nip at her earlobe as her dress sagged and fell to the floor. He turned his attention to her petticoats, discarding them one by one before she felt the ties of her corset release and let out a breath.

"Better?" he murmured as the corset fell away. His large hands smoothed down her sides and over her stomach, his touch gentle.

Evie sighed and nodded, leaning back against him. "So much better."

Louis cupped her breasts, toying with her nipples until they were hard little nubs under the fine cotton of her chemise. Evie whispered his name, aware of the heat of his body burning through his clothes and warming her, and aware too of his arousal, a hard, insistent pressure against the softness of her bottom. She pressed back, hearing his breath catch.

"Take it off," she whispered, glad when he drew the chemise up over her head, leaving her in only her stockings.

"My Evie," he breathed, as he pulled her back against him again, his hands stroking, caressing, mapping her curves as he pressed kisses to her neck. "So, so lovely, *si belle.*"

Once she would have laughed if he had said such a thing, she would have thought that he was being kind, because Louis was always kind, but now she heard the truth in his words and believed it. There was too much sincerity in his voice, too much veneration in the way he touched her, for there to be any doubt.

She leaned back, her head resting on his shoulder, her breathing quickening as his fingers trailed through the dark curls between her legs, dipping lower.

He made an indistinct sound of approval as his fingers slid deeper and found how ready she was for him.

"Lie down," he told her, a rough quality to his voice that made her pulse quicken.

Evie did not need telling twice and hurried towards the bed, glad of the fire that warmed the room as goose bumps prickled over her. She lay down, aware at every moment of Louis' gaze upon her. She undid her garters and cast the ribbons aside, tossing the stockings after them. Louis moved closer, staring at her as she lay still, letting him look his fill. There was hunger in his gaze, a faint flush of colour high on his cheeks and she realised his breathing had quickened. Never taking his gaze from her, he reached for the sapphire pin in his cravat and took it off, setting it on the bedside table.

"No, wait," Evie said, sitting up on her elbows.

Louis stilled at once.

"Don't… Don't get undressed yet," she said, blushing at the understanding in his eyes. His lips quirked, and he sat on the bed beside her.

"As you wish."

"I like you like this," she admitted, touching a finger to one of the mother-of-pearl buttons on his waistcoat. "The elegant, sophisticated Comte de Villen, all perfect and buttoned up. It makes me want to ruffle you," she added, grinning.

"I am at your disposal, Madame," he said gravely.

"And besides, you're rather overwhelming naked, Louis. I think I need to build up to it," which she said partly to amuse him, but also because it was true.

He snorted at that and lay down beside her. *"Non,* you just like being naked with me fully dressed. I have long known you have a wicked soul, *mon amour*. It appeals to you, because it feels naughty."

"Yes, that too." Evie could not deny it, reaching out to smooth a hand over his fine silk waistcoat, down and down to where the placket of his trousers strained against his arousal. "That looks uncomfortable," she observed, watching his face as she caressed him, sliding her palm up and down.

"And growing more so," he growled, taking hold of her wrist and pinning it above her head as he shifted, sliding his thigh between hers, forcing her legs apart. Evie gasped at the pressure and tilted her hips, aroused by the way he held her down, by the friction of fabric against her sensitive flesh, the cold press of buttons and the heat of his body burning beneath the perfection of his clothes.

"Look at you," he whispered, staring down her body with such undisguised lust, Evie felt she would burst into flame if he didn't make love to her. "Never in my life have I seen anything so magnificent as you. *Mon Dieu*, Evie, I have wanted this for so long, I can hardly believe you are real."

"Louis," she protested, sliding her free hand behind his neck and tugging him down to kiss her. "I need you."

He gave her what she wanted, kissing her deeply, urgently, as he took hold of her wrist and held that one too, pinning both hands down. Louis broke the kiss and stared down at her with satisfaction.

"Don't move," he warned her. "Or I'll have to tie you down."

He must have seen something in her eyes at his words, for he smiled and kissed her again, murmuring against her mouth. "Another thing to discover, wicked girl. Perhaps next time. I have too little patience tonight."

She watched as he sat back, smoothing his hands down her arms to her breasts, caressing and squeezing. He seemed quite spellbound, testing their weight in his hands, toying with her nipples until Evie was beside herself. She bucked her hips, trying to move beneath him and Louis sent her an amused look.

"I'm not the only one impatient, I see."

"No!" she exclaimed. "Please, Louis, stop teasing!"

He snorted and shook his head. "Ah, little love, there's slim chance of that for a while yet." But he took pity on her, moving down her body, lowering his head to run his tongue over her breasts, suckling her until she moaned and then his mouth travelled lower. Evie squirmed as he kissed his way down her stomach and pushed her legs wide open.

"The walls of the fortress are thick, *mon amour*. No one will hear you tonight, which is just as well. I want to hear your pleasure. I want to hear you scream for me. You may curse and swear and shout as loud as you please. You can tell me all the wicked, depraved things you want, and I will be glad to oblige, and no one but you and I will know."

Even if Evie had been capable of answering that, the words died in her throat as he put his mouth on her. She cried out, though, loud enough to please him as his wicked tongue searched and found the vulnerable little peak of flesh hidden in that most private place, and set about tormenting it. Evie bucked, overwhelmed, and Louis laughed softly, sliding his hands beneath her bottom and lifting her back to his mouth. He was relentless, teasing her as he had promised to do, worrying the tiny nub until she was mindless with pleasure, beyond thought or words, her existence narrowed to the place where his mouth worked. Though he had warned her not to move, she could not obey a moment longer, reaching down to grasp at his hair, holding on tight, forcing him to stay and give her what she wanted. She heard his growl of satisfaction and that was all it took. She shattered, crying out, calling his name, pulled under by a tide that swept her away into dark, ecstatic oblivion, as waves of pleasure washed over her, leaving her boneless and sated.

She lay panting, arranged in a pliant pose of utter abandon, watching dazedly as Louis lifted his head and crawled over her. With shaking hands, he wrestled with the buttons on his trousers.

"Evie, you must... I can't make love to you like this. I won't last. Touch me, please... *please... Dieu. Oui! Comme ça,*" he choked out as Evie's slim fingers wrapped around him. He braced himself on his arms, staring down at her and Evie's breath caught as she touched him for the first time. This part of him was as beautiful as the rest and the fierce heat of him, the skin so fine and smooth, and the rigid hardness beneath entranced her. He turned his face into his arm, closing his eyes as if he was in pain. Evie stared at him, enraptured by the sight of Louis, always so cool and self-possessed, coming apart at the seams because her hand was on him.

"Like this?" she asked, certain she was being clumsy as she caressed him, moving her hand slowly up and down.

He nodded, apparently beyond words, tension singing through him and his breathing increasingly ragged until he shuddered and let out a harsh cry as he came. Evie gasped at the first hot splash of his seed over her stomach, staring in wonder as his powerful body shook, helpless as the waves of pleasure racked him. At last he stilled, breathing hard, his blue eyes brilliant against the wide dark of his pupils.

"What you do to me," he said, shaking his head. *"Bon Dieu,* Evie, what you do to me."

He collapsed on the bed beside her, and Evie watched him with interest. Louis turned his head and reached out, tangling their fingers together. "Have I shocked you?"

Evie shook her head. "It was wonderful. I like making you feel good, it feels powerful."

He made a rueful sound, his shoulders shaking with suppressed laughter. "You have no idea how hard I have striven to hide just how much power you have over me. I felt it would be disastrous and now I know I was right."

She studied him, aware he was telling the truth and experiencing a thrill of possessive wonder that she had the power to bring this man such pleasure. Louis shook his head.

"Such a glint you have in your eyes," he observed with a sigh. "I'm done for."

He got to his feet and went to fetch a washcloth before walking around the bed and tending to her with such solicitousness that Evie blushed far harder than she had when he'd had his mouth on her. It seemed somehow more intimate, the tenderness with which he saw to her needs. Once he had finished his ministrations, Evie rolled onto her stomach, her head supported on one hand as she watched him undress.

For reasons she could not fathom, he seemed suddenly tense.

"What is it?"

He turned to look at her once he had set his waistcoat aside, dressed only in his trousers and shirt. "I… I have something to show you," he said, looking at her warily.

Evie snorted and smothered her face in the bedcovers.

Louis tsked at her. "Not *that,*" he protested, and she looked up to see him rolling his eyes. "You've just had a very good look besides having seen it before. You couldn't take your eyes off me, as I remember."

"T-True," Evie managed, trying to get herself under control. "I'm sorry, Louis. What do you mean, then?" Her laughter vanished as she realised he really was anxious. "Louis?"

He sighed and stripped off his shirt, tossing it to one side. Evie regarded him as he walked closer, until he turned around and sat on the bed. Evie looked up at the expanse of broad back before her and her breath caught.

"Louis!" she exclaimed, scrambling to her knees. She stared at the design inked into his golden skin with astonishment. "The eagle," she whispered, reaching out a finger to touch the great bird's sharp beak, almost believing it could react, the drawing was so fine.

Louis flinched as she touched him, and she snatched her hand back. He turned his head, looking over his shoulder at her. "Do you mind it?"

Evie stared at him, momentarily perplexed. "Mind it?" she repeated.

He let out an impatient breath. "Society would be disgusted, Evie. In their opinion, only criminals and sailors would mark themselves in such a way. It's hardly the mark of a gentleman."

"Society can go hang," Evie said crossly, daring to touch the tattoo again, tracing the arc of the bird's wings with her fingers. "It's astonishing, and I think it's beautiful. You are beautiful, Louis, and not just for the way you look, but because you are kind and gentle, and you protect everyone you care for. This was important to you, I think, or you would not have done such a thing. It is a part of you now, and I love it, as I love you."

He shifted, turning slightly to look at her.

"Vraiment? You truly don't mind it?"

Evie leaned in and pressed a kiss to his shoulder, trailing a loving hand over the tattoo before leaning down and kissing a path from the tip of one wing to the other. Louis sighed.

Evie slid her arms about him, pressing her body against his back. "How did they do it?"

"Slowly, with a needle and ink."

"Did it hurt?"

"Like the very devil," Louis replied with a laugh.

"Let me see the rest of you," she whispered in his ear.

It seemed he needed no further encouragement and shucked off his trousers and small clothes, getting on the bed beside her. He laid down, one arm crooked behind his head, watching her with interest now, curiosity in his eyes. Evie, who was far too impatient to touch him to pretend anything like coyness, climbed over him and sat on his thighs. He was hard again, and she dared to trail a delicate finger over the delicate skin. Louis' breath caught and his cock leapt beneath her touch.

"Excitable, isn't it?" she observed with amusement.

"You have no idea," he murmured. "Don't stop."

Evie smiled and ran her hands up his chest, intrigued by a landscape of well-defined muscle that spoke of a lifetime of hard physical activity. She had touched him before and remembered his reaction when she had pinched his nipple. Considering how much she liked it when he kissed her there, she decided to see if he felt the same way. She leaned down, trailing a wet circle around the neat, flat disc of darker skin, pleased at the way his breath hitched and the skin puckered under her tongue. She sucked a little and then tugged at the little nub with her teeth, rewarded with Louis uttering a word she did not understand, but suspected was very rude indeed.

Louis shifted, tugging at her hips until Evie gasped as her still sensitive sex settled snugly against his arousal.

He made a pleased sound and lifted his hips, pressing against her. "Oh," Evie said, bracing herself on his shoulders. She waited for him to do it again, but Louis sat back, watching her, folding his arms beneath his head again, challenge in his eyes.

Evie gave an experimental tilt of her hips and experienced a jolt of pleasure. Flushing, she did it again, very aware of how easily her body slid against his, her excitement all too obvious.

"Oui," Louis said, his eyes extraordinarily dark, only a thin sliver of blue visible around the edge. "Take your pleasure, *mon amour.* Take whatever you need."

She took him at his word, sliding against him until they were both breathing hard, his hands clutching at her hips but letting her set the pace.

"Louis, please, please..." she begged, unable to give any better instruction, but he knew anyway and slid his hand between them. His palm cupped her, two fingers sliding inside her wet heat and Evie shattered, clutching at his arms, feeling the strength in the powerful muscles that had turned to rock beneath her grasping fingers. Her climax had her digging her nails into his skin, holding on for dear life as the sensation that she might fly apart overtook her. She cried and sobbed, nothing but a mass of nerve endings seeking out every last drop of pleasure as Louis gentled his touch. She collapsed on his chest, laughing helplessly, and very aware of how hard he still was.

"Oh... Oh, my," she said on a ragged breath.

"You are spectacular," he whispered, stroking her hair, which had come loose in the throes of her release, and tumbled down her back. "I shall never tire of watching you like that."

"So sleepy," she murmured, her eyelids growing heavy as she snuggled comfortably against him.

"Oh, non. Non, you do not escape me that easily, *mon coeur,"* he warned her. Feeling far too lazy to protest, Evie let him arrange her on the bed, allowing him to place her on her front with a pillow tucked under her hips, dreamily curious about what he would do next. She heard the pop of a stopper pulled from a bottle and a moment later sighed as his warm hands stroked down her spine, the scent of something exotic and expensive filling the room. Louis massaged her back with expert touches and spent a great deal of time caressing the generous swells of her bottom.

"You have, without a doubt, the most splendid bottom in the history of bottoms," he said with apparent sincerity.

Evie giggled and buried her face in the pillow. When she could speak again, she forced the words out between gasps of laughter. "That bottom has been the bane of my life, I'll have you know. It's far too big."

Louis tsked. *"Non!"* he said sharply. "I am your husband, and you must listen to me about such things, for I am always correct. This is undoubtedly one of your finest features, and there are so many to choose from, I am quite overwhelmed."

"Louis!" she protested, torn between laughter and such a burst of love and affection for him, her eyes prickled.

"I mean it," he said, and she felt the heat of his body all over her as he pressed against her, nuzzling her neck and murmuring the words in her ear. His arousal nestled against the crease of her behind and she heard his breath catch as he moved, sliding back and forth. "So soft, *si doux,* quite perfectly splendid."

The words were ragged, his breath hot against her nape.

Evie, who would have sworn she was too tired to move a muscle, was suddenly alight with anticipation all over again, that aching, clamouring sensation gathering faster than ever before.

"Do you want me inside you?" he asked, the words hoarse and tinged with desperation.

"Yes," she said at once, without a moment's hesitation. "Yes, yes, please. Now!"

He huffed out a laugh and tugged at her hips, raising her bottom a little more. "Patience," he said. "Though I must tell myself the same thing, I fear. I want to be inside you so badly."

Evie gasped as she felt the blunt head of his cock nudging at her entrance, and closed her eyes, eager to feel the heat and weight of him inside her. He rocked his hips, inching forward until the head of his shaft settled inside her and then reached around with one hand, sliding it between her thighs.

"Louis, I want…" she began trying to take him deeper, shifting to impale herself upon him but he held her still.

"*Non.* I do not wish to hurt you and it will be easier for you if you do as I say. Once more for me and then I shall make love to you. I'm going to beg you to hurry this time, too. Believe me, I cannot wait a moment longer."

Evie shook her head in protest. "No, I want you now," she said, almost petulant, she needed him so badly.

"Once more," he insisted and despite herself, Evie felt it happening, felt her muscles clenching as his fingers worked like magic, as if he understood her body far better than she did. She gasped and shuddered, whimpering with pleasure, all the time aware that there was more to come and wanting it now.

Louis was of the same mind, it seemed, and turned her onto her back, finding his place between her thighs.

"Evie," he whispered, kissing her tenderly as he entered her once more, slowly at first and then with one hard thrust that found him settled deep and snug inside her. Evie gasped, her eyes flying open as she clutched at his shoulders.

Louis waited, staring down at her. *"Mon amour?"* he rasped, the effort of keeping still evident in his taut expression and the fine tremble running through him.

"Yes," she whispered, relaxing upon a sigh of pleasure. "Oh, yes."

He moved then, and all that had come before seemed to her as if he had only laid the tinder and kindling for a fire that he lit now, until she was burning out of control. The way she abandoned herself to him, to her own passion, might have frightened her if he had not taken such time, prepared her and allowed her to trust in him before this moment. As it was, she let herself go, forsaking any notions of propriety, of how one might expect a young woman to behave on her wedding night. She took from him as much as she gave and demanded more, more kisses, more of his love, harder and faster until she thought she would die of it. Louis broke first, crying out and shaking as he spent inside her, his desperate shout calling to something inside her that clenched with pleasure.

When she came apart, she felt she would not be the same when the pieces of her returned, if they ever did. She felt she had been shattered and flung among the heavens, glittering among the stars until she fell back to earth. Some change, some alchemical reaction had taken place, and she was entirely different, stronger, bolder, happier, and she knew without a doubt who she was, and what she wanted.

She tightened her hold on Louis, aware of the slick heat of his skin, his breath harsh and uneven.

"Mon Dieu," he murmured, resting his forehead against hers. *"Mon Dieu."*

"We didn't break the bed," she said, trying to give him a reproving look. "You promised me broken furniture."

He gasped, choking on a laugh, and then buried his face in her neck. "Give me a minute," he mumbled helplessly, his shoulders shaking. "I'll try to do better next time."

She laughed, and he groaned, withdrawing from her body and rolling to her side. Evie followed him, pleased when his arms wrapped around her and she snuggled close, utterly content. *"Je t'aime,"* she said, pressing a kiss to his chest.

Louis sighed and shifted so they were face to face. "Say it again," he whispered, his voice drowsy now.

"Je t'aime, Louis, mon mari," she added, smiling as he closed his eyes.

"I like that, being your husband. *Je t'aime aussi.* So much," he murmured, and she listened as his breathing steadied and she followed him into sleep.

Chapter 15

*La Comtesse de Villen. That is who I am now.
I have discovered she is brave and bold and
not afraid to be a little scandalous. I think I
like her very much already, and I cannot wait
to see what she does next.*

I am so happy I think I shall burst.

**—Excerpt of a diary entry by Evie de
Montluc, Comtesse de Villen.**

**4th February 1826, Rue de la Bièvre, 13th Arrondissement,
Paris, France.**

Louis is thirteen years old.

*"You told him!" Louis raged, so furious he did not know what
to do with himself. "You told him all our plans?"*

*Nic swallowed, obviously wishing he had spoken to Louis first
now, but it was too late. He shrugged, looking guilty. "It seemed
like a good idea at the time. He just looked so old and frail I felt
sorry for him. It's still a good idea," he said cautiously, obviously
not having banked on the depths of his brother's anger. "Louis,
he's sick, there's hardly anything he can do to interfere any
longer, and his endorsement will make the place. I know you don't
like it—"*

"Don't like it!" Louis repeated, his fists clenched. "Oh, that's one way of putting it. How could you?"

"I don't know, I... He's said we can use his property, though. Can't you see how perfect that is? He'll keep the first house for himself, but he knows he's not got long left. That last attack weakened him, but he's so bloody proud, Louis. This is something he can still do. It's not like you won't be involved at all, just not publicly, but if the club is a success, it will mean you're secure. There will be money enough to repair the properties that belong to you. You could go home, Louis, and he wants to see it happen, he needs to know the line will carry on once he's gone, that the title—"

"Home," Louis spat, tempted to start breaking things with his bare hands. "As if such a thing exists. They're just empty buildings, Nic, and I don't want them. And as for the title... on the one hand, he forbids me to have anything to do with a gambling den because I can't sully my name, and on the other, he wants to invite all his friends to his illegitimate son's exclusive club. So I'm to stay away, to sit back twiddling my thumbs and have no part of it, when it was my idea in the first place, and now he'll take over the whole damn thing when it's ours, Nic. It was ours, and you—"

Louis made a sound of frustration and snapped his mouth shut before he said something unforgiveable. It was rare that Louis lost his temper at all, but never with his brother. When he and his father got into it, the fights were vicious and left them both ragged. At first, Louis had simply been glad the comte did not dare to hit him any longer, but those brutal, bloodless rows were somehow worse.

"I'm sorry," Nic offered, raking a hand through his hair and Louis could see he felt wretched. His anger drained away, replaced with a weary acceptance of something he could not now change.

"Can't you see what he is, Nic?" Louis asked him, still not understanding why his brother wanted the man's acceptance so

badly after everything he'd done. "Why do you want him to approve of you so badly?"

"I don't," Nic protested, flushing hotly at the accusation.

"You do," Louis replied, his voice flat. "You think this is something you can do for him, to make him proud. That's why you did it, and it makes me wild. Because you are ten times the man he will ever be. You don't need his approval, Nic. You need nothing from him. Neither of us do, not any longer. We have each other, and that's enough. At least, it's enough for me," he added, before stalking out and leaving Nic alone.

Louis returned to the fortress after his last performance of the year. Winter was here and it was too cold to perform again until the spring. He did not know how he would bear the time in between. He was constantly moving, constantly in need of distraction, as if he feared what might happen if he stayed still for too long. Changing once again from the nondescript outfit he had worn to leave the circus into the fine clothes of the Vicomte Sainte-Apre, he prepared to go out for the remainder of the evening. It was getting harder and harder to slip away unnoticed, but he did not care. He would not give up performing, not until there was no other choice.

Sorting through a thick pile of invitations, he chose the one that looked the least tedious and went out, though it was already gone eleven. Paris was just waking up, and the amusements would continue until dawn.

All of society knew Madame Du Pont for her lavish soirees and rather risqué entertainments. Her parties were an extravagant mix comprising the cream of the aristocracy, artists, intellectuals, dancers, and courtesans that Louis found far more stimulating than other society events. His father would not have approved, which naturally made it the only invitation that was of any interest.

Louis endured the first hour, where he had to be an entertaining guest and speak to everyone important in Parisian society, ensuring he flattered and charmed, and solidified his position as the most popular and original young man in the city. Both he and his father had downplayed his youth as he now looked far closer to eighteen than fifteen, which suited him. As heir to the Comte de Villen, he was due respect, but his wit and sharp tongue had gained him many followers who found him amusing company.

Once he had been as charming as he could stomach, he neatly sidestepped demands from all sides from people wanting his attention whilst ruffling no one's feathers. It was with a sigh of relief that he found himself in the card room and back among the safety of the gambling set.

He played for the next two hours, winning steadily, but careful not to humiliate anyone who might decide he needed taking down a peg or two. It was all a balancing act, every bit as dangerous as walking the highwire. One false move and his house of cards would come crashing down.

Louis was gathering up his winnings whilst everyone else was leaving the card rooms for supper. The lavish meals Madame Du Pont supplied were hard to resist, but Louis had already decided he'd had enough; it was almost three in the morning and the night's performance was catching up with him. The rustle of fabric behind him made him turn in his seat, to find Madame Du Pont herself regarding him with interest. She was a beautiful woman, a very young widow of perhaps not quite thirty years. Her ambitious parents had married her off to a wealthy man many years her senior when she was little older than Louis was now. She looked at him with interest, studying him with an intent gaze that made him nervous. Her hair was dark and lustrous, her skin as pale as cream, and it was rumoured she changed lovers as often as her dresses.

"You're a lucky young man," she said, her voice pleasantly husky as she gestured to Louis' winnings.

"Oui, apparently so," Louis replied, wondering what she wanted of him, under no illusion that she had caught him alone by chance.

She smiled, tilting her head to one side as she gave him an appraising up and down look that made him feel hot and cold all at once. "You really are extraordinarily beautiful."

Louis looked away, uncomfortable. He stood, pocketing the money, and picked up the diamond pin he'd won. She plucked the pin from his hand, turning it this way and that so it glittered in the light.

"You like pretty things, don't you?"

"Doesn't everyone?" Louis replied carefully, taking a few steps away, stilling as she moved between him and the door.

She walked closer, so close the scent of flowers enveloped him, stirring a memory he had repressed for a long time of a beautiful woman in a pink dress, and of the desperate longing for her to want him to stay. He knew it was not the same, but the memory hovered, the sense of living in an illusion falling over him like ribbons of silk.

Madame Du Pont reached out with an elegant hand, heavy with jewels that sparkled in the lamplight. She put the pin into his cravat, forcing him to tilt his head back to allow her to do so. Once satisfied it sat properly, she traced the line of his jaw, touching a finger to his lips.

"I like pretty things too," she whispered. "And you are very pretty indeed."

Louis' heart sped, the scent of flowers dragging him into the past, impossibly caught between the desire to run and the need for her to want him to stay.

"We are alike, you and I, you know," she said, her voice gentle. "There is much I can teach you about surviving in this world, and your father is not so wealthy as he once was. I doubt he

has the funds to buy you all the things you truly desire. But I am a very wealthy woman, and a generous one to those who please me. Shall we help each other, Louis? Would you like that?"

Louis could not speak, afraid of what he might say. There was something inside him that wanted very much to please this woman, but another part of him wanted to run, to get as far away as he could go.

She leaned closer, so close her lips touched his cheek. Louis' breath caught. "Do you think I am pretty?"

"Vous êtes la plus jolie femme que j'aie jamais vue." The words came from nowhere, as if the practised response had been waiting only for this moment, for this woman to demand he say it again.

She laughed then, her eyes sparkling with delight. "The prettiest you ever saw? Such a sweet boy, how delicious you are. Come along with me and let us talk together. I have been watching you and I can see you are an extraordinarily clever young man. You play the game well, but not yet well enough. If you are not careful these people will eat you alive. With the right advice, though, you shall have Paris at your feet. I should like to help you. Will you let me?"

Louis swallowed, nervous now, shaking his head as her hand slipped into his. "But your guests, Madame, I should not keep you from them. I really ought to—"

He gave a little tug, but her grip only firmed.

"Nonsense, my guests are entertained and well fed. Come along, Louis. We have much to discuss."

Louis glanced at the door, heart thudding, but knew there was no way out of this. She had trapped him in a silken web and if he struggled, it would only get worse. Madame was powerful, and not a woman he wished to scorn. He had nothing like power enough to withstand her criticism if she took against him. Not yet, and Madame wanted him to stay. There was something about that fact that pleased him more than he wished to consider. Well, then he would stay. For now, and learn whatever she would teach him.

"It's astonishing," Nic said, turning in a circle as he took in the sight before him.

Louis grinned, knowing the club looked exactly as he had dreamed it would. The work had been lengthy and expensive, but now, after so many months of problems and delays, it was finally ready. Rouge et Noir was lavish, opulent but stylish, decorated with no expense spared, but there was an edge to it too, something that was not quite respectable, that courted scandal and danger. They had joined all the houses together for the club, except the one their father lived in, knocking down walls and rearranging the rooms until they had one vast space and various other private rooms. The central room, painted blood-red, bore erotic frescoes of gods and mortals disporting themselves, feasting and drinking and generally getting up to no good. The entire room was presented like a Roman temple, with great marble columns and Bacchus himself presiding over them. The young man bore more than a passing resemblance to Louis, and gazed down at the revellers from his position, painted reclining lazily on a throne on the far wall opposite the entrance. He wore a Roman style toga, his chest and arms bare, a glass of wine dangled negligently from his fingers. Bacchus had a knowing look in his eyes and was obviously foxed. His crown of grapes and vine leaves sat a little askew, suggesting he was aware of the ridiculousness of his crown and did not much care. Their father had not seen it yet and Louis did not doubt it would give the old man an apoplexy. He could only hope.

"Putain!" Nic exclaimed as he caught sight of it. He turned to stare at Louis. "Are you insane?"

Louis shrugged. "It's my place too, whatever he says."

"It is not your place," snapped an aggrieved voice from behind them. "These are my buildings which I have gifted to Nicolas. He will manage it. It's all in his name, not yours. Neither of us can have our names attached in any other way but as patrons. Men of our class cannot be seen dabbling in... in trade," their father added in disgust.

The comte took a breath, about to continue his diatribe, when he caught sight of Bacchus on the far wall.

Louis smirked, satisfied to see the colour leave his father's face.

"You son of a bitch," he growled, turning on Louis. "You get that painted over at once."

"Non," Louis replied, holding his father's gaze. "This is my place, mine and Nic's. We stole the jewels that financed it. It was my damned idea and Nic has run himself ragged, ensuring the work got done in time. I am a part of this, Père. I am going to run it with him. People will come to play me. You know they will."

"As a member, not as an owner of the club, you arrogant prick! You think society won't look down on you if you treat him as your equal when he is not? He will drag you down in the mire."

The comte spoke with no regard to Nic's feelings and Louis felt his temper snap.

"You think I give a goddamn what society thinks of either of us? He's my brother, and if they don't like it, they can go to hell!"

The comte sneered. "Oh, very noble, and where will you be when society decides not to come here because you don't measure up to their standards?"

"They'll come," Louis said, glaring at the man.

"They'll not come and see my son, my heir, painted on the wall, looking like a damned whore, even if that is what you are. You think I don't know, don't you? Think I don't know about Madame Du Pont, except she tired of you soon enough, did she *not? No surprise there. You're nothing but a frivolous boy. You'd think that pretty face would please them for a while, but you're of no use to anyone. They all tire of you quick enough, don't they, eh? Who was it she passed you to next, Madame Amboise? Did she buy you lots of pretty trinkets for licking her quim? Is that your greatest achievement, mon fils?"*

Louis felt his cheeks heat, humiliation burning and the desire to lash out at the man who called himself his sire overcame him.

"What's the matter, Père? Are you jealous it is no longer you they turn to?" he said coldly, using a precise imitation of his father's clipped accent. "And madame's pretty trinkets paid to fill the cellars with the best champagne so you can cease your sneering for you could not afford to pay for it, could you? Incidentally, you can stop fretting about what people think of your heir in years to come, for it will be far worse than you can possibly imagine. I shall never do as you please. I shall not marry, shall not give you the heir you want so badly. I'll sire bastards the length and breadth of France and support every one of them as you ought to have supported Nic, but there won't be a legitimate heir. There will never be another in our line. I will be the last of our blood and I'll let the buildings crumble to ruins, and all your hopes with them. So go to hell and I'll see you there, monsieur."

Louis saw his father gasp with outrage, saw him clutch at his chest as his brother ran forward, but Louis did not move, only watched as his father crumpled to the floor.

Casino Rouge et Noir was an extraordinary success from the moment it opened, just as Louis had predicted. Nic saw at once what his father had not realised during their last dreadful fight. Louis was society's darling, and they adored him, perhaps all the more for not being entirely respectable. But their father had not been in society much in those last months, and since that fight he had not left his bed. Nic sat with him when he could, explaining

how great a success the club had become to ease his father's worry in his last days.

Louis was now in control of it all, for the comte could do little more than eat soup fed to him with a spoon, and even brief conversations left him exhausted. Nic ran the floor, monitoring everything that happened. Several heavily muscled men stood silently in dark corners, exuding an air of quiet menace that was enough to dissuade anyone from starting fights. They silently ejected those foolish enough to try, and persuaded them not to come back again if they could not behave.

The money that was passing through the club was enough to make Nic's head spin, but Louis seemed to take it all in stride. His instinct for money, for how to spend it to encourage more and more people to the club seemed ingrained and Nic could only watch his brother with increasing awe as his confidence grew and he came into his own. Louis fed most of it back into the club, making it ever more exclusive, employing more staff, offering more entertainments. He even employed some of the circus entertainers now the winter months were upon them, a move which Nic at once approved and made him exceedingly nervous.

These were people that they both trusted to keep Louis' identity secret, yet the overlapping of those two worlds seemed a dangerous idea to Nic and he feared someone talking. At least Louis could not perform again until the spring, but that in itself was a problem. Louis was restless and all on edge, despite the terrific success they had achieved already and all that was at their fingertips. It seemed nothing could satisfy Louis, no matter how successful he became. Nic knew his brother was unhappy, but he did not know how to fix it.

"Louis, please. He's dying."

Louis was lounging back in his chair, feet up on the large oak desk of the room that served as their office at the club. He did not look up from the book he was reading. English poetry again by the looks of things. Though he never admitted it—for learning English had been at their father's insistence—Louis delighted in English literature and usually had his head stuck in a book when he could.

"You say that like I should care," Louis replied, picking up his wineglass and taking a sip, never looking at his brother.

Nic sighed, knowing he needed to tread carefully. "Non," he said, shaking his head. "I say it because there is a part of you that does care despite yourself, and I do not wish for you to have any regrets. You owe him nothing, Louis. I know that. He's treated you abominably, abused, and hurt you at every turn. I know that too. I've seen it, but the truth is you have a kind heart, and I do not want you eaten alive by hatred for a sick old man who can't hurt you any longer. It's you that will suffer if you don't let go of your anger."

Louis regarded Nic over the top of the book he held. Nic's heart ached. Louis' eyes held a weight of experience and cynicism that ought not be present in one as young as he was, but if it hadn't been for that stubborn determination, he'd likely not be here at all. Louis had decided to survive, no matter what. Nic had seen the change in him of late, the desire to take control and be the one in power, the one people obeyed. He could hardly blame his brother for that, but he feared what would become of him if he hardened his heart too far.

"Non. You go if you must. You'll say all the right things, I know. Do what you think is right, whatever means you can sleep at night, but do not drag me to his deathbed. I won't do as he asks, won't agree to anything. He's still the same man he always was, and dying does not change that. He made his choices, lived his life as he saw fit, and now I shall do the same. That is his legacy."

Louis returned his attention to his book, and Nic knew that was the end of the conversation.

Yet that night, Nic held his father's hand as his breathing rattled and grew laboured. He held his hand and gave his word to the old man that he would ensure Louis was established as the Comte de Villen. Nic promised he would see Louis become respectable in society's eyes, see him marry and produce an heir, and then he turned to see his brother standing in the doorway as their father's breathing stilled. Louis was chalk-white, his eyes stark and hollow, his gaze on Nic full of reproach as he turned and walked away.

Chapter 16

My dearest Eliza,

I have found my brother and Evie. They are both safe. I attended their wedding and can only tell you I never saw two happier people in my entire life, not counting you and I, of course. I miss you dreadfully, and being in Paris without you seems all wrong, but I need to sort things out with Louis and figure out exactly what is going on with him. I will return to you as soon as I can.

—Excerpt of a letter from Monsieur Nicolas Demarteau to his wife, Lady Elizabeth Demarteau.

22nd July 1842, Rue de la Bièvre, 13th Arrondissement, Paris, France.

Louis woke late the next morning to discover his wife, a soft warm weight snuggled against him. He stared at her, at her long dark hair tumbling in a silken wave over her back and across his chest. Tenderness rose inside him, a wave of love and protectiveness so fierce he did not know how he would contain it. Fear came too, as he'd known it would. If you had something precious, there was always the risk someone or some cruel quirk of fate would take it from you.

He had thought, or perhaps only hoped, that marrying Evie would put his feelings into perspective and they would lose a little of their power. With chagrin, he had to admit that was not the case. Instead, knowing what it was to be with her, in a way he had only dreamed until now, had only made things worse, had made his feelings unwieldy and unmanageable and that made his chest tight with anxiety. He pushed the sensation away, aware it would cripple him if he allowed it to take hold. He could not keep Evie a prisoner in the rooms of the fortress just to make himself feel better, even if he had to admit to that it would. Etienne was still out there somewhere, and that was something Louis could not allow to continue. Etienne would have hurt Evie in order to hurt him, and that was terrifying and quite unacceptable. For now, though, she was safe and in his arms, and Louis was in a daze of happiness so profound he hardly dared believe it was real.

Yesterday they had woken again, ravenous, and devoured the supper that they had abandoned before. Louis had made love to her again, though he had intended to leave her in peace, assuming she would need time to recover. However, Evie had harboured other ideas entirely, which had delighted him. The night had continued thus, sleeping for a few hours and waking to kisses and touches and pleasure so intense he hardly knew what he'd been doing all those years, because this felt new and extraordinary in comparison to his previous affairs.

Evie sighed, snuggling closer into his arms. Louis watched her as she woke. She smiled, the sight of the dimple flashing in her cheek making him grin with an expression he knew must be hopelessly fond and besotted… not that he gave a damn. She pressed a kiss to his chest and his body reacted at once, stirring to life. Louis admitted surprise, because even by his standards he'd thought he ought to be sated for a little while yet, but no. He could not seem to get enough of his wife, and the merest touch or look was enough to have him reaching for her. This time, however, he was stalled by the loud and insistent sound of her stomach grumbling.

Evie blushed scarlet, groaned, and buried her face against his chest.

"How mortifying," she complained, tugging a pillow from the bed over her head.

Louis laughed and pushed the pillow aside, rolling her onto her back. He tugged the bedcovers down and shifted to kiss the gentle curve of her stomach, nuzzling the impossibly soft skin. "There, there, *mon amour*. We shall get you something to eat before I ravish you some more."

He climbed from the bed and put on his dressing robe before ringing the bell pull. A moment later there was a knock at the door and Louis ordered them some breakfast, ensuring to instruct the servants in exactly how to arrange the tea things properly for his English wife. When the tray arrived, he prepared the tea for her, adding milk and sugar the way she liked it, aware of her watching him and enjoying the chance to take care of her, even in such a small way. She sat up in bed, propped up on pillows, the covers barely covering her splendid bosom as she chewed contentedly on a croissant taken from a selection of pastries on a large plate before her.

He handed her the cup of tea. She took it from him, sipped, and gave a happy sigh.

"Must you do everything perfectly?" she asked, shaking her head.

Louis shrugged and climbed onto the bed beside her. "It's a curse," he replied sadly, leaning over to steal one of her croissants.

"You're getting crumbs everywhere," she said, laughing as she brushed them off his robe, chasing a golden flake of pastry that settled on his chest with her tongue.

"The sign of an excellent croissant," he replied, pulling her closer for a kiss. "They are impossible to eat with any degree of elegance."

Evie murmured her agreement with this statement as she bit into another and tried to catch the shower of crumbs with her hand.

Once they had eaten and shaken the worst of the crumbs from the bed, they settled back together, relaxed and content. Evie tugged at the silken tie of his robe, opening it and sliding her hand over his chest, settling her fingers along the line of a scar that ran across his side. Louis stiffened, uncomfortable with her scrutiny. He told himself it was vain and idiotic to have such a thing as a small scar embarrass him, but it did, for so many reasons. It was a visible reminder of yet another moment in his life when he had been helpless, when someone else had needed to save him. After that, when he had recovered enough to think clearly, he had sworn it would never happen again. He would never be helpless again, and he never had been.

Evie bent and pressed a kiss to the scar, making him shiver.

"Tell me the rest, Louis," she whispered, looking up at him through thick, dark lashes. There was too much understanding in her green eyes, too much compassion. It made him feel vulnerable all over again, to expose those moments when he had been helpless, to her of all people. "You promised you would tell me everything."

Louis frowned, wanting to deny her despite his promise. Those memories would only upset her.

She pressed a finger to his lips. "I'm on your side, Louis. Always. No matter what. I only want to understand, not to judge. I need you to trust me, as I've given you my trust."

"That's blackmail," he grumbled, but she only laughed softly and kissed his cheek.

"I'll use whatever means necessary to ensure our happiness, our future together, so you had better get used to the fact I can be ruthless where you are concerned."

"Very well. If you insist, but don't say I didn't warn you," he said, aware his voice had turned brittle, but Evie tangled their fingers together and he could not hold onto his irritation.

So, he told her all of it this time, not just a recital of facts, but returning to his life under the cruel hands of Monsieur and Madame Boucher, and explaining about Etienne and André. He told her about Nic coming for him, about his father and the circus and, as he spoke, Evie listened. She heard his story without judgement, with unwavering sympathy and understanding, and the more her told her, the easier it became to remember as the past caught up with him again.

"I wish your father were not dead," Evie said hours later, doing her best to contain the barrage of emotion that filled her chest. "I would have a great deal to say to him."

Her tone must have alerted Louis to the depths of her anger, and he shifted to look down at her. "How fierce you are. You truly would defend me with all you have, wouldn't you?"

"Of course I would!" she exclaimed, getting to her knees, ignoring the sheet that fell in a puddle about her hips. They had spent the entire day in bed, talking mostly, except for when Louis got distracted, as he was doing now. "I could murder him for how he treated you. He was a cruel, unfeeling brute, and so damned selfish. Oh, Louis, I am so desperately sorry."

But Louis was preoccupied with stroking the generous curves of her breasts and only shrugged. "It was a long time ago, *mon amour*. He is dead, and I am not."

As if to illustrate the point, Louis pushed her down onto the bed and covered her with his body, his arousal hot and insistent between her thighs.

"Louis," she sighed, stroking his hair. "But you haven't finished your story," she protested, though mildly enough that he was not fooled into believing she wanted him to stop. In case he had any doubts she widened her thighs, tilting her hips and welcoming him inside her with a gasp of pleasure.

"Later," he growled, and Evie did not feel like protesting any more as they lost themselves in each other and the pleasure they found together.

22nd July 1842, Hôtel Westminster, Rue de la Paix, Paris, France.

After a fruitless morning of trying to speak to someone at Rouge et Noir, Barnaby had returned to his hotel for something to eat and to consider his next move. There was clearly no point in trying to gain entry to the club until it opened that night. The place had been shut up tight and there was no one around to make enquiries of. He was uncertain what to do until then.

Barnaby moved to the window of his hotel room and cast a surreptitious glance down at the street below. Drat it. There he was again. It *was* the same boy, Barnaby was certain of it this time. A little shabbier and more travel worn than he had first appeared to be, perhaps, but nonetheless the same. At first, he'd thought he was being fanciful. Why anyone, least of all a boy of indeterminate age, would want to follow him about was beyond him. But this morning Barnaby had been aware of an anxious, unsettling feeling about the lad and, the more he thought about it, the more concerned he became. He told himself he was being utterly foolish and more than a little fanciful, and yet the anxiety had solidified into a hard little knot in his belly and refused to shift.

Aware that there was every possibility he would make a twit of himself, Barnaby picked up his hat and gloves and hurried downstairs. He was about to burst out of the front of the hotel when he realised that whenever the boy caught him looking, he mysteriously melted into the shadows. So this time, he endured the raised eyebrows of the staff at his request to use a back entrance, and made his way in a circuitous route around to the front of the hotel. He approached the boy with great caution and as much stealth as Barnaby felt he was reasonably capable of... which was a limited supply, it seemed, as he tripped over a paving slab on his way.

His muttered oath caused the boy to turn in surprise, but Barnaby's fears coalesced into certainty as a pair of startling blue eyes met his.

"Miss Agatha!" he exclaimed in horror, recognising at once the elfin face and unruly mop of dark curls beneath her cap.

"Ssssh!" the wretched creature said, hurrying up and giving him an irritated shove. "I'm Pete Glover, come to visit my aunt, who married a Frenchman."

"No, you're not, you're Agatha Smith and you've no business being in Paris all by yourself. What the devil are you playing at?"

Agatha rolled her eyes at him. "Same as you I imagine. Monsieur is in trouble, and I've come to help him."

Barnaby opened and closed his mouth, too outraged to find the words required to tell her exactly how ridiculous she was being. "You might have been.... Good God, Miss Smith, the mind boggles at how much trouble you might have got into. A female, travelling through France all on her own, and...where exactly have you been sleeping?"

Agatha sent him a look of such scorn Barnaby suspected it could have etched glass. "Don't give me that. I lived a good deal of my life on the street, not like some pampered gentleman. Do you know how many times I've saved you from having your watch or your money purse lifted on this journey? Honestly, you're a babe in the woods and no mistake."

Barnaby bristled, indignant at being given a set down by a child.

"Oh, don't look so wounded," she said impatiently. "We're here now and the truth is we need each other's help."

"Oh-ho, do we indeed?" Barnaby said. "Give me one good reason why I should not find you a chaperone to take you straight back home."

"Because your French is execrable, and you don't have a clue where Louis might be. Mine is excellent, and I do… have a clue, that is."

"I'm going back to his club, and I'm sure someone there will speak English and get a message to him," Barnaby said, aggravated.

"Oh, please, Mr Godwin. I know where he is, but no one there will take me seriously. Please come with me. He's all I've got, and I know he's in trouble. *Pleeeeeeassse!*" she said piteously, drawing out the *please* for so long and at such a pitch Barnaby thought his ears might bleed.

"Oh, Jupiter," he exclaimed, taking off his hat and running his hand through his hair. "Well, this is a pickle and no mistake. Fine, fine. You'd better come with me, but ought you not…?"

He made an uncertain gesture towards her appearance.

"What?"

"Put on a frock. I suppose we could say you're my sister," he added dubiously.

"I'll be your cousin, Peter," she said with an imperious sniff. "I've been a boy this long and I won't let you leave me out of things because I'm a girl. It's far too tedious."

"Yes, but… you *are* a girl, therefore you ought to be—"

"What?" Agatha demanded, her eyes glittering in a way that gave Barnaby pause. "What ought I to be?"

"Er... protected," he said cautiously. "Tender sensibilities and all that," he added, feeling a little desperate now.

"Pfft!" Agatha said in disgust and strode off.

Feeling much put upon, Barnaby had little choice but to follow her.

Chapter 17

Dearest Mother and Father,

By the time you read this, I'll be in France. I'm sorry for telling you a lie about going to stay with Ridley. The thing is, I was certain a very dear friend of mine was going to do something dreadfully reckless and when I investigated; it turned out I was right. I simply can't allow her to get herself into trouble, for she is the most troublesome creature on earth, and it is bound to happen. So I've gone after her. Please forgive me. I have plenty of money and I will take the greatest of care, but I simply had to go. I hope you understand.

I shall, of course, accept any punishment you see fit upon my return.

—Excerpt of a letter from Lord Frederick Adolphus to his parents, Their Graces Robert and Prunella Adolphus, The Duke and Duchess of Bedwin.

28th June 1829, Casino Rouge et Noir, 7th Arrondissement, Paris, France.

Louis is seventeen years old

Nic watched Louis out of the corner of his eye as his brother readied himself to go out for the evening. He was still struck, even after all this time, by the fact the two of them were related. It seemed implausible at best. Nic had been told he was handsome a good many times, often enough not to be coy about believing it, but Louis was something else entirely. At seventeen, he lost a deal of the prettiness that had often caused him trouble. Yet the harder line of his jaw and the chiselled perfection of high cheekbones and those astonishing blue eyes had turned him into a man people stopped in the street to stare at. And Louis damn well knew it.

His looks, combined with a lethal charm that he wielded with fatal precision, had turned his brother into something Nic looked on with a combination of awe and deep anxiety. Louis could get pretty much anything he wanted from anyone if he put his mind to it. The trouble was, Nic did not think his brother had the slightest notion what he did want. Women turned up at the club at all hours of the day and night, begging to see him, everyone from courtesans to respectable married women who had far too much to lose to act so rashly. Yet they did, and they continued to do so.

Nic knew that, underneath the façade, Louis was the same person he had always been. He was kind and had a generous heart, but that boy was being eaten up by unhappiness and dissatisfaction and Nic did not know how to bring him back again. Louis was driven by something Nic did not understand, an inner demon that pushed him into recklessness, whether walking the highwire or breaking in to steal jewels, he only seemed happy when he was risking his neck. Of late that also meant drinking too much, going to places that were not the least bit respectable or safe, and living too hard. He was burning the candle at both ends and Nic did not know what to do about it.

"Come with me," Louis said again, tugging on his gloves.

Nic shook his head and saw impatience flash in his brother's eyes. He always preferred when Nic went with him, for despite their differences, they were still close. Nic knew he was the only

*person Louis was close to despite the legions of friends and lovers
that followed Louis slavishly about. But Nic did not have the heart
to watch Louis play the part of Comte de Villen tonight.*

*"It only makes everyone uncomfortable when I'm with you,"
Nic replied. "And I can't stand all those snotty devils in one place.
Gives me the pip."*

*"To hell with them, then. I don't care. We'll go and find a
game," Louis offered.*

*Nic shook his head. "There's no point in playing cards with
you," he said, laughing.*

*Louis huffed with impatience. "The club is fine, Nic. We have
managers. You can take time off without it falling down."*

"I know that, and I do. I just don't want to tonight, d'accord?"

*"Then I'll stay in," Louis said. "The wine from those new
suppliers in Bordeaux is waiting for us to try. I'll get the kitchens
to send up some bread and cheese and—"*

*"No! Go out. You want to go out, you're all dressed up. Be a
shame to waste all that effort now. The women of Paris will begin
throwing themselves in the Seine if you don't make an
appearance."*

*Nic had been trying to be jovial, not wanting Louis to feel
sorry for him and like he had to stay in. But too late, he saw the
flash of hurt in his brother's eyes and the now familiar mask slide
back in place.*

*"Of course, that would never do," Louis said coolly. "I have a
reputation to uphold, do I not? The Comte de Villen must be seen
at all the right places. Excuse me, Nic. I shall leave you to your
evening. Bonne soirée."*

*It was early by Louis' standards when he called it a night and
made his way home. Madame Du Pont had made a grand spectacle*

of herself, throwing herself at him and weeping, begging him to return to her. The entire scene had left Louis wretched and uncertain of what he was feeling. Madame Du Pont had been his first lover, at a time when he would have happily not had one at all. He had been out of his depth, and she had taken advantage of his vulnerability. Louis still resented her for that, for making him feel like something that could be bought and sold, especially for how she had passed him around between her friends. To see the woman reduced to weeping in public over him was humiliating to them both and had left him feeling profoundly disturbed. He ought never to have come out tonight. It would have been far nicer to stay in with Nic, just talking and drinking wine and making plans for the future, but Nic did not want him constantly hanging about his neck and Louis understood that.

Nic had his own life, the running of the club, whereas Louis… drifted. He had finally given in and distanced himself from the running of Rouge et Noir, though everyone knew Nic was his brother and that the two of them were inseparable. But Louis was a wealthy patron, not involved in the club's operation, as far as the world knew, and the world knew nothing about Louis other than what he wanted them to know. Sooner or later, those worlds were bound to collide, and there was a large part of him that wished it would happen at once, exploding the brittle façade he wore like armour.

"Louis?"

The soft, anxious voice had Louis stiffening and spinning around. He could defend himself as well as any young man who had fought to survive, and he was quicker and stronger than most. But he looked like a wealthy young toff, foolish enough to walk about Paris alone at night and in a less than salubrious neighbourhood. Any villain might fool themselves into believing he was an easy mark. They'd be wrong.

Louis' hand slid to the pocket where he kept a small, folded blade, just in case, but as he stared through the darkness, nothing stirred. Yet all the hairs on the back of his neck had stood on end and he did not drop his guard.

"Louis, it is you!" exclaimed a wondering voice, and Louis' breath caught as a young man slid out from the shadows and stepped out into the moonlight.

Louis stared, certain he must be mistaken. It could not possibly be... and yet the resemblance was unmistakable. He was older, of course he was older, and his clothes were shabby and worn, hanging off him as if he'd lost weight recently.

"Etienne?" he said, his heart picking up.

"Louis!"

To Louis' shock and consternation, Etienne flung himself at Louis and hugged him tightly.

"Oh! You do not know how happy I am to see you. Mon Dieu, Louis, I have been so afraid. I was at my wits' end. I thought I would die in Paris, alone and forgotten and..." Etienne scrubbed at his eyes, which were wet with tears, and stared at Louis. "But look at you. You... My word, Louis, you really are the Vicomte Sainte-Apre, aren't you?" he said in wonder, as if he truly had not believed it before now.

Louis pulled away, out from Etienne's grip.

"Non. My father is dead. I am Louis César de Montluc, Comte de Villen." Louis replied in his haughtiest voice, retreating behind the façade he had built for himself as his past collided with his present just as he had feared. His head was spinning, his heart racing. If Etienne was here, was his father here? Did he know Louis was here and had taken his rightful place in the world?

Etienne whistled, staring at Louis with undisguised admiration.

"Oh, my father would have an apoplexy if he could see you now," Etienne said gleefully. "The old bastard would shrivel up and die."

"Where is he?" Louis demanded, fighting the urge to look about himself and search the shadows in case the monster crept up on him unawares.

Etienne snorted. "Oh, still mouldering back in Périgueux. I ran away," he said proudly, which might have been more impressive if he was not a man of one and twenty.

Louis relaxed a fraction at that information. "Why?"

Etienne shrugged and rubbed the back of his neck, turning in a circle and staring, wide-eyed, about him as if he was not entirely sure how he'd come to be there. "It was bad after you left, Louis," he whispered, glancing at Louis and then back at the street again. "Père, he... he was so angry. So angry," he said again, frowning, as if he was speaking to himself.

"What did he do?" Louis asked uneasily. Though he did not like or trust Etienne, the boy had been as much a victim as Louis in his own way. What chance had he to become a decent human being with such people for parents? Louis had never seen them show anything resembling love or affection for their son, or for anyone or anything, even for each other. It had been a house entirely devoid of love or any kindness.

Etienne gave a nervous laugh and dragged a hand through his hair, apparently forgetting he wore a hat as it tumbled to the floor. He stared at it in surprise for a moment before snatching it up again.

"Oh, he... he was very angry," he said again. "But I don't want to talk about him. Louis, we're free! Both of us. We're free of him, and Maman too, the spiteful bitch. Oh, my Lord. I am so, so happy to see you. I... I don't suppose you would help me. Please, Louis? I've run out of money. My rooms are paid for until the end of the week, but I haven't eaten since... the day before yesterday, I think. I'm starving."

Louis bit back the urge to remind Etienne that he had often gone longer than that without eating under his parents' roof, but

Etienne's eyes were shining with such relief and happiness that he didn't have the heart.

"I'll buy you supper," he said with a nod, before taking hold of Etienne's arm and squeezing hard. Though Etienne was still taller and broader than Louis, there was little muscle under his grip. "But listen to me, Etienne. If I help you, it's on one condition. You never, never tell your father you found me. Do you hear?"

Etienne looked at him like he'd run mad. "Whyever would I tell him? I spent my entire life wanting to be free of the old bastard. I was never good enough for him and after you left, he… Louis, I won't. I wouldn't. Word of honour."

Louis searched his gaze and saw nothing but sincerity, so he nodded. "All right then. Come along. Let's get you something to eat."

15th June 1830, Casino Rouge et Noir, 7th Arrondissement, Paris, France.

One year later…

Louis is eighteen.

Louis watched the floor of Rouge et Noir, and especially the place where Etienne was laughing uproariously with two beautiful courtesans. He was obviously drunk and gesticulating madly, waving a cigar about as he illustrated some point he was trying to make. Those damned cigars were an affectation that Etienne had adopted the moment Louis had begun paying his way. They cost a fortune, a special blend of tobacco of Etienne's devising that he seemed to have chosen with the express purpose of making Louis ill. He could not abide the smell of them. Louis studied the man dispassionately. Etienne looked at once far better than he had a year ago, and far worse.

Thanks to Louis, he was dressed like a gentleman, and yet his skin was sallow, his eyes holding a glint which bothered Louis more than he liked to admit. That Etienne had become an opium addict was only a part of the problem. Louis turned as Nic appeared at his side, glowering down at Etienne from their position on the balcony.

"I know," Louis said with a sigh of frustration. "But what am I to do?"

"Stop paying for him. He's taking the piss, Louis. He spends half of what you give him on opium and the rest he loses here."

"Well, at least it comes back to us," Louis said with a snort.

Nic shook his head. "You pay for his entire existence, from what I can see. His lodgings, his clothes, the food he eats. The bastard is nothing more than a parasite and you need to deal with him. No one likes him unless he's buying them drinks. He's overbearing and obnoxious, and I wouldn't trust him father than I could throw him."

Louis groaned. "I know, I just feel sorry for him. Besides, if I ditch him, he'll tattle to his bloody father."

"So what? You're not a boy anymore, Louis. He can't touch you. You're the Comte de Villen, for heaven's sake, and you've fought bigger and angrier men in your time, I know. By the way, I hear Monsieur De Lancey is looking a little the worse for wear?"

"Oh, for heaven's sake," Louis said in disgust. "The man is an imbecile, not to mention cruel. He has not touched his wife in five years. Five! He barely acknowledges her existence, and then he beats her black and blue for taking a lover. No one even knew until he made such a damned fuss about it. It was not to be borne, Nic. Truly. He deserved it."

"So why care if that miserable bastard, Boucher, turns up? If he does, either you or I will teach him what a mistake he's made."

Louis hesitated, wondering how to explain Monsieur Boucher was not an ordinary man, that he had taken root in Louis' mind in the shape of a monster that haunted his dreams, but that sounded so preposterous he could not bring himself to say anything of the sort. So instead, he shrugged.

"I don't know. Of course, you are right, Nic. I'll deal with it."

"See that you do."

"Etienne, it's time to go. You're drunk," Louis said, taking the man's arm and hauling him up.

Those around him at the club shot Louis glances of gratitude, as Etienne was becoming loud and belligerent and his manners, which were provincial at best, were increasingly worse when in his cups. Rouge et Noir was a success for many reasons, but in no small part because it was a place where the highest in society could rub shoulders with those from all walks of life—providing they could afford to. But Etienne lacked the necessary charm to get by when his ignorance of polite society's rules failed him.

"No, Louis! I don't want to go. Come… have a drink with me. Champagne! I'll buy us some champagne," he insisted, apparently oblivious to the fact Louis paid all his bills. He clamped the cigar between his teeth and tried to gain the attention of a server. "You. Boy, a bottle of your best champagne at once."

Louis shook his head at the young man, who melted into the crowd.

"Come, Etienne, you're making a scene. I'll walk you out."

Etienne got to his feet, grumbling but aware he could not wriggle out of Louis' grasp. Louis guided him out of the crowded room and towards the staff exit, propelling Etienne through the dim corridors towards the back of the club and the yard beyond.

"Let's go upstairs and play cards," Etienne said, blithely unaware of the fact Louis wanted him out of the building and as far away from him as possible.

"Not tonight," Louis said firmly. "You need to go home and sleep it off."

"Oh, but Louis, you're so dull these days. Come out and have some fun with me. Do you remember when we were boys? We had fun then. Such friends we were."

Louis stared at him, wondering if there really was something wrong with the man. Still, he did not want to fight with Etienne, especially not with him in this mood. He never had trusted him, and nothing had changed.

"We were friends, weren't we? Until that... that boy..."

Suddenly, Etienne stopped in his tracks and turned, pushing Louis with surprising force until he pinned him against the wall. Louis reacted instinctively, pushing him back. Etienne stumbled away a few paces and Louis stared at him warily, pointing a warning finger.

"Non," he said, shaking his head. "You're drunk, Etienne. Go home."

Etienne's face darkened. He pointed at Louis, the cigar in his hand trailing a thin line of pale smoke. "You always were a tease. You just want everyone to want you, don't you, Louis? And when they do, you toss them aside."

Louis stiffened. "That's a lie."

"Non," Etienne shook his head. "My father is a bastard, but he was right about you. You use your looks to get what you want. The devil made you look like that, to tempt the innocent into sin. You are the serpent in the garden of Eden. Just look at me. Look what you did to me, Louis." He made a sweeping gesture and laughed, the sound raising all the hairs on the back of Louis' neck.

"I did nothing to you," Louis insisted, and yet wasn't there some truth in what Etienne said?

"You did. You made me into this... you made me love you when I didn't want to. It's wrong, Louis... I...." Etienne's face *crumpled, and he began to cry, great heaving sobs that echoed through the narrow corridor.*

Louis looked about him in case anyone could overhear them, but the corridor was empty. Etienne sobbed harder and Louis did not know what to do. Etienne's words profoundly disturbed him, but he could not help but pity him.

"I do not believe love is ever wrong, Etienne. God knows there's little enough of it in the world, but I do not feel this way for you. I am sorry."

Etienne stopped crying abruptly and stared at Louis, his gaze hard and ice cold. "Perhaps if you were not so beautiful, it would break the spell," he mused, his gaze moving to the cigar in his hand. He turned it this way and that and then raised it to his mouth, taking a slow draw that made the end glow red in the dim light of the corridor. He let out a long stream of smoke and then advanced on Louis.

"It's for the best, Louis. Someone needs to bring you in line, someone must spoil all that perfection so you cannot hurt anyone else."

Louis' heart skipped as Etienne lunged forward, holding the cigar as a brand. Louis knocked Etienne's hand aside with ease and he saw the cigar hit the floor with a shower of red sparks. Etienne gave a roar of fury and shoved Louis hard, catching him off guard. Louis stumbled, his head smacking against the stone wall behind him.

Cursing, Louis clutched at his head, momentarily dazed and unprepared, when Etienne snarled and lunged at him again.

"Diable!" he growled, pinning Louis down as he pressed his mouth against Louis'.

Louis' senses revolted: Etienne's grasping hands and the scent of cigars sickened him. The feeling of being restrained sent his mind reeling back in time and panic rose inside him as Etienne's wet mouth, tasting of ash, worked against his. Louis raised his

Emma V Leech

knee, hard, and Etienne gasped, falling back and clutching at his balls.

"Touch me again, and I will kill you," Louis said, breathing hard, wiping his mouth on his sleeve in disgust. He stepped forward and ground the heel of his boot against the cigar, trying not to choke as the acrid smoke filled the narrow corridor. "Get out, Etienne. You'll not get another sou from me, so I suggest you find another way to survive. I don't want to see you again. You're not welcome here."

Louis stalked away, more than relieved when the door at the end of the corridor opened, and his brother appeared.

"Nic," he said, hurrying forward.

"Louis? What happened?" Nic grasped Louis' shoulders. "You're white as a sheet."

Louis shook his head and gestured behind him. "Get someone down here to deal with Etienne. He's leaving, and he's not coming back."

Nic gave a satisfied nod and patted Louis on the back. "At once, brother. Come along. You look like you need a drink."

Chapter 18

Dearest Prue,

We arrived safely in France this morning. Please don't worry. I'll have Agatha and Fred back before you know it. They're both intelligent children, if reckless. I admit I am torn between shaking Fred until his teeth rattle and telling him how very proud I am of him for going after Agatha as he has. Of course, if he had confided in me, we might have saved all the dramatics, but boys do love a heroic adventure. I hope he is enjoying himself, for he won't be leaving Beverwyck again until he's thirty.

Kisses to you, my love.

—Excerpt of a letter from Robert Adolphus, The Duke of Bedwin to his wife, Prunella Adolphus, Duchess of Bedwin.

22nd July 1842, Rue de la Bièvre, 13th Arrondissement, Paris, France.

"But I want to see the club," Evie protested, pushing Louis' hands away as he tried to distract her. He was exceedingly good at distracting her, but this time she was digging her heels in. They had spent the entire day in bed, which had been quite delicious, but the temptation to see Rouge et Noir for herself was niggling at her. She had heard so much about it, now she needed to see it with her own eyes. "Just for a little while."

Louis made a sound of amusement and reclined back against the pillows with a sigh. "You just enjoy rejecting me and making me feel sorry for myself, and don't give me that. Once inside the club, I'll have the devil's own job getting you to leave before dawn, I know."

"Rejecting you," Evie repeated with a snort of outrage. "I'd like to know when exactly I've done that since we married."

"Why, this very moment," Louis replied, tucking his arm behind his head, and watching her steadily.

Evie could not help but stare. He was quite naked and seemed to be as much at ease in that state as he was when fully dressed, and why not? She could stare at him all day and never grow tired of looking at his long, elegant limbs, and the musculature of a man who had worked his body hard all his life. Quite simply, he was glorious to behold. He had consigned the covers to a tangled heap at the bottom of the bed, refusing to let Evie cover herself up, either. At the first sign of her self-consciousness or uncertainty, he showed her in no uncertain terms just how beautiful he thought her. Evie had really no choice but to believe him now and, for the first time in her life, was perfectly comfortable with her own generous curves. After all, if a man like Louis looked at her with such undisguised lust in his eyes, why on earth should she have the least doubt that it was true? Just because some might not judge her beautiful by whatever warped standards they held, did not make them right.

"If you are going to look at me like that, you really ought to do something about it, *mon amour.*"

He looked dreadfully smug, knowing full well she was aching with desire all over again, and Evie opened her mouth to tell him he was a wicked devil, before stopping herself. He did not like being called that, she realised, even when spoken in jest. She knew why now, and understood how people had tried to use his own beauty against him, by telling him it was something to be ashamed of, by undermining everything else he was until he believed it was the only thing people valued in him. He was wrong, of course, he was so much more than that, as Agatha and Mr Godwin and so many other people would tell him given the chance. He was kind, and generous with his time, and always ready to offer help someone who needed it. Just as he had made her see her own value, her own beauty, she determined that she must do the same for him.

So instead, she lay down beside him and opened her arms to him. He moved at once, covering her with his body and burying his face in her neck.

"You smell divine," he murmured, inhaling and nuzzling the tender skin beneath her ear.

Evie giggled as he nipped at her ear. "I love you, Louis. You have made me very happy."

He stilled and stared down at her, looking absurdly pleased with himself. "I shall never tire of hearing you say that."

A sharp knock at the door made him curse. *"Allez-vous en!"* he yelled crossly.

"Louis, I'm sorry, I swear," responded a deep voice from outside.

"Wolf?" Louis said furiously. "Go away!"

"I would, I swear, but… I think you need to come down."

"What the hell for?"

"Ummm. Well, there's a fellow here by the name of Godwin and he's with a boy who insists he's your daughter."

"Barnaby? A boy…? My *daughter… Mère de Dieu!"* Louis leapt out of bed and began snatching at his clothes.

Evie followed him, running about and trying to find her stockings and shift. "Louis, do you think that—"

"Oui," he said grimly, tugging on his trousers. "I very much do think, and I am going to murder her."

Louis hurried down the stairs, Evie's hand clasped tightly in his as they made their way to Wolf's office. He burst through the door, but had barely a moment before a small figure flew across the room and flung itself at him, holding on tight. The force of the embrace—or attack, he was not yet quite certain—made him take a step backwards to steady himself.

"Monsieur!" sobbed a tight voice from somewhere in the vicinity of his waistcoat.

Louis got to his knees and stared into the face of his ward. "Aggie," he said, all the air leaving his lungs in a rush as he considered what might have befallen her, alone in a city like Paris. Except she wasn't alone. Louis looked up at Barnaby, who gave him an uncertain smile.

"She turned up outside my hotel this morning," Barnaby said, his gaze travelling between Louis and Evie and Wolf. "Followed me all the way from London, it seems, not that I realised," he added hastily.

Louis muttered an oath and looked down at his ward. "I think you have a great deal of explaining to do, *mon enfant,"* he said quietly.

"I do?" Agatha said, pushing out of his embrace and stamping her foot. "How could you! How could you run away and leave me?"

"Aggie!" Louis said reproachfully. "I did not run away for good, you foolish creature. As if I would leave you behind. Surely you know me better than that? If you had only waited, you would have received my letter explaining."

Aggie sniffed and wiped angrily at her eyes. "I w-was so worried about you. Everyone was saying such h-horrid things and I couldn't stand it. I knew it wasn't true, so I came after you. I was so f-frightened you were in trouble."

Louis pulled her back into a hug. "Aggie, *ma puce.* Don't upset yourself so. And here was I thinking you were safe at school with your friends, or I too would have been out of my mind." Louis shook his head and sighed, taking the cap from Aggie's head as it was listing alarmingly to one side. His eyes widened in shock. "What did you do to your hair?" he demanded, regarding the shock of short dark curls which had been down past her waist when he had last seen her.

"Cut it off," Aggie said defiantly, folding her arms. "I couldn't be a boy with long hair, could I?"

Louis bit back his dismay at the loss of her lovely hair, aware of the way her lip was trembling. She had done this for him. She had cut off her hair and set off on a perilous journey alone, all for him. So, instead, he looked at her anew. The short style rather suited her elfin features and the stubborn set of her up-tilted nose. "It's very becoming, *mon enfant.* I like it."

"Y-You do?"

"I do. Very much. Now, I think you must be tired and hungry."

"I am rather," Aggie admitted, looking suddenly younger than her thirteen years and so fragile Louis could not help but hug her again. *Dieu Merci.* Thank God she was safe.

He kissed the tumble of curls on top of her head and looked around at Evie, who was watching proceedings with a misty-eyed look that made Louis feel dreadfully exposed.

"Alors, you had better go with my wife and see if she can find you something to eat."

"Your...?" Aggie said, before giving a squeal of delight and attaching herself to Evie like a limpet. "How splendid! Oh, I'm so happy. I knew you loved him. I just knew you did!"

Evie laughed and hugged Aggie back and suddenly Louis' throat was tight.

"I did indeed, how clever of you to have realised. Now come along with me. Madame Moulin will find you something delicious, and then we'll arrange a bath and an early bed, for I'm certain you must be worn out after your adventures."

Louis got to his feet and darted a look at Wolf, who had been watching the proceedings with interest.

"Still picking up waifs and strays, then," he said, giving Louis a wide smile.

"She tried to pick my pocket," Louis retorted indignantly. "And her skills were lamentably poor. What else could I do? I tried to train her, but—"

"But by then you were fond of her and didn't want to let her live on the streets," Wolf guessed.

Louis sighed. "Something like that, but would you give us a little privacy now, please? I have a feeling my dear friend Mr Godwin here has a few things to say to me."

Wolf glowered and shot a look at Barnaby, who put his chin up. "You see? I *told* you. He's my friend," Barnaby retorted, crossing his arms, an irritated look in eyes which rather impressed Louis, considering Wolf was... well, Wolf, and not a little intimidating.

Wolf made a growling sound that seemed to imply discontent, but went out and shut the door behind him.

Louis rubbed the back of his neck, feeling awkward. "I'm so sorry, Barnaby," he began, a little startled when the man crossed the room and embraced him.

"Thank God," Barnaby said with feeling, before abruptly letting Louis go and folding his arms again. "I'm really a little vexed with you, old chap."

Louis laughed and held Barnaby by the shoulders, kissing him soundly on both cheeks. "Only a little? *Mon ami*, you are well within your rights to be exceedingly vexed, but let us have a drink and you can reprimand me to your heart's content."

Barnaby sighed and nodded. "A drink would be welcome, and… and you *are* married?"

"Oui," Louis replied, unable to keep the pride and happiness from his voice. "I am."

"I am glad of it," Barnaby said, accepting the glass of cognac Louis poured for him. "But why did you run off like you did? You've caused one hell of a stir, I don't mind telling you."

Louis grimaced. He had not wanted to allow the real world to intrude just yet, but he had known it was inevitable. "I can imagine, and I *may* have behaved rather selfishly, but I cannot pretend that I regret it."

"I should say not, if Evie is happy with the arrangement."

Louis snorted. "Ah, she was not to begin with, let me assure you, but sit down, Barnaby, and I shall tell you what happened."

By the time Louis had explained himself and Evie and Madame Moulin had arranged suitable accommodations for their guests, it was growing late. Louis said goodnight to Aggie and Barnaby, both of whom looked in need of a good night's sleep and was looking forward to returning to bed with his wife, when Elton arrived on the doorstep.

His poor valet appeared worn to a thread after the trials of his journey, but his eyes lit with relief when he saw Louis. "Oh, monsieur, I was that worried. Is all well with you? The young lady—"

"The young lady is my wife," Louis said, smiling at Elton and shaking his hand warmly. "I fear I have caused you a deal of distress, and for that, I am truly sorry. I am beside myself with delight to see you, though. You would not believe the tedious amount of second-rate shaves I have endured in your absence, not to mention my boots."

Elton's gaze flew to the offending items, and he gasped. *"Monsieur!"* he said, his voice heavy with reproach.

"Forgive me, Elton, I am a mess without you," Louis said with a sigh, knowing that this was the swiftest way to soothe any ruffled feathers Elton had suffered to get here. "Though I did not need the proof, I know now that you are a prince among valets, for I have had the evidence impressed upon me forcibly these past days. Welcome back, *mon ami.*"

Louis embraced him and kissed him on both cheeks, causing Elton to blush scarlet. Flustered but pleased, Elton bustled off, intent on seeing to his master's wardrobe with no trace of his earlier weariness in evidence.

"You are such a peacock," Wolf muttered, shaking his head.

Louis shrugged. "We all have our little indulgences, Elton is mine. Besides which, he truly is the most loyal and good-hearted of men. I was lucky to find him."

"Well, I think your luck might have run out," Wolf said, a glint in his eyes.

Louis groaned. "What now?" he demanded, aggrieved.

"Come with me," Wolf said, waiting until Louis had followed him back into the office and closed the door. "Your wife's father is in Paris, throwing his considerable weight around and demanding to see you."

Louis muttered an oath. "*Merde*. Not that I didn't expect it. He's been to the club?"

"Naturally, though Jacques didn't let him in. No one is speaking to him, of course, they know better. He'll not track you back here, but your new wife might not be happy if she discovers her darling papa is on her doorstep, and you didn't tell her."

"Well, I wouldn't have to know if you hadn't told me," Louis retorted irritably.

"Oh, so I'm to keep such things to myself now?" Wolf said, folding his arms.

"Oh, stop looking all wounded," Louis said, rolling his eyes. "I can have more than one friend, you know. Barnaby has been kind and loyal, a far better friend than I deserved. Be nice to him, Wolf."

Wolf's expression darkened. "And so you'll all go off back to England, you and your wife and your friend, and your adopted daughter—that you never mentioned—and what? You all live happily ever after and I get to stay here and keep everything running for you?"

Louis took a breath and tried to hold on to his patience. "Wolf, I have never demanded you do anything of the sort. You took over the business, you made this life for yourself, I thought you were happy? Are you telling me that you're not?"

Wolf glowered at him from under thick, dark brows. "You said if I came to England, you'd kill me," he said, the reproach in his voice perfectly audible.

"*Non.* Only if you messed things up with Evie," Louis amended. "And now I am married you are at liberty to come with us too, if that is what you wish. Indeed, I will welcome you, you know that, but you also know what kind of reception you're going to receive. It won't be pretty."

Wolf sat down in the chair behind his desk, put his head in his hands and sighed, and the weariness and sorrow of that sound struck at Louis' heart.

"Can you miss something you've never had?" Wolf asked him, an uncertain note to his voice that Louis recognised too well.

He, after all, was not the only one who played a part, who knew how to hide behind a mask. If the men who lived in fear of Wolf's anger knew the real man, Wolf might not have lived this long.

"Oui, certainly you can," Louis said, taking a step closer to the desk and studying his oldest friend.

Wolf glanced up at Louis, a look in his eyes that was at once defiant and sheepish. "Well, in that case… Louis, I want to go home."

Chapter 19

Dear Lord Montagu,

Sultan is really most terribly sorry for the dreadful incident yesterday morning, as am I. It was an embarrassing breach of etiquette on his part, and I promise you I was never more mortified. Please let me assure you, I will pay for any damage caused by his appalling behaviour…

—Excerpt of a letter from Lady Cara Baxter (daughter of Luke and Kitty Baxter Earl and Countess of Trevick) to The Most Hon'ble Lucian Barrington, Marquess of Montagu.

20th April 1831, close to Pont des Invalides, 7th Arrondissement, Paris, France.

Louis is nineteen.

Louis stepped down to the street and closed the door on the elegant carriage and smiled as the woman on the other side of the window blew him a kiss. The carriage had deposited him some way from home, but it would not do for Monsieur le Duc to catch wind of the affair with his wife. Not that the duc was interested in his wife, being far too occupied with debauching every opera dancer and ballerina in Paris. Nonetheless, the duc would represent a *formidable enemy and, whilst Louis' position was becoming one of increasing power, it did not do to take such things for granted. So, discretion was all.*

With that in mind, Louis chose the path that ran beside the river towards Pont des Invalides despite the chill wind that whipped over the water and snatched at his coat. Walking along the silent path had his instincts prickling and Louis glanced over his shoulder. Strange parcels had begun arriving for him at Rouge et Noir only days after the altercation with Etienne last summer. From cheap religious icons to dead rats, with each month that passed, the parcels had become increasingly disturbing. The one that had arrived this morning had contained a live adder. The poor creature had clearly been deeply unhappy at its incarceration and Louis had narrowly avoided getting bitten. Inside, written in Etienne's familiar, clumsy hand, was a note:

'Diable, mauvais esprit, démon, serpent dans le Jardin d'eden'. The devil sent you from hell to tempt the innocent to sin. Someone must act before you tarnish everything you touch. Someone must cut the head off the snake and save you from yourself. Let me help you, Louis.

Louis had burned the note, though it had taken him an hour to get the damned snake back in the box so he could release it outside, somewhere no one would get bitten. He had hidden it from his brother, though Nic knew as well as he did Etienne was sick, not right in the head. Louis had not realised just how sick until now. And yet he had not told Nic, and he was horribly aware that it was because he feared there might be some truth in the words. He told himself that was stupid, that he did not believe in the devil any more than he believed in God—not any longer. Yet his stomach turned and something like fear stirred in his heart as those damned words circled around and around, and though Etienne had written them, he heard them spoken as he had always heard them, in Monsieur Boucher's deep voice.

The wind picked up and Louis shivered, though it was not the cold alone making his flesh creep.

As he grew closer to the bridge, he became aware of an altercation in progress. Not that such things were uncommon at this hour of the night, and certainly not in such a place, but the sound of a young woman in distress was not something he could turn a blind eye to. Silently, he crept closer to gauge what exactly was going on before he decided what to do.

A powerfully built man, who had his back to Louis, was dragging a young woman—little more than a girl—in his wake. She was crying and struggling to get free as a boy berated the man in English, pleading for him to let the girl go.

"Please, please. Don't take her back there," the boy said, trying to intervene and getting a casual backhander that sent him sprawling across the ground. Louis had to admire the lad's courage, for the man was far bigger and stronger and the boy tall but scrawny, no more than fifteen. "No! I won't let you. She doesn't want to go back to your damned whorehouse. You lied to her about everything, she didn't know what kind of place it was."

"Shut your mouth, boy," the man groused, but otherwise took no more notice of the boy's distress than he might an annoying blue bottle.

"S'il vous plaît, non, non," the girl cried, tugging against the man's cruel grip on her wrist.

Though he knew in the pit of his belly, this would not end well, Louis could not leave the girl nor her courageous protector to their fate. He remembered all too well what it felt like to be pushed about by someone bigger and stronger and he could not walk away now.

"What is going on here?" he demanded in English, keeping to the shadows.

The tableau stilled, all eyes swivelling in his direction, and Louis was glad for the obscurity of the darkness beneath the bridge as moonlight hit the man's face. His stomach lurched as he recognised at once the man who had come to the Bouchers' household with the hard-faced woman. His cruel features had been indelibly printed upon Louis's mind, and there was no doubt that it was him. This was the man who would have made a whore of him. And now he was trying to do it to this poor girl.

"Let her go," Louis said, his tone implacable.

"I don't think I shall," the man snarled in response. "Go about your business, boy, or you'll find yourself in more trouble than you are ready for."

"Ah, but I am no longer a boy Mr — Forgive me, we were never properly introduced." Louis stepped out of the shadows and into the moonlight. The man gasped and let go of the girl in shock.

"You!" he exclaimed, his expression so stunned it might have been funny if the circumstances were different.

"Run," Louis told the two hapless children, who were staring at him in astonishment. They didn't move. "Run!" he shouted in frustration.

The girl did as he bid, dashing away into the darkness, but the boy put up his chin, and shook his head.

Louis tsked impatiently but could spare the boy no more attention as the man before him was moving closer.

"Well, well, and after all this time, my beautiful Louis César. You caused me a good deal of trouble, young man, not to mention expense. Quite aside from that, I was so very, very disappointed."

"It appears you got over it," Louis replied, never taking his eyes from the man.

"Ah, but I never did. I have searched for you for so very long. I paid Monsieur Boucher a great deal of money for you, and the fool had already spent it all when I came back to discover you gone. I was forced to make him work for me. An unhappy arrangement on all sides, you understand."

"I can imagine," Louis replied dryly, aware of the boy following too close to the man, as if he could stop him from hurting Louis any more than he'd been able to protect the girl.

"Still, all is well that ends well. I have lost the girl, but now I have you instead."

Louis snorted. "Oh, I am afraid you are mistaken there."

"I think not," the man said, removing a wickedly long blade from inside his coat. The knife glinted in the moonlight and Louis' heart skipped, but he was too angry to be as afraid as he ought, too focused on vengeance to walk away. The idea of letting this man go free so he could prey on others who were too weak, too vulnerable to defend themselves was not one he could live with.

"I think it is high time we got better acquainted," the fiend said, as if they were having a normal conversation. "For now, you may call me Charles. We shall leave proper introductions until you are feeling a little more… friendly."

The man called Charles walked towards Louis, his face set and before Louis could react, the boy ran forward, lunging at the man, tugging at the arm holding the knife. The man growled with annoyance and elbowed the boy in the face before turning to him. "Don't interfere, you spineless little sod, or you'll take his place. Do you want that, eh, boy? You want to service the clients on your knees?"

"No, but you can't take him either, you can't! Leave him alone, you brute!" the boy insisted, scrambling to his feet and, with more courage than sense, launching himself at the man again. Louis could see the flash of the knife as the unequal struggle ended with the boy crashing to the ground and the man hitting him so hard Louis heard the crunch of bone. The boy whimpered as the man raised his hand again.

"You bastard," Louis growled and stopped the fist before it could make contact, pushing Charles off balance. "Leave him alone."

Charles only sneered and strode back, delivering a kick to the boy's head that made him go still. Louis stared in shock, appalled by the casual brutality of it, but there was no time to worry about the boy as Charles lashed out with the knife, swinging wildly. Louis leapt away, keeping out of reach, dragging the man farther from the boy in the dim hope he still lived. He lunged again and Louis kicked the arm that held the knife and heard the metal clatter as it hit the ground. The man only chuckled and reached out to take hold of Louis, who dodged and threw a punch that made Charles stagger. He stopped, touching his jaw and testing his teeth with his tongue. Charles spat blood on the ground, regarding Louis through narrowed eyes.

"Well, you've got a bit of fight in you, I'll give you that."

"You have no idea," Louis snarled, circling the man warily. It was not an even match on the face of it. This man outweighed him by almost double, and he was clearly not averse to violence, but Louis was young and fit and quick, and he was relying on that to keep him alive.

"Come now, Louis," Charles said, coaxing now. "You know this is a fight you cannot win. Why, you are just a boy still. Perhaps in a few years, when you have filled out a little more, but why spoil that pretty face or risk doing yourself damage? Come along with me now and I'll take such good care of you."

"In your dreams," Louis replied, revolted.

Charles shrugged. "Ah, well, some people like scars, though it pains me to hurt you, boy. I swear it does, but you'll come with me whole or a little cut up. That, or you die. That is your choice for you'll not slip through my fingers again."

Louis' heart skipped, but he refused to contemplate losing to this brute. He had outmanoeuvred this devil last time, and he would do it again. "Come on then, old man," he taunted. "Come and get me."

Charles lunged again, missing Louis by a mile as Louis laughed and dodged behind and to the side, delivering a blow to his kidneys that made Charles stagger. Anger flashed in the man's eyes, and he tried again, grazing Louis' jaw with his fist, and then stumbling away as Louis tripped him. With a growl, he straightened and circled around to where the knife had fallen, snatching it up again.

Louis eyed the boy as they circled each other, wondering sickly if he were dead. He was so very still. Rage filled him for the young man who had been trying to protect the girl, to protect Louis—a man he didn't even know, and putting his own life in danger to do so. He was so damned tired of seeing this, of seeing the weak trodden down by the powerful. Someone had to do something. He had to do something.

A pained moan emanated from the injured boy, momentarily distracting Louis, enough for Charles to lunge and grapple with him, putting the knife to his throat. Louis slammed his elbow into the man's thick gut and heard Charles gasp. The arm holding the knife fell away from his throat and Louis threw his head back, biting back a curse of pain as he smashed against the man's nose. Charles staggered back and dropped the knife, but then lunged again, using his weight to take Louis to the ground. They fell heavily, with Charles crashing down on Louis and knocking the breath from his lungs.

What happened next was a blur of fists and then Charles' hands were about Louis' throat, squeezing and squeezing. Louis struggled, lights dancing behind his eyes, his lungs burning. "The knife," said a shaky, desperate voice alongside the sound of metal skittering over cobbles. "The knife, reach out your right hand."

Panic surged through his body and with dizzy certainty that he was going to pass out at any moment, Louis reached out his hand, searching the damp cobbles until… yes, the blade. With fingers that did not seem to work as competently as usual, Louis' hand grasped the hilt of the knife and plunged it deep into the man's side.

Everything stopped except the sound of Louis' heart thudding in his ears. Charles' eyes widened. He gazed down at Louis with undisguised shock. The hands about Louis' neck slackened as Charles sat back, staring indignantly at the knife sticking out of his side.

"You killed me," he said in wonder, and then gasped, clutching at his chest fighting for breath, his eyes growing wide as he struggled, clawing at his throat now. Louis pushed at him, scrambling out from under the man's weight as Charles fell sideways, dead, his head hitting the cobbles with an unpleasant crack. Louis stumbled away, breathing hard, staring at the man whose eyes looked out at nothing, glassy and surprised as his blood pooled like thick black ink between the cobblestones.

"Putain," Louis said, staring down at his hands. They were shaking badly, and blood... oh, God. There was blood on his hands.

"Monsieur! Monsieur..."

The boy crawled over to Louis, blood streaming from his nose and from a wound on his head. Louis swallowed down a wave of nausea as the sight and smell of blood all around him and the knowledge of what he had done made his stomach churn.

"Are you hurt?" the boy demanded, and Louis stared at him incredulously, this boy who had tried so bravely to help, who had nearly died.

Louis shook his head. "No," he rasped, discovering as he tried to speak that his throat hurt, the feel of the man's hands still tight about his neck. "Quick, help me. Before someone comes."

Between them, they dragged the body to the river's edge. The water below slid past, thick and black, the Seine swollen and angry after a wet winter and a wetter spring.

"Wait," the boy said, and Louis halted as the boy tugged a gold signet ring from the man's finger. "It's mine," he said defiantly, staring up at Louis as though Louis might judge him for it.

"Take what you want," Louis replied, not about to do anything of the kind.

"The ring belongs in the family," the boy said, tucking it into his pocket.

Louis shook his head impatiently. "Child, you cannot give that ring to the family without implicating yourself in his death. Pawn it if you will, but go to the other side of Paris and hide your face when you do so."

The boy gave a mirthless laugh as they heaved the body into the water. It fell with a splash but was quickly dragged away, disappearing beneath the inky surface.

"I was his family, monsieur. I'm all the family he had," the boy said, staring out at the river, though Louis was uncertain he saw it, his expression was so bleak and unfocused.

Louis went cold, staring at the boy in shock. "What do you mean by that? Who was he?"

"My father," the boy whispered, as his eyes rolled up and he fell to the ground.

Louis stared at him, too numb, too horrified to react.

"Monsieur, s'il vous plaît!"

Louis spun around, appalled to see the girl had returned. She stood dithering on the spot, staring about them. Putain, she must have seen what Louis had done.

"You must leave. Now! Before anyone else sees you here," she pleaded.

Louis nodded, forcing himself to move. Somehow, he got the boy over his shoulder, discovering he was remarkably heavy despite his skinny frame, and carried him away. The girl followed, trotting meekly at his heels like a lamb. Though later, he did not remember how he did it, or even what streets he took, he made his way back to the fortress, entering through one of the secret tunnels that ran below the thick walls of the ancient chateau, so nobody saw them.

Running on instinct, Louis stripped off his blood-soaked clothes and burned them, washing and dressing at speed, whilst the girl cleaned up the dazed young man as best she could. As soon as they were reasonably respectable—though the boy's face was a mess—Louis had them moving again, back out of the tunnels, heading for Rouge et Noir.

"What's your name?" he asked the girl, who was all enormous eyes and was trembling hard now.

"Margot Allard, Monsieur le Comte," she said, her voice quaking.

"You know who I am?"

She nodded. "Oui, my brother works at Rouge et Noir, in the kitchens. He is very proud, monsieur. He says it is a good job, and he is well treated."

"Would you like a job there too, Mademoiselle Allard?" Louis asked, uncertain of whether the girl would cause him trouble in the future. She had plenty with which to blackmail him if she chose. He pushed the thought away, choosing to believe she would not do such a thing, though experience told him he was naïve. Either way, the girl needed help, and having her close would be the best way of keeping an eye on her.

She blinked at him, hurrying to keep up as they strode through the dark streets, keeping to the shadows.

"Truly?" she asked in wonder. "You would give me a job?"

"If you want one."

Her eyes filled with tears and though they walked at quite a pace, she grabbed Louis's hand and raised it to her lips. "You are the very best of men, monsieur. You have saved my life twice over this night."

"I'm reasonably certain good men do not commit murder," he muttered and waved this away, uncomfortable with the adulation shining in her eyes. "Just keep your mouth shut about everything you saw this night, and perhaps we shall all escape unscathed."

Margot nodded and followed him unquestioningly as the three of them made their way to the Casino.

At Rouge et Noir, Louis went straight to his rooms and poured himself a large drink, handing another to the young man and offering one to the girl. She shook her head and sat down only when Louis insisted, her posture stiff with uncertainty, staring around his lavishly furnished rooms with wide eyes.

Once Louis had downed enough cognac to steady his nerves, he rang the bell to call for a servant. A young man appeared a moment later and Louis asked for the man to fetch his brother, and the three people he trusted most on the staff at Rouge et Noir.

Nic arrived shortly after with Jacques and Alan, the two men in charge of security at the club and Madame Fournier, who acted as housekeeper for Louis and his brother.

Nic took one look at Louis and strode into the room. "What is it? What's happened?"

"I do not wish to speak of it at present, Nic. I only need you all to listen. If anybody asks you, Mademoiselle Allard here arrived late this afternoon to apply for a job at the club and was immediately engaged. She worked the night shift and has only just finished. Jacques, you will escort Mademoiselle home now and ensure she has all that she needs."

No one questioned him, which was a relief, though Louis knew Nic was going to demand answers the minute the girl had gone. Jacques simply nodded his understanding and gestured to the young woman to go with him. Margot turned to stare at Louis, who nodded.

"You will be quite safe with Monsieur Toussaint. Come back tomorrow afternoon and Madame Fournier will explain your duties to you."

"Oui, monsieur, and thank you so much, for... everything," she said, eyeing everyone with trepidation before she hurried out.

"What the hell is going on?" Nic demanded the moment the door closed.

Louis ignored him for the moment. "Alan, Madame Fournier, if anybody asks, I have been at Rouge et Noir all evening. Earlier tonight there was an altercation outside of the club where this young gentleman was set upon and robbed. As this terrible act happened in front of our property, I invited him in to recover and offered him a bed for the night."

Madame Fournier, who was an intelligent woman, nodded at once. "Bien sûr. Truly, I do not know what the city is coming to, monsieur, when decent people cannot set foot outside unmolested. But I shall fetch some steak, for the young gentleman's eye is swelling quite prodigiously."

The lady bustled out, leaving Alan and Nic. Alan nodded at Louis. "You've both been here all night. Saw you with my own eyes."

"Good man, Alan," Louis said, sitting down heavily once the man had seen himself out.

Nic looked from Louis to the battered young man huddled miserably in the chair by the fire and back to Louis again. He folded his arms.

Louis sighed. "We had a little... difficulty tonight, Nic, and that is all I shall say on the matter. The less you know, the better."

"You're not serious?" Nic said in outrage.

"Perfectly serious," Louis snapped and then took a breath. "Forgive me. It has been a rather trying night, my nerves are somewhat frayed. Please, brother. Leave it."

Nic's jaw tightened, and his eyes flashed with indignation. "Fine. For now," he said, clearly unhappy, before stalking out of the room and closing the door with a little more force than was necessary.

Louis poured another drink and sat down, eyeing the miserable huddle in the chair opposite him with resignation.

"Alors, out with it. Tell me the worst. You are English, and that ring you took off your father's finger belonged to a rich man. A rich nobleman, if I had to guess. I am praying you will tell me he stole it."

The boy looked up, and truly he was a mess. He was not at first glance a good-looking young man. His arms and legs were too long, his features too big, from the prominent nose and thick dark eyebrows to the harsh line of his jaw. That his nose was bloody and broken and his eyes swelling shut did not help.

He shook his head and something cold and anxious solidified in Louis' gut.

"Then who the hell are you?" Louis demanded. "Out with it."

The boy sat back and stared at Louis, his expression defiant, yet Louis saw the fear in his eyes, a lost look that he recognised all too well.

"Wulfric De Vere, and now my father is dead—Viscount Latimer."

"Putain," Louis whispered, the breath leaving him in a rush. Somehow, he got to his feet and went back to the decanter. He lifted it, but his hands were shaking too badly, and he set it down again.

Louis turned as the young man appeared at his elbow and poured the drink for him. His hands were remarkably steady as he handed Louis the glass.

"Merci," Louis replied. "You must forgive me, but I have never murdered an English lord before. I find it has the most detrimental effect on my nerves."

"You had no choice," the boy said, his voice soft. "If I could have, I would have done it myself. I wish... I wish that I had been able to. He was evil, and now that I know who you are, I think you know that, too."

His voice trembled and Louis turned and met his eyes and wondered what this poor boy had suffered at the hands of such a father. He nodded.

"He was, and you were most courageous. You fought bravely to protect the girl, and to protect me."

To Louis' alarm, the boy shook his head, his eyes filling with tears. "I w-was terrified," he stammered, sobbing now. "And now I d-don't know what I shall do because it isn't over. You d-don't k-know—"

Louis pulled the young man into an embrace, for he was shaking and shivering as the horror of the night caught up with him. "Taisez-vous, hush now. One thing at a time. We shall deal with it all, I promise you."

"We?" the boy looked up and in that moment he looked absurdly young and afraid, and Louis' heart went out to him.

"Of course. I have just deprived you of a father, no matter that he was a sorry excuse for a man, let alone a sire. I will help you as best I can, my word on it. Now, how do I address an English lordling?"

"Just Wulfric," the boy said thickly. "I don't want the damned title. It's tainted."

"Ah, 'petit loup', it seems we have a good deal in common."

"Little wolf?" the boy said indignantly, straightening up and wiping his eyes. "I'm as big as you are!"

"Oui, and perhaps a third as wide, but no matter, you will fill out. And oui, little wolf, for you fought bravely to protect those around you. But come now. It has been a long night and we both need to sleep, if such a thing is possible. The rest can wait until morning. Agreed?"

Reluctantly, the boy nodded, and Louis smiled, ruffling his hair.

"All will be well, my word on it," he said again, and this time Wulfric relaxed, taking the words at face value. Louis knew he ought not to make such promises, but he saw too much of himself in the boy and wanted, for once, to prove to himself that he could make things right.

"I believe you, and you can call me Wolf if you want to," he added with a crooked smile.

Louis nodded and prayed he could do as he had just promised.

Chapter 20

Dearest Helena,

Is there any news? I know that you will forgive me for saying so, but despite all the trouble he has caused, I truly believe Louis César is a good man with a good heart. I believe he has been lost and alone, and if that is so, then Evie is everything he needs. I never in my life met anyone so desperate for a loving family or more incapable of knowing how to accept that love. But he will learn. Evie loves him, we both know this, and she is brave and strong, though she might not realise just how strong yet. As was true of us all at that age. But she will learn, as we all learned, that we are capable of far more than we realise if we trust in ourselves.

If she was not a willing accomplice to their flight, I suspect she gave him hell, and indeed, I hope that she did. For as fond as I am of that young man, I suspect he gets his own way a great deal too often. It will do him good to discover that his wife is not nearly as biddable as he imagined.

In other news, I received a letter this week from Georgiana. She has delivered Rochford's heir and by all accounts the fellow is in alt. Georgie is happy and well and writes that her son is a fine healthy creature with an admirable set of lungs. They have named him James Emilius Gordon Maitland Seymour, Marquess of Drelincourt.

—Excerpt of a letter from Prunella Adolphus, The Duchess of Bedwin, to her sister-in-law, Lady Helena Knight.

23rd July 1842, Rue de la Bièvre, 13th Arrondissement, Paris, France.

"So that's why you called him *petit loup*," Evie said, turning in Louis' arms to kiss his jaw.

Louis laughed and nodded. "Well, I did say he would fill out."

"You weren't wrong," Evie replied with a snort. She was sitting in his lap, her attention on him absolute as they talked. He had shocked her, as he had expected, but she had not yet run away screaming as he had feared. Louis turned to look at her, finding her gaze on him, full of love and understanding.

"I'm not going anywhere, Louis. You were protecting people who could not protect themselves, and you put yourself in harm's way to do it. That is the mark of a hero, not a villain, and so you must stop thinking of it in any other way."

Louis let out a breath, a hard knot of tension releasing in his chest at her words.

"Foolish man," she whispered. "How could you think I would view it any differently?"

"It's just all so…" He waved a hand, unable to explain how he felt tainted by the past, how he had feared her seeing how the dirt of everything he'd lived through clung to him still.

"Tragic," she finished for him. "It is certainly that, but you are a good man, Louis César, and I love you."

He smiled and pulled her close for a kiss, so ridiculously happy to have her with him with no secrets between them, that he could not help but wish he had been courageous enough to have shared everything sooner, but it had seemed so impossible, so terrifying to lay himself bare like that. Not any longer.

"*Je t'aime,*" he murmured, desire rising as she kissed him back, pressing closer. "Touch me," he said, wanting to feel her hands on him, to let her chase all the dark memories away as she did so easily when she was near.

Her hand slid beneath the heavy silk robe and began lazily stroking his cock, her touch unhurried, her kisses slow and tender, quietly driving him to distraction. She enjoyed teasing him now, refusing to let him take her but making him wait. Not that he minded, he enjoyed her newfound confidence as much as she did.

Evie gave him a wicked smile and shifted down to kneel on the floor before him. Louis hurried to undo the robe fully and swallowed a groan as her warm mouth closed over him.

She had devoted herself to finding how best to please him and now set her considerable talents to good use with tantalising kisses and caressing hands, trailing her tongue up and down his sensitive shaft and grazing the pulsing head with her teeth until he was gasping and aching with the need to come.

"Evie," he gritted out, torn between closing his eyes to savour the moment and watching his cock disappear in and out of her lush mouth.

Watching won, and she glanced up as she worked him, such a smug glint in her eyes as she looked up the length of his body to find him arching beneath her, his hands clutching at the arms of the chair as he struggled to hold on. He didn't want this to end, not yet, but, oh, *Dieu*....

There was no one but her, no space in his heart or his memories for anyone but his wife. All traces of the women that had come before were chased away, replaced by her, always her, his Evie.

Just when he thought he would lose his sanity for good, she released him, climbing over him to straddle his hips. He gasped as the sweet, tight heat of her fitted snugly around him, stealing his breath. She made a soft sound as she tried to take him deeper and had to go slowly, easing onto him by degrees, allowing her body to accommodate him and making him harder still as he watched the pleasure reflected on her face. There was no uncertainty or restraint as she began to move on him, nothing but her desire for him, her love for him, as she took him inside her, loving him with all that she was, abandoning herself to her own desires. Her full breasts pressed against his chest as she sought his mouth, kissing him deeply and passionately before sitting back, her eyes closed as she found the rhythm that pleased her most. Louis held her hips, guiding her as she rode him with increasing fervour. He watched her with something close to awe as the morning sun rose behind her, gilding her glorious curves and casting her in shades of gold, like a goddess come to life.

Her cry of pleasure shot straight to his groin, and it needed no more than that for him to follow her, shuddering with the joy of it as he spent inside her with a shout of triumph, happiness bursting inside him as she collapsed in a sprawl across his chest, laughing and exhausted as her long hair cascaded around them.

Louis gathered her closer while their breathing settled, relishing this time together and the decadent pleasure of a lazy morning. He had not slept well and had already woken Evie during the night, needing her touch, needing to make love to her and reassure himself that all was well. The past was dead and gone, and ghosts did not exist.

Etienne was real and alive and needed to be dealt with, but he was not a ghost.

"Well, that's better," he said, once he could speak again.

Evie laughed as she got up and slipped behind the screen to wash. "I'm glad," she said, her face becoming serious again when she reappeared and climbed into the bed. Louis got up and went to her as she patted the mattress beside her. "I want to make you happy after everything you have endured. My poor darling Louis. I am so sorry for everything that happened, everything you have lived through."

Louis shrugged, uncomfortable with her pity in the circumstances. "I do not believe the old viscount enjoyed it much either, seeing he was murdered and tossed in the river."

"It was not murder, and it seems to me he earned such a fate," Evie said fiercely as she snuggled back against him. "For I know you have not told me everything. What was it Wolf was so worried about?"

Louis sighed. "I ought not—"

"Sully my innocent ears, yes, we've done that, Louis. If you have endured all this, hearing it will not send me into fits of hysteria. What a feeble creature you think me!"

Louis could not let that stand and rolled Evie onto her back, staring down at her. "I think nothing of the sort," he said, angry that she should accuse him of it. "You know I do not. I only wish that you need not know everything that I have done and all the wickedness that exists in the world. I wish to protect you and keep you safe, is that so wrong of me?"

Evie sighed and reached up, stroking his face. "No. Of course not, but I want to know, and I know well enough evil exists. Now, what was he worried about?"

Louis groaned and flung himself back against the pillows, scowling at the ceiling. Evie shifted closer, insinuating herself under his arm and kissing his cheek. "Stop sulking," she ordered him. "What happened next?"

With a resigned huff, Louis carried on. "His father had a whorehouse."

"Well, we knew that," Evie replied.

"*Oui,* but it was exclusive, exceedingly expensive. He specialised in offering beautiful young people, whether or not they were willing. He would auction off their virginity to the highest bidder. That was what he had in mind for Mademoiselle Allard. That was what he had in mind for me," he added, unable to keep the anger from his voice. "The viscount's body was found three days later and there was an investigation into his death. Because I gave Wolf an alibi, suspicion fell upon me, but nothing could be proven. I was fast becoming one of the wealthiest men in the city and, with Rouge et Noir, Nic and I held the debts of many powerful men. It was not as difficult as I had feared to make the problem go away."

"I see," Evie said, her tone thoughtful.

"Have I shocked you at last?" he asked, watching her as she shook her head, though her gaze was piercing.

"Everything my father said about you was true, wasn't it?"

It wasn't really a question but a statement, and there was no judgement in her voice, more a confirmation of what she had already known at heart.

"I told you it was," he reminded her.

She leaned in and kissed him, settling beside him again in a way that was familiar and trusting and made his heart feel as if it might burst.

"I'm glad," she said, surprising him as she did so often.

He shifted so he could see her face better, and she raised an eyebrow at his expression.

"What?"

"You're glad?" he repeated sceptically.

"Of course I'm glad. I'm glad that you were powerful enough to protect yourself and those who needed you. Did you think I would say otherwise?"

Louis frowned, needing to clarify exactly what she meant. "I blackmailed lawmen, judges, those people who are supposed to keep the world civilised, into ignoring the fact I'd murdered a man."

Evie made an impatient sound and sat up. "You killed an evil man in self-defence. In the first place, that is not murder. And where were those civilised men when Margot needed them, when you were a boy and you needed them? Until the world comes up with a better way, I shall take your justice over theirs, Louis. Now do stop being ridiculous."

Louis stared at her, taken aback. *"Oui, madame,"* he replied, finding himself in awe of her all over again.

"Now, tell me what you did about the whorehouse? You dismantled it, I suppose? Found better places for the poor people the viscount had harmed?"

Louis hesitated. "Mostly," he said, wondering if this might be too much for her, even though she had taken everything else in stride.

Her green eyes narrowed, and Louis experience a tremor of uncertainty. He cleared his throat.

"We found work for everyone who wanted out. By that time we were extending Rouge et Noir, making it bigger. We had private rooms that people could rent for their own entertainments, and some very exclusive hotel rooms. Some of the most committed gamblers would rent them for weeks or months at a time, and, of course, lovers for illicit liaisons. At Rouge et Noir, we are exclusive, expensive, and above all, discreet."

"I never doubted it," Evie replied, and he heard the smile in her words. "But what did you mean by, *mostly?"*

"You know that at the casino, there is a red door and a black door?"

Evie sat up again, the sheet dropping to reveal all her generous curves to his gaze. Louis sighed and reached for her, only to have his hand pushed away.

"Of course I know!" she exclaimed, her eyes wide and bright. "Eliza told us all about it, but she would never tell us what was behind the door."

Realising he would have no attention from her until he satisfied her curiosity, Louis carried on. "There were some at Latimer's house who were displeased at the loss of their livelihood. Once Latimer was gone, they realised they could make good money, if they could keep it for themselves. I promise you we offered several alternatives, but they were all adults and well able to think for themselves. I did not feel it was my place to insist they change their lives. Mostly they were handsome young men, though there were one or two women among them."

"And so?"

"And so, it had also occurred to me how very many neglected wives and widows there were in Paris. There were so many places that catered to men's needs, but their wives languished alone, unless they found themselves a lover they could trust to be discreet, someone who would not hurt them or blackmail them. And this is not so easy for a woman to do, for though it saddens me to admit it, too many of my sex are not trustworthy in this regard." Louis watched as a slow smile curved his wife's beautiful mouth, and something anxious inside him eased. "You will not think me a pimp? A whoremonger?"

She shook her head, staring at him in delight.

"In truth, I am neither of those things, and nor is Nic. We merely rent the building to them. The house is most competently run by Margot Allard."

"No!"

Louis laughed and nodded. "We discovered the girl had a managing nature and a mind for detail. She is also clever with numbers and is not easily shocked. Of course, she did not take this position at once. It was three years at least before the house evolved into what it is now, but by that time there was no one else we would have considered for the job."

"Well!" Evie said, leaning back against him with a little laugh. "My goodness. I did not expect that."

Louis slid his arms around her and kissed her neck.

"So what of Wolf?"

Louis nipped at her ear. "His father's house was not only for pleasure. It was also a front for a great deal of criminal activity. Luxury goods, tobacco, wine, anything on which tax must be paid, or can be avoided paying if one is not too particular about breaking the law."

"And?"

"And Wolf knew a good deal about how the business ran and…." Louis shrugged. "It seemed foolish to abandon a scheme that had the potential to make so much money. The late viscount was sloppy and dull-witted, more interested in gratifying his own pleasure than anything else. Wolf, however, was quick to see ways to make the whole thing more efficient and less risky for everyone involved. So we joined forces. He was too young to be taken seriously then, but by now Paris believed I had murdered the viscount to take over his criminal activity so my brother and I could control the Parisian underworld. It was well known I had many of the most powerful men in the city in my pocket via their debts at the club. We gained a reputation for ruthlessness, and people feared us. It was both helpful and most disconcerting, but either way, I could do nothing to change it."

In Louis' opinion, that was quite enough talk about his past, and so he shifted, easing Evie down onto the mattress and moving over her.

She slid her arms about his neck, watching him. "You and Wolf are close aren't you. In fact, I would say he adores you," she said with a smile.

Louis chuckled. "Wolf is a conundrum, he is at once intimidating and fierce, and the most ridiculously soft-hearted man I have ever known. He does not let many people close to him, though he loves company and if he is at ease, makes friends everywhere he goes, which does not happen often. However, show him a kitten or a puppy, or, God help me, a ferret, and he's in heaven."

"No!" Evie laughed, clearly incredulous.

"I swear it is true. The trouble he caused at the casino as a boy, forever smuggling in injured animals, or some litter of kittens he'd found abandoned. The night the ferret got loose is one that will live in my mind for years to come," Louis added ruefully. "I thought a certain duke was going to call me out when it ran up his trouser leg. I think he feared he would never produce an heir for a little while there. So did I, come to that!"

By now Evie was laughing so hard tears were running down her face. Louis watched her, his heart so full he did not know how his chest could contain the feeling. He had just revealed so much of what he believed he must hide, and she had not only accepted it, she embraced it, even approved of it… and of him. She accepted him, all the flawed and messy, imperfect parts of him without question, and loved him still. It seemed too wonderful to be true, too precious to be his.

"Je t'aime," he said, hearing the catch in his voice, too much emotion on show, and could not bring himself to care.

Her laughter subsided and her eyes became soft and misty as she pulled him down for a kiss. "I love you too, Louis. *Je t'aime aussi."*

Louis hesitated. More than anything he wanted to forget the world and make love to his wife, but he could not keep secrets from her, not if he wanted to keep her love and trust.

"Evie, there is something I must tell you," he said, wondering what she would do next when he told her.

She stared at him, her expression placid. "Go on."

"Your father is here. He's been to the club."

"Well, of course he's here," she said, giving him an incredulous look. "You didn't think he'd follow you straight to Rouge et Noir?"

"Of course, but...."

Evie sat up, regarding him with interest. "What? You thought I'd go running to him?"

"I suppose so," he admitted.

Louis shivered as she stroked a finger down his cheek. "I will write to him, and you will ensure he receives it. I'll reassure him I am happy—very happy—and well, and I will arrange a meeting so long as he promises not to cause trouble with you."

He snorted at that. "You may write what you wish, *mon amour*, but your father wants my blood, and I cannot say that I blame him."

"Then he will have me to deal with," she said, looking so fierce he could not help but kiss her.

"My courageous love, always so willing to protect me," he murmured, pulling her closer.

Desire thrummed beneath his skin, and though it seemed impossible that he could need her again so quickly, he wanted her beneath him, wanted to sink into her heat, her softness and forget everything else. She allowed it for a moment, melting into his kisses as she always did, but then pushed him away. Louis sighed as she climbed out of bed. He watched with frustration as the view of her magnificent bottom disappeared behind her dressing gown.

"I must write to him now we know where he is, Louis. He'll be out of his mind with worry and that isn't fair."

Louis could hardly argue the point, though his cock could have made a persuasive case for waiting at least another hour, given the chance. Sighing, he stared at the ceiling, waiting for her to come back to bed. A moment later, the covers were stripped from him, and he started in surprise. Evie gave him a long, lingering look that made his burgeoning arousal twitch in anticipation. Louis swallowed at the heat in her eyes as she perused his body with obvious approval.

"I'm just looking," she said cheerfully. "My goodness, you are a sight to behold, husband, but I shall have to wait until later because you need to get up. At least you may console yourself with your devoted valet to fuss over you, now Elton has arrived, but we have guests to entertain. Or had you forgotten Barnaby and Aggie?"

"*Non,* of course not," he said, aggrieved. "But it's only eight—"

"Time you were up and dressed," she replied, interrupting him. She bent to deliver him a quick kiss, tweaked his nipple, which made him suck in a sharp breath, and then the wretch turned away, sending him a wicked smile over her shoulder as she sashayed away to sit at the elegant writing desk.

Louis made an indignant sound.

"Cruel," he lamented, shaking his head. "You are nothing but cruel to me."

His reply was a soft laugh and the rhythmic scratch of her pen as she wrote to her father.

Chapter 21

Dearest Papa,

Firstly, I am well and unharmed and very, very happy. I know you will not attend to the rest of this letter until you know that much. So, be reassured, I regret nothing except the worry caused to those who love me.

Secondly, I am now the Comtesse de Villen.

Everything you told me about Louis was true. Papa, he has hidden nothing from me, but you do not understand the context of the information you uncovered. You do not yet know the cruelty and hardship of the life he has endured, the circumstances of the crimes you accuse him of, nor how far he has come to become the man he is now. That he has done so with his heart intact is a wonder to me, for I think anyone else would have become cold and cynical, and yet Louis is loving and kind, and not only to me. You need only see how he is regarded here in Paris. People adore him, and with good reason. Did you know Barnaby Godwin followed him here from England, and even his ward, Agatha, travelled here alone? They came to ensure he was safe and well and not in trouble. This is the loyalty he engenders in others simply by being who he is.

My husband is the very best of men, Papa, and I know you will love him too if you will only give him the chance. Please give him that chance.

We will meet you tonight at eight pm at Rouge et Noir.

Your loving daughter,

Evie.

—Excerpt of a letter from Evie de Montluc, Comtesse de Villen to her father, Mr. Gabriel Knight.

23rd July 1842, Casino Rouge et Noir, 7th Arrondissement, Paris, France.

Evie watched her husband on the journey to the casino. He was undeniably tense, and Evie reached out and pulled her hand into his lap. One by one, she uncurled his fingers from the fist his hand had clenched into before raising it to her lips.

"There is nothing Papa can say that can change my mind about you or make me regret our marriage," she assured him. He let out a harsh breath, and she smiled. She knew him so well, knew now how his mind worked, and that he usually judged himself far more harshly than anyone else.

"You say that now," he replied, staring out of the window, watching the darkened streets as they slipped past the carriage.

"And I will always say it. I know you've not told me the rest yet, but I also know that you will, that you'll hide nothing from me. I trust you, Louis. With my heart and soul. I would not have married you otherwise."

His brooding expression softened a little, but his voice was still heavy as he replied. "I do not deserve you, and your father knows it."

He raised her hand to his lips and pressed a kiss to her knuckles. Desire sparked to life inside her. Good lord, but how easily he roused her. A look, a touch, the slightest brush of his lips, and the hunger that slept inside her roared to life, insatiable and undeniable. It was as wonderful as it was disturbing. She knew now why so many women had ruined themselves over him, understood well how they could lose their minds and their reason to be with him a little longer.

"But you do," she insisted, leaning closer to him. "You deserve everything that is good in life, my love, and I will do all in my power to see you have it."

He stared at her in wonder, shaking his head as if he did not quite believe she was real.

"Is it true two of your lovers fought a duel over you?" she asked. Evie had heard the rumour years ago when Louis had first arrived in England, but she still did not know if it was true.

"Merde!" he exclaimed in shock, colour cresting his high cheekbones. "You will be the death of me. What a thing to ask!"

Evie laughed at his obvious discomfort. "Oh, come now. Tell me the truth."

Louis shook his head, folding his arms. *"Non,* I should not...."

Evie quirked an eyebrow and he sighed, resigned to the inevitable.

"Oh, if you must know—but it was too ridiculous for words. It is a great enough folly when men act so idiotically, but for two intelligent women… I was never more shocked. I had thought better of them both."

"So it *is* true!" Evie exclaimed. "What happened?"

He tutted impatiently. "Nothing happened. I found out about it and intervened before anyone was hurt, but there were too many witnesses to the entire debacle, and it caused the most spectacular scandal. Nic had wanted us to go to England to find me a suitable bride for some time, but I had resisted. You know I did not wish to marry back then. That, however, forced my hand. It was in all the scandal sheets, I could not take a step out of the house without being besieged by people wanting the story. Everywhere I went, people were talking about it. I needed to get away. By that time Nic was caught up with his own pretty piece of trouble in Madame Lafitte, who was threatening to reveal us as thieves, and so we ran for England."

"Madame Lafitte… she was the one who followed Nic to England?"

Louis grimaced. "Unfortunately."

"And you've not returned to Paris since?"

He shook his head.

"Who were the ladies involved?"

Louis shot her an impatient look, and she shrugged.

"I think if the scandal was so great, people must still speak of it. I would know who I am talking to if I come face to face with an old lover, Louis. I do not wish to be made a fool of."

His expression darkened. "Forgive me, *mon amour.* You are right, of course, and I would not have you made uncomfortable for the world."

Evie smiled at him and shook her head. "I've always known about your women, Louis, and I've always known you were lonely, that you were searching for something. So long as I know you have found it, I do not care a jot for what happened before you loved me, and I trust you to be faithful to me now."

"You know you are everything I have ever dreamed of," he said, sliding an arm about her waist and pulling her close. "I do not want or need anything or anyone else."

He kissed her and Evie sighed with pleasure, but she was not to be diverted, no matter the impulse to let desire come first. It would not soothe her father's ire if she arrived at their meeting all flushed and disarranged. She pushed against this chest, smiling as he returned a look of frustration. "So who were they?"

Louis groaned. "Madame la Duchesse de Sauvignac and La Comtesse de Pomport."

"A duchess and a countess! Oh, my, Louis, no wonder there was a scandal."

He flinched and hunched lower in his seat, so obviously mortified that Evie did not dare tease him for it, though the temptation was tantalising.

"Oh, dear," she said, struggling to keep her voice from trembling with the effort of not laughing. "My poor Louis. Never mind, my love, I will keep them all away from you. From now on, they will not dare glance in your direction for fear of my wrath."

He shot her a wary look, trying to judge if she was sincere or not, and Evie could not help the laugh that escaped her. Louis sighed.

Jacques Toussaint, the manager of Rouge et Noir, was at the back door of the club waiting for them as Louis guided Evie inside.

"Monsieur," Jacques said, beaming and shaking Louis' hand vigorously. He spoke in rapid French. "It is so good to see you here again after so long. Paris has missed you. Everyone asks of you still and demands I tell them when you will return. We must celebrate in style if you will allow it, to welcome your return, and especially as you come with your lovely comtesse. Madame," his eyes lighting up when they fell upon Evie. "I am honoured to make your acquaintance."

"*Enchanté*, Monsieur Toussaint," Evie replied, as the man bowed low to her. "I have heard much about you," she added, and Louis felt a glow of pride in her for speaking in French when he knew she was nervous about doing so with people she did not know. She glanced at Louis, who gave her an approving smile and took her hand before returning his attention to Jacques.

"He's here," Jacques said, keeping his voice low so only Louis could hear. "And fit to be tied. Shall I come in with you? I think he would like to separate your head from your shoulders, given the chance."

Louis shook his head but squeezed Jacques' shoulder in gratitude. *"Non, merci, mon ami.* This is a confrontation I have earned and must face, but I appreciate your loyalty, as always. Leave me to deal with this, and do not come in, no matter what you hear."

Jacques grimaced, but nodded. "As you wish, but I will remain close by if you need me. He is waiting in one of the private rooms, as you requested. Number seven."

Louis nodded, returning a crooked smile. "Lucky for me," he said dryly, and escorted Evie to where her father awaited them.

Room number seven was a large parlour, elegantly but sparsely furnished. It was the type of room they let out to bachelors who wanted to party privately, drink too much, and gamble. The furnishings were sturdy, not too easily broken, and there were few ornaments that could be picked up and thrown or smashed. It had seemed prudent not to give Gabriel Knight too much ammunition for weaponry, just in case.

"Papa!" Evie cried upon seeing her father, and flew across the room into his arms.

For a moment, Mr Knight's attention was entirely for his daughter. He hugged her tightly, his eyes closed as he let out a breath Louis suspected he had been holding since the night she disappeared.

"Evie, sweetheart," he said, his voice thick with emotion. "My God, I have been to hell and back these past days."

"I'm so sorry, Papa," Evie said, tears in her eyes as she saw how pale and tired her father was. "Truly, I am, but I do not regret marrying Louis. I won't have you fighting with him, Papa."

Her father said nothing, only bent and dropped a kiss to her forehead. "You're well?" he demanded. "He didn't hurt you?"

Louis bristled, gritting his jaw, well aware he was being slighted by the fact Knight had not deigned to even look at him yet. He reminded himself Evie was the man's beloved daughter, and he had stolen her away, causing a deal of heartache and worry, and held his tongue.

"Papa!" Evie said, reproach in her voice. "Louis would never hurt me."

"Yet he took you against your will," her father said, his voice grim.

"Yes, but there is an explanation," she said hurriedly, but her father's gaze had turned to Louis, and it was dark with anger.

"I'll just bet there is," he murmured. He let Evie go and crossed the room.

Louis braced himself, knowing what would come next. He resolved to let the man vent his anger, hoping it might make him feel better. Even though he had expected it, the blow was a shock, the fist coming out of nowhere and snapping his head back. Louis staggered, crashing back into a sideboard, and sending a decanter of cognac to the floor with an explosive smash.

"No!" Evie cried, rushing between them, pushing at her father's chest. "Don't you touch him!"

"He kidnapped you!" Knight raged. "Everyone said you were unconscious when you were carried out!"

"That wasn't Louis' fault," Evie shouted, pulling at her father's sleeve. "He didn't drug me. It was someone else, someone who wanted to hurt him and knew that he cared for me."

"Then it was still his fault," Knight said through gritted teeth. He picked Evie up, setting her aside, and advanced on Louis.

Louis stood, ready to defend himself. "You get one blow because I know I deserved it, but I won't stand meekly by and let you break my neck."

"Stop this, both of you!" Evie demanded. "Papa, I love you, but if you don't listen to me, do not expect me to speak to you again!"

Louis and Knight both started at her words, Louis as shocked as her father was. Though he knew she loved him, he had not expected her to estrange herself from her father, knowing how she idolised the man.

"Evie," Louis said, shaking his head. "Don't. You know that would only hurt you."

"Yes, it would," she said, her voice trembling. "But if my father thinks me a fool whose judgement cannot be trusted, then what choice do I have?"

Mr Knight looked stricken and turned back to her. "Evie, love, it's not that—"

"Isn't it?" she demanded. "Isn't it that you think I've been seduced by a handsome face and pretty words because I'm too young and naïve to know when someone truly loves me? Or do you think I'm not beautiful enough for Louis to love?"

"No!" her father returned at once, his anger and shock at the accusation written in the appalled expression he wore. "My God, Evie, look at you! You... You're stunning," he admitted and then let out a breath. Raking a hand through his hair, he moved to the nearest chair and sat down heavily, everything about him speaking of a man thoroughly exhausted and at the end of his tether.

Louis went to the door and called for Jacques. "Bring us another decanter of brandy and something for Mr Knight to eat," he instructed, before turning back to the room. "Perhaps you ought to let us speak alone, Evie," he suggested.

Evie glared at him. "Not on your life," she retorted. "You can both sit down with me, and we shall have a conversation like civilised people. It's clear I can trust neither of you to behave like gentlemen tonight. If the two men I love insist on acting like children, I must play the part of governess."

Louis sighed inwardly, having known that—or something similar—would be the answer, and sat down as Mr Knight looked up, staring between them both with interest. A tense silence filled the room until Jacques came in, bearing a decanter of brandy and a bottle of chilled white wine. Servers entered behind him, one hurrying to sweep up the broken glass as another mopped up the spilt cognac. Another carried in a tray with a selection of cheeses and fresh baguette, grapes and nuts, and another of charcuterie with a little dish of butter. Once Jacques had arranged the repast to his satisfaction, and had served Evie with a glass of wine, he looked to Louis, who was touching the tender spot on his jaw where Knight had hit him with tentative fingers. Louis nodded for him to leave.

"Who drugged you?" Knight asked Evie, as Louis poured them each a generous measure of cognac.

"Louis," Evie said, her voice soft. "May I tell my father a little of your past, please? I need him to understand."

Louis frowned. It rankled more than he wanted to admit, the idea of this man knowing how helpless he had been, but he could deny his wife nothing.

"As you wish," he replied, though his discomfort must be obvious.

"A man called Etienne Boucher," Evie replied. "Louis' father was exiled from France by the king and abandoned Louis when he was a little boy. He was left to the mercy of a man the late comte had tried to destroy. Mr Boucher took his revenge upon Louis. He was abused and humiliated, treated like a slave, forced to sleep on the kitchen floor and eat scraps like a dog. He lived like this for seven years, Papa. It is their son, Etienne, who has become obsessed with Louis. He both loves and despises him and… I believe he has already tried to kill him."

Louis looked up sharply. "I never told you that," he said.

Evie's glance was soft and full of sympathy. "No, you didn't need to. I saw the scar, and from what you had said, it was obvious enough that Etienne was the most likely culprit."

Louis said nothing else, uncertain of what he could say. It was strange and wonderful and slightly unnerving how well this woman knew him, how much of him and his tangled past had been revealed to her, and how none of it had ever swayed her devotion to him. He reached for the cognac glasses and offered one to her father, who took it and downed half of it in one large swallow. Louis didn't blame him.

"And where is he now?" Knight asked.

"Here in Paris, I imagine," Louis replied. "Or at least on his way here. I do not know if he has any funds at his disposal, so the journey might take him a while."

This time, Evie gasped in shock. "You know this?"

Louis shrugged. "I have no proof, but he followed me to England. The man is deranged, obsessed, where else would he go? He means to see me dead."

"And you brought my daughter with you, knowing this?" Knight growled.

"I had no choice," Louis replied, though his stomach roiled with a noxious mix of guilt and regret. "I had a few minutes to decide what to do. Everyone had already seen me carry her away, she was ruined no matter what I did. I could return Evie to her family or bring her with me to France. I knew I could keep her safe here," he said fiercely.

"And so you did not stop to consult my daughter or consider what she wanted."

"I did not," Louis replied, holding her father's disgusted gaze without flinching. "She was unconscious, and I made a selfish decision. I admit it. I knew she did not wish to marry yet, and I forced the situation—though you know well enough that, if she wished to remain in society, it was her only option. Yet, I know it was wrong of me, and I deeply regret causing her a moment's distress or disregarding her wishes, but I cannot and will not regret the outcome."

Knight snorted. "You've caused a damned scandal, when you could simply have taken her home and allowed us to deal with the fallout."

"Ah, yes," Louis replied, reigning in his temper with difficulty. "You would have dealt with it by taking her away from me. You would have told her she must keep away from society until the scandal died down, hiding her so well I would never find her again. You think I did not know this? Well, I won't let you or anyone keep me from the woman I love. *Jamais!"* he added furiously.

"And now she has married the notorious Comte de Villen, you are both scandalous figures, and your pictures in all the print-shop windows. Do you think that is what Evie wished for?" her father raged, equally angry?

Despite himself, despite the situation, Louis' lips quirked, and he darted a look at his wife. She was biting her lip and as she met his eyes, she put her hand over her mouth to smother a laugh.

Her father looked at her in astonishment. "You think this is funny?"

"Well, P-Papa, y-yes, a little," she managed, failing to hide her amusement. "There were all those beautiful debutantes chasing Louis about, and all those notorious married ladies vying to be his mistress, and it's me he runs away with. Little Evie Knight, who never put a foot wrong or said boo to a goose."

"Non," Louis said, shaking his head. He reached out and took her hand. "That is not what is funny. I have told you before, those women cannot hold a candle to you, *mon amour.* You must stop comparing what is incomparable. What is funny is the idea that anyone would think you would shy away from making a scandal. That anyone could know you and not realise how bold and headstrong you truly are."

She smiled at him and, for a moment, Louis simply basked in the warmth of her affection and approval. He had always admired Mr Knight, and that the man loathed him did not sit easily, but the older generation of men in his life had always despised him, so he could bear it for Evie's sake. He looked up to discover Mr Knight watching him intently.

"Evie, love, I think your husband and I need a moment alone together."

Evie shook her head to deny him, but her father held up a hand. "I'll not cause trouble, Evie. I'm tired to my bones and I can see with my own eyes that you are happy. I cannot say that I am, but you are married now. If that pleases you, then I must accept it."

Evie got to her feet and went to her father, kneeling before him and taking his hands in hers. "Papa, I am so very happy. Truly. I love him, so much, and I know he loves me. It would mean so much to me if you could be friends. Please, Papa."

Her father studied her face and sighed. "It is hard for a father to let his little girl go, Evie, especially in such a way. I was not ready, and I did not think you were either."

"Neither did I, but I think perhaps we both underestimated me," Evie said. "Louis never has, you know. He has shown me I am neither weak nor helpless. Louis listens to me, Papa, like you listen to Mama. He does not disregard my feelings—or at least, not since taking me away," she added with a crooked smile.

"Hmmm." Mr Knight glowered but Evie only laughed.

"I have punished him for that—quite thoroughly, Papa, I assure you—and he has promised never to do such a thing again. I believe him. He will always discuss things with me and never assume he knows what is best. He will make me happy. I know that he will."

"He had better," Mr Knight said darkly, but then his expression softened. "So be it, then. Your happiness is all I have ever wanted." He leant forward to kiss his daughter's cheek.

Evie got up and turned to look at Louis, who nodded and got to his feet. "I will behave, *mon amour.* I want peace between us, for your sake, if nothing else."

Content that they would conduct themselves like gentlemen now, Evie headed to the door as Louis hurried to open it for her. He looked out to find Jacques hovering nearby as he'd promised to do. "Jacques, see that my wife is made comfortable and has everything she needs while I speak with her father."

"At once, monsieur." Jacques gestured for Evie to follow him with a warm smile. "Comtesse, this way, if you please."

Louis closed the door and turned back to Mr Knight, eyeing him warily.

"I want to know about the men you killed," he said with no preamble.

Louis had known this would be an interrogation, but all the same, the blunt question was startling. He'd had years of practise at hiding his feelings, though, so he simply nodded, returning to his seat. "The first was Wolf's father."

"Wulfric De Vere," Gabriel replied, his expression unreadable. "I admit I did not immediately make the connection. The De Vere family is extensive, but there are few who dare show their faces in society. and I was unaware Viscount Latimer had sired a son."

"That is the way Wolf preferred it," Louis replied with a shrug as he returned to his seat and poured another drink. "He has never used the title. His father was an evil bastard."

"He was also the man responsible for leaving one and half thousand English soldiers to the mercy of the French after the battle of Talavera," Knight replied, his revulsion unmistakable.

"He was," Louis replied. "You would need to try hard to find a more disgusting excuse for a man and I do not regret killing him, but if it soothes your concerns, it was self-defence."

"What did he want with you?" Knight demanded.

Louis' jaw tightened, but he had promised Evie to do what he could. "Monsieur Boucher, the man Evie spoke of, sold me to Latimer when I was eleven years old. He wished for me to be one of his whores at an exclusive house he kept for such disgusting purposes. He provided certain specialties for which some in society would pay a high price."

"Christ," Knight cursed under his breath and Louis avoided his eyes. It was one thing to be despised, but he did not think he could bear this man's pity.

"For once, fate was kind, and my brother came for me before he could take me away. The night I killed him was some eight years later, here in Paris. He was trying to abduct a young girl and Wolf was not old enough or strong enough to stop him, though he made a courageous effort. His father was a large man, though, and Wolf was doomed to failure. I intervened and Latimer produced a knife. We fought. He lost."

Louis shrugged, unwilling to relive the events of that night in greater detail. Even now he could smell the blood, feel it sliding through the fingers of the hand that grasped the knife, warm and sticky.

"I see," Knight said, his expression troubled.

Louis carried on, uncomfortable with the way Evie's father was regarding him now. "We disposed of the body, but it got about that I was responsible for his death. I was still only nineteen and people believed my brother and I assassinated him in order to take over his criminal activity. In point of fact, we did take over, but that was incidental, not by design. But we gained a reputation for being ruthless and dangerous and it suited me well enough to let people believe it. Nic was furious with me, but he could not stop what had already begun."

"And the other two men?"

Louis swallowed. "It appears there was only one other man, not two. Sadly, I was not as thorough with the last as I had believed. Evie was correct that Etienne tried to kill me, and very nearly succeeded. I'm only here because Wolf got me out of a burning building, and we assumed Etienne had died in the blaze. We were wrong."

"The other man, the one you killed. I assume that was his father, this Monsieur Boucher. The man who abused you."

"Oui," Louis said succinctly. "And I would do it again, given the chance."

Chapter 22

Dear Alana,

I was looking forward to coming out, but honestly, it's been a vast disappointment. I'm so on edge trying to remember all the wretched rules about what I must and must not do, it gives me a headache. And though it is lovely to wear beautiful gowns and dance all night, all the most interesting men are the ones I'm not supposed to speak to. I was even warned about speaking to Jules so freely, for he has a shocking reputation these days. But I have known him since I was a baby, and it seems so silly to be formal just for the sake of it.

As for the other men, except for those within our circle who we know and trust, most of them spend their time gazing at my bosom. I mean, I know it is a splendid bosom, but really, you'd think they might at least pretend to be interested in what I have to say.

By the way, what has happened to Ashburton? I heard Leo Hunt say that he's disappeared from society. Is that true?

—Excerpt of a letter from Lady Cara Baxter (daughter of Luke and Kitty Baxter, Earl and Countess of Trevick) to Alana Cadogan (daughter of Jerome and Bonnie Cadogan).

17th May 1832, Casino Rouge et Noir, 7th Arrondissement, Paris, France.

Louis is twenty…

Louis hurried down the stairs of their private apartment at *Rouge et Noir*. If he didn't leave now, he would be late for an assignation with Madame Polignac. Madame was a lovely and very merry widow who had been chasing him for some weeks. Last night, she had sent him a ridiculously expensive diamond cravat pin, and a letter promising every manner of decadent pleasure if he would meet with her. Having drawn the anticipation out for some time, he figured he ought to give her something for her trouble before the poor woman did something foolish and ruined herself. So, he had booked a suite of rooms in an elegant little establishment known for their discretion and sent her the details. As he reached the bottom step, his foot met something soft, and he lifted it instinctively as a furious yowl rent the air and a small, fluffy object dashed up the stairs. From the step below, two more fluffy creatures leapt in fright, and one climbed up his leg, needle-like claws piercing his skin and startling him so much he lost his balance and fell on his arse. The kitten—as that was what it appeared to be—settled itself in his lap, mewled piteously at him and began kneading his silk waistcoat, immediately pulling a thread.

"*Wolf!*" Louis yelled, trying to detach the creature from his person as gently as he could, but it was like a blasted barnacle and as soon as one claw was free another hung on for dear life.

Wolf loped around the corner, his long-limbed gait fitting his nickname to perfection. He had filled out considerably over the past year, now he had someone who gave a damn whether or not he ate and a kitchen of mouth-watering food to choose from. He was also taller than Louis now and alarmingly showing no signs of stopping growing. At this rate, Louis suspected he would be far bigger than his father had been, and lamented the fact he would need yet another new coat before the month was out. It was generally a toss-up as to whether Wolf would outgrow his clothes first or rip them to shreds in fights or misadventures, into which he seemed to fall with startling ease.

"There you are!" Wolf exclaimed with a grin as he laid eyes on the kittens, deftly unhooking the tiny ginger one in Louis' lap and cradling it carefully in his big hands. Louis turned around, gesturing to his back. "There's another one," he said with a sigh as sharp claws sank into his shoulder.

Wolf laughed and took that one too, looking up the stairs as the third kitten cried to be reunited with its siblings.

"That one just lost one of its nine lives and I nearly broke my neck," Louis said, trying to sound severe but instead finding himself amused as Wolf allowed one of the kittens to climb up and sit on his shoulder like a parrot. "For heaven's sake, I said you could keep them if they stayed in the storerooms."

Wolf pulled a face. "They don't like it down there. It's dark and they're all by themselves."

Louis rolled his eyes. "They're cats; they can see in the dark, there are three of them, and they have that big space to explore and all the mice they can eat. Cat nirvana, I should think."

"They miss me," Wolf insisted, stubbornly returning the same argument they'd had only that morning.

"Oh, fine," Louis said, for admittedly the creatures were adorable, and Wolf was clearly smitten with them. Louis knew Wolf had experienced little enough love and affection in his life so

far, and Louis would not deny him the kittens if they made him happy. Despite his size, he was still only a boy. "But the first time they piss on the floor, or worse, you're clearing it up, and they go back to the cellars."

Wolf grinned in triumph, lifting one kitten up to look at it. "See? I told you he was a soft touch."

Louis huffed and shook his head. "I am nothing of the sort, just keep them in order."

"I'm going to make them their own little door so they can go outside when they want, and they're really very clean already. They won't be any bother."

"You said that about the ferret," Louis said darkly.

Wolf flushed and looked sheepish. "I said I was sorry about the ferret."

"Hmmm," Louis replied, and carried on his way.

It was a fine evening, the first touch of spring warmth in the air, and so Louis decided against a carriage to take him the short distance to the hotel and walked instead. He had gone barely two streets before he realised he was being followed. Without looking back or speeding up, he walked around the next corner and ducked into a doorway to wait. Louis heard a muttered curse, the voice so familiar, his blood ran cold.

As the figure slipped past the doorway, Louis reached out and caught the man by the neck, slamming him face first against the wall and wrenching one arm behind him to keep him still.

"I told you to stay away from me, Etienne," Louis snarled as Etienne struggled to get free. He was skinnier than Louis remembered, and he reeked of opium and stale sweat. His hair was lank and greasy, and his clothes had not been laundered any time recently.

"S'il te plaît, Louis. I didn't mean any harm. I'm desperate. Please. I've not eaten in days," he said, whimpering piteously.

Louis let him go, not wanting to dirty his hands for a moment longer than he had to. "Why should I give you anything?"

"I'm sorry," Etienne said, clutching his arms about himself. "I'm sorry. Forgive me, Louis. Please. We were friends once, good friends. Can't you forgive me?"

Louis snorted. "You were never my friend." Yet despite everything, he could feel nothing but pity and revulsion for what Etienne had become, so he reached for his money, removing enough for what he would need tonight and handing the rest to Etienne. "That's all you're getting from me. Spend it on opium or do yourself some good and get yourself together, I really don't care. Only, don't come near me again."

Etienne looked at the money in his hands. It was not a fortune, but more than enough to get himself cleaned up, get decent lodgings, and feed himself for a month, or more if he was not too extravagant. His lip curled. "That's it? You're worth a bloody fortune and that's all you'll give me?"

"You threatened to kill me, you've already tried to hurt me, you send me vile parcels and ranting letters, and now you think I should help you? Go to the devil!" Louis said in disgust.

Etienne's eyes lit with a passionate, evangelical gleam that made Louis take an instinctive step away from him. "I was trying to help you, Louis. You must understand that. God will forgive you if you repent of your sins. He'll forgive us both. But you're evil, don't you see? Look what you did to me, look how far I have fallen, and I never harmed you, I was your friend. You hurt people, Louis, you taint them with your evil."

Louis stared at him, his skin crawling with alarm. He was insane. Whether it had always been inside him, waiting to break free, or whether the opium had broken his mind, Louis did not know, nor care. He just wanted to get away.

"I am not your friend, Etienne, and you were never mine. Friends do not betray each other, as you have betrayed me

frequently. We're done. The next time, I shan't react so kindly. Do yourself a favour and keep away from me."

Louis strode away and did not look back.

"Non, no more, I must go now," Louis said, trying to disentangle himself from Madame Polignac so he could leave her carriage where it had stopped, a few streets from Rouge et Noir.

He had been seeing her for a couple of months but now it was time to break it off with her. She had that misty-eyed look that suggested feelings were becoming involved, and that would only lead to trouble. Besides, it wasn't real. The women he dallied with wanted romance and pleasure, and that much he could provide, but anything real, anything lasting, he did not know how to give. He only had a limited number of tricks up his sleeve. He was good in bed and a generous lover, and he could be amusing company. But it was all a veneer. They did not know who he truly was. If they did, they would run a mile. And he could not pretend forever. They would inevitably grow tired of the shallow façade, and he had no wish to see disappointment in their eyes, or worse, pity, if he allowed himself to feel anything for them.

"S'il vous plaît, Louis," she wept, clinging to him and sobbing.

"Arrêtez ça maintenant, ma chère," he said, gently but firmly pulling away from her. "You knew this was how it would be. I warned you from the start. I do not stay. It is only for a little while. We had a lovely time together, but now it is over. You must find someone else, someone who deserves you, for you deserve far more than I can give."

"Non, non," she sobbed harder, shaking her head, her hair in disarray and her eyes red and puffy from crying.

Louis hardened his heart, though he felt like a brute as he always did, but it was for the best. "I am not worth your tears, madame, I promise you. I suggest you cry on the shoulder of Monsieur du Malfourat. He admires you very much, you know, and he is a kind man. A generous one, too. You could be happy with such a husband."

"I could be h-happy with you if you would let me!"

"Non, that is not true, and in time you will see that. Goodbye, madame. I am sorry for any distress I have caused you."

Louis climbed out of the carriage and shut the door, giving the driver sharp instructions to take the lady directly home. Yet the foolish woman leant out the window for all to see, still sobbing and pleading for him to change his mind as the carriage drove away.

Swearing under his breath, Louis closed his eyes. God, but he was a bastard. Was this really all he was good for? Yet he did not know how else to live, and he got so damned lonely. Every time an affair ended, he promised himself he would not begin another, and yet the women kept coming, and they were kind and loving and attentive and, for a little while, he felt like he mattered. For a little while he could pretend that he belonged somewhere, and to someone, and even though he knew it was an illusion, it was all that he had. How pathetic.

Disgusted with himself, he determined to find solace in the bottom of a bottle of cognac and turned to walk the short distance home, only to stop in his tracks. His heart, which had sat heavy in his chest until this moment, leapt to his throat as a dark figure detached itself from the shadows. A chill of terror shivered down his spine.

"Well, dog. It seems you are every bit the vile whore I knew you would be."

Louis stiffened, ready to defend himself but the blow came from behind him, pain exploding in his head as his vision whited out, and then there was nothing more.

The first thing he noticed was the cold. The floor beneath him was freezing and there seemed to be little between him and it. Next was the pain. Louis groaned, nausea swirling in his guts as the agony in his head made him want to vomit. He took a deep breath, trying to still the desire to empty his stomach and to force his brain into action. Something was horribly wrong, that much he remembered. There had been Madame Polignac, and she'd been crying and then....

He jolted, scrambling upright so fast his head spun, and smothered a cry of pain. The room was dark apart from a shaft of moonlight, and his vision seemed strangely blurry and unfocused. Louis blinked, certain he was not alone.

"He's awake, Pa," Etienne's voice came out of the darkness, filled with what sounded like childish delight, and the horror of his situation made Louis' heart thunder.

Non. Not this. Not to be at the mercy of this man again. It was unbearable. He knew better than to show any fear, though, or any reaction at all. Louis studied his surroundings, looking for weapons, for a way out, for any hope.

He did not know where he was, but he did not think it could be far from the club. From the little sliver of sky he could see through a small, broken window, he could tell it was still full dark and a long time till morning. The air smelled damp, the floor beneath him only packed earth. A cellar, then.

"Did you see? Did you see his back? He's marked himself with a great bird of prey. That's proof of devilry, surely?" Etienne demanded of his father, sounding beside himself with excitement.

Louis shivered, realising they had stripped him to the waist. Etienne's doing, he suspected, his skin prickling with aversion at the idea of the man's hands on him.

"Shut up, you vile creature," Monsieur Boucher said coldly, regarding his son with open revulsion. "You are worse than he is

because you are weak. At least he never begged. Show a little backbone for once in your life."

"But it's his fault," Etienne snarled, savage all at once. "He did it! He corrupted me. I would never—"

"You stole from me and ran here of your own free will to revel in debauchery. You sought him out. Any rot is your own. The two of you disgust me. That you are a son of mine is my greatest disappointment. I should end you too, put you both down like the dogs you are."

Etienne stilled at the words and grew quiet, though Louis saw his eyes glint with malevolence. Monsieur Boucher turned his attention back to Louis. The man sat on a chair, the only furniture in the room, and now he leaned forward so the shaft of moonlight fell over his harsh features. Louis tamped down a swell of panic, the hopelessness and terror he had always felt in this man's presence threatening to overwhelm him. He reminded himself fiercely that he was not a helpless child any longer. Louis was a man, and he knew how to fight, knew how to survive. He could survive this, endure this as he had endured the rest.

Louis steadied his breathing, trying to slow his racing heart. Monsieur Boucher's face was haggard; he looked older than Louis remembered, though he was still an intimidating presence, and there were two of them. Still, Louis was cleverer than Etienne and quicker than either of them, or at least he had been before that blow to the head. Now his brain seemed sluggish, dull with pain. He suspected if he tried to stand, the room would spin.

"Well, Louis. It's time for a reckoning. You caused me a great deal of expense and trouble, leaving like you did."

"Well, most pimps and madams know better than to spend the money their whores earn before they've earned it," Louis said, holding Monsieur Boucher's gaze.

"It was the best place for you," Boucher said in disgust. "You're still a whore, no matter how you present yourself to the

world. You taint everyone you touch. That poor woman tonight will burn in hell for what she let you do to her."

Louis snorted. "I see you've found religion in your old age. Hedging your bets, old man? That was always your bitch of a wife's refrain."

There was an ominous click and Louis saw the moonlight glint on the barrel of a pistol. He forced himself not to react.

"I was too soft on you, that was the trouble. Perhaps I should have simply drowned you when you were a snivelling little boy, and saved myself all this trouble."

"You should have," Louis agreed softly. "For you will die this night."

There was a bark of laughter. "I don't think so. I'm the one holding the gun."

Louis forced his limbs into a relaxed pose, his expression placid. "Alors, but you are still a fool, and a short-sighted one at that. You do not know who I am, do you? You do not know what you are dealing with." Louis laughed, leaning his head back against the wall and snorting as Boucher's obvious indignation and fury at his words made him feel better, stronger.

"So, you have a title, what do I care for that?" Boucher sneered.

Louis sighed, waving this away with a dismissive hand. "I do not mean the title itself, but my name means something in Paris. Even supposing you manage to kill me—and I am not so certain you have it in you—you won't last the night. Once word gets out, you will be hunted down like the dog you made me. They will make you suffer first, for what you did."

"Ridiculous," Boucher scoffed, clearly disbelieving.

Louis smirked, an expression precisely calculated to infuriate the man. "Ah, but you are king of your little pile of shit, and you never poke your head out far enough to look beyond it. Here, I rule. I killed your friend the viscount, by the way. Did you know that? I threw his body into the Seine and took over his business. I closed his vile house, and I made his pitiful little enterprise into something that employs hundreds of men. All loyal to me. And my brother will set every one of them to the task of ending your life. I hope you can sleep with one eye open, for you'll have no peace after this."

Boucher glanced at his son, who was nervously turning a knife back and forth between his hands. "Is this true?"

Etienne shrugged and ran a hand through his filthy hair, avoiding his father's eye. "I suppose," he said, his expression that of a sulky boy.

"And you didn't think to tell me?"

"You wanted him found!" Etienne retorted. "You never asked me for anything more than to lead you to him. I didn't realise you were a coward."

Boucher leapt to his feet and backhanded his son, the move so quick and brutal that Louis knew he could not underestimate him. Still, he got to his feet while the man was distracted, leaning against the wall and breathing hard as his head and stomach punished him for moving.

Etienne huddled on the damp ground, whimpering and clutching at his jaw as blood trickled between his fingers.

"Enough of this," Boucher said, his voice firm. "You ruined everything for me, and I'll have my revenge now. Latimer screwed every sou I ever had from me, and I've little enough left that I don't much care what happens next, but I'll send you to the devil if it's the last thing I do."

"Oh, it will be," Louis promised him.

"Get moving." Boucher gestured with the pistol.

"Where are we going?" Louis demanded.

"There is a nice deep hole waiting on the other side of the yard there," Boucher said with a nasty smile. "It's all ready for you. All you need to do is die."

Louis moved forward. Down in the cellar there was little chance of escape, but outside, he might get lucky, or someone might see and send for help.

Once outside, Louis realised he had been correct. They were close to the club and on a plot of scrub land surrounded by abandoned buildings, which were due to be demolished any day now. Someone must have seen the two men carrying him away, surely? But this was Paris, and people disappeared every day. Most knew better than to interfere when turning a blind eye was so much safer. It was unlikely anyone would know he was missing until tomorrow afternoon. So, he was on his own.

The ground was littered with broken glass and bricks, and Louis knew this was his best chance. Boucher kept him walking ahead of them, the gun pointed at his back. Louis saw a fresh mound of earth up ahead in the moonlight. His blood ran cold at the sight, and he pretended to stumble, falling to one knee, and earning himself a kick before he staggered to his feet again, half a brick clutched in his fist. The move had been too fast for Boucher to notice him snatch it up, and he held it close to his chest, awaiting his chance.

They were perhaps five feet from the grave when Louis spun around and smashed the brick down upon Boucher's wrist. The man yelled in pain as the gun clattered to the ground and Louis kicked him in the balls. Etienne shrieked as his father fell to his knees with a groan, and then lunged for the pistol that had been flung at his feet. To Louis' astonishment, he levelled it at his father.

"Ha! Not so weak now, am I, Pa?" he crowed. "Kill him, Louis," he demanded, reaching into his pocket and removing the knife he'd been playing with earlier. He tossed it to Louis, who lost no time in picking it up.

"Kill him yourself," Louis said, never taking his eyes off either man.

"No! You're the devil, you do it! Make him burn, Louis. I'll help you burn him once he'd dead. Just cut his throat for me," he added, with a grin that made all the hairs on the back of Louis' neck stand on end.

Etienne was not grinning for long, however, as his father grabbed his ankle and pulled. Etienne fell hard, smashing his head on the floor. He lay there groaning as his father got to his feet. Louis lashed out with the knife, cutting Boucher's upper arm before he could close his fingers around the pistol. Cursing, he staggered back, and Louis kicked the pistol farther away, not daring to take his eyes off him, holding the knife out.

"Leave, now," Louis said, praying he would not black out before this was done, for his head was exploding, the pain making it hard to concentrate on anything else. "Leave and go back home, and forget you ever knew me, or I shall kill you."

"Non," Boucher said, his gaze black with hatred. "Not now. This ends tonight."

Louis nodded, knowing there was no way out. Only one of them was going to walk away from this. Boucher ran at him, and Louis tried to dodge, but his head was spinning, and he stumbled, the man crashing into him and sending him to the ground. They grappled, Boucher smashing the hand holding the knife against the ground, and Louis gasped as he felt something break. The knife fell from his injured hand. With all his remaining strength, he hit Boucher in the side of the head as pain radiated through his knuckles. For a moment, Boucher swayed, stunned, and Louis flipped them before scrambling away and snatching up the pistol. Boucher roared with fury and came after him, knife raised, and Louis fired.

Monsieur Boucher stopped in his tracks as a dark stain bloomed on his chest. Louis stared, heart thundering as the man swayed, and crashed down like a felled tree.

Louis could do nothing but breathe and endure the searing pain in his head. The world seemed to grow dark around the edges as he fought to stay conscious.

"Oh, Louis," Etienne's voice whispered in the darkness. "You did it. You killed him."

Louis swallowed hard, fighting the desire to throw up, but the pain was dizzying, and he knew Etienne was going to kill him if didn't get away and fast. Drunkenly, he lurched to his feet, almost falling again as the ground seemed to shift beneath him. He reached out, steadying himself against the wall of what had once been a warehouse. Though he had known it was inevitable, he saw the glint of the knife in Etienne's hand with increasing desperation. He would not get out of this alive.

Using the wall to keep himself upright, he backed up, trying to put distance between him and Etienne, who was standing over the body of his father, staring down at it with a look of unrestrained delight. Dieu, what a family.

"Oh, don't go, Louis," Etienne called, sounding almost cheerful. "We're not finished yet. I'm still going to save you, because I promised I would, didn't I? And I always keep my promises."

Louis ignored him and kept moving as fast as he could, breaking into a run as he heard Etienne crashing about behind him.

"Wait for me, Louis. It's not like you can start without me," he added, laughing now.

Louis forced himself on, fighting through the pain, concentrating on staying conscious as the world blurred and spun. There... There was the abandoned building where they'd held him. The street was on the other side and if he could just get there... He crashed inside, falling to his knees and pulling himself upright again on the remains of a broken chair, but Etienne was right behind him.

"Louis, wait!" he shouted. "Don't run away. We're friends, remember?"

Louis stilled as his body refused to obey him. There was the strangest sensation in his side, and he was suddenly cold, so very cold. He fell then, too broken to move, to try to escape. Looking down, he saw the hilt of the knife. It was not such a very large knife, not like the one he had killed Latimer with, but it would do, he supposed. He looked up to see Etienne staring at it too, his expression sympathetic.

"It won't hurt for long," he promised, his voice soft. He sat down cross-legged beside Louis and reloaded the pistol. Glancing at Louis, he shrugged. "Just in case, seeing as how you've got my knife," he added with a chuckle, as though it were quite normal for Louis to have a knife stuck in his side.

Louis stared at him and then decided he did not want Etienne to be the last thing he ever saw, so he closed his eyes and tried to remember something good. He thought about his brother and the life they had led at the circus, which had felt something like happiness for a while. Then he thought about Wolf and the kittens, and the damned ferret, and he smiled. He was glad Nic was there to look after Wolf, and vice versa. They would mourn him, at least, and he was sorry for it, but glad too, to know someone would think of him kindly.

Etienne's voice intruded again. "Your teeth are chattering, but you'll be warm enough soon. Oh, yes. We'll both be warm, and the fire will cleanse our souls of all the bad things, and we'll go to heaven, you and me. We'll be together again, like when we were boys, when we were happy."

Louis could smell smoke, and hear the crackle of flame, but he shut Etienne's voice out. He was too tired, and it hurt so damned much. He hoped he'd be dead before the flames reached him.

"Louis!"

Louis' eyes flew open as he saw Wolf in the doorway. Panic swept through him at the idea Etienne would kill him, too.

"Wolf, no! Look out!"

Etienne stood, raising the pistol, aiming at Wolf. Louis forced his body to move, crying out as the movement sent the knife deeper into his flesh. He reached up, grabbing Etienne's arm and pulled down hard. The pain was so intense he fell back immediately, but Etienne staggered and dropped the pistol, which was all Wolf needed. For a moment Louis could do nothing but pray as he saw the two figures struggling, backlit by flames, as the fire took hold of the old, dry timbers and climbed higher.

"Wolf, get out... get out!" he ordered, desperate that he not be responsible for killing the boy too. If there was such a thing as hell, he did not doubt that was where he was going, but if Wolf died because of him, he'd go willingly. Desperately, he reached for the pistol, dragging himself across the floor and almost vomiting as pain ripped through him. Fighting to stay awake, Louis grasped the gun in a shaking hand and did his best to aim.

"Wolf," he rasped, needing the boy to get clear, but Wolf could not hear his voice over the flames. He tried again. "Wolf!"

Miraculously, Wolf heard and stumbled away. Louis fired. Etienne screamed, clutching at his thigh as blood poured from the wound. His face twisted with savagery, he turned on Louis, but Wolf tackled him to the floor, smashing his fist into his face over and over until Etienne lay still. Coughing and choking as the smoke burned their eyes and throats, Wolf stumbled to his feet and ran to Louis.

"Louis! My God, we need to get you out of here."

Louis shook his head. The fire surrounded them, the heat of the flames searing his skin, and he knew they'd not both get out of this. "Go," he said, too tired to fight anymore. "It's all right. Tell Nic I'm sorry. Just go."

"I won't leave you, so you can tell him yourself!" Wolf said, his voice thick, though whether from emotion or the smoke that was filling the room, Louis did not know. "Damn you, Louis, don't you die on me! I'll never forgive you."

Wolf tried to get him to his feet, but it was too much, and Louis could not stand. Pain and exhaustion pressed down upon him, and he fell back. The last thing he remembered was the crackle of the flames, the acrid smoke burning his lungs, and Wolf's furious voice shouting at him from a long way away, commanding him not to die, until even that faded, and everywhere was silent.

Chapter 23

Dearest Cat,

I thought I had best write and let you know I am well and safe in Paris with my guardian. Please don't believe all the horrible things they said about him. It is all nonsense. He and Evie are married, and I am so happy for them. For myself too, for Louis has promised I shall have a home with them.

I had the most marvellous adventure coming out here; it was very exciting. I met with Mr Godwin, who is a very nice man, for he came to make sure Louis wasn't in trouble, which was very good of him. He is lucky I found him, though, for he is far too trusting. How he doesn't get his wallet or his watch stolen every time he sets foot out of doors is beyond me.

I wish you were here too. What fun we could have in this marvellous city.

—Excerpt of a letter from Miss Agatha Smith to Lady Catherine 'Cat' Barrington (daughter of Lucian and Matilda Barrington, The Most Hon'ble Marquess and Marchioness of Montagu.)

23rd July 1842, Casino Rouge et Noir, 7th Arrondissement, Paris, France.

Evie laughed as Jacques made a great fuss of her, treating her as though she were the queen herself come for a visit.

"Really, Monsieur Toussaint, this is unnecessary," she said, gaining a little confidence in her French as the man seemed to understand her without difficulty. "Please do not worry about entertaining me. Though, if you would like to indulge me, I should enjoy visiting the kitchens."

The man's eyes grew round with surprise. "The kitchens?" he repeated, as though she'd asked to tour the sewers.

Evie nodded and lowered her voice conspiratorially. "You know as well as I do, all the best gossip can be found in the kitchens."

He stared at her for a moment and then burst out laughing, delighted. "Ah, monsieur has married a clever woman, I see. In that case, the kitchens it is." He gave her a flourishing bow and offered her his arm.

Evie took it with a regal nod, adding, "And if there is the slightest chance of a cup of tea and some cake, we shall become the greatest of friends."

Monsieur Toussaint grinned at her. "We have learned how to make perfect English tea, Madame la Comtesse, for we have many English lords and ladies who visit us here. As for *gateaux*, the finest in France can be found at Rouge et Noir. Let us see what our chef can tempt you with."

"It will take very little in the way of temptation, I assure you," Evie said gravely, and went happily along to view the culinary expertise of their chef.

Half an hour later, Evie had the undivided attention of Monsieur Alfonse, who—much to her delight—was everything her

305

imagination believed a French chef ought to be. He was a short but rotund man with a ruddy face, a luxuriant moustache, and an extravagant way of expressing himself. His pride in his work and his kitchen was clear.

"Oh, no, monsieur. Pax!" Evie cried as the chef brought her yet another exquisite creation to try. His face fell, and she laughed, shaking her head. "Oh, my word, very well. But this is the last one," she scolded him, wagging a finger as he set down a beautiful creation adorned with tiny wild strawberries and meringues and spun sugar and… well, it looked far too good to eat. Not that she would let that stop her. She took up a clean fork and cut off a mouthful, which comprised a strawberry mousse and cake and something with a little crunch.

"Bon? C'est bon?" he demanded, looking agitated as he waited for her response.

Evie sighed. "Oh, it's heavenly. Divine. Truly, Monsieur Alfonse, you are a marvel. I have half a mind to steal you away and take you back to England with me."

Monsieur preened, grinning at her, and giving an expansive sweep of his hand as he bowed. "For you, madame, I would go."

Evie laughed, but a commotion outside the kitchen took her attention. "Whatever is going on?"

Monsieur Alfonse scowled, clearly displeased by the interruption and he strode through the kitchen scattering staff as he went. Evie followed, for wasn't that was an English voice she heard shouting. Not her father, surely?

The chef stormed out of the kitchen and through a scullery to a corridor. Here in the open doorway that led to a large, paved yard, was the commotion.

"Get your hands off me, or I'll break your nose!" returned a furious voice in clipped, precise English before it reverted to French. "Take me to Monsieur le Comte. I am Lord Frederick Adolphus, I tell you…."

"Fred?" Evie said in alarm, pushing through to see the boy standing in the yard outside, with two security men on either side of him, scowling.

"Evie! Oh, thank heavens I've found you," he said, breathing a heartfelt sigh of relief and shoving irritably at the two men trying to restrain him.

"Fred!" Evie said again, looking him up and down in horror. "Whatever happened to you?"

Poor Fred blushed scarlet and pushed his sodden hair out of his eyes, one of which was swelling shut. His trousers were torn, one coat sleeve was hanging on by a thread, and he was soaked to the skin. "I had a bit of disagreement. A couple of lads down the road thought they'd relieve me of my purse, and I thought they wouldn't. I persuaded them in the end, but not before they'd pushed me in the fountain."

"Good heavens. But how are you here at all? Where is your father?"

"Never mind that," he said impatiently and then added in a rush: "Begging your pardon, but have you seen Miss Smith?"

Everything became clear to Evie as she saw the worry in the boy's eyes. "Oh, Fred. You came after her. What a sweetheart you are. Yes, Agatha is safe and well. Don't worry."

All the tension seemed to leave the boy in a rush, and he let out a sigh. "Oh. Oh, that's… that's jolly good. I-I was rather worried," he added, and then gave a slightly hysterical laugh.

Evie's heart ached for the poor boy, who must have been beside himself to have taken off on such a madcap adventure in pursuit of her. "Well, never mind Agatha for the moment," she said gently. "You'll see her later. For now, let's get you dry and find you something to eat."

"Yes, please, I'm famished," he admitted, looking relieved to have someone else take charge for a bit.

"Do you not have any luggage?" Evie asked, looking about for a bag or something, for surely, he'd brought something with him.

"Yes, thankfully, I kept hold of it. I think it got tossed over there when those two brutes started trying to make me leave. Though there's not much left, or I would have changed before arriving dripping wet on the doorstep. I suppose I do look rather a sight. It's no wonder they didn't believe who I was, but I had to pawn a few things in the last town," he admitted ruefully.

Evie looked over towards what looked like a series of large storerooms and saw a dark shape in the open doorway of one of the buildings. His bag, no doubt. She turned back to Fred.

"Oh, dear. It sounds like you've had quite the adventure." Evie nodded towards Madame Fournier who had come to see what the commotion was about. She was housekeeper of the private apartment Louis and Nic kept next to the club and Jacques had introduced her earlier. "Madame Fournier, this is my young friend Lord Fredrick, the Duke of Bedwin's son. He's had a very trying evening. Could you arrange a bath for him and something to eat, please?"

"Of course, Madame, at once. If you would like to follow me, my lord," she said to Fred, gesturing for him to follow her. Fred turned back to Evie, uncertainly.

"It's all right, Fred. You go inside and get cleaned up. I'll fetch your bag and have it sent up. We'll talk later."

"So Etienne escaped the fire?" Mr Knight replied, his gaze on Louis intent.

Louis nodded. "Sadly, though how is beyond me, for Wolf swears he was unconscious when we got out, and we barely made it."

"You are close, the two of you. To risk your lives for one another speaks of a deep bond."

Louis nodded. "We understand each other and have much in common. We were both born to titles which should give us entry into society, but neither of us really fit. Wolf never even had the chance to try, though truthfully, I did not know he wished to until recently. Now he has it in his head to return to England, but I fear what kind of reception he will receive."

"The son of a traitor, and a notorious criminal in his own right? Oh, I think we know what kind of reception he'll receive," Knight said with a snort.

"Quite. I think they will shun him at every turn, and I do not wish to see him hurt," Louis said, frowning. He laughed at Mr Knight's expression.

"Wolf is every bit as terrifying as you might have heard, when the occasion warrants it, but to those he cares for…." Louis shrugged. "Many of us show a face to the world because it is what is expected of us, because we must survive, and it is the only way. If we do not, we have no place at all, but it is not always who we are."

"So, you mean to tell me that your womanising days are behind you, and you will be a devoted husband to my daughter, and that the king of the Parisian underworld is really a decent fellow and only misunderstood?" Mr Knight asked sceptically.

Louis' lips quirked, but he nodded. *"Oui,* exactly that."

Mr Knight sighed and shook his head. "Well, my daughter seems to believe in you, and despite what she said earlier, I do not believe her the least bit foolish. Young, yes, and perhaps a little naïve, but she is a good judge of character. I saw the way she spoke to you earlier, and the way you listened. Perhaps I should take a leaf out of her book and admit I may have judged you a little harshly. Only a very little, mind."

Louis shook his head. *"Non.* I have thought much of this of late. I have thought about the fact that one day, if we are lucky, I may have a daughter as lovely as she is. What would I have felt if a man like me appeared and tried to carry her off?" He blew out a harsh breath, a shiver running down his back at the idea. *"Non,* Mr Knight. You have done nothing I that should not have done myself in your place. Indeed, I think you have been most decent. I believe, in your position, I may have had the fellow disappeared, never to be seen again."

Mr Knight laughed, and finally he seemed to relax, smiling with what looked like genuine amusement. "Then, I shall pray nightly that she delivers you with a surfeit of daughters and consider that a fitting revenge for the trouble you have caused me."

"Dieu, you are a hard man," Louis replied with a pained expression.

"I'm afraid so, but I think you had best call me Gabriel, or we shall have Evie scolding us for not being friends."

"Are we friends?" Louis asked cautiously.

Gabriel shrugged. "Perhaps not yet," he admitted. "But I'll get used to the idea, given time. After all, I nearly killed Henry when I discovered him with Florence, and he *was* my friend."

Louis opened his mouth to reply when shrieks and shouts echoed from outside the club. *"Que diable*—excuse me, Gabriel. I must see what is going on."

Louis hurried towards the staff exit that led to the kitchens and storerooms and then outside. By the time he got to the door, Jacques was running to find him and clutched at his arms, his face white with fear.

"It's Etienne," he said. "He has the comtesse. I swear I did not know, monsieur, but she went outside. I do not know why she went, but he must have been hiding in the storerooms."

For a split second, Louis thought he could not possibly have heard correctly, for Evie was safe inside the building, behind layers of security and guards and....

He ran.

Bursting out onto the courtyard, he found it bristling with those same guards, not one of whom could do a thing without the risk of hurting his wife. Etienne had hold of her and was backing her up towards a waiting carriage. One arm was lashed tight about her upper body, shielding himself with her, a gun pressed to her temple.

"Etienne," Louis said, as terror held his heart in a vice. He knew he must keep calm, knew he must do whatever it took to keep Evie safe, but it was so hard to think straight when he saw the fear in her eyes. He wanted to kill Etienne with his bare hands, but he could do nothing to put Evie at risk. Louis forced himself to speak, to sound calm and reassuring. "It's all right, Evie, don't be frightened. Etienne won't hurt you. He does not want you, do you Etienne? You want me. That's why you came, isn't it? You came for me. Because we're friends, yes?"

Louis could hardly recognise the man, the burns to his face were so severe. His hair was patchy on one side, and he held himself at a slightly odd angle.

"I am your friend," Etienne agreed, his voice calm though his eyes burned with a febrile intensity that boded ill. "Though you're not mine, are you, Louis? You left me to burn alone. You were supposed to be there too. But it's all right, I forgive you. I know you can't help it, you were born evil, that's all. It's not your fault. But I'm going to help you now, because I cleansed all my sins away in the flames, and now it's your turn. You really must, Louis. I am God's messenger, you see. He sent me to save you from the devil, and I must do it. I *must* save you."

Louis nodded, holding out his hands. His heart was beating so hard he felt sick, and it was hard to breathe, hard to force the words out when he was out of his mind with fear for Evie. "I know, Etienne. I know, and I will come with you. I'll come willingly, but first you must let Evie go. She's innocent, you see. Like you were, remember? I tricked her. I seduced her and stole her away from her family. Her father is here, he's inside, waiting to rescue her, to take her home...."

"Louis, no!" Evie cried, tears rolling down her face. "No, that's not true."

"It is true!" Louis said harshly, staring at her, silently pleading for her to understand that he *must* do this. For, if Etienne took him, there was still a chance for them, but if anything happened to Evie, they were both doomed, for he would not live with such a loss. He had endured a good deal in his life, but that he could not survive.

"You see, Etienne," Louis said, his voice thick as he saw the misery in Evie's eyes. "She's bewitched, she does not know what she is saying. You remember how it is, don't you? She can't help it, any more than you could, the poor child."

Etienne's expression softened, and he stroked Evie's hair with the barrel of the gun. "Poor deluded child. She thinks she loves you, but it's the lure of the devil. He's the serpent, don't you see? He's the wicked snake in the garden of Eden."

"No, that's a lie," Evie retorted and elbowed Etienne savagely in the gut, struggling to get free. "You're the evil one, not him!"

"Non!" Louis cried, running forward as Etienne snarled in fury but he only tightened his grip on Evie. "Don't hurt her, Etienne. I'm here. Remember? I'm the one you want. I'll come with you. I'll do whatever you want, but let her go," he pleaded, willing to do anything Etienne wanted so long as Evie was safely away from him.

"Very well," Etienne said, though he was staring at Evie with undisguised malice now. "Get in the carriage, Louis."

"Let her go first," Louis insisted, but though Etienne had never been very bright, he was sly enough to know better than that.

"Oh, no. If I let her go, those men will shoot me the moment I do. We all three get in the carriage and I will let her out around the corner, *if* they don't follow us," he added, raising his voice so everyone could hear.

"Very well," Louis said, watching as Etienne struggled to get in the carriage backwards, dragging Evie up behind him. Louis climbed in after them and sat opposite, never taking his eyes from Evie.

Slamming the door shut, Etienne shouted to the driver. "*Allez, Monsieur Franklin.*"

The carriage took off at speed and Louis gritted his teeth, desperate for a moment when he could get to Etienne without putting Evie at risk. But the bastard held her in his lap, the gun aimed beneath her chin, and Louis did not dare move. Slowly, he reached his hand out across the gap, twining his fingers with his wife's. She held on tight, her hands cold as ice.

Louis held her gaze, trying to tell her without words everything he felt, the joy she had brought to his life, the knowledge of what it meant to love and be loved in return.

"I love you," she whispered, and the tears sliding down her lovely face made him want to howl with misery. "Please, please don't let him hurt you."

Louis did not know what to say, how to say goodbye to this woman when he did not want to ever leave her side, but Etienne meant to see him dead. Louis was not about to make it easy for him, but the last time had almost killed him. It had taken him months to recover, and only then because his brother and Wolf had nursed him so diligently. He did not know if he could be that lucky again, or if his luck had run out.

"*Amour de ma vie,*" he said, so quietly Etienne could not hear, but he hoped Evie did. He bent his head and pressed a kiss to her fingers, only to jerk back a moment later as Etienne kicked out at him.

"Leave her be. You've hurt her enough," he snarled. "There, there, pretty English lady. You're safe now. Franklin, *arrêtez-*

vous!" he yelled, kicking at the door of the carriage. They halted abruptly and a moment later, the door opened.

"Louis!" Evie cried, as Etienne shoved her violently out of the door.

Louis exclaimed, trying to reach her but Etienne cocked the pistol and Louis knew he'd as soon shoot him in the guts as leave him be. To his relief, the driver who had opened the door caught Evie, steadying her fall.

"You bastard," said a furious English voice. "For Christ's sake, you said nothing about an English woman, just the comte. I'll have no more part in this."

"You'll drive to the destination, as agreed, then you may do as you please," Etienne snarled. "Now leave her and get moving."

Cursing, the man slammed the door shut and hurried back to the horses while Evie tried to pull the door open again.

"Louis!" she cried, banging on the door, but the carriage moved off, and Louis watched as she disappeared into the distance.

He let out a breath. He did not doubt that someone was following. Not close enough behind to be seen, but close enough that Evie would not be alone for long. Now, all he needed to do was survive.

Chapter 24

Dear diary,

I am horribly worried about Aggie. I do not blame her for going off in pursuit of her guardian, for if my Papa was in trouble, I would not hesitate to go after him. Nearly all the books make it so that the men have grand adventures and save the damsel in distress while that poor creature just weeps and faints, and that's just hopeless. My mama would not sit by if Papa was in trouble, and I should not either if anyone I cared for was at risk. Besides, I should enjoy a grand adventure.

I suppose I must admit that I am a bit put out that Aggie did not ask me to go too, especially now that I hear Fred has gone after her. I should have expected that, as he always worries about us making spectacles of ourselves or getting into trouble. Though he usually blames me, which is most unfair, as Aggie is quite capable of being every bit as naughty as I am. He makes her cross with his fussing though and she seems to drive him mad half of the time. The other half they are the very best of friends. I hope he is safe too, for really, Aggie is probably far better equipped to make such a journey than Fred, who has never lived on the streets as she did.

Oh, I want them home safe and sound, and then I can just be cross and tell them how horribly jealous I am that they went off and had adventures without me.

One day I shall have a grand adventure all by myself, and I won't let either of them come along!

—Excerpt of a diary entry by Lady Catherine 'Cat' Barrington (daughter of Lucian and Matilda Barrington, The Most Hon'ble Marquess and Marchioness of Montagu.)

23rd July 1842, an unknown destination, 7th Arrondissement, Paris, France.

"Where are we going?" Louis asked as the carriage drew them over the river.

Etienne shrugged, never taking his gaze from Louis. "Not too far. Somewhere quiet. I chose the perfect place for us before I followed you to England. I wanted to make sure it was just right this time, so it's all ready and waiting. You see the care I took to do this for you?" he added, as though he had planned a wonderful treat.

"I do see," Louis agreed.

Etienne sat back with a sigh, regarding Louis with a dreamy expression. "It's strange, isn't it, how God works, because now, I'm ugly on the outside, and beautiful inside, and you're beautiful outside, but…." He gave a delighted laugh. "But not for long, so don't be jealous."

Louis hoped he could keep the revulsion from his face and answered as civilly as he could manage. "I shall endeavour not to be."

Finally, the carriage stopped, and the driver came back around to open the door. Louis had recognised the name Franklin earlier, but it had taken him a moment to place where he had heard it. This was the man who had tried to murder the Earl of Vane. How he'd fallen in with Etienne, Louis could not fathom, but then rats often ended running together. He held his tongue, not wanting the man to know Louis had guessed who he was. It did not seem prudent to give Franklin a reason for wanting him dead, too. For now, all Franklin wanted was to get away from Etienne, and that suited Louis fine. With Etienne alone, he stood a chance.

"*Sortez,*" Etienne said, gesturing with the pistol for Louis to get out.

Any hope that he could escape vanished as he saw Franklin also held a gun.

"Fine company you keep, sir," he said in English.

Franklin's jaw tightened, but he ignored Louis, turning to Etienne, who threw a pair of iron handcuffs to him. Louis' heart sank as Franklin caught them in one hand. He gestured for Louis to hold his hands out.

"No tricks, *mon ami,*" Etienne whispered in his ear, and the press of cold metal at the base of his skull told him Etienne was ready to blow his head off the moment he did not go along with his plans.

Reluctantly, Louis held out his hands and Franklin tucked the gun in his waistband whilst he secured Louis' wrists.

"*Voila,*" he said in disgust, turning back to Etienne. "Now, we're done. I'll have no more part in your damned schemes. If you try to blackmail me again, I'll bring you down with me."

Etienne only laughed. "Oh, there won't be anything more. We're going away, aren't we Louis?" He reached out and stroked Louis' hair and Louis jerked away from his touch. He turned to Franklin.

"You know he's quite mad? He means to kill me. Does this not trouble your conscience?"

"My conscience?" Franklin repeated with a bitter laugh. "My life is over. Why the hell should I give a damn about yours? Good luck, monsieur. You'll need it."

With that, Franklin climbed back into the carriage and drove off.

Louis cursed inwardly, but took stock of his surroundings. They were close to the river here and before him was an area of abandoned slum housing in the midst of demolition. Most of the properties were little more than rubble, but in the centre were some larger buildings, warehouses which the workers were still using for storage by the looks of the heavy locks and chains securing the doors. The building on the end was dilapidated, however, listing drunkenly to one side, and this was the one Etienne guided him to.

Louis' stomach churned as they entered and he recognised the overpowering stench of camphine, usually used for lighting oil lamps. Etienne really had prepared for this, he realised, his gaze falling on the carefully prepared bonfire, the wood all neatly arranged. The entire building was one great tinderbox.

"Keep walking, up the stairs," Etienne said, gesturing with the gun. "There's a lovely view of Paris from the rooftop. It should be quite magical in the moonlight. Romantic, really."

Louis kept his mouth shut, looking desperately around for a means of escape, but there was a look in Etienne's eyes that he did not underestimate. He'd shoot Louis with the slightest provocation. Not to kill him, but to incapacitate him, and Louis could not have that. He would not be at this madman's mercy. If he could get out of this alive, he would, but he would not be Etienne's to toy with, like a cat with a mouse.

He climbed up the stairs, which creaked ominously beneath their weight, and opened a door to find himself on a flat roof. The view was indeed lovely, as Etienne had told him, but Louis was more concerned with getting down. He glanced over the side but there was little in the way of footholds. Nothing but a sheer drop and a smooth brick wall. Instead, he looked to the side, to the neighbouring building to judge the distance. It must be at least fifteen feet. He'd never make it if he tried to jump, certainly not restrained as he was, but it looked like his only hope. He needed to get these handcuffs off.

"It is beautiful, Etienne," he said softly, forcing himself to look at the view and appear relaxed. "You're right. It's peaceful too, away from the world."

"See, I told you," Etienne said, grinning at him.

Louis nodded, hoping the smile he returned looked genuine, for it sat ill and stiff upon his face. "Do you remember when we were boys, and we used to go fishing down by the river?"

"*Oui!*" Etienne said, his eyes lighting up. "I always caught the bigger fish, and you were so cross."

This was news to Louis, but he laughed softly and nodded. "Ah, well, you were more patient than I was. I never could sit still for long."

He sat down on the low wall that edged the rooftop, hoping Etienne might sit beside him and give him the chance to push him off, but Etienne stood watching him from a safe distance and did not lower the gun.

"I remember creeping into your room at night so you would read me bedtime stories," Etienne said wistfully. "I didn't like to read by myself, and no one had ever read me stories before, but you made them come to life. You did all the voices, and it seemed so exciting. Though the best were the ones you made up. Do you remember? About knights rescuing princesses, and so many grand adventures? I always thought we might have grand adventures when we grew up, but my father never let us have any peace, did he?"

There was a break to his voice as he said the words, an echo of real regret Louis recognised as the truth.

"Non," Louis said sadly. "He never gave us a chance."

He meant it this time, as he looked at Etienne and saw a glimmer of the man he might have been, in a different life, with a different father, but what was done was done, and Etienne had drifted too far into madness to return now.

Etienne's eyes filled with tears and the moonlight reflected in the glimmer, giving him a strange, otherworldly appearance against the waxy shine of his scars.

"I'm sorry, Etienne. I'm sorry for what has happened to you," Louis said. "I understand why you do this."

Etienne nodded and dashed away a tear with irritation. "I want to help you, to save you." he said, his voice choked. "To save us both."

"I know that," Louis replied, "But do you think you might take these off me? It is a little undignified for me, you know. A man has his pride, even if it is a sin."

Louis watched, his heart crashing about behind his ribs as Etienne considered him, weighing up whether it was a trick. Finally, he nodded.

"Oh, very well. I never could refuse you anything, and you are so terribly vain, but you can't help it, can you?" He fished about in his pocket for a moment and tossed Louis the key. "There you are. *Alors je m'en vais.* That fire won't light itself, will it? I'll be but a moment."

The second Etienne turned his back, Louis scrambled for the key. There were sounds from below the building, wheels and horses and men's shouts, and he glanced down, seeing two carriages arrive and his heart leapt as he saw Wolf and his brother explode from inside one. *Merci Dieu.*

"Ici!" he yelled, seeing the horror on his brother's face as he looked up.

A door banged and Louis turned to see Etienne had run back up, smoke billowing up behind him. Louis had no illusions that anyone was getting in or out via the stairs now. The building would be a furnace in seconds. He tamped down the panic growing inside him, concentrating on getting the blasted cuffs undone, which was damned difficult when his hands were shaking. Finally, he got one hand free, and the other was easier, but instead of discarding the cuffs, he held on to them, for they were made of iron and weighed a ton. As good a weapon as he was likely to get.

"Oh, dear, your friends are here, and your wife," Etienne said conversationally as he peered over the edge.

Louis started, horrified to see Etienne was correct, there was Evie with her father. She screamed as she saw him, clutching at her father's arm. Louis' heart contracted. Damn the man. What was he thinking bringing her here? He did not want her here to witness whatever was going to happen. To his left, a thunderous sound began, and he looked to see Wolf and Nic smashing down the doors to the building beside them with sledgehammers. They had come equipped for a rescue this time. Jacques was there too, a heavy rope slung over one shoulder. Louis' heart lifted. Perhaps he could survive this, with a little luck.

An explosion rent the air, the force of it knocking Louis from his feet as the door to the roof blew apart, flames and smoke billowing out as the fire reached whatever fuel Etienne had left waiting below.

Etienne yelled with pain and shrieked as he saw a large splinter had struck him in the arm. He yanked it out with another cry, the pain causing him to drop the gun. Louis lunged for him, tackling him to the floor and smashing the cuffs down against his temple. Etienne fought like a wildcat, scrabbling to get away and thrashing madly but Louis struck again and suddenly he was still. Louis got to his feet, searching blindly for the pistol but the smoke was too thick, and his eyes burned. Etienne was out cold, though, which had to be good enough.

"Louis!"

Louis turned towards the voice that had come from the next rooftop. Blindly, he ran to the edge to see his brother, Wolf, and Jacques.

"Look out," Nic yelled and swung the rope. They'd attached a brick to the end, and it clattered onto the roof. "Where's Etienne?"

"Unconscious," Louis shouted back and lost no time in grabbing hold of the rope, searching for a place to secure it and settling on a narrow chimney that looked a little like it might collapse at any moment, but was the best he could do.

"C'est fait!" he called as Nic hurried to secure the other end. Louis sat, coughing as the acrid smoke filled his lungs but he had no hope of walking across with his boots on. Tugging them off and throwing them over the side of the building, he thought somewhat hysterically that Elton would be beside himself, though perhaps he might not mind the loss of the boots if his master survived. Coughing harder, he took off his coat and waistcoat and tugged off his cravat, tying it around his face and nose to counter the smoke.

"It's ready!" Wolf shouted across the gap. "Come on, move your arse. That building won't last much longer.

Louis did not doubt the truth of that. He could feel the heat searing the soles of his feet and leapt up onto the low wall. Looking across, he saw his brother and Wolf watching him.

"Come on, Louis, you can do this!" Nic called fiercely, though they both knew the wind was blowing, which would be a problem, and the rope was not tensioned properly.

Added to that was the billowing smoke and the sparks that settled on him, burning through his shirt and stinging his skin. This was not like walking the highwire in the circus, where everything was just as it ought to be to minimise the danger.

Finally, Louis glanced down to where the carriages were. Gabriel Knight was holding Evie in place, stopping her from running to him, but she was watching, her hands covering her mouth.

"Je t'aime," he whispered, and blew her a kiss, watching with a smile as she returned the gesture, before stepping out onto the rope.

Evie did not know what to do. She called to Louis as he stood on the building's edge, staring down at her, but doubted he heard. When he blew her a kiss, she wanted to scream and weep but she held still, needing him to know she believed in him. So, she blew him a kiss in return, and told him she loved him too, and prayed that she could tell him again, a thousand times over, when he reached the other side. But she could not bear it. Could not bear to watch and yet could not tear her eyes away. The idea of standing there doing nothing was beyond her.

"Papa, I can't…" she cried, and tore from his grip, moving so fast and suddenly he did not have the chance to stop her, though she knew he followed. She flew to the building that Nic and Wolf had entered, hiking up her skirts and running as fast as she dared. As she got closer, she felt the heat from the building next door, saw the flames licking out like scarlet tongues from the openings, sending sparks and thick black smoke rising far into the night sky, blocking out the moon.

Louis was up there. He was walking that damned rope and, though she knew he had done it a thousand times, she needed to be there, needed him to know she was waiting for him, not standing beneath like a spectator while his life was in the balance.

Please God, please God, she prayed as she ran up the stairs. Louis might not believe any longer, but she did, and surely Louis had endured enough in his life, surely it was time he had a chance to live instead of merely surviving. *Give him the chance. Please, please, please....*

Though she wanted to burst out onto the roof, she knew better than to cause any sudden movement or do anything to distract Louis at such a moment. So, she opened the door quietly, stepping out with her heart in her mouth and smothering a gasp when she saw he was still there, suspended in mid-air with only the rope to hold him, still moving forward, his gaze focused directly ahead, though smoke clouded around him, and sparks danced in the darkness.

She walked slowly closer, praying all the while, holding her breath, and never taking her eyes from Louis. That was almost her undoing as she stumbled, nearly falling to her knees. Glancing down, she saw a pile of things the men had discarded: ropes and weaponry. Knives and pistols. She'd heard no shots, so she had assumed the explosion had killed Etienne. For a horrifying moment she had feared Louis dead too, but then she'd seen him standing on the edge of the building and had wept with relief. He could do this, she told herself. She knew he could. He would find his way back to her.

She looked up, horrified to see how the rope swayed back and forth, Louis' concentration absolute as he focused on balancing. His brother, Wolf, and Jacques stared at him too, as if they could keep him on the rope if they willed it hard enough. Wolf and Nic lent over the edge of the building, arms outstretched, reaching out across the divide to grab Louis the moment they could. So it was that they did not see the figure appear behind Louis, emerging from the smoke like a wraith from the depths of hell. They did not see Etienne raise the pistol.

Evie did not even think. She bent down and picked up one of the guns the men had set down and raised it. She did as her father had taught her when she was a little girl and spared the crucial second to focus on her target. *Better to hit true than waste the shot, Evie.*

She fired.

Louis had never been afraid of walking the hire-wire, not since the first time he had performed in public. Adrenaline took over and practise did the rest. You could set fear aside if you focused, if you had confidence in your own abilities. Usually this was enough, but tonight —with the damn rope swaying and the wind buffeting him, the smoke blurring his vision and making him want to cough— tonight he was afraid. He refused to think about falling, but fear climbed his throat. Louis kept going, one small step at a time. *Evie.* Evie was there, waiting for him. Everything he had ever wanted or dreamed of was waiting for him, if he only reached for it. The woman he loved, a home, a family. He needed only to manage a little farther, just a little farther.

"Goodbye, Louis."

Etienne's voice came from behind him, thick with tears, and Louis knew he was going to die. Foolish of him not to have finished the job when he had the chance. Ah, well, the mad bastard had won in the end. He held his breath.

The shot exploded through the darkness and Louis jerked, waiting for the pain, waiting for the moment his limbs ceased to obey him and he fell. He swayed violently, fighting to keep upright, too focused to wonder why there was no blood, why he was not dead as the rope jerked, giving way. It sagged, and he knew he would fall. He stepped off the rope.

"Louis!"

Voices screamed as he grasped the rope in both hands before he fell, the coarse hemp burning with no bindings to protect his skin. Hand over hand, he closed the distance to the building.

His brother's voice cried out in panic. "Louis, hold on! The building is—"

But suddenly the rope gave way. Louis held on tight. He smashed hard into the side of the building, and it knocked the air from his lungs as pain vibrated through his bones. The noise sounded like the end of the world, the vibration of the building tumbling down enough to weaken his grasp on the rope as his lungs filled with dust and smoke and he fought to breathe, fought to hold on, but there was a pain in his side, something broken, failing him now, draining his strength. He tightened his grip, determined not to fall, not now, not when he was so very close.

"Pull!"

Voice from above shouted, and Louis felt strong hands grasping him, pulling him over the wall as he collapsed in a heap, gasping and fighting for breath.

Shouts of triumph rang out and suddenly his face was being peppered with kisses.

"Louis, Louis! My love, are you hurt? Oh, my God! Louis, please… tell me!"

Louis could not speak, he could barely breathe, but he pulled Evie into his arms and held on tight despite the pain, hoping that was enough to reassure her. She collapsed against him, sobbing her heart out as she clutched at him until he could find enough air to speak.

"Mon amour. I am so very glad to see you," he said, his voice cracked and raspy.

"You ought to be," Gabriel Knight said, looking down at him. "My daughter just saved your life."

Louis stared up at her father, not understanding for a moment and then his heart sank as he realised. He cupped Evie's face in his hands. "It was you? The shot?"

Evie nodded, wiping her eyes, and leaving a black swipe of soot on her cheek in its wake. "He was g-going to shoot you. I had no choice. I c-couldn't let him…."

"Oh, Evie," he said, holding her to him and wanting to weep for what he had done, the life he had dragged her into. Gabriel must want to pitch him over the side of the damned building himself. "I'm so sorry. So sorry you had to do that."

Evie pushed away from him, scowling. "I'm not!" she said furiously. "He would have killed you! You think I would turn away from something ugly if it meant saving someone I loved? He was wicked and mad and broken and, if he had been an animal in such pain, you would call it a mercy. I do not regret it, Louis, and it will not break me or damage me. I will not regret it or let it haunt me. Neither of us will. We have too much to live for."

Louis stared up at her in wonder. *"Mon Dieu*, my Evie. I pity anyone who dares to underestimate you again. I shall spend the rest of my life anticipating what you will do next."

"I shall love you, Louis, through all of it, no matter where we go or what we do," she said staunchly, sniffling and wiping her wet cheeks on her sleeve.

"I should hope so," he murmured, holding her to him.

"Look, I'm sorry to interrupt as it's all very romantic, but do you think we could get out of this bloody smoke and off this roof? I want to go home," Wolf grumbled.

Louis gave a choked laugh and nodded as Gabriel lifted his daughter to her feet and Wolf reached for Louis, helping him to stand.

"Oh, that hurt," Wolf said, regarding Louis, who had sucked in a breath and suspected he'd just turned a startling shade of alabaster. "What did you break?"

"Ribs," Louis said through clenched teeth.

"Nice. That's got to be the third time," Wolf said, rolling his eyes as he helped Louis down the stairs as everyone else followed. "Honestly, do you think we could go for a few years without me having to rescue your sorry arse, or carry you out of a burning building? I'm getting tired of saving your life."

"I saved yours first," Louis retorted, stung.

"Yes, but my rescues were far more heroic. I mean, I carried you out unconscious through the flames. I have *scars,*" Wolf added proudly.

"So do I!"

Wolf shrugged, clearly unimpressed. "Yes, but mine were heroically earned. You were idiotic enough to let Etienne stick you with a knife."

"Like I had a choice!"

"God, you two are exhausting," Nic muttered from behind them as they reached the bottom of the stairs. "Evie, tell them to shut up and stop bickering. It's like listening to a pair of debutantes bitching."

Evie only laughed and shook her head, and to everyone's surprise, ran to embrace Wolf and kissed his cheek. "You *are* heroic, and I have been wanting to thank you so much, Wolf, for what you did that day. If you had not, I should never have had my dearest friend and the love of my life. I owe you everything. We both do."

Wolf beamed, looking appallingly smug. "There, see?" he said to Louis. "You owe me everything."

Louis groaned. "Evie! Now he'll be unbearable."

"No, he won't," Evie said, smirking. "Because if he is, I'll tell everyone he can't resist kittens and puppies, and ruin his fearsome reputation."

Wolf opened and shut his mouth, staring at Evie, and then turned to glare at Louis. "What did you tell her?" he demanded.

Louis laughed and then gasped as pain shot through his ribs. Evie ran to him and took his hand, raising it to her lips.

"He told her the truth by the sound of it," Nic answered for him, clapping Wolf on the back. "The big bad Wolf is nothing more than a fraud."

"I am not a fraud. I am exceedingly scary, I'll have you know. Grown men weep at the sight of me!" he added with obvious indignation, scowling harder as Nic snorted. "I'm not joking as you well know. They tremble and beg for mercy at the mere sound of my name," he insisted.

"Yes, you are very scary, I'm sure," Evie said soothingly. "You scared me when I first saw you, if it makes you feel better," she added helpfully.

Wolf glared at her.

"I'm not speaking to any of you," he said darkly and helped Louis to the carriage without another word.

Chapter 25

Dear Cat,

I don't know what the devil is going on. I'm in the Comte de Villen's study. I got to Rouge et Noir this evening and found Evie here. I think she married the comte, but as soon as I arrived, I was shown to my room to clean up (I'd had a rather trying evening) and since then everyone has disappeared, and no one will tell me what is going on. It's most frustrating. Aggie is in Paris too. Safe, thank heavens. Honestly, I am so tired and fed up it might be as well if I don't see her for a day or two, or at least until I've had some sleep. I don't think I trust myself to speak to her. I might wring her idiot neck for being so cork-brained as to set off across France alone. I've worn myself to a thread worrying about her these past days, and to think, I always assumed you would be the one to lead her into trouble. I apologise most humbly, Cat, for ever believing such a thing.

She's a reckless hoyden and if she's knocked a decade off my life expectancy, I shan't be the least bit surprised.

—Excerpt of a letter to Lady Catherine 'Cat' Barrington (daughter of Lucian and Matilda Barrington, The Most Hon'ble Marquess and Marchioness of Montagu) from Lord Frederick Adolphus (Son of Robert and Prunella Adolphus, Their Graces The Duke and Duchess of Bedwin).

23rd July 1842, en route to Casino Rouge et Noir, 7th Arrondissement, Paris, France.

Evie sat in the carriage, holding onto Louis as tight as she dared whilst trying to avoid his injured side. Wolf and Nic had gone with her father in his carriage to give them some privacy for which she was grateful. She breathed in the scent of him, able to discern the familiar fragrance of his expensive aftershave beneath the smoke and the sweat and trying her hardest not to cry. He was alive. He was alive and Etienne was dead and would never hurt him again.

There was a part of her that still could not believe she had killed a man. She had learned to shoot with her siblings when she was a girl, and had been a reasonable shot, but nothing more than that. Today, the bullet had struck Etienne in the centre of his forehead. He'd been dead before he hit the ground.

There had been a moment when she had wondered if she would faint, or become hysterical, but then Louis had fallen and her world had stopped, and then hung suspended in time until she discovered he was still holding the rope. She had been unable to breathe, not knowing if he would fall. But Louis had lived, and Etienne had died, and she could not let what she had done colour everything else. She had taken a man's life, and that was a terrible thing, but she would not dwell upon it, would not let Etienne spoil another moment of Louis' future, of their lives together. In any case, Etienne would have died moments later when the building collapsed, so she had only shortened his life by seconds, and he would have stolen Louis's entire future if she had not. She would not think of it any other way, but put it behind her and move forward, hoping and trusting the future for them was bright.

Life was always like that, she reflected, walking into the unknown, taking chances or turning away from them, playing it safe or daring to face something dark because it was worth the risk. Balanced on a highwire, with nobody knowing what might happen with the next step forward. But you had to keep moving, keep looking ahead, confident that everything would be all right, because if you doubted, if you stopped or looked back, you were far more likely to fall.

"I can hear you thinking, *mon amour,*" Louis said, his voice heavy with exhaustion.

"Can you?" she said lightly. "I was making plans for us."

That was not entirely true, but she had been thinking of it earlier in the day, and she did not want to discuss Etienne with him again.

"Ah. Do they include staying in bed for the next month? For I shall agree wholeheartedly if they do."

Evie laughed and pressed a kiss to his cheek. "Indeed, they do. I was thinking a little more long term, however."

"Oh?"

"I wish to stay in France."

Louis cracked open his eyes, looking at her with interest. "You do?"

Evie nodded. "Not forever, but for longer than just a visit, as I said before. Months, at least, maybe even a year or so. But after that, I would prefer to live permanently in England, close to my family, if you do not mind too much, though we could come back whenever you wished to."

He laughed at that and then winced, so Evie stroked his cheek to soothe him. "I had anticipated that. In fact, I hope you will not be cross with me all over again, but I bought a property for us some time ago," he said, watching her cautiously.

"How long?" she demanded.

"Nearly a year," he said, and then relented with a sigh as she narrowed her eyes at him. "A bit more than a year."

"Louis!" she said, doing her best to sound annoyed when, in truth she wasn't a bit cross. "You're telling me now because you think I'll let you off now you're hurt, aren't you?"

"I am quite shameless," he admitted.

She snorted, shaking her head. "Lucky for you, you're right, you dreadful man. How presumptuous of you to buy a house without consulting me!"

"I know, but it is beautiful and romantic, and it's called Heart's Folly. What else could I do but buy it for us when I was so hopelessly in love with you?" he protested.

"Oh," she said with a sigh, tears prickling her eyes as she recognised the romance of the gesture. "Well, yes, of course you had to buy it. I quite understand. Will I love it?"

"You will," he promised, raising her hand to his lips and kissing her fingers. "Now tell me why you want to stay in France?"

Evie rested her head on his shoulder. "Because this is where you were born. I want to go to the place that ought to have been your home and make it a home for you. If we have a son, it will be his one day, and I want it to be a place he adores, filled with wonderful memories and love, so that he will live in it with his own family one day, and share the stories of his life growing up there. I want to banish the past, chase away all the ghosts and the darkness from your life."

He reached out and traced the line of her jaw with the back of his fingers, his touch reverent. "You did that a long time ago, *mon amour*. You are the light in my life."

"Then you don't mind?"

He shook his head. "How could I mind the picture you paint of our future? It is everything I have ever dreamed of."

"But you've never gone home, have you?"

"Non," he shook his head. "I have not been there since I was five years old. I paid to have the property repaired and maintained. There is an estate manager to oversee things, and it is well looked after, but it sits empty. Nic and Eliza have stayed there, but I could never bear to go back. Now, though, with you… well, everything is different."

"Then we can go?"

"We can go," he agreed.

"And will you show me the rest of Rouge et Noir too?"

He laughed. "Of course, though perhaps not tonight. We will return there but to my rooms, and I have no intention of leaving them for some time."

"That's fine. I can wait," she said, content now as the carriage drew them back to the club. "We have all the time in the world."

Louis returned to the club feeling about fifty years older than he had when he'd arrived with Evie earlier that night, but he was happy. There was no longer anything to fear. Those people with the power to hurt him were dead. Evie was his at last, his wife, and it appeared her father no longer wished to murder him. He had a future with the woman he loved, and he'd endure any number of bruises and broken ribs to make that a reality.

As they entered, Madame Toussaint, the manageress of Noir, came running along the corridor.

"Monsieur, you're hurt? We were so worried, and Madame la Comtesse?" Her eyes flew between Louis and Evie, filled with concern.

"*Oui, Margot, merci.* We are both well, if rather tired and dirty," Louis assured her.

"I'll have the staff prepare baths at once," she said, and then gave a sigh of relief when she saw her husband. "Jacques?"

"*Oui,*" Jacques said, giving her a swift kiss on the cheek. "I'm fine," he assured her before they hurried off about their business.

"Jacques and Margot married," Evie said, remembering that Louis had instructed Jacques to walk Margot Allard home the night Viscount Latimer had tried to abduct her.

"They did," Louis said with a smile, and then paused as a ruckus began from a room down the hallway. "*Merde*, what now?" he demanded. "Am I to have no peace?"

"Oh, dear," Evie said, realising she recognised Aggie's voice.

They hurried down the hallway and Louis opened the door of what looked to Evie like his private study and walked into an argument between Fred and Aggie that appeared to have been going on for some time. Barnaby, who was also present, ran a hand through his hair in frustration, his relief at seeing Louis obvious until he saw the state he was in, torn and bloody and covered in soot. Evie was certain the pervading stench of smoke came with them.

"Louis?" Barnaby exclaimed. "What in blazes happened?"

"Not now, *mon ami*," Louis said, shaking his head. "But I might ask you the same question."

Barnaby threw up his hands. "Someone sent word that Lord Frederick had arrived and what must Miss Agatha do but set out at once, despite the late hour. I tried to stop her, but short of tying her to a chair…."

Louis rubbed a weary hand over his face, scowling at his palm as it came away black and sooty. "Do not trouble yourself, Barnaby, I am well aware of the child's stubborn nature, I assure you."

Evie turned from Louis and Barnaby to listen to the argument.

"*I'm* cork-brained?" Fred was saying in outrage. "Well, I like that! There's you, a female all on her own, travelling through France and you think I'm the foolish one? The devil take you, Aggie, you could have been murdered, abducted… Good God, do you have any idea how terrified I've been?"

"You're an idiot!" Aggie insisted, her eyes bright with tears. "I lived on the streets, you great lummox. I know how to steal and how to survive, not like some pampered aristocrat."

"I am *not* pampered!" Fred shot back, twin flags of bright red staining his cheeks, as he stood a little straighter.

Aggie snorted and folded her arms.

"I am not! You take that back," Fred insisted, looking truly hurt and upset.

"Oh, of course you are, Fred," Aggie said, but now she sounded far more as if she might cry than as if she wanted to murder him. "You are so obviously an aristocrat, it's painful. It's you that was in danger, don't you see? You might have been kidnapped and held to ransom every time you opened your mouth. Lud, any fool need only look at your profile, never mind the quality of your clothes. You're the son of a duke, Fred and I… I'm n-nobody," she finished as her voice quavered and turned to run as tears fell down her face.

"Aggie!" Louis intervened, stepping into her path and hugging her to him, and Evie winced on his behalf as Aggie flung her arms about him. Louis closed his eyes for a moment and paled, but said nothing as the girl sobbed into his chest. "You are most certainly not no one, *mon enfant*. You never have been. You belong to me."

Aggie sobbed harder and shook her head and Louis turned to look at Evie, who knew what he wanted to ask her without him having to say a word. She had wanted to speak to him about Agatha but there had never been a moment to do so. Now, though, she smiled at him and nodded. "Yes, Louis. Of course."

Louis' expression was one of such love and gratitude, Evie felt winded by it. Would she ever get used to the power of that smile, of those startling blue eyes?

With only a slight intake of breath, Louis got to his knees and held Agatha by her shoulders, forcing her to look at him. "You belong to me. Now I am married, I will claim you as my own, Agatha and you shall live with Evie and me."

Agatha stopped crying abruptly to stare at him. "B-But everyone will think I'm your bastard," she said. "They'll think you abandoned me and denied me all this time, when it isn't true. They'll talk about you."

Louis shrugged. "What other people think of me is of no matter. People have always assumed it, so let them think it. Let us make it true, Aggie. Would you like that?"

Aggie made a hiccoughing sound and stared at Louis uncertainly, as if she did not dare believe it.

"I don't want people to think badly of you when you've been so good, so very k-kind. You're the best person I've ever known."

"Aggie," Louis protested, his eyes growing very bright. "Indeed, I am not. I am horribly selfish. Just ask Evie's Papa if you don't believe me. Besides, Montagu adopted his illegitimate niece, did he not? People always gossip and murmur that she was really his daughter, and I've seen how he deals with such scurrilous tattlemongers. If anyone so much as implies I did a thing wrong, I shall take a leaf out of his book and give them a glacial stare until they go away."

Aggie was trying hard not to cry, her cheeks red as she asked hesitantly, "I-I could call you, Papa?"

Louis swallowed hard, and Evie knew he was struggling to keep his composure too. He knew what it was like to belong nowhere, to no one, and he did not underestimate what he was offering Aggie, though he had given her his loyalty and his love for a long time now. He cleared his throat and nodded.

"Oui, ma fille, I should like it very much if you did."

Aggie gave a sob and launched herself at him, almost knocking him down. Though Evie knew he must be in pain, he only hugged the girl tightly, his eyes closed as a tear escaped and tracked through the dirt on his face. Evie was less restrained and accepted the handkerchief her father handed her so she could wipe her streaming eyes and blow her nose. They did not have more than a moment to enjoy the tender scene, however.

"I want to see my son!" boomed an imperious voice from outside the room and everyone turned in alarm as the door flew open and the imposing figure of the Duke of Bedwin filled the doorway.

"Mon Dieu," Louis said faintly, shaking his head. "I do not think I can take much more."

"Father!" Fred squeaked, his voice suddenly a little higher pitched than it had been a moment ago.

All at once the furious expression on the duke's face was gone, replaced by one of such joy and relief the change was startling. Without a word, Bedwin crossed the room and embraced his son tightly.

"Thank God," he said, and let out a breath as he looked the boy over. "Whatever has happened to you?"

"Nothing much... at least, only a little scrap, it's not as bad as it looks. I'm fine, honestly, and—I'm very sorry, sir," Fred said once the duke let him go.

Bedwin cleared his throat and shook his head. "No. No regrets. It was rash and foolish, but you acted honourably. A young woman was in danger, and you wished to help her without getting her into further trouble. I'm proud of you."

Fred stared up at his father in surprise. "You are?"

The duke nodded. "I am. Though you've turned me grey, and your mother is worried to death, which was unkind of you. Perhaps next time you are in such a fix, you might turn to me instead of taking it all on yourself. I would have helped you, Fred. You don't have to do such things alone. No matter the trouble, I will always help."

"Thank you, sir," Fred said, looking a little awed and exceedingly relieved. "I shall not cause you such worry again."

Bedwin laughed. "Yes, you will," he said, ruffling the boy's hair. "But that is to be expected."

Evie turned away as a shadow fell over the already crowded room and Wolf appeared.

"Louis," he whispered, pointing at the duke. "Look who it is."

Louis, who was already pale with fatigue under several layers of soot and grime after stresses of the night, blanched. *"Non,"* he said, shaking his head.

"Is it still in your desk drawer?" Wolf asked, his eyes glittering with mischief.

Louis shook his head, an expression of panic in his eyes. "Wolf, *non!* I forbid you…"

"Bedwin," Wolf called across the room, folding his arms.

"Oh, *mon Dieu,"* Louis said, pinching the bridge of his nose.

The duke stiffened as his gaze fell on Wolf, who looked every bit the reprobate he was after the events of the night. "Do I know you?" he asked, curiosity in his eyes.

"We've never been formally introduced," Wolf said, grinning rather too broadly. "I'm Wulfric De Vere, Viscount Latimer. Yes, the son of that Latimer, though don't hold it against me. He was an evil bastard."

"Wolf, children present," Louis hissed, looking more uncomfortable with each passing moment.

"And you are…*Le Loup Noir,*" Bedwin said slowly.

"You've heard of me," Wolf replied, looking pleased. "Well, good, but I've been wanting to return something of yours to you for some time."

Louis made a pained noise, and Evie went to him, taking his arm. She gave him a questioning look and Louis gave another quiet groan. "I know you've already done it once tonight, but save me, Evie, please, I beg you."

Too entertained to do anything of the sort, Evie watched the scene unfold as Wolf went to Louis' desk drawer and searched about until he withdrew a heavy gold fob watch. He handed it to the duke, who stared at it, turning it this way and that in astonishment. "My grandfather's watch," he said, his voice disbelieving. "But I lost this years ago. Here in Paris, actually. Someone picked my—"

He broke off, his gaze narrowing on Wolf.

"Oh, don't look at me, I was only the distraction," Wolf said with obvious delight, despite the fact Louis was glaring daggers at him.

Bedwin turned to Louis, who looked perfectly mortified. "I beg your pardon, your grace," he began. "I was… a little…."

"He was drunk out of his head is what he is trying to say," Wolf supplied cheerfully. "Well, to be fair, we both were. I'd not known him long and his brother had told me how quick and clever he'd been as a lad at picking pockets. Then we were out one night, and I saw you and that shiny gold watch and… well, it was irresistible, really. I dared him to lift it. You never even knew it happened, did you?"

Bedwin shook his head. "Not until I got home and realised it was gone, but I remembered the incident afterwards—the drunken young man who waylaid me on the street. I remember you," he said to Wolf. "Not you, though," he said to Louis in wonder.

"He's quick," Wolf said proudly.

"Your grace," Louis began again.

Bedwin hushed him. "You did not think to tell me this before? When we had that little revelation about you and your brother's past?"

Louis shook his head. "Nic was in enough trouble with you, and when you relented and let him marry Lady Eliza… I did not want to risk making matters worse. I am sorry. It was a foolish dare, nothing more and I ought not—"

"A dare," Bedwin said with a sigh. "I might have known."

Evie giggled.

"You might laugh, you've not taken yours from the hat yet, I believe," Mr Knight said in amusement. "Though, frankly, what else could you possibly do that you've not already done? No, I take that back. I don't want to know. I'm going to bed. Goodnight, everyone. For God's sake, keep her out of trouble, Louis."

With that, he kissed his daughter's head and took himself off.

"Come along, Fred. I think we shall go too," Bedwin said with a sigh. "I've had about as much excitement as I can take for the next six months."

Fred nodded and cast Aggie an uncertain look as he followed his father out, but Aggie ran to him and took his hand.

"Thank you, Fred, for coming after me," Aggie said. Shyly, she pressed a quick kiss to his cheek before blushing furiously and running from the room.

Fred touched his cheek with his fingers and then turned scarlet. He darted a glance at his father, who grinned. "Well done, son," he said with approval, and led the boy out of the room.

Evie glanced at Louis, whose eyes were shadowed and taut with fatigue and hurriedly ushered everyone else away too, promising to see them again in a few days when Louis had rested. Finally, they were alone.

"My poor Louis. You're exhausted."

He shrugged, pulling her into his arms. *"Oui,* I am, but I have never been happier all the same."

"Nor I," she said, resting her head on his chest.

He kissed her temple before resting his chin on her head. "You don't mind about Aggie?"

"You know that I do not."

"Je t'aime, amour de ma vie," he whispered. "You are everything I ever dreamed of."

"It's not a dream any longer, Louis. It's real. Let us live every moment of it."

He smiled and nodded, his extraordinary blue eyes warming for her, and her alone. "And so we shall, but first—and, I promise you, it kills me to say this—but *please,* may we go to bed and get some *sleep?"*

Evie laughed and kissed him. "Well, maybe just this once."

Epilogue

Dear Evie,

I am so jealous! Rouge et Noir sounds scandalous and exciting and the party your husband threw for you sounds so very sophisticated and romantic. I wish I could have been there and am a revolting shade of green with envy. How lucky you are to visit such places now you are married. I am not surprised everyone made such a fuss of you though, for so they should. You have quite the dashing reputation now, you know. How smug you must have felt when all those French ladies saw you were the Comtesse de Villen. Even in London, the scandal sheets reported how the female population of Paris wept at the news.

Oh, how I wish I could run away to France with a man who loved me like your comte loves you. It's so very romantic. This season promises to be tedious with all the same faces and how horribly spoiled I am to complain about going to parties and dancing until dawn. Except it isn't nearly as exciting as I hoped it would be.

I want an adventure, Evie. To be swept off my feet and carried away. The only person who carries me away isn't a person, but Sultan. He saw a rabbit yesterday morning and pulled on the lead so hard I fell flat on my face. I was never more mortified. I had to get up with mud on my dress and grass in my hair while all the elegant ladies muttered and sniggered behind their fans. Then the wretched beast lopes back with his tongue hanging out, looking so pleased with himself despite the rabbit getting away, and I had not the heart to be cross with him.

Perhaps I shall run away with Sultan and have an adventure. Just the two of us, far away from spiteful debutantes and men who insist on talking to my bosom. For, outside of my family, Sultan is the most loyal male I have ever encountered, and I have grave doubts of ever meeting one better.

PS. Cat is wild that you never took a dare. We have all tried to mollify her by telling her of all your daring exploits, but she would not be placated. So she took one for you. Please see enclosed.

—Excerpt of a letter to Evie de Montluc, Comtesse de Villen from Lady Cara Baxter (daughter of Luke and Kitty Baxter, Earl and Countess of Trevick).

10ᵗʰ October 1842, en route to Périgueux, Dordogne France.

"I do not understand why I was forced to dress in my finery and set off on a mystery tour at the crack of dawn," Louis grumbled for the tenth time since they'd left that morning.

Evie smiled and shared a conspiratorial look with Wolf, though she was nervous. Wolf was adamant that Louis would be pleased, but she feared upsetting him by raking up the past. Wolf insisted it was not raking but burying, and that it would give Louis peace. She prayed he was correct.

"It's a surprise," Wolf said, giving the same answer he'd given on each occasion. "And don't make out like you don't enjoy dressing in your finery. You're such a blasted peacock."

Louis shrugged. "What can I say? I have style, unlike some. There are other colours than black, you know."

"I am *Le Loup Noir,* this *is* my style," Wolf retorted, folding his massive arms and glaring at Louis.

If Evie did not know him, the look might have been terrifying, but she did, so she only laughed, much to Louis' amusement and Wolf's consternation.

He huffed and pointed a finger at Evie. "When we go to England, if you so much as mention kittens, I shall…."

"Yes?" she replied, lifting one eyebrow.

"Well, I shall think of something," he grumbled.

Smirking, Evie got the letter from Cara out of her reticule. It had arrived that morning and she'd not had time to read it before she left. She broke the seal and opened it.

"What's that?" Wolf asked as a piece of paper fluttered out. He bent down and picked it up, squinting at the writing. "It's all faded. What does that say? Dare to be… *wicked?* Dare to be wicked!" he repeated, eyebrows flying up.

Evie reached out and snatched it from him, stuffing it in her bag. "That's private," she said, blushing, having guessed what it must be. Louis looked at her and quirked an eyebrow.

"Hush," she warned him, knowing he knew full well about the hat of dares.

"What is your wife up to?" Wolf demanded.

Louis shrugged and returned a lazy smile. "With a bit of luck, I shall find out later," he said, sending Evie a challenging look that made her feel hot and muddled up inside. She knew she was blushing.

"Spoilsport," Wolf grumbled.

Evie ignored them both and settled back with her letter. When she got to the bit about Sultan, her heart went out to poor Cara, though she could not help but laugh.

"What's so funny?" Wolf asked.

"My friend, Lady Cara, she's wonderfully amusing, though the poor creature is struggling to find a good husband."

Louis took her hand and pulled it into his lap. "Not everyone can be as lucky as you, *mon amour,"* he said gravely.

Evie snorted and rolled her eyes. "Dreadful man," she said fondly, before returning to the letter and shaking her head. "Why is it that some men cannot appreciate a woman's intelligence as well as her figure? I know Cara is a great beauty, but she's clever too, and kind, and terribly funny. But no, they must gawk at her bosom and talk over her and treat her like she's a ninny. She's threatening to run away with Sultan if things don't improve."

"Who is Cara?" Wolf asked, perking up, his expression curious. "And Sultan of where?"

"Lady Cara Baxter, daughter of the Earl of Trevick, though I know of no Sultan," Louis replied, turning to regard Evie with a frown.

"Sultan is her dog," Evie said with a laugh. "A Great Dane. A monstrous immense beast, though it adores her and she it. She begged and begged her father for a puppy in the spring and, of course, he can deny her nothing. Sultan is as big as a pony now, though, and has not yet learned his manners. She has got into several scrapes because of him."

Louis stiffened, his expression growing sharp as he looked out of the window. Evie set the letter down on the seat beside her as her nerves leapt. Well, this was it. He turned back to glare at Wolf.

"Where the devil are we going?"

"I have something to show you," Wolf said.

Louis shook his head. *"Non. Non,* I do not wish to see."

"Louis. It is a good thing, I swear. Just for a moment, and then you may go home. Please," Wolf said, his dark eyes on Louis full of understanding.

Evie watched as Louis turned to her, his expression reproachful. "You knew about this."

She nodded, guilt stirring in her belly. "I did, and I was anxious, but I think Wolf has done a good thing, Louis. I think you will be pleased when you see. He did it for you."

Louis huffed out a breath and sat back and Evie took his hand, tangling their fingers together until the carriage stopped outside the house where Louis had lived as a boy. The house that had belonged to Monsieur and Madame Boucher and their son, Etienne. A footman opened the door, and they got out. Evie clung to his hand as Louis stared up at the house where he had been so dreadfully unhappy. From inside, they heard children's voices. They were singing. A newly painted sign hung outside the door.

Montluc Ecole Communal de Garçons.

Louis' grip tightened on Evie's hand as he turned to look at Wolf. "You did this?"

Wolf nodded. "When I came here to question Madame Boucher, it was clear she'd not last much longer. I may have bribed the *notaire* into letting me buy the building the moment she died. After all, Etienne had been declared dead years earlier. She might have realised that was not true. She certainly knew it when I visited, but she never made it official, so he could not inherit."

"Why?" Louis asked, his voice scratchy.

Wolf shrugged. "I intended to have the place torn down at first. But the building is decent, and you told me what Evie said, about making a home and chasing the ghosts away. I suppose the idea struck me as a good one."

"It was," Louis managed, staring up at the building. He let out a slow breath and Evie felt the tension leaving him as he nodded. "It was a good idea."

He turned to regard Evie, who leaned into him. "No more ghosts," she said.

Louis smiled and bent to kiss her. "Not a one. You chased them all away. You both did," he added, looking at Wolf.

Wolf grinned, obviously pleased with himself. "Don't I get a kiss?" he demanded, dark eyes sparkling wickedly.

"No, but I'll hug you if you like," Louis offered with a laugh.

Wolf held up his hands and shook his head. "Not in public. Your wife has done enough damage with her talk of kittens, I can't have you going around hugging me in broad daylight."

"Do you want to see inside?" Evie asked him.

Louis shook his head. "Perhaps, but not today. I will, but... I would like to come when I am more prepared for it. Today, I am touched and happy that this has been done in my name, and that is enough. Thank you, Wolf."

"There is one more thing," Evie said sheepishly. "Because you know very well that you have a promise to keep."

"I'm not sure…." Louis said awkwardly as Evie tsked and gave him a little shove towards the carriage. "Go. You promised and you always keep your promises, remember?"

Louis climbed out again a few minutes later as the footman opened the door. The carriage they'd come in was a new one, black and glossy and emblazoned with Louis' coat of arms: a gold eagle and a unicorn with a crest of bright blue held between them. Four matched black horses drew the carriage, which was accompanied by footmen dressed in dark blue and gold. In the middle of the busy marketplace, everyone stopped to stare, men and women gathering closer to get a better look. People came out of their houses to gaze at the fine carriage and four, and the grand nobleman who had deigned to stop in front of one shop in particular.

It was an elegant shop, clean and brightly painted, with the owner's name in bright blue letters over the door. Behind the gleaming windows was a display of mouthwatering cakes and pastries, which had drawn a cluster of children to press their noses against the glass. They had been looking at them with longing but now they turned and gawked at Louis, who felt rather ridiculous, but he *had* promised.

A bell jangled, and the door opened, and a man came rushing out. He was slender and shorter than Louis, with dark blond hair and grey eyes, and he stared and stared with his mouth open.

"You still have freckles," Louis observed, not knowing what else to say.

"Louis!" the man said in a choked voice, and then ran to Louis, hugging him tightly for a moment before stumbling away, looking horrified. "Monsieur, I'm so sorry… I did not mean—"

"André," Louis said, shaking his head and grasping him by the shoulders. "Don't be foolish. I do not think I would be here

349

without you, and I made you a promise a very long time ago. So, here I am, carriage and all, just as you asked for."

"You remembered," André said, laughing, his eyes bright with emotion. "I cannot believe it, and the shop, Louis. It was you, wasn't it? It was you that bought it and sent me the deeds."

Louis nodded. "My luck changed, *mon ami,* and I wanted to share my good fortune with someone who deserved it. You've made a splendid job of it, too. The best patisserie in Périgueux, as I knew it would be."

André gave a shocked laugh and covered his mouth with his hand, then his expression sobered, and he stepped closer to Louis. "I know this sounds mad, Louis, because we all heard that Etienne died, but not long ago someone broke into my home. I thought nothing had been taken at first, but…." He blushed before hurrying on. "The lock of hair you gave me. It was taken, and who else would take it if not him?"

Louis nodded. "*Oui,* it was Etienne. He tried to cause me some trouble, but that is all over now."

"Oh," André sighed with relief. "I was sorry to have lost it," he admitted.

Louis chuckled. "Well, if my wife does not object, I shall give you another."

André's eyes lit up and he stared at the carriage. "Your wife? You married? Congratulations, Louis. I'm so happy for you."

"*Merci, mon ami,* I am a very fortunate man."

André shook his head in wonder. "Will you come in, Louis? I have so much to tell you, and you… my word I want to hear everything," he said, laughing with all the exuberance Louis remembered in him.

"I would love to, but you have customers to serve," he said, gesturing to the children who were bored with staring at Louis and had gone inside the shop. "Perhaps I could call again, though. If you wouldn't mind? I should like to sample some of those delicious creations in the window, and my wife has something of a sweet tooth," he added with a smile.

"I should like that," André said. "And to meet your comtesse," he added hopefully.

Louis turned back to the carriage and held out his hand. Evie took it and stepped down. André bowed low, blushing a little. "Madame, it is an honour."

Evie shook her head and held out her hands to him. "The honour is mine, *monsieur*, to meet the man who was so very brave and kind to my husband when he so badly needed a friend. He has told me so much about you."

André looked at Louis in surprise.

"Did you think otherwise?" Louis said gently. "I never forgot you, André."

"Nor I you, Louis," André said with a smile. "You'll really come again soon?"

"I promise," Louis replied, knowing that André knew he meant it.

"Where is Wolf?" Louis asked when they returned to the carriage.

"He said he would make his own way back," Evie replied, settling next to him. "He said he had things to do here. But where is my letter?" she added, searching the seat for Cara's letter to no avail.

In the end, she gave up, assuming it must have fallen out when she'd got out to greet André.

Louis fell quiet for a while, staring out of the window. "You were right. It was not the place I despised, but the life I lived here, the people who hurt me. But André believed in me, he gave me hope and made it bearable. I'm glad I came, thank you, Evie."

"You more than repaid him, by the looks of thing. You are a good man, Louis César," she said softly, and kissed his cheek. She rested her head on his chest and watched the streets pass them by for a little while until the sun glared in her eyes. Reaching out, she tugged the curtains closed on each side, giving them privacy.

"You're very quiet," Evie observed.

Louis smiled and shifted to face her. "Just thinking."

"A penny for them," she whispered, reaching out to stroke his beautiful face.

His eyes darkened, a wicked glint in the depths of the blue as his sensuous mouth quirked. She touched the curve of his bottom lip with her fingertip, and he nipped at it.

"I was thinking," he said, and his voice was low and intimate now, making her insides quiver with excitement. "That you have been issued a challenge."

"Oh?" she said, striving to sound nonchalant.

"*Oui, Madame la Comtesse.* I was also remembering how much you liked the idea of being wicked in a carriage. You did like the idea, didn't you?" he teased her, sliding a hand down her thigh to her knee. "That's why you ran away."

"Of course," she said, her breathing growing ragged as he tugged at her skirts, bunching up the material until he found her silk clad leg.

"You liked the idea of doing something very naughty whilst the world carried on beyond the window, just a few feet away."

Evie glanced at the door, where through a small gap in the curtains she could still see the busy streets of Périgueux as they passed by, people shopping and hurrying about their day. She nodded, unable to speak as his hand drifted higher, finding the soft skin of her inner thigh.

"Spread your legs for me," he commanded, and Evie obeyed without question, sighing as his clever fingers tickled through her soft curls, seeking and finding the delicate bud hidden beneath.

"Louis," she said on a gasp, leaning her head back against the squabs. Pleasure unfurled inside her as he caressed her, leaning in to steal a searing kiss that scattered what remained of her senses.

"More?" he asked, drawing back to look at her.

"Yes. More. Much more. Everything."

One finger slid inside her, and Evie moaned, closing her eyes.

"Tell me what you want."

Evie licked her lips, wondering if she dared.

"Dare to be wicked, *amour de ma vie,*" he said softly.

She met his blue eyes, seeing the love and desire burning there and knowing he would do whatever she asked, whatever would please her, and he would love doing it too. "Get on your knees, Louis."

He flashed her a sinful smile and did as she asked, dropping elegantly to the floor of the carriage, and pushing up her skirts. She spared an anxious glance at the tiny gap in the curtains, and he laughed.

"No one can see," he reassured her, pushing her legs wider and kissing the tender skin of her inner thigh. "Probably," he added, before parting her intimate flesh and applying his mouth.

Evie bit back a cry, remembering the driver and the footmen were just outside, but she did not want him to stop. It was wicked and exciting, dreadfully naughty and quite exquisitely wonderful.

Her breath caught as he worried her delicate flesh with his tongue and his fingers slid inside her once again.

"More, oh, yes… don't stop," she breathed, and then had to bite down on her hand as he suckled gently, and the world flew apart. She had hardly caught her breath, still dazed and giddy when Louis tugged her across the carriage onto his lap.

"Hurry," he admonished her as she fumbled with his buttons, trying to release him as his arousal strained against the cloth of his trousers. "Evie!" he protested, his urgency making her laugh.

"Anyone would think you were desperate," she said, snorting with laughter at his look of outrage.

"You think I'm not? Take me inside you for the love of… *Oh, oui,*" he said in relief, his protests disappearing as she sank down onto him.

Evie gasped as he filled her, the pleasure that had barely ebbed flooding back as he urged her to ride him, hard and fast.

"Take what you want," he told her, holding her hips, their gazes locked together. "You can have it all, Evie, everything, all of me."

She laughed again then, knowing she had it, she had this man and his love, and he would change the world for her if that was what she demanded of him. Not that she would. She had all that she wanted. He was imperfect and wicked and a little bit broken, and he was kind and wonderful and entirely hers, and all she could ever want.

"*Je t'aime,*" she told him as the pleasure took them over, shutting out the world outside until it was just the two of them. "*Je t'aime pour toujours.*"

"Always," he agreed raggedly. "I promise."

And she knew he meant it.

Next in the Daring Daughter Series...

Wildly Daring
Daring Daughters, Book Fourteen

A bold Miss and her beloved dog...

Lady Cara Baxter is a scandal waiting to happen. She knows it. Her family know it. The only question is when and what kind of scandal she will fall into, though undoubtedly her dog, Sultan, will be at the heart of it. Cara doesn't care. The marriage mart is a bear bait, and not half so much fun as she thought it would be. Sultan might be badly behaved, but outside of her family he is the only male in her life that truly loves her.

A criminal with a heart of gold...

Wulfric 'Wolf' De Vere, Viscount Latimer, is a conundrum and he knows it. To all the world, he is *Le Loup Noir*, king of the

Parisian underworld. If you want silks, spices, alcohol, or anything of an exotic nature, you go to Wolf. If you wanted someone to disappear, you go to Wolf. If you want a favour, you go to Wolf, but only if you are prepared to pay the price, and that price is high.

Everyone knows he is not a man to be crossed, but they do not know Wolf.

An irresistible temptation…

When Evie describes her lovely friend and her naughty hound, her description captivates Wolf. Having stolen the letter Cara wrote her friend, Wolf begins a correspondence with a girl he has never laid eyes on. Signing himself only as 'W', an unlikely friendship begins.

An adventure with a man she ought not to trust…

When Cara discovers her wicked W is none other than the infamous Lord Latimer, newly arrived in London, nothing will keep her from the man she has fallen in love with one letter at a time. She does not care about his terrible reputation, nor that it will ruin her to be discovered in his company. Nothing matters, but being with the man she adores, and anyway, falling into scandal was inevitable so she may as well be…

Wildly daring.

Pre-Order here: Wildly Daring

And coming in **2023**, an exciting new series based on the male children of the Girls Who Dare…

Their mothers dared all for love.
Their sisters did the same.
Something wicked this way comes…

The first book in the **Wicked Sons** series….

The Devil to Pay
Wicked Sons, Book One

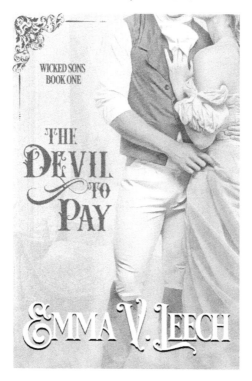

To be revealed

The Peculiar Ladies who started it all…

Girls Who Dare—The exciting series from Emma V Leech, the multi-award-winning, Amazon Top 10 romance writer behind the Rogues & Gentlemen series.

Inside every wallflower is the beating heart of a lioness, a passionate individual willing to risk all for their dream, if only they can find the courage to begin. When these overlooked girls make a pact to change their lives, anything can happen.

Twelve girls—Twelve dares in a hat. Twelves stories of passion. Who will dare to risk it all?

To Dare a Duke
Girls Who Dare Book 1

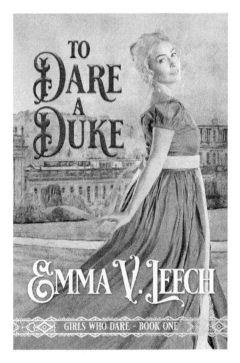

Dreams of true love and happy ever afters

Dreams of love are all well and good, but all Prunella Chuffington-Smythe wants is to publish her novel. Marriage at the price of her independence is something she will not consider. Having tasted success writing under a false name in The Lady's Weekly Review, her alter ego is attaining notoriety and fame and Prue rather likes it.

A Duty that must be endured

Robert Adolphus, The Duke of Bedwin, is in no hurry to marry, he's done it once and repeating that disaster is the last thing he desires. Yet, an heir is a necessary evil for a duke and one he cannot shirk. A dark reputation precedes him though, his first wife may have died young, but the scandals the beautiful, vivacious and spiteful creature supplied the ton have not. A wife must be found. A wife who is neither beautiful nor vivacious but sweet and dull, and certain to stay out of trouble.

Dared to do something drastic

The sudden interest of a certain dastardly duke is as bewildering as it is unwelcome. She'll not throw her ambitions aside to marry a scoundrel just as her plans for self-sufficiency and freedom are coming to fruition. Surely showing the man she's not actually the meek little wallflower he is looking for should be enough to put paid to his intentions? When Prue is dared by her friends to do something drastic, it seems the perfect opportunity to kill two birds.

However, Prue cannot help being intrigued by the rogue who has inspired so many of her romances. Ordinarily, he plays the part of handsome rake, set on destroying her plucky heroine. But is he really the villain of the piece this time, or could he be the hero?

Finding out will be dangerous, but it just might inspire her greatest story yet.

To Dare a Duke

Also check out Emma's regency romance series, Rogues & Gentlemen. Available now!

The Rogue
Rogues & Gentlemen Book 1

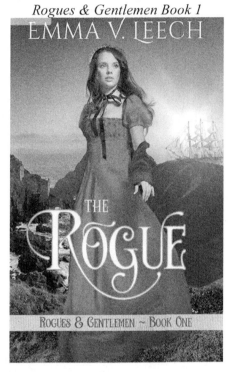

The notorious Rogue that began it all.

Set in Cornwall, 1815. Wild, untamed and isolated.

Lawlessness is the order of the day and smuggling is rife.

Henrietta always felt most at home in the wilds of the outdoors but even she had no idea how the mysterious and untamed would sweep her away in a moment.

Bewitched by his wicked blue eyes

Henrietta Morton knows to look the other way when the free trading 'gentlemen' are at work.

Yet when a notorious pirate bursts into her local village shop, she can avert her eyes no more. Bewitched by his wicked blue eyes, a moment of insanity follows as Henrietta hides the handsome fugitive from the Militia.

Her reward is a kiss, lingering and unforgettable.

In his haste to flee, the handsome pirate drops a letter, a letter that lays bare a tale of betrayal. When Henrietta's father gives her hand in marriage to a wealthy and villainous nobleman in return for the payment of his debts, she becomes desperate.

Blackmailing a pirate may be her only hope for freedom.

**** **Warning**: This book contains the most notorious rogue of all of Cornwall and, on occasion, is highly likely to include some mild sweating or descriptive sex scenes. ****

Free to read on *Kindle Unlimited*: The Rogue

Interested in a Regency Romance with a twist?

A Dog in a Doublet
The Regency Romance Mysteries Book 2

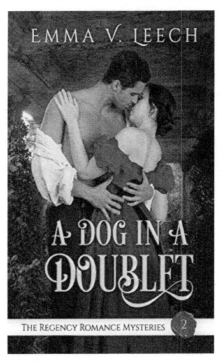

A man with a past

Harry Browning was a motherless guttersnipe, and the morning he came across the elderly Alexander Preston, The Viscount Stamford, clinging to a sheer rock face he didn't believe in fate. But the fates have plans for Harry whether he believes or not, and he's not entirely sure he likes them.

As a reward for his bravery, and in an unusual moment of charity, miserly Lord Stamford takes him on. He is taught to read, to manage the vast and crumbling estate, and to behave like a gentleman, but Harry knows that is something he will never truly be.

Already running from a dark past, his future is becoming increasingly complex as he finds himself caught in a tangled web of jealousy and revenge.

A feisty young maiden

Temptation, in the form of the lovely Miss Clarinda Bow, is a constant threat to his peace of mind, enticing him to be something he isn't. But when the old man dies his will makes a surprising demand, and the fates might just give Harry the chance to have everything he ever desired, including Clara, if only he dares.

And as those close to the Preston family begin to die, Harry may not have any choice.

Order your copy here. A Dog in a Doublet

Lose yourself in Emma's paranormal world with The French Vampire Legend series…..

The Key to Erebus
The French Vampire Legend Book 1

The truth can kill you.

Taken away as a small child, from a life where vampires, the Fae, and other mythical creatures are real and treacherous, the beautiful young witch, Jéhenne Corbeaux is totally unprepared when she returns to rural France to live with her eccentric Grandmother.

Thrown headlong into a world she knows nothing about she seeks to learn the truth about herself, uncovering secrets more shocking than anything she could ever have imagined and finding that she is by no means powerless to protect the ones she loves.

Despite her Gran's dire warnings, she is inexorably drawn to the dark and terrifying figure of Corvus, an ancient vampire and master of the vast Albinus family.

Jéhenne is about to find her answers and discover that, not only is Corvus far more dangerous than she could ever imagine, but that he holds much more than the key to her heart...

Now available at your favourite retailer.

The Key to Erebus

Check out Emma's exciting fantasy series with hailed by Kirkus Reviews as "An enchanting fantasy with a likable heroine, romantic intrigue, and clever narrative flourishes."

The Dark Prince
The French Fae Legend Book 1

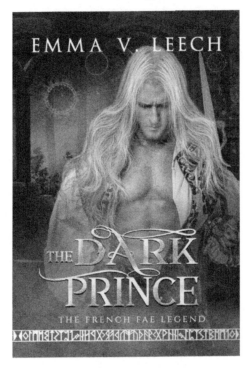

Two Fae Princes
One Human Woman
And a world ready to tear them all apart

Laen Braed is Prince of the Dark fae, with a temper and reputation to match his black eyes, and a heart that despises the human race. When he is sent back through the forbidden gates between realms to retrieve an ancient fae artifact, he returns home with far more than he bargained for.

Corin Albrecht, the most powerful Elven Prince ever born. His golden eyes are rumoured to be a gift from the gods, and destiny is calling him. With a love for the human world that runs deep, his friendship with Laen is being torn apart by his prejudices.

Océane DeBeauvoir is an artist and bookbinder who has always relied on her lively imagination to get her through an unhappy and uneventful life. A jewelled dagger put on display at a nearby museum hits the headlines with speculation of another race, the Fae. But the discovery also inspires Océane to create an extraordinary piece of art that cannot be confined to the pages of a book.

With two powerful men vying for her attention and their friendship stretched to the breaking point, the only question that remains...who is truly The Dark Prince.

The man of your dreams is coming...or is it your nightmares he visits? Find out in Book One of The French Fae Legend.

Available now to read at your favourite retailer

The Dark Prince

Want more Emma?

If you enjoyed this book, please support this indie author and take a moment to leave a few words in a review. *Thank you!*

To be kept informed of special offers and free deals (which I do regularly) follow me on *https://www.bookbub.com/authors/emma-v-leech*

To find out more and to get news and sneak peeks of the first chapter of upcoming works, go to my website and sign up for the newsletter.

http://www.emmavleech.com/

Come and join the fans in my Facebook group for news, info and exciting discussion…

Emmas Book Club

Or Follow me here…

http://viewauthor.at/EmmaVLeechAmazon

Facebook

Instagram

Emma's Twitter page

TikTok

Can't get your fill of Historical Romance? Do you crave stories with passion and red-hot chemistry?

If the answer is yes, have I got the group for you!

Come join myself and other awesome authors in our Facebook group

Historical Harlots

Be the first to know about exclusive giveaways, chat with amazing HistRom authors, lots of raunchy shenanigans and more!

Historical Harlots Facebook Group

Printed in Great Britain
by Amazon

13518999R00222